DEPTHS OF VANALF

GRIMNIR CHRONICLES 1

BRADY HUNSAKER

LIGHFIRE PUBLISHING

CONTENTS

Dedicated to Stanley Hunsaker. A man who endured many pains but always maintained hope.

He had a love that knew no bounds, and a tender spot for those who suffered. Though he was a man of few words, he could fuel dreams and inspire the best in others.

He was my father, and a piece of his soul will always be a part of this story.

AVSKILD
SEGLSATT
DALSTAVA
VANALF
EVERGROVE
KJAKITH
HEMTVED

CHAPTER ONE

TO DREAM

Hallik

There were a hundred ways to get killed by monsters, but perhaps the most exciting way was to enter their den, travel to the bottom of it, and hope to make it back out alive with a slim chance of survival, all for the purpose of emerging with magical powers. This was a task every initiate committed themselves to when they joined the Grimnir school around the age of ten. By eighteen, they would enter the monsters' realm, Vanalf. Hallik was one such initiate, and now, with a year of training remaining, he sought the opportunity to enter the depths of Vanalf early. To do that, he needed to prove himself.

The leather grip of his wooden practice sword felt hot in Hallik's palm as he faced off against Storr. The other boy was taller and thicker, and he came from the final year class, while Hallik was one year his junior. Arenda, their combat instructor, stood to the side, arms folded, feathered wings tucked behind her back.

This was Hallik's chance to prove himself. If he could beat Storr, that should be evidence enough that he could enter Vanalf a year early. Then he could emerge from the cave a Grimnir, a survivor gifted with one of four magical classes. He was tired of being a student. Going off to discover what happened to his father was completely unreasonable without having the strength of a Grimnir.

Arenda nodded, and the battle began.

Storr was no fool. He knew of Hallik's reputation among his own age class. His first move was careful, a step forward with a practice swing arcing harmlessly in front of Hallik.

Though he was only seventeen, Hallik had been training his whole life to become a Grimnir. Storr was the same, though a year older.

Storr was at the top of his class, just like Hallik, but the younger man was convinced he was the better fighter. Hallik took his own experimental swing, keeping the sword in his right hand, knees slightly bent as he twirled the dull blade. If left unimpeded, the swing would have thwacked Storr on the wrist, but the older boy twitched his hand to the side and countered with his own attack.

Hallik parried.

Storr swung three times in quick succession, but Hallik batted each attack away with his own sword. Energy pulsed in his veins, urging him on. A crowd of students had gathered around the courtyard, knowing that this was a fight not to be missed. They held their breath in utter silence.

Hallik took in his own sharp breath and swung up. Storr moved to block, but Hallik feinted and switched the trajectory, aiming his sword tip for Storr's elbow. The older boy tucked his arm in just enough that Hallik's wooden sword barely grazed the skin. Storr stabbed for him, but Hallik brushed the stab away with the hilt of his sword. The wooden point of Storr's sword passed right by Hallik's cheek.

Too close. Though not enough to make Hallik back down.

With a spin, Hallik closed the gap between them, bashing the pommel of his sword against Storr's shoulder with a thunk. The older boy kneed at him, but Hallik dodged back with a skip, parrying Storr's swinging blade at the same time. He hammered down at Storr with a flurry of strokes, and for a moment, Storr kept pace, but his reactions were too far behind. Eventually, one of Hallik's swings took Storr on the upper thigh.

Storr shouted at the pain, but it wasn't considered a killing blow. Hallik batted away Storr's sword before pushing the point of his sword up against his opponent's chest. The students roared, many of those from his own class jumping and cheering louder than the rest.

"Dead," Hallik said, unable to keep the smile from his face.

Storr scowled at him, but gave no rebuke, so Hallik clasped the boy's hand to help him rise.

"Good fight," Hallik said, raising his voice to be heard over the tumult.

Storr rolled the shoulder Hallik had bashed and offered a curt nod. Hallik might have felt the same if he'd been beaten by one of his youngers.

Arenda nodded her approval to Hallik.

Hallik smiled at her, approaching to make his bold request. "Perhaps now you will consider letting me go through Vanalf this year."

Arenda narrowed her eyes, lips twitching. "You want to enter Vanalf so badly?"

Hallik nodded. "Yes. Of course." Excitement climbed his chest like cold water, pushed with a strong current. There was no way she could deny him. Not even Lind, the head instructor, could say no after today's display.

Arenda seemed to deliberate before she looked down. A second later, her fist shot forward, exploding toward Hallik's nose.

Instinct was all that saved Hallik. He jerked his head to the side, dodging the punch. Eyes wide, he stumbled away from her. With his practice sword still in hand, he raised it warily.

The students gasped before going silent. Instructors sometimes sparred with the students, but the sudden attack was unanticipated.

Arenda stooped to pick up a practice sword at the edge of the circle formed by the onlookers. "You want to enter Vanalf, do you?"

Hallik nodded, though he kept his sword up, her intentions unclear.

"Have you fought against monsters before?" she inquired, stepping within reach. The muscles of her arm flexed. Arenda was a Valtyra, one of the four Grimnir classes, and the class best known for creating the ideal soldier. Among other things, she was blessed with strength, endurance, and the ability to fly.

"No," Hallik said, taking a step back. "I have not."

Arenda swung for Hallik with her practice sword, the attack coming with blinding speed. Only his distance saved him as he stepped back, sword failing to deflect the attack.

The wood whistled in front of his nose. By the depths, was she trying to injure him? She swung again. This time, their swords connected, and the impact of it sent tremors up Hallik's arm. She was powerful. He took another step back.

"Monsters are faster than you," Arenda said. "They are stronger." She swung twice more. Hallik deflected the first blow, but it nearly dislodged the sword in his hand. He dodged the second, taking another step back as he ducked, but his back was nearly touching the crowd of silent students behind him.

He understood she was trying to make a point, but he did not intend to be made a fool. With a snarl, he stepped forward. He thought to surprise her as he began to attack, but a smirk lifted the side of Arenda's lips. She countered each of his attacks with ease before hammering against Hallik's sword with a hit so jarring that his fingers went numb with the impact. Before he could even blink, the wooden blade was pressed up against the side of his neck, cradling his throat stone. If it had been a real sword, she would have torn straight through him.

Besides Hallik's panting, a few hushed whispers were the only sound. A bead of sweat trickled down his eyebrow as he blinked up at Arenda, waiting to hear her verdict.

"Next year," she said, withdrawing the wooden sword. "Now rest. Tomorrow morning we have more training to do."

Hallik dipped his head to her, trying not to let his frustration show. He'd fought like a child, and like a child, he'd been defeated.

Elowyn, one of Hallik's fellow students, caught his eye. She beckoned him over with a jerk of her head, blonde hair pulled up in a tail. Her skin was tanned by long hours in the sun, and her green eyes were placid, soothing. Calmness melted across Hallik's being.

The crowd dispersed as he tossed his practice sword into the pile. Hands on hips, he stopped before Elowyn. "I may have lost, but at least I looked good doing it, right?" he said, trying to play off the disappointment he felt.

Elowyn raised an eyebrow. She knew him too well. "Remember that she is one of the best fighters in Avskildian history. You did fine."

"I know," Hallik said, brushing off his tunic. "I just wish she hadn't used that as a point to keep me back from entering Vanalf this year."

"It's a silly notion anyway," Elowyn said, shaking her head at him. "I too am eager to enter, but everything has its time for a reason."

Hallik scoffed. She was right, of course. She almost always was—not that he was about to tell her that.

"We should rest as Arenda suggested," Elowyn said. "I need to spar you tomorrow after we run. Catch you when you're tired so I have a chance." She flashed him a smile before heading inside the keep of Castle Vrodr without waiting for him.

Hallik looked up to the darkening sky. At times like this, the milky film that kept their island shielded would sometimes shimmer in the fading light.

Tomorrow, he would train. And the next day, and the next. In one year, he would become a Grimnir to remember.

CHAPTER TWO

ONE YEAR

Elowyn Galdre

Some of the songs claimed that victory had created the island nation of Avskild, but Elowyn knew the songs herself. It wasn't victory that brought their people here. It was defeat. It was likely only a matter of time before monsters found their way here again, and then it would be all the more imperative for her to become a Grimnir. No matter how grave the risk. Magic was the one thing that would keep them safe.

She sprinted hard, knowing that every bit of training she did would increase her chances of surviving when she entered Vanalf. That was the price one paid to gain magic. There was no other way for her to become a Voyager, those who could activate portals. The ground practically glided away beneath her feet, warm wind carrying the scent of saltwater. She skimmed the edge of a short cliff, running parallel to it. A dark, sandy beach stretched out below.

Her destination, a ruined heap of an ancient castle on the cliff, was just ahead of her. The castle was from another age, when war was common and the need for Grimnirs was much greater.

The other Grimnir students from her age group raced behind her, all twenty-four of them. At the very rear of the group would be Arenda, the combat instructor.

Elowyn passed beneath the crumbling archway of the old castle, slowing to a stop as the soft grass changed to pebbled dirt.

"I win," Elowyn said with a huff.

Hallik clomped up right behind her, coming in second place. "You cheat," Hallik said through his panting, placing hands on hips as he walked toward her, gray eyes narrowing. He whipped his blond hair out of his eyes and added, "You're not even human."

He wasn't exactly wrong. Elowyn smiled. "I'm more human than you."

"What is that supposed to mean?"

"By the smell of it, your father was a troll."

Hallik laughed with a shrug, white teeth flashing. "Seeing as I never knew my father, you may be right."

The two of them walked in circles around what would have been the castle courtyard to cool down as the other students filtered in.

When the remainder of the students had entered the wide space, Arenda came last, her face calm. Her large brown wings were folded behind her. She was a Valtyra, one of the four Grimnir classes, distinguished by the wings that always appeared on their backs after emerging from their trial in Vanalf. When a student entered the cave, there were only two outcomes: they'd emerge as a Grimnir, or they'd never emerge at all.

"You are one year away from entering Vanalf," Arenda said, her voice steady as though she hadn't been running for the last hour. "You must be prepared to face whatever challenges may confront you while inside. Feats of endurance and combat are not uncommon." She withdrew the wooden practice sword from her belt.

Arenda said practically the same thing every day, or some variation of it, as if they needed any reinforcement for why her training was necessary. Elowyn respected combat training, but she had no desire to become a Valtyra, the warrior class. She couldn't fathom the inconvenience of having large wings protruding from her back, though Arenda appeared so graceful with them.

Elowyn's aspirations were different. She wanted to be a Voyager, one who could move between the realms. There hadn't been a new Voyager for eight years straight. All the previous ones had disappeared.

The students knew what to do. Each of them had their own practice sword they'd brought with them, and they started pairing off.

"You'll duel me then?" Elowyn asked Hallik.

Hallik rolled his broad shoulders. "If you don't mind losing."

Elowyn shrugged. "The best way to learn is to practice with someone who's better than you."

"So does that mean my skill will degrade by practicing with you so much?" He smirked, thinking he was clever.

"I'm sure I could teach you a thing or two."

"Alright then," he said, holding his practice sword out to the side. He loosened the lace of his plain brown tunic where sweat still glistened on his tanned chest.

The sun was high. The air was humid, and a light breeze coming up from the bay did little to cool them off.

Elowyn tucked a stray strand of her bright blonde hair behind her ear and pulled out her own sword, falling into stance. Other students around her started their duels as Arenda paced around them, watching and providing corrections.

Hallik's gray eyes were focused on Elowyn as she stared back at him. His lips pursed, square jaw tightening as he made a couple practice flicks with his sword. Yesterday had proven that he was the best fighter among all the students, and whenever Elowyn didn't rope him into dueling, he often practiced directly with Arenda, something Elowyn had only done a few times. Though Arenda's little show with him yesterday was evidence that she normally went easy on him.

Even if Elowyn didn't want to be a Valtyra, she certainly wanted the skill to rival Hallik. Thankfully fighting was the *only* thing he truly bested her at.

Elowyn let out her breath in short bursts as she struck at Hallik. He deflected three strokes from her before trying three of his own. Elowyn matched his rhythm, blocking each attack. She tried again, but he feinted a block and dodged instead, stepping in and striking low. Elowyn caught it with the tip of her blade, but Halik tapped her elbow to taunt her before spinning away with a smile.

She refused to let that slide. She lunged toward him, breaking the rhythm to find her own stride. The sound of clattering wood filled the air as their weapons clashed again and again. She swung at his shoulders—once from one side, then the other, in quick succession—before going for a jab. He jabbed as well, his blade poking the top of her chest as her blade caught him in the ribcage.

"Either you're getting rusty, Hallik, or Elowyn has finally become a fair match," Arenda said, folding her arms as she stood beside them.

"I'm not rusty, Arenda. You've said so yourself. I can't expect to win every fight. Every soldier gets injured eventually." He withdrew his weapon.

"Oh, let her compliment me, Hal," Elowyn said. "I still have more to teach you."

"You're fast, Elowyn," Arenda said. "Use your advantage. Keep with the quick strokes. When battling someone like Hallik, focus less on killing blows. A blade to the wrist, elbow, or knee can ensure a victory when using a real weapon. A stab to his liver would do you no good if he pierces your lung at the same time." She gave Hallik a narrow-eyed glance. "Don't go easy on her."

Hallik nodded his acquiescence and readied his weapon again.

Arenda turned her attention away, providing advice to another pair nearby.

Elowyn took the advantage and stepped toward Hallik, taking a quick jab. He deflected it easily and threw in his own swings, wielding his wooden weapon as though it were a longsword. Elowyn kept up, trying to take Arenda's advice to use faster strokes, but Hallik matched the rhythm. If speed was supposedly Elowyn's advantage, then Hallik certainly wasn't letting that show.

She attempted several more strikes but Hallik only smirked, which annoyed her more than it should have. This was her choice after all. Didn't she want to train with somebody who was more skilled than her? In one quick flash, Hallik deflected Elowyn's attack and struck her across the forearm, wooden sword batting at her flesh.

Elowyn groaned and stepped back.

Hallik shrugged at her. "Something like that," he said. "Take the easier hits where you can get them."

Arenda had since moved on to instruct other students, but she nodded in their direction.

Hallik and Elowyn sparred for another hour, and, true to his word, Hallik didn't go easy on her. An accumulation of bruises slowly built up along her arms and shoulder. She'd at least been able to strike Hallik once on the ankle, but he'd otherwise held the advantage.

"That's enough for now," Arenda said.

The students all sighed with relief. Except for Elowyn. She was as determined as ever to strike another blow against Hallik.

But they weren't in the clear yet. They still had to run back to the castle, not that Elowyn minded that at all.

Endurance was another of her strengths. Rather than place her wooden sword back through the loop at her waist, she held onto it as she took the lead, starting at a light jog back toward the castle.

"You're getting better," Hallik said as he jogged behind her.

"Don't patronize me," Elowyn said.

Hallik laughed. "I'm not one for patronizing, El. You know that."

When she didn't respond, he went on. "Really though. I'm sure if you sparred with any of the other students, you'd be more than a good match for them. I wouldn't be surprised if you come out of Vanalf a Valtyra."

"Nature's rays," Elowyn cursed. "Let's hope not. The last thing I need is a set of wings."

Hallik laughed again. He knew how much she feared the idea of emerging as a Valtyra. So much for not patronizing.

She shook her head, instead focusing on her breathing, and on the salty scent near the ocean. They were too far away from the beach to feel the misty air as waves crashed on the sand below the cliffs to her left. A long plain of short grass stretched out before her with a thick, dark forest to the right, jagged peaks rising above the tree line.

After jogging for a while, she switched the wooden sword to her other hand, wiping her sweaty palm on her pants. The path ahead curved away from the cliffs and back toward the forest. On the other end of it was the city of Dalstava. Home.

Even from the distance, the great Tower of Tarn rose over the edge of the trees, its dark gray surface blending against the mountainous backdrop.

As Elowyn passed beneath the branches of the old forest, the air cooled, and a humid stillness surrounded her. Ancient magic resided here. It was embedded in the very fabric of Dalstava.

A set of small fairies darted across the path ahead of her, one disguised as a leaf, another as a feathery seed, and the last a butterfly. Elowyn always found their choices of disguise humorous. Because of their inconsistency, their disguises were too obvious.

In her eagerness to get home, the rest of the students fell farther behind as her pace increased. Something about the forest itself invigorated her, filling the tired muscles of her legs with renewed strength that added to the euphoria of exertion. She was positive that at such a rate, she'd be able to run to the other side of the mountains and beyond.

But she wouldn't need to go that far. She'd already reached the other side of the short strip of forest that stood between the cliffs and Dalstava. The gray stone of Dalstava's walls stood as a massive blockade. It had been centuries since the city had been attacked, but in the stories of old, even the greatest of trolls could not penetrate them.

A stretch of land, bursting with green grasses, lay between her and the city wall, but she veered to the right toward a stout fortress embedded on the side of the wall, two thick, rounded towers breaching the edge. Castle Vrodr.

The stocky fortress was set apart from the rest of the city, though their walls connected. One thick keep stuck out from the middle, its slanted roof protected by dull, red shingles. The other smaller structures of the castle were hidden behind its walls.

Elowyn slowed her pace as she jogged toward the open gate. A single sentry, Latshal, stood outside the gate, armed with an iron spear, her brown hair jutting out the back of her leather helmet. Latshal functioned less as a warrior and more as a lookout, waiting for the various classes to return to the keep if their lessons took them outside the castle walls. She was a Watcher, one of the four classes of Grimnirs, with sharpened, supernatural senses. Latshal's counterpart, Khanak, would be somewhere atop the ramparts. He too was a Watcher.

Latshal nodded to Elowyn as she drew close, though her narrowed brown eyes looked over Elowyn's shoulder as if she were seeing something else. Elowyn glanced back, though she knew she wouldn't see whatever Latshal sensed.

"Welcome back," Latshal said, her voice tinged with a subtle rasp. "Everyone survived today's training?"

Elowyn let out a huff, looping the wooden sword into her belt as she reduced to a walk. "Mostly. Can't say they'll all run back safely though." Pride flavored her tone.

"They're your team, Elowyn. Your greatest strength is standing together." Latshal's eyes locked with Elowyn's as she passed.

"Yes, Latshal," Elowyn said, absorbing Latshal's wisdom. It was something all the instructors often reminded her of as well.

She proceeded through the open castle gate, its double portcullises hanging overhead like two rows of sharpened teeth. The walls were thick, and the cold shade offered a bit of respite from the warm exertion of her run. As she emerged on the other side, the scent of thick pine and forest receded and was replaced with that of moist clay and fresh berries. A cobbled path led from the gate to the opening of the keep, a moderate courtyard stretching between, interspersed with the manicured, bushy foliage of a well-tended garden.

A black and gray banner hung from a low parapet of the keep, bearing the crest of the Grimnirs, all four classes represented. Wings and sword for the Valtyras, an eye for the Watchers, an open book with a flame set on top for the Vitugrs, and a compass for the Voyagers.

She needed to become a Voyager, one of those gifted with the ability to travel and activate the portals. Their island, Avskild, was built of magic, secluded in its own realm, safe from most dangers. The Voyagers were meant to be able to maintain the security of the portals and enchantments that kept Avskild alive, but all the Voyagers had disappeared, and new ones were rare. It was a strange phenomenon, since Voyagers were once the lifeblood of Dalstava. Where had all the Voyagers gone?

Elowyn did not like mysteries. Especially not one that hung so cryptically over their heads like a dark cloud that no one wanted to acknowledge.

Her fellow students, and even the instructors, all suspected she'd become a Vitugr, one of those blessed with a sharp attunement to arcane spells and magic. Though she hoped that wouldn't be the case, it was rumored that Vitugrs still had a means of opening the portals, but such a spell would take years to master.

Years she didn't want to lose.

On the topic of Vitugrs, Lind Hjordis emerged from a low building protruding from the side of the wall, thick brown hair bouncing just above his shoulders, face grizzled with a rough beard. Lind was the instructor who oversaw much of the coursework regarding both magic and creatures. Arenda would hand the students off to him for the afternoon. An axe dangled from his waist, his broad shoulders bouncing as he walked toward Elowyn. She suspected him of being a greater warrior than he was a magi, but she never questioned his knowledge. His brown eyes lingering on her for only a moment before he nodded and redirected his gaze at the gate.

The other students were returning, Hallik at the head.

She knew he could have run much faster to keep up with her, but he hadn't. It was always his tendency to stay with the others. Something she felt less inclined to do.

She let out a breath. One more year before she could enter Vanalf. One more year before she could become a Voyager.

CHAPTER THREE

DARKNESS EXISTS

Hallik

Hallik brushed his hair back from his eyes, breathing steadily as he led the rest of the students to the well near the center of the courtyard, Castle Vrodr looming beside them. What looked like tiny, rounded bushes shimmied away from him and the others. In truth, they were little creatures called bushnings that aided in cultivating the castle gardens. Despite trying, he'd never been able to figure out what they looked like. They'd pop right back into their bush-like shell whenever he tried to pick one of them up.

Lind stood with arms folded across his broad chest, smiling at the students as they shuffled toward the well, each of them breathing heavily.

Elowyn's attention was turned away from them, instead looking up at the Grimnir banner as she often did. She was always thinking, that one. He could never guess what about.

Hallik had taken the jog easy. At first, during their run, he pressed Elowyn from behind, knowing she'd run even harder just to lose him. Once she took off at a faster pace, he slunk back until the rest caught up with him. His fellow students were a strong bunch, the hardiest youth of Dalstava.

He reached the well and wheeled up a bucket of water. Several cups were already laid out, awaiting the students' return. He poured water into the cups as others held them out, nodding to his classmates in turn.

"I can't wait until I have my wings and don't need to run anymore," Svea said, heaving a breath as Hallik filled her cup. Her shoulders, both marked with dark, swirling tattoos, sagged. Her thick brown hair was coiled into a braid around the top of her head and pinned into place.

Hallik huffed a laugh. "You realize flying takes considerable exertion as well, right?"

"At least it's faster." Her light gray eyes blinked at him lazily before she nodded her thanks and withdrew with her cup.

Hallik smirked and helped everyone else before they shuffled toward Lind as he led the way into the castle.

After successfully handing them off, Arenda jumped into the air, massive feathered wings carrying her to an upper tower where the Valtyras made their roost.

"You always make yourself to be a leader," Elowyn said, nudging Hallik with a knuckle as she fell in beside him at the rear of the class.

She was teasing him about his tendency to serve out the water or hang back during the runs. "Grimnirs need captains, do they not?" Hallik said.

Elowyn laughed. "Ambitious."

"There's nothing wrong with some ambition. You too are ambitious. It's one of the reasons we make a good friendship." He dropped his wooden sword in a pile beside the door to the castle. A couple of the castle staff would take care of them from there.

"Who says we're friends?" she said, lowering her eyebrows at him.

Hallik shook his head and poked her with his elbow. "I do. Which means there's no way out of it, I'm afraid. Unless you start besting me in combat, then we may need to become rivals."

Svea looked back at them over her shoulder. "I wouldn't mind being your rival if it meant besting you at swordplay, Hal." Elowyn nodded to Svea in mock-serious agreement.

Hallik balked. "You would trade friendship for dominance?"

"Just *your* friendship, Hal," Svea said, smiling at Elowyn. "Rivalries are more fun anyway."

Hallik grunted as they went through the castle's wide stone hallway. The nooks were heavily decorated with relics from years past. Sconces burned with heatless, magical light, captured within upturned, hollowed goat horns. Massive wooden beams stretched across the top of the ceiling. The hallway ended at a large atrium that stretched three floors tall, but instead they entered a room to the side, lined with windows that filled the room with warm light.

Dusty tomes filled a bookshelf on one side of the room, and dark green wallpaper covered the walls, hinting at a time when the island was not closed off to the rest of the world. The students shuffled into three long benches that faced the windowed side of the room where Lind went and stood beside a small podium.

This class was what Hallik considered the most difficult part of becoming a Grimnir. Using magic had such varied intricacies to understand, and it was more difficult when considering the fact that none of them had any magic yet. Not until they could pass their trial through Vanalf.

Pass or die.

It was no surprise Grimnirs were a dying breed.

Lind smiled at them all through his thick beard until each student was seated.

As difficult as it was to keep his mind sharply attuned to the lessons Lind taught, Hallik knew the information would be invaluable. How else would he know what to do if he were to come across trolls, water sprites, or elves?

Lind's smile disappeared as he went straight into his lecture. "Today we will learn of draugrs."

"The drowned," Elowyn murmured from beside Hallik.

Lind nodded. "Yes. The drowned." He carefully lifted a leather parchment from the lectern before him and held it up for everyone to see. Tattooed into the leather was a crude depiction of a person with boned hands and tattered clothing, the face sunken and skeletal.

Did the air seem colder? Hallik brushed his hands across the skin of his arms. A quick glance at the other students showed that they too began to fold their arms and cross their legs.

Lind was a Vitugr, able to cast various spells, and he was known to do so during lectures to add an extra element to his storytelling.

"Many years ago, long before Avskild was formed, there were two brothers, Glemor and Reti. Their father was a great warrior in possession of many treasures, and both his sons were jealous of his wealth. The three of them went sailing with their families to find a new land for themselves. The first night at sea, a strong storm created mountainous waves. Water sloshed into the raft, and everyone struggled to keep the boat afloat. Reti, who stood at the back of the boat with his father, saw it as a terrible chance to rid himself of his father to claim his treasures for himself. He drew his sword and stabbed his father up through the back, piercing the lungs. He pulled the rings from his father's fingers before shoving him off the boat.

"Glemor saw Reti pushing their father into the sea right as it happened. In his fury, he charged back toward his brother, preparing to avenge his father. But Reti cast a savage blow across his brother's face with the tip of his blade. Disoriented, he lost his footing as another wave crashed into the boat, and Glemor was swept away with the water, captured by the sea, vengeance pounding in his heart, a yelled curse lost in the roar of the wave."

Lind's expression had darkened, an uncommon expression on the face of an otherwise cheery man. "Reti and the rest of them made it safely to a new land. Nobody else had seen Reti's treachery, so after mourning their losses, they appointed Reti as king. But a darkness hung over them. Often in the mornings, gray clouds hung low over the sea, and many said they saw the mast of a black ship hidden among the dark shadows. Days passed. Then weeks. Then months. Some said they could hear Glemor's voice shouting at them from the ocean, or whispering to them in the wind, always demanding vengeance, but for what, they knew not.

"All except Reti. The voice haunted him even more than the others. So early one morning, he took his sword and strode onto the beach till the waves were lapping at his knees. 'Face me,' he cried out to the ocean, slashing his sword across the water."

Lind slapped the parchment onto the lectern and stepped closer to the students, eyes scanning across them before he continued. "Then, from out of the water, a desiccated figure emerged and stood before Reti, a familiar voice echoing in the air like a distant storm from the sea.

"It was Reti's brother. Glemor."

"The first draugr," Elowyn whispered, her voice barely discernible.

Lind's inclined his head ever-so-slightly. "The first draugr." He took a deep breath. "Overcome with terror and madness, Reti was unable to defend himself against Glemor. He was dragged out to sea, disappearing from the eyes of the others who watched from the shore. Vengeance was dealt. A short while later, the dark clouds lifted and the voices faded from haunting the young village."

Hallik stroked his chin as he pondered the significance of the tale. "Why does this matter now?" he dared ask. "Does a draugr only seek vengeance if wronged in life?"

Lind nodded with a grunt. "Hallik poses a good question. The story of Reti and Glemor does not provide all the insight, but there have been many other draugrs. They do not always live for vengeance alone. Sometimes hatred. Sometimes simply an unwillingness to die. It is important to know that they are born of evil. Evil deeds. Evil thoughts. As future Grimnirs and defenders of Dalstava, you should know how to defeat them."

"They do not feel pain or suffer from wounds," Elowyn said.

"Yes," Lind said. "And they carry with them the skill they had in life, so warriors are more competent in battle. Then they may also employ whatever dark magic helped form their creation. Their power has a tendency to tug at the mind and drive people toward madness when haunted by a draugr or when trespassing in their territory."

"Have we had draugrs here on Avskild?" asked Trygge, his hazel eyes wide.

"Infrequently, yes," Lind answered. "I have destroyed one myself that haunted the burial grounds, though I was able to use fire magic, making it easy work. Most of you will not have the same advantage."

"So how do we kill them?" Trygge asked.

"Again," Svea added with a smirk.

Lind's smile returned. "Fire is good. Swords and axes can still sever their limbs, but whatever dark curse keeps them alive can be broken by separating their heart from their brain."

"Decapitation," Svea stated, her smirk widening to reveal her teeth.

"Indeed," Lind said, though he held up a hand. "But it should be noted that more than flesh holds them together. The curse makes them hardier than you would think, so severing the head can potentially be more difficult. Sometimes piercing the heart or brain can work, but it is not a guarantee. Fire ignores their curse and burns them straight through."

Fire. Hallik rubbed his chin. Another good reason to become a Vitugr, not that he'd be able to choose what type of Grimnir he'd become. At least kindling was already a staple supply of his.

But there was something about today's lesson—something about Lind—that left Hallik sitting at the edge of the bench. Lind liked to add dramatic flair to his stories since it was effective at helping the young students remain rapt, and it certainly helped Hallik who might otherwise fall asleep, but there was still something that made Hallik almost uncomfortable. That jovial light in Lind's eyes had been gone.

As soon as the class was over, Hallik lingered after, exchanging parting words with his fellow students.

"Are you coming tonight?" Elowyn asked before leaving. Hallik often visited her home at the edge of the forest to eat dinner with her and her mother, and still frequently stayed the night. It wasn't the same there as when he was much younger though.

Hallik popped one of his knuckles. "I told Sefrid I'd help out at the beach tonight. I don't know how long it will take." He swatted at Sefrid as the smaller boy walked to the door.

"All night," Sefrid joked, smiling as he attempted to dodge Hallik, but he was too slow. One of his front teeth was chipped in half from when a rope had snapped on their boat, causing a mast support beam to smash into his face. His brown hair was pulled into a loose bun at the back of his head and trimmed short everywhere else.

"I could help," Elowyn said.

Hallik narrowed his eyes at her but said nothing. It was uncommon of her to offer help in her free time.

"Excellent," Sefrid said. "I'll see you both at the docks later then." He rushed out the door.

Elowyn's eyes lingered on Hallik for a brief moment before she too left the room, leaving Hallik alone with Lind.

The mountain of a Grimnir stood beside his lectern, arms folded across his broad chest, eyebrows raised in amusement. "Is there something you wanted to talk about, Hallik?" Lind asked.

Hallik shifted his feet, unsure how to ask the question. "Are you... well?"

"Of course," Lind said, widening his arms, "but your question is deeper than that, is it not?"

Hallik smiled. Straight to the point, then. "I like to think of myself as perceptive. I've seen many lessons from you over the years. Something seemed different about you to-day when you spoke of the draugrs."

Lind nodded with a sigh. "Perceptive indeed. While there are many creatures or beasts, it's a rare thing to have them born of evil. A draugr is such a creature. Their existence is a direct result of abhorrent deeds. It's only a shame that such deeds exist, but," he paused to shrug, "our job is to slay the beast, and I have taught you what would be needed to do that. Darkness exists. Now just see that all your battles are not fought for jealousy, pride, or envy." Lind gestured to the door. "Have peace." There was still a hint of sadness in Lind's eyes, but that seemed to be all he had to say.

"Have peace," Hallik said and headed for the door. *Darkness does exist*, he thought, clenching his fist. As a Grimnir, he would fight that darkness.

UNEASE

Mikel Vigsen

Captain Mikel Vigsen of the Grimnir Guard placed his hands on the stone parapet atop Castle Grim. The great Tower of Tarn rose like a spike behind him. He stroked his black-and-gray peppered beard as he gazed out toward the mountains. His vantage high atop the castle allowed him to see across the entire city, but it wasn't the citizens of Dalstava that worried him.

As captain, Mikel oversaw all defensive and scouting operations for the entire island, a massive undertaking were it not for the fact that they'd had relative peace for over a century. All native threats had been nullified well before his time.

But Mikel was a Watcher. He experienced a supernatural connection with life. He could sense it. Feel it.

And something in the mountains, perhaps the forest itself, was… uneasy.

A fluttering in the air caught his attention as ink-black wings propelled in his direction. It wasn't an unexpected presence. Serena, his closest companion, was a raven of utmost intellect. Their bond had been instantaneous and powerful, from the very moment Mikel first sensed her in the forest nearly twelve years ago. They connected so well that Mikel could essentially see from her eyes if need be. He sensed her anxiety as she approached, and he held out his arm to receive her.

Serena croaked as she landed on Mikel's arm. Her wings continued to shuffle, legs bouncing as though she were unable to settle.

"Peace. What have you seen?" Mikel muttered, stroking her with his free hand. His own vision blurred as he connected with her, replaying her memory of gliding over the forest. The images revealed nothing, but it still brought with it a sense of disquiet.

He pursed his lips, wary of what these feelings could mean.

Another presence approached. One he did not expect.

Serena took to the air. He turned around and stood at the edge of the stairs that led back into the castle's keep. His hand settled over the pommel of his sword. It wasn't that he expected violence, but the unease must have gotten to him.

The door to the keep opened, revealing none other than Lind Hjordis, one of the instructors at Castle Vrodr. He seemed slightly out of breath, and Mikel could only imagine how long it had taken the large man to travel all the way up to this level.

"Lind," Mikel said. "I've been meaning to come visit Castle Vrodr for a while. I hope you'll excuse my absence. My thoughts have been elsewhere."

Lind waved his hand and shook his head, waiting to reach the top step beside Mikel before huffing and catching his breath. "I understand. Mine have as well. That is why I have come to speak with you."

Mikel pinched his beard and regarded his old friend, waiting for him to say more. Though Mikel was a full decade older than Lind, the teacher was still a mentor of sorts. Becoming an educator at Castle Vrodr did something to Grimnirs that Mikel would never understand.

Serena landed on the roof nearby and cocked her head down at them.

Lind let out another long breath before speaking, blue eyes flickering about as he sought the right words. "I'm not sure how to word it, but I've been feeling this sort of…"

"Unease?" Mikel finished, voice grave.

"Yes," Lind said, eyes narrowing. "You've felt it too?"

Mikel nodded.

"Any idea what might be triggering it?"

"I have sent Serena scouring the woods, but to no avail." Mikel's eyes switched to Serena, who remained at her perch on the roof, watching the conversation. "She senses it as well, but nothing is discernible."

Lind tugged his belt with a thumb. "I believe it's deeper than that. Potentially external. I have half a mind to visit Vanalf or check the portals."

Lind was right. Mikel patted his old friend's shoulder. "A wise suggestion, of course. I should have done so already. I will send Valtyras and Watchers to check the portals immediately. Could I rely on Castle Vrodr to assess Vanalf? That is your specialty after all."

"I will check it personally," Lind said without hesitation, leaving no room to question his urgency.

Mikel whistled to Serena. She took off, shooting up toward the Valtyra perch. She would signal them to meet with Mikel. He would need to alert the others. Create assignments. Issue orders. His pulse quickened, resolve settling over him like a familiar blanket. He doubted there would be dangers from beyond the portals. Nothing had breached Avskild's defenses in centuries, and even then it was only because of betrayal—a Voyager who'd been corrupted, opening the portal for others to pass through.

But now there were no Voyagers.

He cleared his throat, returning his attention to Lind. "I'll see to our defenses, my friend." He jerked his head toward the stairs in dismissal. "Peace."

Lind smiled and swatted Mikel's shoulder. "Peace." Then he ran back down the stairs.

Unlikely as an external threat would be, checking for any potential weaknesses there should have already been standard protocol, and Mikel would not be known as the captain who let dangers slip into Avskild. It was also a good reminder to send another party deeper into the mountains. Perhaps near the old ruins where the forest had grown thick. Pairing a Vitugr with a good Watcher would be effective there. He pursed his lips.

Peace indeed.

THE UNDEAD

Elowyn Galdre

E lowyn scolded herself the entire way down to the docks of Dalstava. Why in the realms would she volunteer to help haul and sort fish? She wanted to be angry about the idea, but she knew why. *They're your team, Elowyn. Your greatest strength is standing together.* Latshal's words had stuck with her.

She'd struck out on her own for too long, something she'd caught from her reclusive mother. But she could be a friend. She could be a part of a team. But did that really mean helping at the docks, of all places? Unfortunately, she could not turn back now.

The salty smell of the sea drifted up to her on a cool breeze. Several ships were moored at Dalstava's large docks, some massive, though most were smaller craft meant only for fishing. The biggest ships had been pulled ashore, as they were not often used. With whatever magical barrier it was that separated Avskild from the rest of the world, one could not sail away from the island no matter how hard they tried, nor could any outsider penetrate the barrier. It was rumored that Avskild was essentially in its own dimension, thus the need for Voyagers to be able to travel the portals in order to get anywhere else. That explanation didn't make complete sense, and she wasn't sure Voyagers could have created a separate realm. It was more than likely they were simply cut off physically. Sailors always said a wall of dark stone kept them from going too far.

But where did the Voyagers go? She was determined to uncover such mysteries.

Her feet made little sound as she stepped lightly on the wooden docks, scanning the row of boats until she spotted Hallik. They were not at the docks where she expected them, but instead they were pulling the boat toward the sandy shore, standing up to their waists in the water.

Elowyn jumped down from the docks and jogged toward them, worried she might be too late. She waved at the distant pair to catch their attention.

Sefrid laughed. "Ha, she came!" His voice carried over the susurration of gently crashing waves.

"I told you she would," Hallik shouted back, clearly intending for Elowyn to hear. He flashed that devilish grin of his.

Sefrid gestured toward a pile of crates and barrels stacked on the shore. "Bring one of those crates here toward the edge of the water," he shouted at her.

Elowyn did as requested without a second thought, rushing to grab a crate. She hurried to the edge of the water as Hallik and Sefrid stopped pulling the boat. Sefrid's mother, Glenda, and father, Kaf, jumped out of the boat, one to either side.

"She'll help fill the baskets," Sefrid explained to his parents.

Glenda and Kaf smiled at Elowyn, both muttering something she couldn't hear. They started lifting up strings of fish from the boat, holding them out to Hallik and Sefrid. The boys were armed with thick, curved knives that they used to unhook the fish before tossing them to Elowyn.

Elowyn grunted and deflected the fish into the basket. The fish no longer wriggled, now still and lifeless. Once the first basket was filled, they moved on to the second, then the third. They were working on the fourth as the sun got low, and Elowyn spared a glance toward the sea where gloomy clouds hung low above the surface of the water. It seemed like it would rain soon, but she hoped they would finish shortly and she'd be back at home before that happened.

She thought she caught sight of something within the shifting, nebulous clouds, but a fish nearly hit her in the face as Sefrid tossed one over.

"Sorry," Sefrid said, even though Elowyn was the one who was distracted.

Elowyn dropped the fish in the basket before returning her gaze to the skies. She saw it again, something even darker than the clouds. Another tossed fish from Hallik drew her eyes away once more, but when she looked back out over the ocean, the apparition was gone.

Hallik's eyes narrowed at Elowyn before he glanced over his shoulder and cast her a questioning look. "What is it?" he asked, as perceptive as always.

But Elowyn kept searching the misted skyline. If her eyes hadn't deceived her, then perhaps those weren't just clouds.

Sefrid's parents worked on the last two fish, walking toward Elowyn to put them away themselves rather than having Sefrid and Hallik toss them.

"Let's carry them over here," Kaf said as he dragged a full basket further up the sand, oblivious to the turmoil that simmered in Elowyn's gut.

Hallik stepped toward her, looking back at the sea one more time before his eyes settled on hers. "El? What's wrong?" he said.

Elowyn brushed a stray lock of her too-smooth hair back behind her ear. "I thought I saw..." She chewed her lip, hoping she wouldn't sound crazy. Knowing Hallik, he'd come up with some kind of joke. She shook her head and spoke anyway. "It looked like the black sails of a massive ship."

Hallik didn't even smile. Instead, he glanced down at the water where the small waves seemed to be building, then back over his shoulder. "Sefrid! Let's pull your parents' boat up and secure it."

Elowyn's breathing quickened. If Hallik was taking her seriously, then something was truly amiss.

Sefrid ran over and helped Hallik pull the boat in. Even Elowyn rushed into the water to tug at the rope hanging over the front. The frigid water chilled her to the bone.

A rush of cool wind burst across them as the murky clouds drew nearer, causing the hair on Elowyn's arms to rise. There was a mystical aura to the fog. Avskild had always been a magical place, but this was a type of magic that she didn't feel keen on exploring. Not yet, at least. As if sharing her sentiment, a flock of birds flew out from the mist, squawking as they retreated toward land.

The water level rose, stretching up the beach to the edge of the barrels before it stilled without receding. They pulled the boat up higher. Kaf loaded all the fish onto a cart while Glenda tied one of the boat's ropes around a thick boulder protruding from the sand.

"Get out of the water," Elowyn said, backing away, eyes scanning the surface of the water as the fog and darkened clouds drew closer. Wind tore through her hair with the sound of a giant heaving a sigh.

"I've never seen such a thing before," Kaf said, eyes wide as he retreated from the water, pushing the cart ahead of him. "What is happening?"

Of the five of them, Elowyn was the most likely one to be able to answer such a question. She'd read every book at Castle Vrodr that she'd been able to get her hands on, and her mother often sang the chronicles, endless tales of ages past. Had she heard of such a thing before? Of waves stilling along the beach? She couldn't recall any, but she had learned plenty about ominous clouds or fog, and none of those were good.

They all fled to the edge of the water, dripping wet. Hallik and Sefrid still held the fishing knives. Elowyn's blood pounded through her, making her fingers tingle with anticipation.

The surface of the sea was as still as a mirror, reflecting the dreary skies above. Oppressive silence replaced the sound of the waves.

A head burst from the water, no more than a couple paces away from Hallik. It was a place far too shallow to have been hiding an entire person. The head rose straight up until a corpse stood before them, sallow, water-logged skin hanging from its body, eyes pale white, shattered teeth protruding behind tight lips that barely existed. Tattered clothes hung limp from its body, and long, wet hair sagged past its shoulders.

"Draugr," Elowyn said, voice barely a whisper. She could hardly believe her eyes.

The draugr tilted its head and lurched toward them.

"Run!" Hallik bellowed.

Sefrid's parents were quick to oblige. They had no combat training and were probably the last people who would want to face up against a creature born of dark magic.

The three young Grimnirs-in-training stood their ground, though Elowyn was completely unarmed.

"Elowyn, that means you too," Hallik said, barely sparing her a glance as he widened his stance, preparing to battle the draugr.

"We will fight together," Elowyn said.

"No," Hallik said. "You need to run and warn the guards. We need Grimnir magic to fight this, and you're the fastest runner."

Elowyn ground her teeth. "Then we should all run!" Frustration boiled in her chest.

The draugr drew a rusty, curved sword from its shell-encrusted belt. The cool wind blew stronger and rain began to patter against Elowyn's skin. A dark feeling of despair crept along her neck like an insect. She swatted at it, but the feeling remained. The draugr took two more steps in their direction, and Elowyn subconsciously retreated equally as far back, gritting her teeth even harder.

"There are people all over the docks," Hallik said. "Sefrid and I can hold it back, but you must go quickly."

The draugr made a sudden movement, lunging forward, weapon slashing. Hallik lurched to the side, dodging the attack.

"Go, Elowyn!"

Elowyn growled, fists clenched. "Don't die while I'm gone!" Elowyn punched her palm and turned away, sprinting up the sandy beach. Sefrid yelled from behind her, but Hallik was right. They needed help.

CHAPTER SIX

GOODBYE

Hallik

Hallik dodged around two quick slashes from the draugr. Sefrid was bold enough to attempt a jab at its side, but it deflected his fish knife and lashed back at him. He jumped away just in time to avoid the saber's edge. Hallik was still stunned. Never in his wildest imagination could he have conceived that such a deteriorated body would move so quickly.

Hallik ducked under another slash, dragging the edge of his knife across the draugr's wrist. The blade tore at the exposed flesh and grated against the bone beneath, but the draugr was undeterred. It stabbed toward Hallik's midsection as Sefrid took a low swing that scraped against the draugr's hip.

Hallik stepped backwards, nearly tripping over a discarded crate. He looked over his shoulder at Sefrid's retreating parents. Elowyn had already caught up and would be well beyond them in no time. It was extremely fortunate that she'd chosen today to start being more considerate.

"Did you notice how your parents ran away without even saying goodbye?" Hallik asked without looking at Sefrid.

"Of course not," Sefrid said. "Goodbyes are for the dead, and I am very much alive."

"Goodbye, Sefrid!" his father's voice yelled back at them from the docks.

Hallik grunted. "That doesn't bode well."

A slash from the draugr caught Sefrid on the upper arm, a bit of his blood flicking into the air. He gasped and stumbled back. "No, it does not." His eyes were wide.

The draugr's jaw unhinged mechanically to one side and its pale, milky eyes widened as if excited to see Sefrid's blood. The air grew colder as the wind increased, rain coming down ever harder.

Neither Hallik nor Sefrid had been in a real fight before. Sure, they'd accidentally drawn blood, but nothing like this.

A deep groan escaped the draugr's throat, and it attacked with unending vigor. It stepped into each of its swings, drawing closer to Sefrid. Hallik attempted to attack from behind, but it was always able to whip back toward him with unnatural speed. He snatched up a crate and hurled it at the draugr, shattering it across the creature's back. It may as well have been a grain of sand, for the draugr paid no mind.

Sefrid continued backing away, dodging as best as he could against the draugr's onslaught. They needed to last long enough for Elowyn to get the Grimnirs.

A slash of the draugr's sword nearly took off Sefrid's head, but he ducked away just in time.

Hallik took a tentative jab at the draugr's back, blade cutting cloth and scraping against its ribcage. Undaunted, it raised its sword in both hands before battering down on Sefrid. Sefrid used the knife to deflect the blow just well enough for him to roll to the side, but his weapon was knocked from his grip, stabbing into the sand.

The draugr didn't slow. It hacked again. Sefrid barely moved in time, pulling his legs away as the sword dug a thin trench where his body had been.

Hallik needed to end this. They wouldn't last long enough for the Grimnirs to arrive. He gripped his fish knife in both hands and leapt at the draugr's back.

Still ignoring Hallik, the draugr stomped down on Sefrid's leg, preventing him from getting away.

Hallik came down, driving the weapon hard toward the draugr's neck. It ducked at the last moment, its weapon whipping across Sefrid's chest. Hallik missed his target, the knife burying into the muscle around the draugr's scapula.

The abomination no longer ignored Hallik but slammed its arm back, cracking Hallik across his chest. He was thrown back by the force, slapping down against the cold, wet sand while more rain pummeled against his face. His breath came in short gasps as he rose up on his elbows. Sefrid had gotten to his feet, stumbling away, holding a hand over his wound.

The draugr lurched toward Hallik, its jaw moving as though words would emerge. Speech came after a slight delay, as if it took great effort to summon air from whatever desiccated lungs it had. A deep, whispering voice rushed across Hallik's face, but he couldn't understand the words. His knife was still embedded in the draugr's back. He grasped around him, hoping to find something to fight with, but his fingers only closed around the slippery flesh of a fish that had fallen from a basket in their haste to retreat. Not much of a weapon.

That left him defenseless.

If only he were already a Grimnir. Why did they need to wait before entering the cave? This whole fight hadn't lasted long enough. They'd barely bought any time for Elowyn to alert the guards. If they abandoned the beach now, the draugr would be free to wreak havoc on the docks. He couldn't let that happen. But he also couldn't let the draugr kill his friend.

Something about the draugr's voice made Hallik's limbs feel sluggish. He huffed and struggled to his feet. As the draugr came and stood in front of him, Hallik held the fish out in his hand as though it were a weapon.

The draugr paused, looking at the fish, mouth agape as if considering whether or not it was a threat. Its voice faltered.

"Run, Sefrid," Hallik shouted, but a quick glance showed that Sefrid had fallen to his hands and knees only a few paces away. Perhaps that wound had been worse than he'd thought. Without another thought, he hurled the fish at the draugr, its wet, scaley body slapping against its face.

Hallik dodged around the undead creature and sprinted toward Sefrid. He dove to one knee, scooping his friend up from under his arms, helping him to rise. "Let's go. I think we've delayed it long enough," he said.

"You should go, Hallik," Sefrid said, eyes sad. "I will die."

Hallik shook his head. "No." They only took one step before something wet and hard crashed into the back of

Hallik's knee, dropping him to the sand. The fish. The draugr had hurled it at him.

The draugr's voice came again, stronger this time. Hallik's limbs grew cold in an instant. He groaned, losing his grip on Sefrid.

Hallik looked back, but the draugr was already upon them. He dropped to dodge a swing of its sword, but it turned its blank eyes to Sefrid, who rolled to his back, looking up at his demise.

"No," Hallik muttered.

Sefrid gave Hallik one last look before saying, "Goodbye."

CHAPTER SEVEN

A BIT OF FIRE

Elowyn Galdre

Fire burned in Elowyn's legs as she pounded up the docks. "Grimnirs!" she shouted. "We're under attack!"

There were over a dozen people milling about the docks with their evening chores, most transporting fish or crabs. Some were repairing nets or preparing line for the next day. They paused to stare as she ran past.

"Flee the docks!" If her words weren't enough, the heavy rain that followed in her wake must have sent an adequate message. People started leaving their work to rush toward the city.

She wanted nothing more than to stand beside Hallik and Sefrid to fight, but unarmed as she was, she wouldn't have been any help. Never again would she be caught without a weapon.

Elowyn was well ahead of Sefrid's parents. She tried to observe every person she passed, hoping beyond reason that any of them were Grimnirs. Her best bet was to head straight for the guard post that oversaw the docks. When she arrived at the two-story building, she threw open the door. A single man stood inside, looking out the window at the rapidly changing weather. He opened his mouth to speak, but Elowyn interrupted him.

"Draugr on the beach," she panted.

The man's eyes widened. He did not wear the sigil of Grimnir and would thus be of little use to Elowyn.

"What?" he said incredulously.

There was no time for this. For all she knew, the draugr had already butchered her friends and would be approaching the docks any moment. The very concept of them fighting against that monster with little more than fishing knives made her breath quicken with panic. Hallik was good with a sword, but that knife would certainly not be sufficient. Elowyn scowled and gritted her teeth as she spotted an axe and a spear on the wall, hung up across a rounded shield. A lamp burned at the table, the small flame winking in the wind of the open door. "Alert the Grimnirs. There are people in danger."

"Are you certain?" the man asked, clutching a hand to his chest.

"Go!" she shouted at him. This was no place for courtesy. She snatched the axe off the wall and grabbed the lamp.

"What do you think you're doing?" the man said, though he had barely moved one step from his place beside the window.

Elowyn growled. "Saving my friends. Now go! Alert the Grimnirs." She didn't bother looking back as she ran outside. The docks were nearly empty already. It seemed they had more sense than the watchman. Word would spread quickly. The Grimnirs would come. They had to.

But Elowyn needed to ensure that her friends were still alive by the time that happened. She tucked the axe in her belt and used a hand to protect the flame of the lamp as she rushed back down the docks, heading for the beach. She ignored the burning heat that sizzled at the flesh of her palm. It was a small price to pay if it meant saving a couple lives. The axe handle bounced at her side as she sprinted.

A tangle of weeds and rocks blocked Elowyn's view of the place where the draugr had attacked Hallik and Sefrid. When she finally rounded it, she saw the draugr stepping toward her friends as they crawled away from it on the ground.

Rain pelted Elowyn's face as she gasped in horror, her legs pumping even harder after she leapt off the wooden docks and sprinted across the sand.

Hallik narrowly dodged a jab from the draugr just before Elowyn arrived.

The darkness in the air was almost as palpable as the rain, pressing in around her with a chilling weight. It slammed down against her like the cold of snow, fatigue gripping her muscles. She groaned against the sudden pressure and yanked the axe from her belt.

The draugr ignored her presence and swung again, this time at Sefrid. Sefrid barely managed to kick at the sword, deflecting the blow, but he yelled in pain. It must have sliced into his foot.

Keeping one hand holding the lamp, Elowyn hurled the axe. The weapon flipped end over end until its tip hacked into the draugr's back, wedging just beneath its ribcage. It was a magnificent throw. A triumphal energy coursed through Elowyn from the moment the weapon struck. Even the cursed air loosened its frozen grasp on her.

The draugr halted its advance on her friends and turned to regard her with its ghostly eyes, thin lips pulling back in a sneer.

Trickles of fear crawled up Elowyn's skin like the legs of a hundred spiders.

Fire. She needed to use the fire. It would negate the monster's magical aura and allow them to kill it.

The draugr stalked toward her without any regard to the axe in its back. A knife jutted out near its neck as well, a sign that her friends were equally disarmed.

How could she use the fire? With the rain pounding down, it would very likely go out as soon as she pulled her hand away. Even the wood nearby was soaked through. It would be impossible to create more fire under such conditions.

Lind had not prepared them for this kind of scenario.

"Elowyn," Hallik shouted. "What are you doing?"

"A team works together." Elowyn said, taking a few steps back as the draugr drew near. It did not run, but strode confidently toward her.

Hallik got to his feet while Sefrid remained on the sand, groaning in pain. "What about the Grimnirs?"

"They will come," Elowyn said, hoping beyond hope that they would arrive in time.

Guttural words issued from the draugr's mouth as it reared back its weapon, preparing for a mighty blow.

With little thought, Elowyn flung the entire lamp straight into the draugr's chest. Chunky oil spattered across its body, the flames expanding, burning with a blue-orange light. But it swung for her, unperturbed.

Elowyn dropped, diving to one side, but the draugr was relentless, jabbing again and again. Thankfully, she was quick—her one advantage—but the draugr attacked tirelessly. Her heart pounded with all the intensity of battle as the draugr's blade whooshed around her. It even tore the fabric at her sleeve. She was barely dodging in time to avoid each swing, but she would tire eventually.

From behind, Hallik rammed into the draugr's back. It stumbled to one knee, and Hallik flopped to the ground as though he'd just run into a tree.

With all the anxious energy burning through Elowyn's body, she wanted to rush the draugr, but the glint of the axe in its back drew all her focus. In spite of the fear that still crawled across her skin, she took one firm step toward the draugr and leapt, throwing her hands up. She clapped one hand down on the draugr's lowered head, using it as leverage to flip herself over its body. With her other hand, she gripped the axe. As soon as her feet hit the ground, she yanked the axe free. Expecting more resistance, she stumbled back.

The draugr shot to its feet, turning on her, sword slashing in a wide arc. She was far enough away that she dodged it easily then jerked forward, throwing all her weight into a mighty swing. All of her training had encouraged her to avoid such a risky move, especially when speed was supposed to be her advantage, but weaker attacks would not help her against the draugr's dark magic.

The axe came down hard, crashing into the draugr's still-burning chest with a sickening crunch.

Hallik was on his feet behind the draugr as well, and he wrenched the knife from its flesh, jabbing at the draugr's neck once again. Its flesh tore away, but it elbowed Hallik, throwing him back.

Elowyn dislodged the axe and swung again. She needed to behead the beast. She didn't know how much longer the fire would last, but its disabling voice would ruin them if they didn't kill it quickly. Her axe narrowly missed its neck but battered into the draugr's jaw, tearing the bone away from its face. The jaw hung from one side.

The draugr hesitated, its white eyes somehow widening even further within its lidless gaze. It went to swing its sword at her, but Hallik rushed in and grabbed the draugr's sword arm. He tugged it to the side. The draugr was firm, but it lurched to the side just enough, exposing its neck.

"Now, El!" Hallik shouted.

Elowyn swung the axe as though she were about to split a log and brought it down hard on the draugr's neck. A squelching sigh escaped the draugr's body as its head broke away from its body, thudding into the sand. A pitifully small amount of blackened blood sprayed onto Hallik's arm.

Hallik scrambled away from the draugr's body, hands shaking, lips curled in disgust. "Blegh." He wiped his hands on his soaked shirt. "I'm going to be sick. That was the most disgusting thing I've ever touched. It was like holding wet, shriveled meat."

The draugr's body was completely stiff as it thunked onto the sand. The oily fire on its chest began to dissipate, but the flesh it had touched fell away like ash.

"We killed it," Elowyn said so that her mind would accept the finality of it. The pounding in her chest receded.

Hallik nodded, the disgust on his face shifting to a satisfied smirk. "We do make a good team."

Sefrid groaned. "You got it?"

"Sefrid!" Elowyn had forgotten about him in the thrill of the fight. She ran to his side, falling to her knees to take a quick inventory of his injuries. The cut across his chest would maybe need stitches, but it didn't seem lethal. His other injury, a slash on his foot, wasn't bleeding as much. Relief flooded her, and Hallik came to stand beside them.

"You'll be alright, Sefrid," Hallik said. "I didn't know you could be so brave. Well done."

Sefrid barked a laugh through clenched teeth. "Wouldn't be trying to become a Grimnir otherwise." He poked at the wound on his chest tentatively.

Flashes of shadow flicked past the setting sun far to the west where the clouds hadn't yet reached.

Four Valtyras soared down through the air and landed on the beach, Arenda among them. The three others went straight to the draugr, but Arenda approached the three students.

"We killed it," Hallik said.

"I can see that," Arenda said, her voice and expression stern. Her hair was pulled back, hidden beneath a steel and leather helmet. In her left hand, she held a spear and a rounded shield.

Elowyn shot to her feet. Arenda's expression was not encouraging, and Elowyn worried that something wasn't right. "What's wrong?" she asked. "Are we safe?"

Arenda didn't answer immediately. "We will be."

A much larger group of Valtyras flew down, joining the rest of them, and several other Grimnirs charged down the beach, all fully armed.

Their eyes were fixed on the sea.

Elowyn followed their gaze, squinting against the downpour and darkened clouds.

"You only saw this one draugr?" Arenda asked.

"Yes," Elowyn said, suddenly remembering what else she'd seen. "But I did see what looked like the black sail of a large ship."

Arenda nodded. "Lind and Captain Vigsen are concerned about a breach."

Elowyn swallowed hard. A breach. That would mean the draugr came from outside Avskild altogether. She took a step further up the beach.

Hallik stormed over to the headless draugr and wrested the sword from its grip.

"That could be tainted, Hallik," Elowyn said.

Hallik breathed a laugh. "I'm sure that holding its sword is the last thing I need to be worried about." He gestured at the sickly draugr blood that spotted his arms and shirt. Even under the heavy rain, it did not easily wash away.

Elowyn shook her head, but her eyes were drawn back toward the sea. She thought she could see that black sail again.

A Grimnir leader yelled an order, and the Grimnirs started forming up.

To Elowyn's horror, another draugr head emerged from the water. Then another.

Arenda whistled at a nearby Valtyra. "Take the injured boy to Castle Vrodr." The large Valtyra obeyed and rushed over to scoop Sefrid off the beach.

"We can fight," Hallik said, standing beside Arenda.

Arenda smiled at them, the sternness vanishing from her face. "Indeed you can, but you will leave this to the Grimnirs. We can take care of a ship full of draugrs. I need the two of you to head back to Castle Vrodr. Watch over your friend until we return."

"But—" Elowyn started.

"Go. Now," Arenda said. "This is not a discussion." She switched her spear to her other hand.

A jet of fire launched by a Vitugr engulfed the nearest draugr, making quick work of it as the monster dropped back beneath the water. Two other Grimnirs pushed toward another draugr. In a flurry of blows, it too collapsed to the watery sand, bodiless head soaring back into the sea.

They made it look so easy.

Elowyn's hands tightened into fists.

More draugrs emerged, a whole score of them.

But Arenda was right. The draugrs would be no match for the Grimnir forces. Now was not her time.

She let out a sigh and grabbed Hallik's shoulder. "Come, Hallik. Arenda is right. Let's go keep Sefrid company."

Hallik huffed, wiping his wet hair back from his face. His brows furrowed in a deep frown, but he nodded to Elowyn. It would be unwise to not listen to one of their instructors. Together, they headed for the docks as the sounds of battle rose behind them.

CHAPTER EIGHT

EVIL DEEDS

Lind Hjordis

A burning sensation rippled across Lind's stomach until the jet of flame bursting from his hand died out. The draugr before him fell in a blackened heap. He panted to catch his breath. He was soaked from head to foot, a combination of both perspiration and precipitation.

It was the last of them.

The beach was cleared, though the daylight was a mere memory. Who knew what else lingered in the dark?

He looked to Captain Mikel, who nodded back.

"It's clear," Mikel bellowed, his voice loud enough for their whole company to hear. The other Watchers nodded their confirmation. They would have been able to detect if any draugrs remained.

Lind heaved a sigh of relief, letting his hands drop to his side where his axe still hung. He hadn't had to draw the weapon at all. The fire was all he'd needed, but the magic left a burning sensation along his whole arm that caused him to sweat profusely, and his throat was painfully dry.

A massive, dark shadow grew closer through the fog over the sea, but the Watchers showed no concern, leaving Lind's mind at ease. He'd grown to trust the Watchers' instincts. The air swirled as the dark shape came closer, becoming more distinct until the front of a giant ship appeared. A dozen Valtyras had grabbed onto it, pumping their wings to bring it to shore. Its large black sails fluttered in the wind, and its wooden surface was crusted with age.

Lind's lips curled at the sight of it.

Beside him, Mikel sheathed his sword and shook his head. "An entire ship full of draugrs," Mikel grumbled so that just the two of them could hear. The scowl on the captain's face communicated all Lind needed to know.

It shouldn't have been possible. The ship itself looked like it came from a completely different era, back before Avskild had been separated from the rest of the world, lifted up on its pillar of stone. Lind had only seen sketches of such monolithic ships. Even the few larger, seafaring ships that they'd kept on the docks from hundreds of years ago had practically withered away.

This ship had to have come from the outside, yet there was certainly no way it could have traveled up from the true ocean that rested far below the sea of Avskild. There was no other explanation. It meant that the defenses of the portals had lapsed. And how long had they been open?

Lind stepped closer to Mikel. "If an entire ship could slip through, it makes me worry that we've had other security breaches," he said in a low voice.

Mikel nodded. "Let's hope our discussion earlier today wasn't too late. I've already informed the officers that we'll need to send scouts to the portals. I'll have them depart at first light, though the farther portals might take a day or two before I have results."

Lind grunted a response. "And I need to head to Vanalf first thing in the morning as well. Arenda will be in charge of Castle Vrodr in my absence."

"That is well," Mikel said. "Let us hope that this resolves easily without too much attention from King Knos."

Lind understood completely. Involvement from the king was the last thing they needed. He'd spent more of his reign renovating his own manor than anything else. His hasty, uninformed decisions could very possibly create more issues than otherwise.

Arenda came toward them, along with Irena, the leader of the Grimnir Guard's Vitugr squadron. "We've cleared the ship," Arenda reported. "There was only a single draugr left aboard. The rest of them must have come ashore."

"Burn it and bury it in the sea," Mikel said, gesturing at the ship, "lest any dark magic remains. I want nothing left but ashes."

"Aye, sir," Irena said. She ordered the Vitugrs to burn the ship, and a torrent of their combined magic warped into a blazing wave of fire that crashed into the ship.

Lind moved to join them, but Mikel grabbed his sleeve.

"Not you," Mikel said. "You must check back in on those students of yours. Get some rest. You have a journey in the morning."

Lind regarded the other Vitugrs. Thirteen of them. More than enough to incinerate the ship, even of such a size. He nodded to Mikel. "Peace, then, Captain Vigsen."

"Peace."

Lind strode up the beach. He never imagined that an entire ship of draugrs was possible. Such a case was unheard of, and he was positive he'd read every record they had in the entire city. What kind of evil deed could have created so many?

It was possible, of course, that the ship had been submerged for centuries, the draugrs long dead. If that were the case, then the portals would still be in good condition and their defenses would not have been thwarted. Though that scenario seemed unlikely, unless the draugrs could have been lying dormant for so many years.

He rubbed his forehead. The condition of the portals would give him all the information he needed.

At least the threat had been stopped.

For now.

NORMAL

Hallik

Hallik's footsteps fell heavy as he walked through the darkened hallways of Castle Vrodr. He should have been asleep already, but like the other students who had bunked up in the castle for the night, he'd been restless. He was returning from the well outside, a large mug of water held in one hand.

He and Elowyn had killed a draugr, and they weren't even Grimnirs yet. As a trophy, and extra protection in case he needed it, Hallik had recovered the draugr's saber and kept it looped through his belt. It was certainly in need of a good polish, and it could very well snap in two the moment he blocked a stroke, but he'd never owned his own sword before. He'd only ever used the weapons provided by the Grimnir training program.

"Hallik," a voice hissed from the shadows.

Hallik recognized the voice and paused. Only dim fire-light from the burning hearth at the end of the hall reached them. He even thought he could hear the faint sound of music.

Latshal emerged from a doorway. As one of the two Watchers that kept guard at Castle Vrodr, Latshal would often be roaming the hallways or watching the gate while students studied outside. Occasionally, she taught a lesson, but Hallik had only received a lesson from her in three or four instances over the last few years.

"Stay with the others," Latshal instructed. "Don't wander the halls. Khanak and I will be on alert all night in case there is trouble. You need not worry yourself."

Hallik held up the mug. "I was just getting water for Sefrid."

Latshal raised an eyebrow at him. "Very well, but get some sleep."

Hallik nodded and proceeded down the hall, though the faint music he heard was indication enough that they wouldn't be going to sleep too soon. He walked by the large hearth of the banquet hall and entered another big, elongated room on the opposite side. Some forty students were inside, trying to remain quiet as they listened to one other student who sat on a table at the far end. Kelm was the boy's name, and he was playing a three-stringed lyre, using a horsehair bow to make the deep, humming music.

Latshal poked her head in behind Hallik. "Enough of that," she said. "Get to bed. All of you." She didn't wait to see if they listened, but vanished behind the door once again.

Several students groaned and blamed Hallik for leading her back to them.

Hallik waved them off and sat down next to Sefrid, handing him the water. It had been a few hours since their fight with the draugr. Lind had visited them to let them know that all the draugrs had been defeated, but they'd encouraged the students to remain at Castle Vrodr for safety purposes. Their families were already well aware of the protocol, but Hallik spent most of his nights at the castle anyway, when he wasn't staying at Elowyn's place on the edge of the forest. Elowyn's mother had practically raised him ever since Elowyn had brought him home like a stray animal.

Sefrid took a swig of water before handing the mug over to Svea. Svea took the mug, her face stuck in a permanent pout ever since hearing that they'd fought a draugr without her.

"You heard Latshal," Elowyn said to the other students. "We'll need our sleep anyway. Tomorrow will be like any other day with plenty of training."

The four of them planned to sleep in this room tonight. That way they could all remain together.

Hallik smirked as the kids' voices faded. Most of them shuffled out of the room, heading toward the living quarters. Some of them were as young as twelve years old, though most people enrolled to become a Grimnir at age fourteen. Hallik and Elowyn had both joined at twelve with encouragement from Elowyn's mother. It was the price to pay if they wanted the magic offered by venturing into Vanalf, and the earlier they enrolled, the greater their chances of survival.

Elowyn turned her sharp gaze to Hallik. "That means you too, draugr-slayer."

Hallik pointed at her. "You struck the killing blow."

She smiled and shrugged in response.

"I helped too," Sefrid said, laying back down on the blanketed floor with a grunt.

"You were a very effective distraction," Hallik said, grabbing a spare blanket.

Sefrid breathed a laugh and shook his head.

Hallik was positive that Sefrid would heal as long as his wounds were kept clean, but his mind still whirled at the implications of the day's events. From the way Lind had explained draugrs, didn't they thrive on vengeance? Perhaps it was pure malice without discrimination. The draugr attacked all three of them without particular attention to anyone in particular. The only exception was when it focused on Sefrid, but that was because he was injured. And then there was a ship full of other ones that had attacked the Grimnir Guard. Who were they after?

"At least you got to fight it," Svea whispered to Sefrid as she placed her sword on the floor beside her and laid back. The two of them continued whispering to each other about the fight when Elowyn came and sat next to Hallik.

"Thanks for coming back," Hallik said, placing his hands behind his head. He looked up at her green eyes that glistened in the dim candlelight. "For helping me and Sefrid. It might have killed us both."

She jabbed a finger at him. "It *would* have. But I wasn't about to let it kill you. I'd hate to hear what my mother would say if things had ended differently."

Hallik smiled. "I'm *sure* that was your motivation."

Elowyn's smile faded when she saw the rusty old sword Hallik had kept with him. "Hallik, you need to get rid of that thing. It's hardly even fit to call a weapon."

Hallik scoffed. "Sefrid's wounds would beg to differ." Her distaste for the weapon made it that much more appealing to him. "I don't have a weapon of my own anyway, and this is better than nothing."

"We'll have to fix that," Elowyn said. She blew out the candle, and they all settled down.

Tomorrow would be another normal day. Back to training. Back to waiting. Maybe he'd ask the teachers again if he could go to Vanalf a year early. The mystery around his father was like a hook in his flesh. He wasn't sure how, but he was, for some reason, positive that becoming a Grimnir would provide him with the insight he needed to find his father.

CHAPTER TEN

CHANGE

Mikel Vigsen

Morning rays filtered through the enormous windows that lined the upper walls of the stairway. Mikel's boots echoed on the stone surface of the steps as he reached the top of the stairs. The throne room occupied half of the second floor of the Tower of Tarn. Most of the upper floors were in disuse, and few people ever ventured higher than the fifth floor except for the Valtyras, who could fly to the very top from the outside. It was rumored that the original portal was created within these walls.

Massive wooden carvings extended from floor to ceiling on either side, many of them depicting monsters and warriors from ages past locked in eternal battle. A long history of war littered the past of the citizens of Avskild.

So many years of peace made those ancient wars feel like merely myth and legend.

Some said the Tower of Tarn existed over two thousand years ago, long before the Grimnirs ever came to be. When the Grimnirs came along, they salvaged it. Made it their stronghold. Those were much darker times.

Ahead of him, pacing in front of the throne, was King Knos. Standing. Not sitting. The very fact that Knos was up and ready at such a time was already alarming.

Mikel closed his fists and steadied his breath, steeling himself for what was to come.

Accompanying Knos were his two constant companions, Lorelai, the royal attendant, her rust-red hair tied back into a thick braid, and Daelen, the King's Guard, his stern gaze fixed on Mikel.

A long, elaborate rug stretched the distance from the stairs to the throne, but it did little to mask Mikel's steps as he approached. He'd already imagined how this conversation would go and considered it in his best interest to keep the conversation as simple as possible. All he needed to do was make the king feel as though things were being handled.

Knos paused his pacing and clasped his hands behind him. He was a large man, taller than most, with reddish-brown hair that was shorn on the sides and a short, well-trimmed beard. An intricate sword was sheathed at his waist, though he'd likely never used it. The weapon itself was as important as the crown on Knos's head—perhaps *more* important as a symbol of his position. It had been passed down for generations.

His face lacked expression, though his head tilted slightly to one side. A necklace of silver and gold hung from his neck, and he wore a green tunic laced with gold thread. Knos pursed his lips as Mikel continued toward him and his attendants.

"How is it possible?" Knos asked, his voice low, words spoken with slow ease.

Mikel took a few more steps before stopping, still several paces away from where Knos had been pacing in front of the throne. He used every last step to finalize how he would address the matter with the king. "We have eradicated the entire threat, Lord King. The Grimnir Guard suffered no casualties."

"A boy was injured," Knos said, voice sharpening. "A student at Vrodr. Not slain, certainly, but still a casualty, is it not?"

Mikel swallowed. He wasn't sure how Knos had received all of his information and did not know that such details had reached him. It had been too optimistic of him to assume that this would be an easy conversation. "True,

Lord King. A misguided decision by one of the students, but I will communicate with Instructor Lind Hjordis to ensure that each student has sufficient understanding of protocol."

Knos nodded but kept his eyes fixed on Mikel. "It is well, but you also evaded my question. How was it possible?"

Lorelai, the royal attendant, folded her arms, her dark gray eyes feeling especially sharp as she glared at Mikel. How he answered this question could elicit reactions he did not want to deal with, but he was up to the task. Such was his role as the captain.

Mikel cleared his throat. "The origin of these draugrs is unknown. It seems unlikely that an entire ship of them could have been created here within Avskild. It is most plausible that there was a breach in the portal safety around Avskild."

Lorelai's glare shifted to a disapproving shake of her head; subtle, but he still caught it.

Knos lifted a finger, mouth open. "Not possible," he said. "There has not been a breach of our defenses in over three-hundred years. I have followed the same protocol as the kings and queens before me with even greater devotion than they. So no, do not suggest such folly."

Mikel nodded. "Certainly." That meant he would not be sharing the details about sending soldiers to investigate the portals. If he didn't mention it, then the king could not protest the investigation. "There is the possibility, then, that the ship and the corpses of the draugrs have been resting on the seafloor for these many years. Perhaps a fisherman accidentally recovered something that belonged to them, and this triggered their lust for vengeance. Disturbing resting places can have such effects." He'd made that up, hoping the king was not as well versed in the sagas and stories shared around fires. A spirit could be disturbed in such scenarios, but that certainly would not trigger the summon of a draugr. Such undead were only created through evil acts done to them while still alive.

If a breach in the portal defenses had occurred, the king would be the last man in Avskild to admit as much.

Knos tapped his chin with his thumb as he chewed on Mikel's words. When the king looked to Lorelai, Mikel knew he had to say something else before the woman caught on. She had a reputation for trying to know everything, and he wouldn't be surprised if she were able to catch his misdirection better than the king.

"Lord King," Mikel said hurriedly. "We have not previously had a Grimnir stationed at the guardhouse at the docks. I have already assigned it as a regular station for the Watchers. We've made preparations to have one inhouse and another on patrol during the primary operation time of the fishers and dock workers. We have some Watchers paired with various birds, which will provide good coverage. We'd be able to rally even quicker with that arrangement."

Knos snapped his fingers. "That's the kind of response I wanted from you, Captain Vigsen. But tell me, why were the docks not already manned by Grimnirs?"

Mikel's eyes dropped to the floor. Every year there were fewer and fewer Grimnirs. "We've been stretched thinner these last few years. Each year we have fewer students. Previously, the docks were directed by Voyagers, but... as you know, Lord King, the Voyagers are all gone. We have had some members of the militia fill in for certain roles to compensate. Such was the situation at the docks."

"This could work, but where will you pull the additional Grimnirs from?"

"Patrols to the outer villages," Mikel replied without hesitation. "We just have to reduce frequency with those. I've already issued the orders, and everything should be in place by this afternoon."

Knos glanced at Lorelai one more time, but the woman said nothing. "It is well," Knos said. "Ensure that the militia receives better training as well."

Mikel inclined his head with a slight bow. "Wise counsel, Lord King. I will see it done."

"And no more nonsense about a breach in the portal defenses," Knos said, grabbing Mikel by the shoulder in a tight grip. He was close enough that Mikel could smell the fish on his breath. "Stamp out any such rumor."

Mikel placed a hand over his heart. "Of course, my king. Gossip about such things would only be detrimental." He refused to look over at Lorelai, though he knew she was scrutinizing him.

The very fact that King Knos was so insistent about not considering a breach in the portals made Mikel that much more interested in getting the results from the scouts he'd sent.

"Too true," Knos said, loosening his grip to pat Mikel's shoulder instead. "That should be all, Mikel. Peace."

Mikel bowed his head once again, relieved to hear the king use his first name. "Peace." He stepped away and strode back toward the stairs. He'd long considered himself to be one of the king's trusted advisors, but he'd grown to understand that Knos maintained a very close group. Despite the fact that Mikel was the commander of their army, there were many things the king did not share with him. The refusal about investigating the portals, for instance, was concerning, though he feared that asking why the king was so dismissive would only result in Mikel losing the favor he had worked hard to gain.

In his heart, he hoped the king was merely stubborn. Of course something wouldn't have harmed the portals, and without any Voyagers, there was nobody on the entire island who could open them. Except, perhaps, Irena or Lind. There was no doubt a spell out there that would allow them to open one of the portals, though he'd never been able to get them to confirm if they could.

But then again, there were many mysteries in the world. Things could always change.

CHAPTER ELEVEN

THE HUNTER

Jaysen Bjorn

Bjorn held his breath, listening beyond the sounds of buzzing insects that swarmed the forest. The midday sun gleamed above, beams of light filtering down between the leaves and branches. The tracks he'd seen yesterday certainly did not belong to anything like a wolf or a bear, but perhaps something in between. And the villagers had reported three missing people. This was something larger. More sinister.

Just another creature to kill. Hopefully something he hadn't killed before. There were still several monsters that needed to be marked off his list.

He'd rubbed dirt into his skin to mask his scent, but the air was more humid than usual in this part of the world. It would only last so long before the beast might be able to sense him. He liked being careful, but he also wanted to be quick, and most importantly, he wanted to survive. Everyone died eventually, and he knew his day would come, but there were still plenty of things he wanted to accomplish before then.

Killing this monster was one of them.

His body was equipped with enough weapons to arm a small army. A longsword was strapped to his back, and he had a large collection of knives, of which he was particularly proud. There were nineteen of them strapped all across his body. Some for throwing, others for jabbing or cutting. Even the back of his gloves had a couple jagged points for a quick, painful punch if all else failed. And in his hand he held a small crossbow, loaded with an iron bolt.

He was prepared. Hunting monsters was his livelihood. A lucrative job if someone was efficient, and Bjorn was one of the best, even if he was only twenty years old. He'd been doing this almost half of his life.

There were always monsters to kill.

Crunching of the underbrush drew his attention. He honed in on the sound as it repeated again, farther this time. Then again, farther still. His prey had not caught on to his presence. He smirked and stalked after it. He watched his steps carefully. Without knowing what he was after, he had no idea what it was capable of. From the descriptions he'd received, which weren't the most enlightening, they'd described claw marks, and some had heard growling. This at least suggested that what he was after was not one of the sapient races.

He paused as the sound of its movements stopped, replaced by a different noise, like that of rushing air, but there was no disturbance among the trees. No refreshing breeze to stymie the perspiration that started to dampen his brow. Just the sound.

Something strange was happening. It could be a sign of magic, which would only make the game more complex.

His eyes narrowed as he readied the crossbow and crept forward, sneaking around several shrubs. The tracks in the ground were more evident than ever. Crushed stems and broken branches marked an easy path forward, though he had to place his feet carefully so as not to alert his prey.

A fresh footprint in the moistened soil merited closer examination, but Bjorn did not feel as though he had enough time. It looked like it belonged to a wolf, though it was significantly wider, more like a bear. Whatever he was about to confront, it was no beast he'd encountered before. He'd come to learn that this mattered very little. Many monsters operated the same. Most of them were too confident for their own good. By the time Bjorn got called in to hunt them, they usually already had their taste of humans, and thus they did not fear humans as they should.

They would learn. Bjorn would teach them.

The footprint meant he was on the right trail. It appeared consistent with the ones he'd seen yesterday.

The air before him shimmered as he rounded a tree, as if there was an intense heat burning through it. He took his next step slowly, holding a hand out to touch the air, but nothing felt awry. In the otherwise still forest, the crackle of leaves and branches scraping began again. Leveling his crossbow, he rounded another tree, following the sound.

There.

A slight glimpse of a dark gray tail vanished through the underbrush. So it was possibly more wolf than bear. Not a good sign. Wolf variations always had differing levels of cleverness, but that just meant this hunt could be more fun than his usual experience. It also meant he'd most definitely need more than the crossbow. His first shot would need to be targeted toward maiming to some degree.

The beast made no other sound after disappearing, though the whooshing of wind persisted despite the stillness. Flecks of dust floated through the beams of sunlight stretching down between the leaves, and the shimmering effect on the air made it hard for Bjorn to focus. He was not impaired. His mind felt sharp as ever, but something was warping the scene around him.

The monster was magical. It had quite possibly detected his presence and was now trying to disguise itself.

Clever indeed. But it would not work.

He rushed to the last place he'd seen the beast. The image of the forest around him wavered more, like a mirage or rippling water. This would not stop Bjorn. No such trick had stopped him before. Nothing mattered more than killing his quarry. He was the master hunter, and no mere creature would outmaneuver him.

The signs of its passage were unmistakable. For a clever beast, it made no attempt to hide its path. Perhaps it wasn't hiding at all. The idea sparked a new level of wariness within him. What if this wasn't the only one? Could it be leading him into a trap? If he was up against an entire pack, that would change the game completely. One monster he could handle, but two or three?

He gritted his teeth and bent his knees slightly, exhaling a seething hot breath.

There was no turning back from here. Not for Bjorn. If it was a trap, then so be it. If he died, it mattered little. He'd done his fair share of monster-slaying already. But if he did die, then the village he'd come to help would soon follow in the destruction. The world itself was slowly sinking into a dark abyss. What little he did would not stop the inevitable.

He'd already made his decision long before this moment. He would pursue this monster to the end.

Directly ahead of him, he caught a glimpse of the tail again, catching the ray of a beam of light before it disappeared once more. The time for caution was over. If it was meant to be a trap, then he would take them by surprise and bring as many of them down with him as he could.

He rushed forward. The rippling of the air increased, as though he were disturbing a watery surface. It splashed across his exposed face and hands like tendrils of hair. He held his breath as he continued forward. All at once, the mirage and odd sensation evaporated, and a stilled forest lay before him.

But something was wrong. Something was very wrong.

The trees were evergreens, and the ground was covered in thick moss. The air itself was cooler and less sticky. There was no sight of the monster.

This was not the same forest.

CHAPTER TWELVE

ACQUAINTANCE

Hallik

Water poured over Hallik's head and soaked into his shirt. He flicked the water from his eyes and brushed his hair back, placing the bucket on the ground beside the well for the next student. All the other students milled about the castle courtyard, trying to catch their breath, cheeks red.

He smirked at them.

"You're insufferable, you know," Svea said as she tossed her wooden sword onto the stack. She jabbed a finger at him. "You *and* that smirk of yours."

His smirk only grew.

"Jealousy is unbecoming," Elowyn said. She didn't even look tired, as if they hadn't been running for the last hour.

"It's envy," Svea corrected. "And why shouldn't I be? He could beat everybody."

It was true. Lind was off on some assignment, and they'd been stuck running drills with Arenda all day. Even Instructor Arvid had been called away by Captain Mikel Vigsen for some reason, leaving them with no relief.

Regardless, Arenda's instruction was Hallik's favorite. They'd gone beyond simple duels today and had actually practiced team combat formations. She acknowledged that they would need to adjust the structure a bit once they emerged from Vanalf as Grimnirs, but the general formations would still be relevant. Either way, Hallik was all for it. They needed all the real training they could get. When they entered the cave, Hallik had every intention of working with his team to ensure as many of them as possible emerged alive. This was his team, and as their greatest fighter, some of that responsibility for their welfare rested on his shoulders.

Their island had been at peace for so long, but yesterday with the draugrs proved they still needed Grimnirs.

But today had been fun. In addition to the drills, Hallik had beaten both Svea and Elowyn in duels, and he'd even dueled both of them at the same time, emerging unscathed, much to their chagrin.

"You would benefit from another real duel, then, eh Hallik?"

Hallik's smile disappeared as he turned his head to regard Arenda, who retrieved two wooden swords from the pile. Unsure what she meant, he remained silent.

Arenda tossed a wooden sword to him, which he caught in his left hand. Hushed whispers rippled through the students. There were nearly a hundred of them in the courtyard, and they all shuffled closer to see what their Valtyra instructor was about to do. Surely her show of defeating him yesterday was still fresh on their minds.

Arenda's wings flexed before folding back behind her. She rolled her neck before taking a fighting stance, wooden sword held at the ready.

Hallik's mouth hung open, but once he realized, he snapped it shut and took a deep breath. He wasn't sure if he was supposed to be afraid or excited, but either way, his body flushed with energy. "We are to duel, then?" Hallik asked, still not sure of her intentions. Hopefully this was not just another lesson on humility.

Arenda did not smile. Her expression remained solid as stone. "You need a challenge. I offer you that challenge." She tilted her head at him. "I suggest you take a stance. I doubt you'll be able to defend my barrage with that posture."

So she wanted to play, then. Hallik suppressed his smirk and switched the sword to his right hand as he shifted his right leg back, left hand and foot in front. He held the sword high, prepared not only to defend, but to attack. At the back of his mind, he wondered what kind of punishment she might give him if he hit her with the sword, but the thought fled as she whipped forward, assaulting him with her sword.

Hallik barely moved quickly enough to parry her strikes. This would be a true challenge, not only because Arenda was extremely skilled and experienced, but Valtyras emerged from Vanalf with more than just wings; they had strength and stamina unrivaled. He would need to be creative if he had any hope of defeating her. What he really needed was proper armor or a shield. Her quick, powerful strokes were too much to defend against with a simple sword.

The students formed a circle as they watched their best fighter struggling to keep up with Arenda. Hallik only wished they'd left the circle a little larger, because he was using all the space he could to back up and dodge her attacks. With too little room, he wouldn't have anywhere to retreat. It would come down to blows, which hadn't gone well for him last time. He'd nearly lost his grip on his sword completely.

He knew he needed to switch tactics. Hallik was already exhausted from all the drills earlier, and though Arenda had participated to some degree, she would most likely still be at full strength. He needed to strike.

Hoping to take Arenda by surprise, Hallik stepped toward her next attack instead of away. Their swords met with a terrible crack as he held a firm grip. He'd angled his sword so that it was not a direct hit, but it whipped her sword away. The impact shook through his arms, but he followed through with a whirling blur of attacks, each swing shifting into the next.

Arenda stood her ground, her sword clacking against Hallik's every blow. Her talent thrilled him. It was as though they entered a rhythm, erratic as it seemed, and the reverberating clacks of their swords became like beating drums.

But it came to an abrupt end as Arenda merely feinted one of her own strokes, sword flicking just over the tip of Hallik's. The wooden blade slid up Hallik's arm until the point thwacked against his chest. Arenda kicked Hallik's sword at the same time, jolting it from his grip.

Hallik stumbled back to one knee with a cry. He pressed a hand to his chest where the wooden sword would undoubtedly leave a bruise and looked up at his instructor. Neither of them smiled, but the students forming the circle erupted. All the bushnings that lived in the courtyard shuffled away from the loud humans, bundling up like a walking pile of bushes near the exterior wall.

Arenda gave the slightest nod. "Well fought. It was wise of you to take the offensive. Compared to yesterday, I noticed you changed your tactics with how you blocked or dodged my attacks to better account for my superior strength. Well done." She reached a hand down.

Hallik took her hand, and she helped him back to his feet. She'd been holding back during the duel. When she'd finally struck him, she made it look easy. She probably could have done it at any point during the fight.

"I hope you learned something," Arenda said, raising one of her dark brown eyebrows at him.

Hallik breathed a laugh. "I did. That rhythm we had for a while was... thrilling."

Arenda's second eyebrow joined the first, sliding further up her forehead. "Yes. I matched your pace. It felt rhythmic because you became easy to read. I was anticipating your strikes. It may be fun, but it also makes it easy for your enemy to break the rhythm to their advantage. Which I did." She offered a sad smile. "With ease."

"Noted," Hallik said, lightly running his fingers over the new bruise on his chest. His plain woolen shirt had done little to shield the blow.

Arenda tossed the sword onto the pile. "We may need to duel more. I think you have potential."

Hallik smiled. Was Arenda being sarcastic?

Without waiting for a response, Arenda raised her voice so all the students could hear. "Dismissed. You may return to your homes."

The students devolved into ant-like chaos, some rushing into the castle to gather their things, others heading straight for the gates on either side of the castle grounds.

Hallik put his sword back and caught Elowyn's eyes. Her questioning gaze was all too familiar, and he knew what she was asking even without words.

"I will come by later," Hallik said.

Elowyn nodded and disappeared into the crowd of bustling students.

Hallik entered the castle, navigating the hallways back to the room they'd all stayed in last night.

Sefrid had since been taken back to his home by his parents after a healing poultice had been applied to his wounds. From the looks of it, he'd be running around again within a couple more days.

Hallik retrieved his cankerous sword from where he'd left it in the room. The metal beneath the grime was steel—certainly not what he would have expected of an ancient weapon wielded by a draugr. The idea of carrying his own sword with him was comforting, since his possessions were almost completely limited to the clothes he wore. He wanted to take the sword to the castle's smithy, which wasn't often operated, though it was well-equipped.

He wound his way back out of the castle, wondering what kind of history the weapon had before its owner had become a draugr. How old was it, truly? If it was as ancient as some people had speculated, then he thought it would have looked a lot worse. Sure, there was a bit of rust and some hardened, green crusty stuff, but it looked fine otherwise. He'd also seen bits of metal that had been fished out of the sea before, and those always looked a lot worse. If he had to guess, this weapon hadn't really spent as much time submerged as some of the Grimnirs wanted to think.

That was the danger. It further solidified his idea that the draugr ship had come from outside of Avskild's mystical shield. But he still didn't understand enough to know how the shield worked. Didn't something have to pass through a portal in order to leave or enter Avskild?

He'd have to ask Lind when he got back. Surely he would know.

When he got outside, he went toward the back of the castle where the old smithy was built up against the side of the wall. It was close to the gate that led back into Dalstava. A couple students were just trickling out.

Watcher Khanak stood beside the gate as the two students left, arms folded. He was a shorter man, with a well-trimmed, dark brown goatee, his head capped with short hair. He wore his usual dark gray tunic, both an axe and a sword holstered at his waist. A medallion hung from his neck with the depiction of an eye, the official insignia of the Watchers. He also often wielded a spear, and sometimes a shield. It was like every day he wanted to flaunt a different weapon.

As Hallik headed to the smithy, Khanak smiled and moved to walk beside him. "Decided to clean up that cursed weapon of yours, eh?"

"You heard about this, then?" Hallik said, hefting the blade so Khanak could see it better.

"Lind mentioned it to the rest of us before he left this morning," Khanak said, thumbs looped through his belt. "He did not speak favorably of your decision to keep it. Everything else got burned."

Hallik rubbed the back of his neck. "Right, well, I thought perhaps I could clean it off a bit. Would you mind helping me?"

Khanak gave a boisterous laugh and clapped Hallik on the shoulder. "I wouldn't have it any other way. I couldn't have you in here ruining the smithy." He led the way to the smithy and hefted a clay jug out from under a shelf. When he removed the lid, a strong scent of vinegar wafted up. "It looks like good metal, but we'll want to clean it with this, and then we can work it on the grindstone."

Hallik nodded eagerly. "Let's get to it." From this day forward, Hallik was committed to never being without a weapon. If what he suspected about the shield around Avskild was true, he was going to need it.

***

After working on the blade for over an hour, Hallik decided the sword was about as good as he could get it. There were small things to polish out of course. Some rust still lingered around the crossguard, and it would certainly benefit from some fresh wrap on the handle, but at least he'd learned how to work on it himself when he'd need to.

"You're a true gem, Khanak," Hallik said to the older man as he left the smithy.

"Indeed," Khanak said with a smirk before waving his goodbye. "Peace."

"Peace," Hallik replied, then jogged to the other side of the grounds. Elowyn's house wasn't too far into the woods, but the sun was already getting low, and her mother would have food waiting for him. He didn't have a proper sheath for the sword, so he simply held it in his left hand for now.

He nodded to Latshal who stood guard at the gate before jogging off toward the forest. Rain clouds showered down the higher levels of the mountains, and he guessed they'd eventually shift down toward the city by nightfall.

Elowyn's home was closer to the base of the mountain, but he and Elowyn had walked to and from Castle Vrodr often enough that a small trail had been etched into the ground. There was one spot where a large rock cut off the trail, and Hallik made a point of jumping off it with a flourish every time he passed by. He smiled as he jumped, then jogged into the cover of the trees. From there, the elevation started to change more dramatically as he climbed the foothill. A mixture of trees melded to form a thick canopy, but moss covered nearly every stone. The remnants of an old stone wall had crumbled with age.

Elowyn's mother, Selke, said that this island had once been much larger, and had even been connected to other lands. The portals, the cave of Vanalf, and the rich magic here were much to blame for the changing landscape, but Avskild had supposedly been part of a significantly larger kingdom. The sagas Selke sang had been passed down for generations, far longer than anything Lind had to read in all his papers.

Though Hallik made a point not to bring such things to Lind's attention. Selke enjoyed her solitude—with the exception of Hallik and Elowyn, of course. There were some very specific events where she would be invited as an honored guest to share a song or sometimes sell carvings, but otherwise she did not mingle with other people much.

Hallik breathed deeply, filling his lungs with the forest air. Birds and squirrels chirped happily, and a few small lights darted by, the sign of passing nature spirits. The thickness of life in the forest always felt so invigorating. It was no wonder Selke chose to make her home out here.

He was probably halfway up the hill when he heard what sounded like a distant scream, like a woman in distress. Hallik stopped short. The sound had come from the east, deeper in the forest. His instinct called for him to go help, but he'd been warned about things like this before. A scream coming from deep in the woods? That could easily be a trap. Any number of malignant spirits could be hoping to lure somebody away.

He proceeded up the hill more slowly, listening closely. If he recognized the voice as Elowyn's or Selke's, then he'd not hesitate.

The scream sounded again, more desperate this time, and it cut off at the end.

"Curse it all," he muttered to himself. Then he switched the grip on his blade and ran toward the voice. His better judgment grasped at him, but he forced it away. He was going to be a Grimnir. Wasn't this the sort of thing Grimnirs would do? Besides, he'd faced a draugr. How much worse could any forest spirit be, especially now that he actually had a sword?

Trees whipped past him as he ran. The forest here was thick, the trees tall and ancient. Wisps of clouds passed in front of the sun, plunging the forest into an ever-increasing darkness. He knew he was a complete fool for doing this, but he'd already made up his mind. He continued running for several moments. Surely he should have reached the location of the scream, but he had no idea what he was really looking for. He reached a clearing and slowed to a stop. A break in leaves above allowed more light to enter this part of the forest, but he squinted as he looked around to try and find anything.

"Hello?" His voice came out hollow, disappearing as though it were a distant echo. The forest was still. The only sound was that of his heavy breathing. It was a stark contrast to the hum of life that had been buzzing through the forest near the trail. His heart hammered in his chest.

There was a tangle of vines and branches that formed an odd shape in the middle of the clearing. There was also a large stone, about chest-high. Despite the feeling in his chest that told him this was a mistake, he stepped forward. He'd already committed himself to this. He would not back down.

As he neared the center, he realized the vines and branches formed a large arch. Dull, green light shimmered along the veins of the leaves.

It was a portal.

He was so enraptured by it that he only noticed the body that lay crumpled at the base of the portal when he stepped in a pool of their blood. He growled, looking down at his feet, anger rising as he noticed the Watcher medallion around the body's neck, spattered with blood. The face was unrecognizable. A broken spear lay inches from the Watcher's hand, but the victim was clearly not female. So the scream must have belonged to somebody else. The wounds across the person's body looked like it had been gouged and bitten by a creature. No human could have done it.

Part of him felt inclined to look away, but he knew he needed the details. Wasn't that what Lind's lessons were all about? Knowing his enemy was key to victory, even if his enemy was more powerful.

What did the wounds tell him?

Four claws. Long, massive jaws with larger canines. A wolf?

But a Watcher falling victim to a mere wolf seemed highly improbable.

A deep rumbling sound barely perceptible to his ears filled the space around him. He felt it more than heard it. The air itself shivered. The scent of copper was so thick that he could taste it on his tongue.

Whatever it was, this was no wolf, but he would not be its next victim. His eyes whipped about, scanning the edge of the forest, his back up against the vines of the portal. It was difficult to see through the strange effect that rippled the air, but he set his jaw and spread his feet apart, preparing for a fight.

The sound morphed, becoming more perceivable until he recognized it as a growl. It was coming from his left. He turned, slashing his blade as though he might cut it down, but nothing was there. Now the sound was behind him. He shifted his stance, blade high. Nothing.

It was playing tricks on him.

He could have sworn he'd heard of something like this before in one of Lind's tales, but the details eluded him. This was one of those moments where he needed Elowyn's knowledge, but she wouldn't be coming to rescue him this time. He should have paid closer attention. What good were all his fighting skills if he couldn't even find his enemy?

He inhaled a sharp breath and held it. The sound continued to play tricks on him, but he ignored it altogether. He wasn't sure there were any of his senses he could trust, but he had to assume that everything was a trick, so if the sound came from behind him, then perhaps he needed to look in the opposite direction.

When he tested his theory, he found himself facing the boulder. The portion of it that faced him and the portal was flat, etched with intricate carvings, but from atop it, a gray-black, furry figure glared down at him, one massive paw taking a slow step down the surface of the boulder. Its claws were longer than he would have thought possible, the dagger-like protrusions scratching grooves into the stone surface. One swipe would easily have him completely eviscerated.

The Watcher's speartip protruded from its shoulder, but the monster seemed unfazed.

Hallik shifted to a two-handed grip. The possibility of dying crossed his mind, but that didn't matter. What mattered was the battle, and *how* he died.

The creature watched him, taking one more slow step down the stone. He expected it to pounce at any time, but he suspected it was not accustomed to having its prey stand their ground. The delay allowed him to get a closer look. Its ears were shorter and round, and a thick mane of gray fur coated its neck. Yellow eyes glared at him and its lips gradually raised in a snarl, head lowering.

This was the moment it would strike. Hallik bent his knees and elbows so he'd have enough room to leverage a strike, but he certainly wasn't about to make the first move against an unknown enemy. This was no mere animal. There was clearly something magical about it.

The rippling muscles along its forelegs flexed just before it pounced. Claws reached for him, and its jaws opened wide, everything aiming for his head.

Hallik dropped to his knees, thrusting his sword forward like a hammer. The blade met flesh, and he rolled across the dead Watcher's blood, barely dodging the monstrous creature that crashed down where he'd been standing.

The beast turned without delay and snapped at him. Hallik whipped his sword toward its face, but its jaws clamped down on the metal. It shook its head, wrenching the weapon from Hallik's grip.

Hallik bellowed at the monster, knowing his own death was imminent. It swung a paw at him, which Hallik kicked away with the bottom of his foot, but then it leaped forward, its other paw thunking down into Hallik's chest, full weight bearing down on him. He slammed into the ground, caught on his back as the beast glared down at him, sword still gripped in its mouth. Hot saliva dripped onto Hallik's forehead, and the tips of its razor claws slowly tightened against his shoulder.

With his free hand, Hallik punched at the creature's neck, but it ignored the blows and flicked Hallik's sword away with a twitch of its head. Mouth free, it opened wide, preparing to mangle Hallik's face just like it had the Watcher's.

In the next instant, one of the monster's eyes popped, a stick protruding where its eye had been. Its paw pressed down harder into Hallik's chest, forcing the air from his lungs. Something wet dripped across his body as the beast lurched forward, a roar breaking from its throat, vibrating the air.

There was a blur and flash of steel that drove the monster back. It stepped off of Hallik's body and snarled at its new opponent.

Hallik sucked in air as the pressure on his chest was gone and rolled to the side where his sword had been tossed.

A man stepped in to defend Hallik.

His savior, whoever it was, slashed the beast across the side of its face, then jumped, grabbing the spearhead protruding from its shoulder, using it to swing up onto the monster's back. With one hand, he jabbed his sword down into the monster's snout as it tried snapping at his leg, then with his other hand, he withdrew a dagger and slammed it down into the back of the beast's head, not once, but three times.

By the time Hallik got to his feet, the monster collapsed with a raspy sigh of death. He grunted and lowered his sword.

The other man slid from the beast's back and wiped his blades on its fur. Hallik had never seen someone like him before. He was clothed in full armor of black, hardened leather, additionally reinforced with dark iron on his forearms, shoulders, and shins. Weapons clung to his body in seemingly every available space.

When the man's forest green eyes settled on Hallik, they couldn't have been more disinterested, as if this whole ordeal had been boring. Most of his disheveled, dark brown hair was pulled back. The muscle of his sharp jaw clenched, just visible beneath his short beard. He sighed and said, "So, you managed not to die."

"Thanks to you," Hallik said, glancing down at the monster, blood pooling out from its mouth.

"It's only part of my job," the man said. He couldn't have been more than a few years older than Hallik, but a frown line creased his brow. He glanced around the forest, eyes lingering on the portal.

"Who are you?" Hallik ventured to ask. The man clearly wasn't a Grimnir. Hallik hadn't traveled to all the different parts of Avskild, and though there were other villages, he'd never seen somebody dressed in such a way.

The man's eyes flicked back to him, narrowing in annoyance. "They call me a monster hunter, but my name is Jaysen Bjorn." He pulled a long sheaf of parchment that had been folded several times from a pocket and set it against the flat part of the stone before making a mark on it with a bit of graphite.

"Jaysen?" Hallik said, testing the strange name.

"I go by Bjorn," he said, folding the parchment back up to tuck it away.

"What's that for?" Hallik said, aware that he was asking many questions.

Bjorn's eyes narrowed. "My list." He nudged the monster with his foot. "I haven't killed a liowolf before."

Liowolf. Of course. Hallik had heard of them before, but they belonged only in legends. Such a thing hadn't been seen on Avskild for ages.

Bjorn's head tilted ever-so-slightly. "Your eyes widened when I named the beast. You've heard of it?"

Hallik nodded, finally glad to be the one answering a question. "Heard of them, yes, though I've never seen one before. The Grimnirs will be interested in hearing about this."

Bjorn blanched. "Grimnirs?" His voice came out as more of a growl than a word. More incoherent words escaped his lips. He looked around the forest again with renewed interest, a hand lingering over one of the knives sheathed on the back of his arm. "Where is this place?"

Hallik looked to the portal. The glow he'd seen in the leaves earlier was now gone. Perhaps it had been the after-effects of its magic. One thing seemed certain. Jaysen Bjorn was not from Avskild.

CHAPTER THIRTEEN

CHRONICLER

Elowyn Galdre

E lowyn sat on her favorite pillow, leaning back against the wall of her home as her mother stirred a pot on the other side of the room. Various trinkets dangled from the ceiling, beautiful crafts of birds, bears, wolves, a dragon, and many more. Her mother often carved when she wasn't busy tending to the home and garden. Elowyn loved all her mother's figures. On occasion, she sold something to wealthier citizens of Dalstava, but only when she really needed more money. Her works were always in high demand, though nobody was ever allowed to come to their home.

Mother hummed to herself as she stirred, and Elowyn knew a song was on the tip of her tongue. Mother had a gift for music, like her voice was from the gods themselves.

Elowyn could sing as well, but her own voice seemed to pale in comparison. As the words to her mother's song began, Elowyn was enraptured, as always. All other sensation ceased, wrapped up in each word that filled the room.

Lost, we roamed, defeated
Safety gone, retreated
For many years we wandered, ready for the grave
Lives were all but squandered, until we found the cave
Horrors there we faced,
In terror's dark embrace
Such few emerged victorious, with magic in our veins
Powers strong and glorious, reward for our pains
Those who persevere,
Arise reborn, Grimnir
A thousand years we battled, with monsters cold and heartless
Until the world was shattered, fading into darkness
One hope, a key, a shield
The portals of Avskild

Elowyn could practically feel the air tingle, as if the song itself were some form of magic. Each word weighed in Elowyn's mind, drawing her deeper into the story. There was more to it, and though she felt it in her soul, she did not know how to fully connect it to meaning. It was more a feeling than a conscious thought. One could only experience it through the words of the song.

She had to wonder if there was some enchantment to her mother's singing. Whatever mixed blood flowed in their veins must have left them with something supernatural, despite any of mother's denials.

Wooden chimes outside the home clacked, drawing Elowyn back to the room. She took a deep, sharp breath and found that Mother was staring at her with a subtle smile on her lips. Elowyn blinked quickly, realizing there were tears at the edges of her eyes. The minor tone of the song had left a somber weight in her chest, but it escaped as she heaved a deep sigh.

"Is there nothing but darkness outside of Avskild?" Elowyn asked, still encumbered by the mystery of the missing Voyagers. What purpose did Voyagers have to travel outside of Avskild if there was nothing but death? Perhaps this was why they were no more.

"We do not know," Mother said, ladling out some of the soup. She had three bowls set out.

Elowyn had expected Hallik to be here by now. Knowing him, he was probably off getting killed by another monster or something just to test out the sword. Thinking of monsters, death, and darkness, Elowyn hurried across the room to a wooden wardrobe and withdrew her dagger, a gift from her late father. Supposedly it was of elven make, from a time when the portals were still actively used. It was possibly the most expensive thing in their home, complete with an elaborate sheath of black and silver. The weapon itself appeared like a long, double-edged spike, a thin groove running up the middle. Perfect for stabbing and slitting. Paired with an axe or a hammer, she'd be well equipped to fight most anything. If she was stealthy, anyway. An area in which she had plenty of room to grow.

The chimes outside stilled and mother looked at the door. "Somebody comes."

Less than a second later, the door burst open and Hallik stumbled into the home, eyes wide, his body covered in blood.

Elowyn gasped, but Mother merely furrowed her eyebrows and brought out a fourth bowl. Four?

"Nature's rays, Hallik. What happened?" Elowyn said.

Hallik sputtered for a moment. "A portal must have opened. And we, uh…" He glanced behind him before returning his attention to mother. "I fought a monster—"

"—And I killed it," a man said, stepping up behind Hallik. His eyes flickered between Elowyn and her mother, and he was armed head to toe in armor and weapons, though he held nothing in his hands.

Elowyn kept her dagger held ready.

Hallik gave Mother a nervous smile as he gestured at the man. "This is my new friend."

"I have no friends," the man said, glaring at Hallik.

Hallik grinned. "He's joking, of course. He has an excellent sense of humor."

The man's glare hardened.

"Anyway," Hallik continued. "His name is Jaysen Bjorn."

"Just Bjorn," the man said.

He was not as tall as Hallik, but he still struck an imposing figure, and his brooding expression was tense enough to insinuate that he perhaps had a terrible stomach ache and was struggling to suppress it.

"Hello, Bjorn," Mother said. "I've made some soup, if you'd care to join us."

Bjorn didn't respond immediately, but he scanned the room, eyeing each of Mother's carvings as though they might be traps. Occasionally his eyes lingered on a carving, particularly those that depicted some of the various monsters.

"Sit," mother instructed, pointing at a bench.

Hallik moved to take a seat, but mother cut him off.

"Not you, Hal. Go take that tunic off and wash up outside. I don't need that gore in my home."

Hallik nodded. "Yes, Selke." He rushed outside, loosening his belt before he disappeared.

Mother returned her attention to Bjorn. "You have questions. We will answer them as best we can. Have a seat. Eat some soup."

Bjorn obliged, taking two stiff steps to the bench before sitting down, back straight, feet planted as if ready to bolt at a moment's notice. "You are Hallik's family?"

Mother glanced at Elowyn. "As close to a family as he's got, yes." She handed him a bowl and spoon. "El, could you light a candle?"

Elowyn nodded and quickly drew out a candle, lighting it on the simmering flames beneath the stove her mother had just used to cook.

Hallik returned, shirtless, body glistening with water from the rainwater trough. There were four small wounds on the top of his left shoulder. Red, but not bleeding.

Elowyn averted her eyes and grabbed his spare tunic from the bedroom.

"Hallik, provide us with some context," Mother said.

Hallik coughed a laugh as he took the tunic from Elowyn. "Well, I was on my way here when I heard a scream in the woods."

Mother's sigh was almost palpable. Elowyn couldn't restrain the words. "It's basic knowledge to not chase after a scream in the forest, Hallik."

"I know," Hallik said, holding up his hands. "But it could have been you or Selke. It seemed close enough to your home that I wanted to be sure."

"You wanted to test your sword," Elowyn said knowingly.

Hallik shrugged. "Maybe. Regardless, I chased after the sound until I came to a clearing in the woods that turned out to be a portal. There was a dead Watcher there, and the portal was a little shiny, and a giant wolf-bear-monster started hunting me."

"A liowolf," Bjorn mumbled between sips of soup.

"Yes," Hallik said, pointing at Bjorn. "One of those."

Liowolf. Elowyn had heard about them from Lind's class. "It uses vocal vibrations to distort reality and dull the senses, lulling them into incapacitation before killing them from behind. They're also said to mimic human sounds. That would have been the screaming you heard, Hallik."

Bjorn's spoon was halfway to his mouth, but he stared at her without moving or blinking. "You know of them?"

"Elowyn knows practically everything," Hallik said, giving her an approving nod. "But yes, despite its cuddly appearance, it wanted to kill me. I thought it was using some kind of magic to distract me, but I fought it for a moment before our new friend here made quick work of it."

"It was about to kill you," Bjorn said.

"Also true," Hallik said, "but that's what friends are for. Helping each other not get killed. Thank you for that, by the way. You did have incredible timing. Was that intentional?"

"Somewhat," Bjorn said. "It was a tactical decision, but stop using that word."

"Friend, right," Hallik said with a shrug. "Helpful acquaintance, then."

Elowyn struggled to hide another smile. There was something refreshingly pleasant about watching Hallik interact with someone who was completely immune to his charm.

Mother chimed in. "Well, helpful acquaintance, why don't you tell me how you ended up here."

Bjorn's jaw clenched for just a moment before he responded. "I am a monster hunter. I was in the forests along the shores of Kelig hunting after this monster. I followed its trail here. Simple as that."

"Kelig," mother said, as if to affirm that was what he'd truly said.

A tickle ran down Elowyn's neck. She knew of Kelig. Mother's songs sometimes mentioned that land as a place ravaged by monsters. A place of danger. A place completely separate from the island of Avskild. "He... he is an outsider," Elowyn said, placing her bowl aside, her other hand resting over the handle of her dagger.

"Yes," Hallik said, "but he's... a helpful acquaintance, as we've established."

"And we can reasonably conclude," Elowyn said, "that as he followed this monster through the woods, somehow he was able to pass through the portal in Avskild. That's the only way he could have gotten here through the shield and across the sea."

"Avskild," Bjorn said, his already broody expression becoming even broodier. "So it is not gone."

"No," Elowyn said, ignoring a look from Mother. Perhaps she wasn't supposed to let that slip. "What do you know of Avskild?"

Bjorn shook his head. "It's a legend where I'm from. It was said to be the home of the magicians who held back the tide of darkness, but it vanished, swallowed up by a mountain and an ever-churning storm. We've been ravaged by monsters ever since. Everything has been in gradual decline for the last... however long it's been."

"Are there many people left in Kelig?" Elowyn asked, curiosity piqued. This was the sort of thing she'd been wondering about for years. Perhaps all the Voyagers were gone because monsters slew them when they traveled the portals.

"A few scattered settlements, clinging to life," Bjorn said, frown returning to his brow. "Inevitable destruction awaits us all. I saw the dead Grimnir after coming through the portal. If he wasn't able to defeat the monster then your people will fare no better than mine." He shrugged, eyeing the dagger in Elowyn's lap.

Hallik caught sight of the weapon, and his expression shifted to one of surprise. "You have a nice dagger as well?" Elowyn had never revealed the weapon to him in all these years, keeping it tucked away in her wardrobe.

"Yes," Elowyn said carefully.

Hallik nudged Bjorn, who swatted him away, glare turning into something so fierce it could kill. Perhaps he would. "Bjorn, even Elowyn has a dagger, and all I have is this old sword. You could easily spare one of those two hundred knives of yours."

"No," Bjorn said. "I earned each of these blades, either with my purse or by killing someone. I doubt you've killed anything in your life."

"Nonsense," Hallik said. "I killed a draugr just yesterday, right Elowyn?"

Elowyn wasn't sure what to think of the strange interaction between the two of them, but she nodded. She was much more concerned about the worry manifesting as a tightness in her chest. "With my help, of course."

"A draugr?" Bjorn said, his jaw hanging for the briefest moment before he snapped it shut. "How?"

Hallik pointed at Elowyn. "She threw a lamp at it and caught it on fire. Then I yanked it by the arm, and she hacked its head off with an axe."

Bjorn smirked. It was the first time he'd smiled since arriving. "So she slayed the beast. Not you."

"It was a team effort," Hallik said. "I'm a great team member."

"Sorry to interrupt your banter," Elowyn said, heat tingeing her tone. That tightness in her chest demanded some kind of action. They couldn't sit around here chatting while monsters from the outside world seeped into Avskild. "I think we should inform the Grimnir Guard immediately. They will want to know about the portals malfunctioning. A Grimnir was killed today. By a monster. The entire island could be at risk."

"In the morning," Mother said, rising to her feet. "I won't have any of you running through the forest at night-time. Especially not right now. In the morning, we can head to Dalstava together."

Elowyn glanced outside. She hadn't realized how dark it had gotten.

Mother shared a knowing look with her, a hidden message glinting in her eyes.

"What was that?" Bjorn said, looking between the two of them. "You two looked at each other. Will you be killing me in my sleep?"

Hallik guffawed. "No, Bjorn. Except maybe Elowyn. She might try to kill you out of jealousy that you killed the liowolf instead of her."

Elowyn rolled her eyes. "Hal."

"I believe you are joking," Bjorn said, eyes narrowing. "But I will sleep outside. It's not wise of you to allow a stranger to sleep in your home, especially where I'm clearly more heavily armed than the three of you."

"If that pleases you, but stay close to the home," Mother said. "We will discuss this more in the morning."

Everyone shuffled off to prepare for bed, but Elowyn remained in her spot. The portals were failing. Their *shield* was failing. Elowyn had not even gone through Vanalf yet. She had no magic. She was not ready for this.

She felt as though she needed more time to prepare, but fate would not allow it.

CHAPTER FOURTEEN

CORRUPTION

Lorelai Harkral

As the royal attendant to King Knos, Lorelai enjoyed many privileges. At least, she had once considered them privileges. Over time, the more she learned, the more shackled she became. Especially with her involvement in the king's intelligence network. Though she was privy to most things, she knew that there were many details the king withheld from her. It was wise of him to do so, of course. Lorelai would have done the same in his position. The king was no fool. Despite his supposed disinterest in the affairs of the kingdom, he spent more time working on improvements than most people realized.

One of the secrets she'd come to learn, perhaps one of the strangest of them all, was that King Knos was a Grimnir. Most likely a Vitugr. For some reason, he kept his magic a secret. The only reason she even knew was that she'd gone looking for him late one night because she'd heard a sound outside his room. Checking to see if he was inside, she found his room empty and undisturbed. Before alerting the guards, she'd searched for him, stumbling upon his robe on the stairs leading to the upper floors of the Tower of Tarn.

She'd climbed higher, searching each level until she arrived at the fifth floor, candlelight glowing from one of the rooms. She'd approached it carefully, peeking through the crack of the door to see the king inside, an ancient tome open before him as magical tendrils snaked across the ground. But why keep it a secret? She was sure that no other person knew of his abilities. That meant he'd had to venture through Vanalf all on his own, something Grimnirs were never supposed to do. That, or all who'd accompanied him were dead.

Lorelai shook the recollection from her head. That was when her shackles had truly closed around her. There was nothing she could do about all that now.

The hour was late, but Lorelai had discovered some unfortunate news that she knew the king would want to hear immediately. She did not know *why* the information was unfortunate, only that the king would be displeased by it. The king had a habit of staying up late anyway, so she knew she would not be disturbing him.

True to the point, she found the king in the planning office, overlooking a large drawing of his new estate.

Knos looked up as she entered, his dark blue eyes settling on her unblinkingly. "You couldn't sleep either, I see," his voice rumbled.

"No," Lorelai said, unsure how he would receive her message.

"I'm glad you came," he said, resting the knuckles of his hands on the table before him. "I've been thinking, and I want to get married."

Lorelai's eyes widened, and it felt as though she'd been slugged in the stomach. Sure, she'd worked with the king for years, but she'd never suspected such a thing of him. But he certainly couldn't have meant her. That would not be reasonable. Frustration flared that the thought had even occurred to her.

Knos grunted. "Not to you, Lorelai." He shook his head.

"Of course not," Lorelai said, quickly suppressing the reaction. "You will look at some of the other powerful families in Dalstava. I simply haven't seen you express any interest in marriage before. Such a comment takes me by surprise."

"I wasn't sure much *could* take you by surprise."

"Consider this a rare occasion," Lorelai said, grateful for the moment of reprieve before delivering her news. "What sparks the interest?"

"Dark times," Knos said, standing up straight, one hand stroking the edge of his sword hilt. "The people could use a bit of good news at a time like this."

Lorelai took a deep breath. She needed to tell him. It would be interesting to see his response. She would be direct. "Captain Mikel Vigsen sent Grimnirs to investigate all the portals."

Knos's reaction was subtle. A mere darkening of his countenance, a fierce expression in the dim candlelight. "He doubts me."

This was a topic Lorelai had yet to understand. "Is it not wise to ensure the portals have not been compromised?"

"It's foolish," Knos snapped. "Only Voyagers can open the portals, but there are no Voyagers."

"But there could be," Lorelai pressed. "They've only gone missing. Isn't it possible that a Voyager could be out there acting of their own volition?"

"No," Knos said, his face calmer than she would have expected. "It is not. The Voyagers are all dead, Lorelai." His gaze was even, his voice steady and sure.

He was so certain of himself that Lorelai's mind immediately went to the worst possible conclusion. It all made sense now. She nodded slowly, suppressing the fear that came with the revelation. "I see. You had them killed."

Knos did not deny it. He only blinked at her. "Without Voyagers, the portals cannot be opened. If the portals cannot be opened, Avskild is secure. The only reason we were invaded before was because a rogue Voyager opened the portals to an army of trolls. No such threat can present itself again." He rounded the table and took one step toward her.

Lorelai held her ground. She'd never experienced violence from the king before, but his looming presence made her question his intentions. He wielded magic after all. Even if his skill with a sword was untested in her eyes, she had no idea what he could summon. If he was a Vitugr, as she suspected, then fire was not out of the question.

"Doesn't the magic of the Voyagers also strengthen Avskild and the shield from outside corruption?" she said.

"I have taken care of that as well."

"Not to question your wisdom, King Knos," she said carefully, "but what are your conclusions regarding the draugr ship?"

"You heard Captain Vigsen yourself," Knos said. "It could have been dormant."

Lorelai shook her head ever so slightly. "He said that to appease you. That's not how draugrs work. They do not lie dormant. I've run an investigation on everything there. The condition of the ship, the weapons and clothing of the draugrs. It all suggests they had died only recently, and they were not people of Avskild."

Knos's jaw set, and a growl rumbled in his chest.

She pressed on, hoping to make her point—not just to be proven correct, but for the sake of Avskild. "You must recognize that there are other ways for the portals to be breached. Magic works in many mysterious ways."

"But *I* have secured them," he said, voice quiet but firm. "Of course it would be unwise to assume that everything is foolproof, but I have done more than just execute all the Voyagers."

Lorelai's mind spun, unsure what he could have possibly done to secure the portals. Perhaps it had something to do with him becoming a Grimnir. "What do you mean?" she dared ask. She dropped to her knees before him. "I only desire to help secure the safety of your people, my king. I wish to know so that I can help you."

"You have indeed been loyal, Lorelai, but there are some things that must remain my burden alone."

Lorelai dropped her head, gritting her teeth against the rising fury. She would not give up so easily. "I know you are wise, my king, but surely you recognize that much of the power of a ruler lies not only in their own body and mind, but in the strength and wisdom of those they command as well. I am at your command. Let my strength and wisdom be at your disposal."

"I thought it already was," Knos grumbled. "You have your role. There are administrative tasks that need to be done, like finding me a wife. Work on that. The defense of Avskild is up to me and Daelen. I have divided roles for a reason. It is not necessary for me to reveal everything to you in order to maintain your allegiance, is it?"

"Of course not," Lorelai said, rising back to her feet, but bowing her head. "I only invite you to utilize me for all of my assets."

Knos nodded, eyes narrowing. Perhaps Lorelai had come off too eager. The king was not too shrewd most of the time, but on occasion would display a rare sense of perception. "We will see. Thank you for bringing me this news, but the hour is late. We should get our rest. I expect you to start communicating with some of the other houses tomorrow."

Lorelai dipped her head lower, mostly to give her enough time to hide her displeasure, a craft she was always improving. "As you wish." She flashed the smallest flicker of a smile. "I am eager to see how your courtships progress."

"I'm sure you are." He gestured to the door. "Peace."

"Peace," Lorelai replied as she turned to leave the room, though peace felt far from reach.

Footsteps approached, thudding at a rapid pace. Lorelai held her ground just outside the door, hand ready to withdraw the knife hidden up her sleeve. Who could possibly be charging toward the king at a time like this?

"My king," a voice called, lantern bouncing in his hand. She recognized the voice as Daelen's. She relaxed and stepped aside as Daelen slid to a stop in front of the king, but not before Lorelai caught a glimpse of his expression. Wide-eyed. Shocked.

Daelen took a gasp of breath. "Captain Vigsen sent word. One of the Valtyras has reported that a portal has been destroyed."

Unable to contain herself, Lorelai gasped audibly, clutching a hand to her chest as she gaped at Daelen. Such a thing was unheard of. A tragedy, the consequences of which could very well threaten all of Avskild.

King Knos shook his head as the idea settled in. "How did it happen?"

"No idea. The report was that the site looked... corrupted."

Knos growled and clenched his fists. "Such a thing should not be possible." He slammed a palm against the wall, and his eyes settled on Lorelai. "Perhaps I will make additional use of your wisdom after all, Lorelai."

Lorelai nodded, but something within her felt as though she would regret this night.

CHAPTER FIFTEEN

JOTUN

Lind Hjordis

Lind was up just before the sun. The forest was active with life in the early light. He snapped his finger, his campfire winking out with a final crackle. The path to Vanalf was a winding trail that led deep into a steep valley behind Dalstava. The valley was left without much disturbance on purpose, a wilderness only for those brave souls who entered the cave to acquire its magic or hunters seeking game. He was near the peak of the trail, and today he would descend into the valley and reach Vanalf.

His horse, a dun-colored steed he'd named Davard, was large for his breed. A necessity, since Lind himself was a larger man. Davard was a strong horse, bred for traversing the mountains, and at only eight years old, he was still young and sturdy.

Lind rolled his blanket and wrapped it up before stowing it on Davard's saddle. It didn't take long for him to mount and get back to the trail just as the sun came over the edge of the foggy sea, barely visible on the horizon from his high vantage. He wondered what a true sunrise would look like. One that wasn't obscured by the fog and darkened stone that ringed the sea. Such a thought made him ponder how the rest of the world fared. The lack of Voyagers was concerning. There was always the necessity to travel the portals to ensure the integrity of the magic constructs from the other side, but he had high hopes for the current students. The path through Vanalf was a mysterious one, and he could never be certain about what type of Grimnir a student would become, but he did often have lucky guesses.

Instinct told him that they would have several Voyagers this next time, even though there was no Voyager instructor among the staff any more. Not since the last one disappeared.

Trees faded behind him as Lind neared the crest of the trail. Two distinctive shapes marked either side. One was a wooden pillar, carved from the trunk of a pine. Its surface was etched with men and women locked in combat with various monsters. Many of the people were being consumed by the beasts, arms, legs, or heads torn or completely lost inside the mouths of the monsters. On the other side was a pillar of stone with similar imagery, though the men and women were instead Grimnirs, armed with magic. The people on the stone pillar were victorious, the very peak of the pillar topped with the image of a Valtyra holding the severed head of a serpent. But where the wooden pillar was as clear and smooth as the day it had been carved, the stone pillar looked worn with age, having been scratched and eroded by nature over the years.

As the head of Castle Vrodr, Lind felt the deep inclination to meet with King Knos regarding the pillars to see if artisans could be commissioned to repair the damage. He hated to think what the students would feel to pass such ominous depictions.

Once past the pillars, he began the descent into the valley. This was true wilderness. It was not at all uncommon to see bears, boars, moose, wolves, lynxes, beavers, or any number of deer, making it a favorite territory for daring hunters. Granted, this was the safest valley to hunt in. Other areas of the island were roamed by larger beasts, and a dragon was rumored to slumber in one of the peaks, though it had not been seen in his generation.

Davard kicked up rocks as they descended, the trail getting less gravelly the deeper they went. A barren section stretched before him for a while before the tree line resumed. Lind was making good time. He would likely reach the entrance to Vanalf by midday. From there, it would take only a quick inspection to determine its integrity.

He could still distinctly remember the first time he'd entered this valley. He'd been thirteen at the time. His family was out foraging for berries when he'd foolishly decided to follow a fox. It didn't take long before he was completely lost and decided that finding some high ground would be the best way to determine how to get back to Dalstava. Trees blocked his view until he'd almost reached the entrance to the valley.

It was only then that he'd noticed a strange creature trailing him. The beast was humanoid, only slightly taller than Lind at the time. It lurked about on two feet, and several large gemstones sprouted from its head like hair. With seven eyes in total, its most prominent feature was the massive eye at the center of its face.

Lind had screamed and ran, slipping down the slope into the valley. He'd never even heard of such a creature before, but had since come to learn that they were called dwevores. It had managed to crawl directly out of Vanalf, hunting for magic to consume. But if it couldn't find magic, flesh would do.

It pursued him into the valley and would have caught him, but two Grimnirs intercepted the monster. A Watcher stampeded toward Lind on his horse as a Valtyra dropped from the sky, landing on the dwevore with a thick hack from its battleaxe. They'd saved him and led him back to Dalstava where he was reunited with his family.

That was the same day Lind had decided to become a Grimnir, if only to repay his debt. Ironic that he was blessed with neither the sight of a Watcher nor the stamina of a Valtyra, but with the spellwork of a Vitugr. Perhaps knowledge was simply his destiny. Knowledge would help. And he'd also fought his fair share of monsters over the years. Vitugrs were specifically known as the greatest asset in wars, but Avskild had been at peace for so long that the best Lind could do most days was to pass down that knowledge. If war did come again, the future Grimnirs needed to be prepared.

A small watchtower to his left was the last building he'd pass before reaching the forest floor. When he was younger, that tower had always been manned, and he'd even spent a full year positioned there. The reduction in Grimnirs was not a new phenomenon. Their numbers had been declining for decades. From the records Lind had heard and read, the Grimnir army once numbered 4,000 strong. Now the Grimnir Guard was probably shy of 500. It meant that the safety of their portals was more critical now than ever before. He couldn't envision their enemies outside being any weaker than they were before the shields were erected.

The best thing he could hope for when he reached the cave was that nothing was amiss. Or perhaps that there was a small issue, one that could be handled without too much difficulty, that might inspire a swell in their ranks.

He entered a section of the forest where towering pines as old as time stretched into the sky. The scent of them was embedded in the very essence of this place. He took a deep breath, reveling. Already the closeness to Vanalf tickled his skin with the familiar aura of magic. Not even the senses of a Watcher were needed to detect it. He drew his axe from its holster and laid it across his lap.

Without regular patrols through here, he had no idea what kind of creature could slip out of the cave. Though he could fling fire and ice at will, the axe offered him an extra measure of comfort.

They were two months away from sending the oldest class to Vanalf, a group of eighteen-year-olds. There were only sixteen of them left. It wasn't uncommon for a few students to drop off in the last year. They would get too nervous to take the final step of venturing into the depths of Vanalf, even though survival rates were better than ever before. The death toll, however, made it the riskiest job in all of Avskild, and that was before they ever got their magic.

Lind eyed the forest carefully as Davard plodded along. The sooner this was done with, the better, and perhaps Davard wanted a good trot. Lind clicked his tongue and nudged Davard to a trot, hooves pounding against the earthen floor, softened by fallen needles. A pair of deer bounced out of view. He even caught a rare glimpse of a nymph watching him from the branches before it disappeared behind the trunk. That was only his third time seeing one, and he wasn't sure if it was a good sign or a bad one.

The day was halfway through by the time Lind neared Vanalf. The elevation continued to drop dramatically, and the trees weren't as thick. His favorite sign that he was close was the collection of cloudberry bushes where the trees were thinner. The berries wouldn't be in season for a few more months still, but his mouth watered just at the thought of their sometimes sweet, sometimes sour taste. When they were allowed to ripen all the way, their soft texture was the peak of nature's treats.

He crossed one final stream before stopping and jumping down from Davard's back.

A mountainous formation of rock jutted from the ground ahead of him. Five massive spikes rose up from the formation at geographically inconsistent angles, like the structure of an immense crown. The rest of the structure may have very well been the skull of an enormous giant. The right eye of the skull was merely an indentation, hollowed and dark, but the left eye was a large opening that led deep underground.

Lind tied Davard to a small spruce and approached the formation with firm steps, following the familiar path. He bounced his axe in his hand as the cave came into full view, just at the base of the central spike. Steam issued from the entrance to Vanalf and from other cracks and seams along the surface of the formation. The cave was a dark, gaping hole. If the rock formation was a giant's crown, then the entrance to Vanalf was an eyeless socket.

For all he knew, it *was* the ancient body of a giant, the rest of it hidden beneath the earth. The mysteries of Vanalf were endless. It was a cave that connected to magical realms, never meant to be trodden by mere humans. It was supposed that one could travel all the way to a world of elves, or one of trolls, or one of demigods, but such paths were blocked by unimaginable dangers. Perhaps the kind of paths that only Voyagers could survive.

The sight always left Lind rapt with wonder.

But the wonder was cut short.

Something started to lumber out of the cave. Something dangerously familiar.

Lind dove behind a fallen tree trunk and held his breath. A deep, guttural voice echoed up in a language that seemed like it was from a distant memory. He'd read words that sounded like that before. Such a beast should not have been able to reach Avskild through Vanalf. The magic of the portals was what powered the shield around their island, but it also shielded certain things from entering Vanalf from the other realms.

Clearly, that had failed.

Lind inched up slowly to peer over the edge of the log as even more voices conversed below. He could scarcely believe his eyes when he saw four of the beasts standing outside the cave, squinting up at the midday sun. They were large creatures, humanoid in shape, but their noses were the size of Lind's head, and their eyes were the size of plates. Unkempt hair dangled wildly down to their bellies. Their limbs were long, and they wore mismatched clothing, though one of them had metal pauldrons on its shoulders and wielded a massive axe. Another one had two heads, though its second head had only one eye. Their skin was pale gray, dotted with sickly, hairy warts.

Trolls.

The one with two heads was doing most of the talking, its one-eyed head croaking about the sunlight. From what Lind could understand, it also muttered something about "getting the others."

Lind's grip on his axe tightened, barely restraining himself from rushing out and calling down fire on the monsters. The one thing that held him back was that, despite their hideous appearance, trolls were quite fast, and they could very likely run him down. Those long limbs of theirs were good for something. There was also a sense of mystery to the trolls. Avskildian archives contained numerous accounts regarding trolls. Sometimes they could have a sort of magical resistance. If not for that, he'd probably be able to destroy them in a couple moments. Additionally, the more heads a troll had, the more powerful they were, meaning that two-headed troll could very well have some protections against magic.

He would need to sneak away, ride back to Dalstava, and inform Mikel and King Knos of the threat immediately, before it got any worse.

It was decided. He rolled away, rising to a crouch, fully intent on running back to Davard and riding out of the valley as quickly as possible. When he turned back, however, he found himself face-to-face with a troll bent down on one knee, watching him with a crooked smile on its hideous face.

"I smelled you, crunchy human," the troll said, words barely discernible. The other voices near the cave suddenly began to bellow. They'd be upon him in moments.

Lind flicked his arm, and a flaming ball launched from his palm. The fireball crashed into the troll's chest, exploding into flames. A human would have been incinerated, but the troll stumbled back, flailing and screaming. All subtlety lost, Lind summoned a pillar of earth beneath his feet, launching him into the air. He flipped over the troll's body, five spears of ice launching from each of his fingers. The ice spears stabbed into the troll's face, resulting in a roar that could have been heard through the whole valley.

Lind landed with a roll and sprang straight back to his feet. He sprinted to Davard as footsteps thundered up the hill behind him.

"Time to go," he told the horse as he whipped his reins loose and got into the saddle. A spear the size of a small tree barreled past Lind, shattering the ground in front of him. Davard reared to the side, and Lind barely dodged beneath the swinging axe of the two-headed troll. He heeled Davard around and urged him to a full gallop. Sparing a glance back, the four trolls were mere steps behind him, but they were losing ground. Unable to keep up with Davard's speed, the trolls roared in frustration and hurled their weapons at Lind.

The weapons fell short, and Lind was off at full speed up the trail, heart pounding like the thumping of Davard's hooves.

This was worse than anything he'd expected. Five trolls. Certainly more dangerous than a ship full of draugrs. There was also the likelihood that more had snuck through before he'd arrived. How many more would appear?

The shield around Avskild was not gone. They would have definitely caught such a change in the air, and the foggy appearance on the horizon wouldn't even be there, so the shield had to be operational to some extent, but it was undeniably weakened. There could be no other explanation for the presence of trolls. Even King Knos wouldn't be able to deny such a thing. And if Vanalf was compromised, how would they risk creating more Grimnirs? The dangers involved would be greater than ever before.

Lind heeled Davard again, but the horse did not run any faster. They were already at maximum speed and wouldn't be able to gallop like this for too long. He bit back his frustration and slowed Davard to a trot. They'd ride harder than they ever had before, or all of Avskild could be lost.

TIDES OF WAR

Hallik

Hallik, Elowyn, and Bjorn stood at the side of the forest looking out toward Dalstava. Bjorn had frozen in place as soon as the city came into view.

Hallik could only wonder what was going through the man's head, since he wouldn't say anything at all. "Come on, Bjorn. Please. We've been standing here for a while now."

Elowyn shook her head at Hallik, but he ignored her.

"Can you at least say something? We need to get to the city to let them know about the portal."

"Maybe you should go on," Elowyn said in a quiet voice, touching Hallik's arm. "I can stay here with Bjorn."

Hallik kicked the dirt and placed his hands on his hips. He didn't want to leave Bjorn here. In truth, he wanted

Bjorn to be able to share his part of the story so that Hallik didn't sound like he was making it up. And, though he wasn't sure if he wanted to admit it, he was a little worried about whatever Bjorn was thinking. He didn't feel inclined to leave the fully armed man with Elowyn.

"I—" Bjorn said before his voice trailed off.

Hallik nodded to Bjorn, hoping he'd continue.

"I never imagined I'd see a city like this," Bjorn finally got out. "I always imagined that your people had been eradicated. That seemed like the only viable explanation."

Hallik glanced at Elowyn, but her eyes remained fixed on Bjorn. Hallik found Bjorn a curiosity. How had he been surviving outside of Avskild? His whole idea regarding the world outside was that it was ravaged by monsters, and yet there were still people living out there.

"Tell us, then," Elowyn said. "Tell us what happened from your perspective."

Bjorn shook his head. "As history goes, the magicians, or Grimnirs as you say, were the last line of defense humanity had against the dark, but they were ultimately defeated, leaving the rest of humanity to fend for themselves."

"Defeated?" Elowyn said, head rearing back as though she had been personally offended. "Most certainly not."

"I can see that," Bjorn said, eyes narrowing. "So instead, you abandoned the rest of the world so you could hide behind your own shield."

Elowyn shook her head. "We would never do such a thing," she said, her words biting. "We've been sending Voyagers all along to help maintain peace in the world, but they've all disappeared, probably killed by monsters or uninformed dunces." She shot him a glare.

Uncomfortable with the obvious tension, Hallik stepped between them. "I hate to be the voice of reason here, but these events happened what, 205 years ago? Isn't it possible that there's some lack of context after all this time?"

Elowyn and Bjorn didn't take their eyes off each other, both squinting in equal distaste.

"I know all the songs," Elowyn said.

"And what do your songs tell you about your abandonment?" Bjorn's expression was murderous, but his hands made no movement for his weapons.

Elowyn opened her mouth, but no words came out. Instead, her eyes dropped, and she turned away, eyebrows knitting in a frown.

Even Hallik knew what the songs said. He'd heard them all from Selke's own lips, and he trusted her songs over any record kept in the libraries of Dalstava. "There were no other people," Hallik said. "We thought the world was lost. That's why the portal shield was created. I don't recall any mention of survivors outside of Avskild, but Elowyn is right. The Voyagers were meant to travel the portals, ensure their security, and make contact with any remaining people."

Bjorn grunted. He looked back toward the city and took a deep breath. "Quite possibly a lie." He shrugged. "No matter. If you had stayed to fight, you probably would have all died sooner anyway. Sealing yourselves off and leaving the rest of us to die may have been the right choice."

"That's a rather grim outlook," Elowyn said.

"Fitting, then," Bjorn said. "Now tell me about your city. I want to know what I'm in for before we enter."

"Right," Hallik said, urging Elowyn on with him. He pointed at the Tower of Tarn. "That tall black thing is called the Tower of Tarn. It functions as the headquarters for the Grimnir Guard and also the throne of King Knos, the king of Avskild. Castle Vrodr, just through these gates, is the training grounds for students who want to become Grimnirs."

"Become?" Bjorn asked from behind as Hallik started walking toward the gates of Castle Vrodr.

Hallik smiled. "Yes, becoming a Grimnir requires surviving Vanalf, a cave network connected to the other realms."

"I don't understand," Bjorn said. "Where does the magic come from? Is there an elf or a godkin that gifts it? Just entering a cave seems too simple."

Hallik laughed. "There's more to it than that, though the details we're able to get from our instructors or other Grimnirs are always somewhat vague, like they don't remember all the details. All we know is that you have to go in one way and come out another, and when you emerge, you have one of four powers."

"And annoyingly, you don't get to choose which power you get," Elowyn said.

"Interesting. And suspicious," Bjorn said. "I've never heard of a distinction between different types of magicians. You mentioned Voyagers earlier. Is that one of them?"

Hallik smiled again. This was the most Bjorn had talked since they'd met. He gave Bjorn a brief explanation of each Grimnir class, but mostly he couldn't stop thinking about what life must have been like for the monster hunter. How many monsters had he killed? How did his family survive? "I have a question for you now, monster hunter," Hallik said. "You were surprised by Dalstava. Are there not cities like this in Kelig?"

Bjorn gave his signature grunt. "I don't believe there are cities like this anywhere, unless they're being run by vampires or something."

They neared the gate and saw Latshal beckoning them to the castle with her arms, eyes wide as she scanned the forest behind them. "Elowyn, Hallik. Get inside!"

Hallik reactively started jogging. He'd never seen Latshal behave in such a way, and it reminded him all the more about the news he had to share. He still wasn't certain who exactly he was supposed to share it with, but he was sure it wouldn't take long to figure out. Questions about Bjorn would point him in the right direction in no time.

"What is it?" Hallik asked as they drew up beside her.

"We'll talk more when you get inside," Latshal said, then she dropped her spear, holding it out before Bjorn. "Hold it!"

To his credit, Bjorn simply halted and stared down the haft of the spear at Latshal. Hallik had expected the monster hunter to draw a weapon or at least say something, but he did no such thing.

"This is our frien—uh... our friend*ly* acquaintance," Hallik said. "We have some important news to report."

"That is well," Latshal said, spear unmoving, "but your friend here—"

"I'm not—" Bjorn protested.

"—will remain outside," Latshal continued as though Bjorn hadn't said anything. "Now is not the time to accept strangers into Vrodr. Especially not someone who is armed like a trained assassin."

"If I wanted to assassinate somebody, I would certainly do it without the aid of these children," Bjorn said. "Besides, I don't kill people. Normal ones, anyway."

Latshal tilted her head at Bjorn. "Your companion could learn some manners." She sniffed at him then squinted quizzically before sniffing at Hallik. "You smell like beast. Both of you. Were you hunting?"

"That's what we came to report," Hallik said, distinctly aware of Latshal's magically enhanced senses.

Latshal's lips curled. "A monster." It wasn't a question.

Hallik nodded. "I found a dead Watcher at the base of a portal not far from Elowyn's home. He was... killed by a monster called a liowolf." He pointed at Bjorn. "Bjorn helped me kill the monster."

"I recall being the one who saved your life and killed the beast," Bjorn said.

Hallik shrugged. "He killed it."

Latshal growled. "What were you even doing at a portal?"

"The liowolf lured him there," Elowyn said. "It's a common tactic of theirs to confuse the senses, even from great distances."

Latshal hissed out a long breath through her teeth. "Alright." She withdrew her spear from pointing at Bjorn and used it to gesture to the castle. "Get inside. I need to get word to Captain Vigsen before anybody else hears of this. Hurry." She kept her eyes on the forest as Hallik and the others walked past her.

She seemed like she had more to say, but instead, she held her ground before the gate as the three of them entered Castle Vrodr. Hallik paused to look back at her. "Latshal?"

"Something approaches," Latshal said. She gestured at the gate again. "Get inside."

Hallik stopped just behind the gate, but watched the forest line, hoping to catch sight of whatever Latshal was sensing. He knew it was futile. Her keen senses would be able to detect things for a full mile, after all. But he didn't have to wait long.

Galloping up to the castle came Lind. He kept the horse at full speed, one hand waving at them madly.

"Didn't Lind go to check on Vanalf?" Hallik asked.

"He did," Elowyn said in a grave tone.

Hallik could only wonder what would make Lind, of all people, come riding up to the castle like a madman. His imagination didn't need too much creativity. He'd seen two different monsters in two days. It wasn't hard to put the pieces together. The shields were weak. Avskild was no longer safe. *Nature's rays.* What he wouldn't give to be a Grimnir already.

Lind galloped straight past Latshal. "Close the gates!" he said to her in passing.

She rushed in after them all.

Lind dismounted and patted his horse. By the way he was panting, one may have thought Lind was doing the running. A few other people gathered in the courtyard drew near at the excitement.

"What is it?" Hallik asked at the same time as three others said the same thing.

Lind shook his head. "Secure the castle. Prepare yourselves." His eyes settled on each of the students in turn. "We will soon be at war."

CHAPTER SEVENTEEN

MUSTER

Jaysen Bjorn

Discordant voices bickered, echoing off the tall walls and high ceiling of the enormous room. The walls were like nothing he'd seen before, constructed of dark gray stone enameled with golden inlays, sometimes in the shape of ancient beasts. This Lind character had escorted Bjorn to the Tower of Tarn so that he could give a report to the officers and leaders of the Avskildians. Two guards had stripped Bjorn of all his weapons before allowing him entry into the tower, a painstakingly long process that had Lind muttering curses to himself.

Bjorn still had three knives about his person that they hadn't located, thanks to Lind's persistent urging that they had dire news to report. Now, Lind and the other leaders argued amongst themselves about the information.

Apparently, Lind's report was not dissimilar to other accounts that the captain, Mikel Vigsen, had received already. It had Bjorn wondering how many portals were at Avskild and where they all connected to. Perhaps they were linked to places all across the world.

What Lind had seen seemed like the worst news of all. A troll invasion. Bjorn hadn't killed a troll yet, unfortunately, but what little he knew about them was not good. They rarely worked alone, and if Lind had seen five, that meant there were most likely many more than that. A whole clan of them at least, and clans could measure anywhere from thirty to a couple thousand.

Bjorn stood by himself, arms behind his back. One soldier stood behind him near the door, and most of the other people in the room were armed, a detail he did not fail to notice. Bjorn still did not know how to process being in such a massive structure. He'd thought all such human civilization had long been ruined. *But,* he reminded himself, *although the Grimnirs had not truly been defeated, they were only delaying the inevitable.* From what he'd seen of the rest of the world, it was dominated by monsters and vile creatures. Even if the Grimnirs were as powerful as legend, they wouldn't stand a chance against the innumerable host of wicked beings that fought for control over the realm.

Even Bjorn's efforts in slaying monsters were trivial. It simply offered him a basic sense of fulfillment, a bit of coin, and a lot of fun. No matter how many he killed, however, it made no difference in the ultimate outcome. Night, he'd even saved a town from a couple werewolves once only to have the same town utterly destroyed by a horde of goblins an hour later. It was a cruel world, not that he was bitter about it. He was simply a realist.

A sharp thud brought the discourse to a sudden halt. The captain had slammed the handle of his sword down on the wooden table around which they'd been bickering. His eyes settled on Bjorn.

"Enough," Mikel said to them. "Let us question this man as well, and then we can discuss a course of action." He urged Bjorn forward with two fingers. The captain was what Bjorn expected of a military leader. His expression was hard, his demeanor and posture controlled and intentional. He wore leather armor, intricately designed for aesthetic appeal, suggesting these Avskildians had more time on their hands and money to spare than anybody that still lived outside the island. A fine sword was sheathed at his waist, which was expected. The more peculiar detail was the crow that sat on Mikel's shoulder, its head cocked as it glared at Bjorn with one eye.

The crow was unnatural to Bjorn. It was too tame for a bird. It had an uncanny level of attention, watching people with deeper understanding than it seemed like it should. He suspected it was some kind of changeling.

"Jaysen Bjorn," Mikel said, eyeing Bjorn up and down with a slight frown. "Lind has explained a few things, but I'd like to hear it from you. Where are you from?"

Bjorn took a deep breath. This was not how he'd expected his next few days to be going. He still needed to get back to that village and collect his payment for killing the liowolf. "I am from Kelig, across the sea."

"And how did you come to be here?"

"I was on commission to hunt a liowolf. I followed its trail through the forests. At one point, I simply found myself in a different forest, unlike the one I had been in previously."

Mikel shared a look with the others around him. "Instantaneously? Were there any other conditions? Did you notice any structures?"

"It was instantaneous," Bjorn said. "The liowolf was impairing my senses, so I was hearing the sound of rushing wind, though there was none, and visually, everything was wavering. Once I ended up in the forest here, I did not notice any structure initially. I had to walk a few more steps before I saw the actual portal, so it wasn't like I simply walked through it like a door." This seemed the strangest detail. He would have expected the portal to work as a door.

"And what of the Watcher? Was he already there when you arrived?"

"When I saw the portal, the liowolf was sneaking off into the forest. The Watcher was dead." The last thing he wanted was for them to suspect him of murdering the man. He realized he may have unwittingly subjected himself to their authority, even allowing them to remove most of his weapons. If they treated him unjustly, he would have to seek retribution, but in his experience, humans were so scarce that any animosity between their own people was rare back in Kelig. Things could very well be different in Avskild. He quickly spoke to add more detail. "The portal was glowing, though. There were small green lights, glowing in the vines, and something within the support beams seemed alive."

"That Watcher would have been Riga," said a woman beside Mikel.

"Riga could not have activated the portal," Lind said. "And if the portal was functioning normally, Bjorn would have stepped through the portal directly instead of appearing somehow nearby."

"The liowolf might have had something to do with that," Mikel said. He nodded to Lind. "You are familiar with their unique abilities. Bjorn could have been disoriented. I'm not sure how much of what he says can be trusted on the matter."

Bjorn drew his lips into a thin line. Was such a thing possible? Yes. Perhaps he walked through the portal earlier than he'd thought, but why did such details even matter?

The room continued discussing the implications, again seeming to forget that Bjorn stood there. It was only then that Bjorn became aware of a woman in the room, standing off to the side, observing the whole affair with slight amusement. Half of her red hair was pulled behind her head in a knot, the rest dangling down her back. She wore a dark green dress with metal pinions holding it in place, a dark blue, long-sleeved underdress beneath that. She seemed out of place. The other women in the room were all dressed like soldiers. Where had she come from?

She looked over at the door behind Bjorn just before it opened.

Bjorn stepped back as another man entered, a large, heavily armed soldier coming in behind him.

The new arrival was richly dressed, with elaborately embroidered clothes and a fine fur cloak. Several rings decorated his fingers, a gold bracelet was clasped around one wrist, and two necklaces hung about his neck, though neither of them bore the symbols Bjorn had come to recognize as markings of Grimnirs. Most importantly, a crown rested on his head. This was likely the King Knos he'd heard of.

The room fell silent, all eyes on the king.

Knos stopped just in front of Lind. "I hear you have word from Vanalf."

"Yes," Lind said, dropping his head just briefly. "Trolls came through. I killed one, but there were four others. They appeared to be assembling more from within the cave. I returned here to deliver word. We need to mobilize."

Knos was silent for a moment. A slight twitch in his cheek and his clenching fist hinted at his irritation. "Indeed. They must be eradicated." He nodded to Mikel. "See it done."

Mikel placed a hand over his chest. "As you wish." The bird on his shoulder took off into the air with a caw and flew out the door. "Also, we still do not have word from the last two portals."

"Leave the portals to me," Knos said in a gravelly voice.

The many confused expressions that followed that statement made Bjorn wonder if the king's subjects doubted his ability to secure the portals. Even Bjorn felt suspicious. What would the king do that the Grimnirs could not?

Nothing. That was the truth of it.

Avskild was doomed like the rest of the world.

If monsters could slip through the portals from all across the world as simply as the liowolf had, how long would this place last? The walls were indeed high, and the defenses seemed formidable. It would be able to hold off for some time, no doubt. Perhaps, at least for Bjorn, this would be a good place to at least earn some coin. After all, he'd fared better against the liowolf than one of their precious Watchers.

That woman's eyes were on Bjorn, but she glanced away as soon as he noticed.

"Go now," Knos said. "With haste. Send those fiends back. Hold off the cave." Without waiting for any response, he turned to leave the room. That big soldier went with him, and, interestingly enough, the strange woman followed after the king beckoned to her.

A flurry of activity ensued. Mikel issued orders, and people began to scramble.

"Let me come as well," Lind said to Mikel, but the captain shook his head.

"No," Mikel said. "With all this madness going on, we need you at Vrodr. Those students are the future of Avskild."

Lind gripped the axe at his waist, but nodded, mollified.

Mikel patted Lind's shoulder as the crowd headed for the exits.

A heavy sigh on his lips, Lind returned to Bjorn. "Let's go," he said, voice quiet.

"I don't suppose they would let me fight beside them, would they?" Bjorn asked. Not only was he interested in seeing Grimnirs in battle, but he wanted to mark a troll off his list.

Lind wheezed a laugh and patted Bjorn's shoulder, much to his disdain. "I don't think so, lad. A trained army of Grimnirs isn't going to have a random man join them in the field of battle. You and I have our places."

"But this isn't my place at all."

Lind nodded at that. "True, but for now you're stuck here, like it or not. And while you're here, you're under the government of King Knos and the Grimnir Guard."

Bjorn let out a long, angry breath. He'd never been under anyone's rule before. No real form of government remained in Kelig. They were all just survivors, clinging together as they got picked off one by one. Nothing more.

He held back all of his scathing replies. He'd follow the rules, at least until he got his weapons back, then he'd find a way to get out of this city and go back to paving his own way.

CHAPTER EIGHTEEN

FIRE, BLOOD, AND SMOKE

Lorelai Harkral

King Knos strode at the head of their small party, Daelen behind him, massive body blocking the king from view. Lorelai followed at the rear. They walked wordlessly, their hollow footsteps the only sound in the vast, empty hallways.

Perhaps this was the moment Knos would reveal whatever secret he'd been withholding from Lorelai. She wasn't sure she was ready for it. Nonetheless, a feeling of excitement tickled within her. She couldn't help it. Secrets were interesting. Exciting. No matter how dark the secret, there was this unique sense of power and control in knowing things about people and the world. A power that she scarcely felt in anything else.

Secrets like knowing that Daelen's son was a drunken brawler living in the streets near the docks, his life wasting away. And Daelen knew she knew. It made him uneasy whenever they made eye contact.

There was more power out there. More secrets. And Lorelai could hardly resist. That is what drew her to the king. She knew he was hiding things. His obsession with building his manor was all part of his ruse. In truth, he was deeply ingrained in the goings-on of Avskild.

As Knos led them further up the Tower of Tarn's stairways, she knew she'd finally learn what he'd been up to.

Working her way into a position as the king's attendant had been rigorous. It had required determination, wit, a bit of finesse, and of course, secrets. The king understood the good value of a bit of hidden knowledge. Lorelai was not born into a poor family, nor a wealthy one, but she had obtained certain skills. She could hide, she could sneak, and most important of all, she could listen. And the king loved secrets. She'd actually worked under the militia watch for a while, though she doubted Captain Mikel Vigsen had even known her name until she worked her way up to a watch leader after preventing a couple robberies and finding the culprit for another.

That was when she had opportunities to get into the Tower of Tarn a few times. She took every chance to cross paths with the king until he finally spoke to her. Without any hesitation, she told him one of her secrets she'd been saving just for such an occasion: his cousin had pilfered a golden bracelet from the burial mound of their grandfather. It was something she'd discovered while staying up one night, prowling the rooftops as she sometimes did. But she'd saved this secret just for him. She didn't want anybody else trying to take credit for her work. She'd been under his direct employ ever since.

It was because of her that the king knew Mikel secretly sent Grimnirs to each of the portals. It was her suggestion that had prevented the king from stopping Mikel. Not only would such an action have damaged the loyalty and confidence of his guard, but giving the order himself would have made him seem less in control than he should have been.

Even still, the Grimnir Guard questioned him. They doubted his ability to protect Avskild. She'd seen it in their looks earlier. She hoped it was unfounded. She wanted to believe that King Knos knew what he was doing.

They ascended another set of stairs to the sixth floor. This triggered Lorelai's curiosity the most. There were no guards this high up. No residents. There was no function to this space. The rooms were all but empty, save for a few pieces of old furniture covered with pale sheets. Light spilled in from lofty windows, illuminating specks of dust that drifted through the air. It smelled old. Ancient.

This building had stood longer than the entire Grimnir legacy.

"Are you sure about Lorelai, my king?" Daelen asked.

Lorelai held back a huff.

"We will know shortly," Knos said. "How old are you again, Lorelai?"

Lorelai pursed her lips. She had never told the king her age. Intentionally. But she saw no reason to lie now. "Twenty-three."

Knos looked back at her with renewed interest. "And here I thought you were my age at thirty. You're too keen for twenty-three, Lorelai. Perhaps that's reason enough." They stopped inside a small, dark room. There were no windows. Only the light of the open door illuminated the space.

Knos pulled away a tattered rug that hid a few torches. He selected one and nodded at the door. Daelen closed the door behind them just after Knos lit the torch.

"The Tower of Tarn is ancient, Lorelai," Knos said. "Much older than we know. It's rumored that the building was constructed by magic rather than by physical means, magic that is not accessible to Grimnirs. Some architects who have studied it have documented suspicions that there were lower levels to the tower. There are odd spaces in the structure that seem to have no entrance, and many of them are suspected to merely offer structural integrity. Nonetheless, I had them map out each floor in detail, showing an accurate scale of room sizes and everything. What I found interesting about this information were some unexplainable, inaccessible areas."

Knos paused as if for dramatic effect before holding the now-burning torch to the stone near the bottom of the far wall. "I looked all around them. The only place I found anything interesting was here. On the sixth floor. The stone is a little blacker here."

To Lorelai's utter surprise, the flames seemed to trickle into the bricks. Orange light flowed around, tracing the outline of each brick. Soundlessly, the bricks began to slide back on both the wall and some of the floor. They formed a gaping, sloped hole that descended further.

"Fire is the key," Knos said, stepping into the darkness beyond. "Come."

Daelen handed Lorelai an unlit torch, his expression stern. He held his own, also unlit, and followed after the king.

Lorelai gulped and hurried down after them. She quickly discovered that it was a circular staircase. It was chilly. Tendrils of thick air seemed to coalesce against her exposed skin. When she glanced back, the entrance was simply gone, and all she saw was blackness. She kept her face forward and stayed close to the light offered by the king's torch.

Knos's voice easily carried up the stairs. "I found this place eight years ago, when I was just younger than you. I almost got stuck the first time I ventured in because I wasn't sure how far down the stairs extended. I have since measured it, and based on my findings, I would say it extends well beneath the ground."

Indeed, the steps kept going. If the stairs went below ground, and they only started on the sixth floor up, that meant they had several floors to descend. This was certainly a big secret. One she hadn't anticipated. But the real question remained. What was down there? What would she find at the bottom of an ancient building around which the portal nation of Avskild had built their entire society? The king's excitement was growing the more he shared. She could only imagine that he'd kept this secret pent up for so long, sharing it only with Daelen, who may as well have been a moving pile of rocks for all the personality he offered.

"You've made an amazing discovery, my King," Lorelai said. "I'm surprised you've kept it to yourself this whole time."

"Necessity," Knos said. "You will see when we reach the bottom. The interesting thing about this staircase is that it extends far enough below ground that there's probably another floor between the first floor and this one, but I have found no way to locate an entrance between them. Nor have I found anything that might go any deeper, but perhaps it is not necessary."

More questions boiled through Lorelai's mind. This was all rather intricate. Why go through the trouble of designing an entire building this way? A staircase that connected only two floors, from the sixth to... two levels below ground? It was bizarre to say the least, and being made of stone meant that it was unmistakably intentional.

The original creators of this place had been trying to hide something.

They continued to descend until Knos stopped before a stone wall. "This part was easier to figure out. Massive staircases don't lead to stone walls, so I figured there must have been another key of some kind." His torch hovered over a reddened stone on the last step. He withdrew an elaborate dagger with an ivory handle and jagged edges.

He pricked his finger on one of the jagged parts and then squeezed some of his blood onto the reddened stone.

It reacted in a similar way. A red glow flooded the grooves around the brick and then spread across the others. This time, the bricks folded in on themselves, revealing an open passageway ahead.

Lorelai shielded her eyes against the surprising amount of light that emanated from within. Knos proceeded inside without any hesitation.

"No turning back now," Daelen muttered to Lorelai.

Lorelai set her jaw and gripped the unlit torch in her hand as she followed after the king. The light inside came from glowing spheres encased in metal wiring, caged against the high ceiling. The room was relatively small compared with many of the rooms in the tower, but it was still larger than her entire home. A single stone table jutted from one of the far walls, an assortment of strange instruments laid out across it. Other than that, the only thing in the room was a curved arch that rose all the way to the ceiling and back down. Its smooth surface made it look like it was forged from a dull metal, and it glowed with a faint orange light.

It was a portal. The rumors about a portal hidden within the Tower of Tarn were true.

But the burning question remained. What had King Knos done to secure the defense of Avskild? She doubted it could get much worse than murdering every Voyager.

The magical door through which they'd entered remained open. She wondered how long it would last and if they'd have to use blood again to get back out.

Knos withdrew an ornate dagger from within his fur-lined robe, different from the one he'd pulled out previously. Lorelai had never seen the weapon before. The handle looked like several twisting, knotted cords, and the pommel was a brass depiction of a serpent's head. The metal of the blade itself was so dark it could have been carved from ebony, and there were golden symbols that almost glowed along the middle of the otherwise black surface. Two yellow gemstones were on either side of the crossguard.

"Skuga!" Knos cried. He pounded his free hand against the side of the portal.

To Lorelai's astonishment, a black mist boiled up from the bottom of the portal. Instead of spilling outward, it continued to climb up until it reached the top of the portal, filling its entire shimmering surface. The mist coalesced as though pushing at some unseen barrier that prevented it from leaving the portal.

"He will arrive shortly," Knos said, looking back at Lorelai. He held the dagger up for her inspection. "When I first entered this room, this dagger was the only thing on the floor, just sitting there in front of the portal." He gestured to a place in front of the portal where scratches scarred the stone floor. The scratches did not seem random, but almost seemed to form a symbol.

"It says Skuga's name," Knos said, answering Lorelai's unasked question.

When Lorelai tried to discern any words from the scratches, nothing was legible. Perhaps it was not in their language.

Knos pointed at the word again. "When I came in here, I picked up the dagger and read the name. Then the mist appeared and... well. Skuga came."

Lorelai looked back at the swirling black mist. This was not right. The portal shouldn't have been working to begin with, and yet Knos seemed to have no trepidation about it whatsoever. "Is this... dangerous?"

"No," Knos said with a smirk. "As you can see, the portal is sealed."

"If it was sealed, it wouldn't be reacting at all," Lorelai said. A sealed portal wouldn't be glowing. The magic was active—certainly that was a reasonable conclusion.

"And yet." Knos shrugged. "Nothing escapes. The magic here within the tower is powerful. I think the tower itself is fueling this portal rather than some outside source."

Lorelai was still skeptical, but she did not have time to voice her thoughts.

A sound seeped into the room, like a giant yawning after a long nap. The mist in the portal roiled as if blown by a strong wind. "Ah," the voice said. It was a deep, male voice, almost seductive. A hand, grayish-violet in hue, pressed against the invisible barrier. "King Knos. How may I serve?"

Whatever the voice belonged to, it was certainly not human. And the hand was large enough that it must have belonged to a being much larger than herself. Possibly a troll.

"Skuga!" Knos snapped. His change in tone was violent. "Trolls have entered Avskild through Vanalf, a portal has been destroyed, and several other portals are completely malfunctioning. Monsters are seeping in. You assured me this would not happen!"

"Mmm," Skuga replied, its voice a deep rumble, coming out as if Knos's words brought it pleasure. "You had not returned the dagger. The shield requires power." There was a pause as Skuga inhaled deeply, as if sniffing.

"All the Voyagers are dead," Knos said. "I've brought you their power. Last time, you said it would be enough."

"All of them," Skuga said slowly, savoring the words, "dead?"

Nature's rays. By all the demons of creation, what had Knos done? Lorelai's mind reeled. Knos had not simply been murdering the Voyagers, but he'd somehow been capturing their power and turning it over to this... creature.

"Yes! Just as required," Knos screamed.

The light around the portal pulsed and flickered. Lorelai thought she could see the faint image of a face appearing through the mist, dark orange eyes flickering like flames. Four eyes, not just two.

Knos flailed his arms for effect. "I killed them all myself. Stabbed with Dris, just like the others. What went wrong?"

Mist coiled at the king's feet, but he didn't seem to notice. The orange light within the structure of the portal pulsed more brightly, while the glowing magical spheres in the ceiling grew dim.

"Daelen," Lorelai hissed, eyes wide.

Daelen saw it as well, ripping his sword free of its sheath. He lunged forward, blade arcing toward the mist. "My king!" Daelen shouted in warning.

Knos gasped, looking down just as the mist coiled around his ankle. He jerked back, but the mist had locked onto him like an iron clasp. It pulled him toward the portal, directly into the path of Daelen's swinging sword. Originally intended to sever the mist, Daelen's sword hacked into Knos's shin.

Knos screamed and nearly fell to his back, but another coil of mist clamped around his wrist where he held the dagger, Dris.

"Mmmm," Skuga hummed. "You have done your job well, King Knos."

After recovering from the shock of hacking at Knos's leg, Daelen continued to strike at the mist with his blade as Knos struggled to pull himself back. The sword had little effect on the mist, like the equivalent of Daelen blowing fog away with his lips.

Lorelai had seen all that she needed. If she had to guess, the monster communicating with them was some type of demon, though how it manipulated the dark mist was beyond her. She had no magic to aid them.

The dagger clattered to the floor beside the king as he cried out in pain. She faintly heard the sound of crunching bones.

"Curse you, Skuga!" Knos yelled, spittle flying from his mouth.

Another misty hand stretched out toward the dagger.

If what Lorelai had just heard was true, that dagger could hold a Grimnir's power. Such a tool did not belong in the hands of a demon. Steeling herself, she scrambled forward and snatched Dris away before the hand of mist reached it, her hand smacking against the bloodied stone. She hurried away before the mist could latch onto her, rushing back toward the entrance.

"Lorelai!" Daelen shouted, still somehow convinced that hacking at the mist would make any difference. "You can't leave us here." He stopped speaking, emitting a loud roar as another misty tendril latched onto his shoulder.

She had to get out of here. This place was kept a secret on purpose. Perhaps it was a prison. Wherever this portal connected to, it had been sealed off for good reason. She dropped the tip of her torch to the king's, which had been dropped to the floor, then she sprinted over to the exit. The door had resealed soundlessly behind them, but she found the reddened stone, similar to the one on the other side. The king's blood was still wet on her hand where she'd touched it, so she put her hand down, wiping the blood on the stone. It reacted just as it had before, and the bricks began to fold.

"Lorelai!" Knos screamed at her. When she glanced back, both the king's legs had been dragged into the portal, the rest of his body thrashing around to free himself. Daelen was completely gone. Only his sword remained, left on the floor.

Lorelai tucked the dagger away and started climbing the stairs. She had a long way to go and wasn't about to wait around to see if the demon could pursue her. The king was as good as dead. There was nothing she'd be able to do to save him. Daelen as well. If he'd passed through the portal completely, then he'd have a lot worse than mist to deal with. And without even his sword... she forced away the thought. All she could do was keep climbing, the men's screams haunting her as she panted, climbing higher and higher up the dark, winding staircase.

Her body trembled, from fear or excitement, she didn't know. She had to slow her pace, too exhausted to keep going so quickly. The only sounds were her own steps, her heavy breathing, and the soft whoosh of her torch burning.

After ages of climbing, she reached a wall. She dragged the torch all across the surface, unable to discern where the flames should be placed. Her movements were frantic, breathing still labored. At last, an orange glow reacted to the torch's fire, and the hidden door swung open. She stumbled out, relief flooding her. She wasn't sure if it would work, but she placed the torch's fire against the burn mark on the outside. Thankfully, the magic reacted again, and the door closed behind her.

She stumbled out into the hall, dropping the still-burning torch to the stone floor. She rested her back against the wall and slid down, slumping until her head came down against her knees. It took a long while before her breath stopped coming in deep, heaving gasps. Her fingers still quivered.

So this had been the king's brilliant plan. Kill all the Voyagers, seal their power into some cursed weapon, then take the weapon to a demon. The demon must have promised to use the energy to secure the portals. It was likely doing the exact opposite. How had the king been so foolish? His uncanny ability to read the scratched-out word on the floor was indicative of something strange. Perhaps he'd been manipulated.

If the portals were compromised, what would stop the demon from completely coming through the portal? Would it even be hard for it to figure out how to open the hidden doors? It could come out directly inside the Tower of Tarn and ravage the entire guard if they were unprepared.

Whatever the case, one thing was certain. She shook her head, fighting back the ache that rose in her throat.

Avskild was doomed.

CHAPTER NINETEEN

ALL IS WELL

Elowyn Galdre

Loose strands of hair blew across Elowyn's face as she stood atop the outer walls of Castle Vrodr, gripping Hallik's arm tightly as though he might disappear at any moment.

Together, along with Lind and Bjorn, they watched the army march out onto the path that led to Vanalf.

"We should be with them," Hallik said through gritted teeth.

She was positive that their presence was the one thing holding Hallik back. "We were told to stay, and that's what we'll do."

"Must you always be so obedient?" Hallik said.

"We are not Grimnirs yet, Hal," Elowyn said. "And though I'm sure we'd make valuable assets in battle, the

Grimnir Guard should be able to handle a few trolls." A squad of Valtyras flew out ahead of the army, a few birds, likely Watcher companions, flying with them. They'd be able to scout out the battleground.

"Yes," Hal said, "I know I'm not a Grimnir yet, but I never will be if Vanalf is overrun."

"They'll be fine," Lind said, patting Hallik's shoulder. "I only saw five trolls. I doubt they'd bring more than forty or fifty of them. The guard will hold up against that quite sufficiently. I know we've only just started some of the drills with you students, but combat routines for squads of Watchers, Valtyras, and Vitugrs are quite formidable."

"It would be even better if there were Voyagers among them," Elowyn muttered so only she could hear, but Lind still made eye contact with her from the other side of Hallik.

Bjorn was as stolid as ever, arms folded, watching the departing army with barely restrained boredom. She was genuinely surprised that he hadn't snuck off to join the battle as well. He clearly had more restraint than Hallik, though she suspected Bjorn wasn't here entirely by his own will either.

"Even if they win the battle, it is only a temporary victory," Bjorn said.

"A little bit less of that attitude would be acceptable," Hallik said with a frown, but Bjorn merely shrugged.

Lind chuckled. "Bjorn comes from a place where success is rare. Perhaps we can raise his spirits."

"My spirits are already in good order." Bjorn's face remained neutral.

Elowyn rolled her eyes. "That's arguable."

"I still feel like we should be out there with them," Hallik said.

"No," Lind said. "Our place is here. Battle is never something to be eager about. Sometimes it's necessary of course, and the duty will soon be yours, but the more you chase tomorrow, the more you'll miss today."

Elowyn had to smile and shake her head. Lind was always saying the most profound things. They all continued to watch in silence until the last of the Grimnir Guard disappeared from sight into the forest.

"Was that your entire force?" Bjorn asked as they continued staring out at the forest.

"Practically," Lind said. "Though there will be others like me who have undoubtedly been commanded to remain here. Latshal, Arenda, and Khanak, the other instructors here at Vrodr, have gone with the army. We have far fewer Grimnirs than we did in previous years, so we are supplemented by a few members of the militia, though they probably won't be involved in the fighting."

Elowyn's mind spun with all the logistics of sending out the entire army. Did everyone plan for themselves individually, or did somebody have to coordinate all of their food or equipment as a collective?

"How long will it take?" Elowyn asked, hoping that things would return to normal soon.

Lind shrugged. "Once the army arrives, it won't take long. They'll fight to extermination. Then we'll need to come together and figure out how to seal Vanalf properly. The protection from the portals is only partially effective inside of Vanalf anyway, as it is a direct path to other realms. It doesn't prevent everything from coming through, which is probably by design. I'm not sure people would emerge as Grimnirs when venturing inside otherwise. But I'd say we take the next year of students through the cave as soon as it's secure. We will need Voyagers, no doubt."

Bjorn grunted. "Nobody has explained Voyagers to me yet. Why are they necessary?"

"They have the power to open portals," Elowyn blurted. "They can travel planes, and they have some magic over space and even time in some cases."

Bjorn grunted again, clearly missing how significant Voyagers were.

Elowyn rolled her eyes again and turned away, looking back toward the city on the other side of the parapets. She squinted, looking up toward the Tower of Tarn, its dark spire absorbing the sunlight. She could have sworn there was the faint shade of a cloud hanging around it, like a small stream of smoke.

Hallik looked at her then squinted out at the tower as well.

"I thought I saw something," Elowyn said, answering Hallik's unasked question. Whatever she'd seen, it was gone.

Hallik nodded. "Alright, Jaysen Bjorn," he said, turning to face the monster hunter. "Since we have to wait here, let's go duel so I can show you how skilled I really am with a sword."

"There's a lot more to fighting than simple swordplay," Bjorn said. "Duels can only teach you so much until you get more experience fighting in the heat of the moment."

"Sure," Hallik said. "But at least dueling is better than wishing I was out there."

Bjorn shrugged. "Very well."

Elowyn decided to join them, but Lind remained on the wall.

"I will remain up here for a time," Lind said, then he too squinted at the Tower of Tarn, brows furrowing. He caught Elowyn's eyes. "All will be well, Elowyn."

Elowyn nodded and smiled before following after the boys, but something in her gut felt uneasy. So much had already gone wrong. And if they didn't get more Voyagers soon, then what would happen?

CHAPTER TWENTY

BATTLE

Mikel Vigsen

Captain Mikel Vigsen rode near the head of the procession as the army marched through the forest. They were just about near the peak that would lead them down into the valley where Vanalf was. A few soldiers rode in front of him so that he was safe to focus in on his connection with Serena, her sight allowing him to scout ahead.

From above, Serena could see signs of troll activity, but they were being discreet. A true idea of their numbers was difficult to ascertain, and the thick trees were probably hiding more than he cared to admit.

The Valtyras had braved a quick landing to get a view beneath the tree line, but Mikel didn't want them getting ambushed. Depending on where they were, it could be difficult for them to take to the skies again. He couldn't really direct them from this distance, but thankfully they didn't stay on the ground long and headed back to report.

Serena trailed behind them, eyes mostly on the forest below. They'd be back soon.

The Grimnir Guard was five hundred strong, but trolls were extremely dangerous. Much more dangerous than a few draugrs. This day likely wouldn't end without casualties. Even as a Watcher, trolls were sometimes difficult to detect. They were known for their proficiency with masking and camouflage, though some were admittedly much better at it than others. They wouldn't be able to hide completely, and Mikel would want to clear this entire valley. Trolls would not be tolerated anywhere on Avskild.

Trolls were practically their sworn enemy. Their kinds had been at war with each other since the first Grimnirs emerged from Vanalf. This island used to have a whole settlement of trolls on the north end, and they'd been known for murdering, eating, and kidnapping people throughout all of human history. For sapient beings, they were malicious, vile monsters. If not eradicated, they would prey on the citizens of Avskild as long as they remained.

The downside of today's battle was that none of them had fought against trolls before. The last time anybody had fought a troll was just over a hundred years ago. Though they were a mandatory topic of study during training to become a Grimnir, everything they knew about trolls came from the songs and what little writings were kept on them in Castle Vrodr.

As a warrior, Mikel had to recognize that studies only went so far. Firsthand experience was immeasurably more valuable.

The pass between the valleys was just ahead, the two carved columns to either side signaling their arrival. There was an odd comfort in seeing the artwork from their past, but it was a grim reminder at the same time. Humans forever at war with a host of monsters. Defeat was depicted on one pillar, victory on the other. Magic was the deciding factor. The integrity of Vanalf was critical to human survival. Defending it was the cause Mikel had taken up when he'd first joined the Grimnir initiates as a boy.

And the trolls wanted to take it from them.

The squad of Valtyras came toward them from the north, flying low. The ridge ahead was quite barren of trees, so the Valtyras landed to the side of the road and waited for Mikel to reach them.

Marhen, the Valtyra squad leader, stood at the front of the group, her gray and white wings stretching behind her as she rolled her shoulders. She wielded her signature trident in one hand with a small buckler in the other. Her light brown hair was tied back in a thick braid, her skin bronzed and leathery from countless hours in the sun. She'd been tall and strong *before* going into Vanalf, but after emerging as a Valtyra, her strength was remarkable.

Mikel made a gesture to Marhen with his hand, indicating that he did not want to stop. She nodded and moved to walk beside him as he rode. "I am ashamed, Captain," she said, her expression a wrinkled frown.

"Report," Mikel said, not sure what she meant.

"We could not get a good indication of their numbers and didn't want to risk roaming through the trees too much for fear of being attacked."

"That's reasonable. I didn't want you venturing too far into the brush anyway. Better to have us all fight together than to have you ambushed. But what can you tell me?"

Marhen nodded. "They have not erected any fortifications from what I can tell, though according to Lind's report, they're expecting us to come. There are many more than the four he'd left behind. We counted at least twenty, but we know there are plenty we weren't able to detect. Perhaps we should have brought a Watcher with us."

"Aye," Mikel said. They were so out of practice that he'd forgotten the simple tactic of having them carry a Watcher between two Valtyras. Those enhanced senses would have been quite valuable in a fly-over. Mikel could only discern so much through his connection with Serena. "You flew around the whole area though, did you not? How have their forces disseminated?"

"Still heavily concentrated around the entrance to Vanalf. If I had to guess, they know our pattern for taking new students through the cave, and they may have been hoping to set up a bulwark before next month. Lind's inspection must have come as a surprise."

Mikel grunted. "I could see them attempting a stunt like that." They had started the descent into the valley. Fresh rain during the night left an earthy smell in the air, and wisps of clouds rolled slowly across the sky. A good day to fight. "Let's keep a couple Valtyras in the air for additional reconnaissance if we need, but the remainder should walk with us to maintain their strength. We'll need it. Anything else?"

"That's all I have, Captain."

He saw the grip on her trident tighten. He could practically smell her anxiety and anticipation. Humans were emotional beings, and his practice as a Watcher had made him sensitive to their shifts in feelings. He dismissed her with a wave of his hand.

They were basically going in blind. At least twenty was the best guess Marhen could give, but Mikel assumed there could be upwards of forty or fifty. Valtyras were strong, but trolls were stronger. They'd be able to hurl small boulders and trees. Even with Vitugr spells, there wasn't much they could do to stop a tree from smashing them.

Grimnirs would die today.

And it made him angry. Perhaps this could have been avoidable if they'd maintained the regular patrols. He hated to admit it, but even he had grown more complacent over the years. King Knos had rubbed off on him.

He motioned for Irena to come ride beside him.

The Vitugr squad leader heeled her small horse forward until they were side-by-side then peered up at him, awaiting orders.

"Let's stick with earthen spells during this engagement," Mikel said. "Avoid fire. I don't want the whole valley in flames."

Irena nodded. "We have an arsenal of conjurations in mind."

"Good. And I suspect that we'll want to start with wall formations, but the trolls are hiding, so we should anticipate surprises."

"Ah, so patrol formations?"

"Exactly," Mikel said. Patrol formation was where they'd make teams of six with two of each of the three surviving Grimnir classes. They'd stick together if things got dicey, and the combined skills would allow them to function with more versatility. It was a common unit formation—the same one used for island patrols. "Let's get all the units together before we hit the tree line, and then we'll leave the militia with the horses and proceed on foot."

Irena rushed to fulfill Mikel's orders, going down the line and spreading the word. The Valtyras joined the procession, thinning out among the others as they all started getting paired up into their units.

Each passing second brought them closer to battle. Mikel thumbed the pommel of his sword and started mentally flipping through all their practiced battle tactics and which ones would be most effective against trolls.

Serena flew just over the edge of the forest, circling the area in case there was an early ambush set up, but she saw nothing. As they neared the edge of the forest, nothing smelled amiss, suggesting the trolls hadn't ventured this far. They were waiting.

"Dismount," Mikel ordered, hopping down from his own horse. "Militia will remain here. Grimnirs will proceed in formation."

Most of the soldiers were not mounted, but those who were quickly dismounted and tied their reins to smaller trees. The militia began setting up. They would need to defend the horses if any trolls got around and tried to attack from the rear. None of them wielded any magic, but, as those three students had recently proven at the beach, humans without magic could still fight, even if their odds weren't as good. He thought back again to the images on the pillars they'd passed just over an hour ago and shivered. Hopefully the trolls wouldn't think to sneak around the back.

Serena flew down to land briefly on Mikel's shoulder. She gave him a small nod before snapping her beak and flying off into the trees. She'd stay close but provide an aerial view in case they needed it. Mikel took the lead, taking his round, wooden shield from off his horse, unsheathing his sword, and walking at the head of the army.

Mikel made sure to breathe deeply as they walked. He found that it helped him tap into his power. The magic of Watchers and Valtyras was different than Vitugrs or Voyagers. For the most part, he didn't have to cast spells or activate anything. His power was mostly an enhancement of natural senses. His connection with Serena was also natural, but being able to tap into her senses was an activated spell. There were also at least two other spells in his arsenal. He cast *detect magic*. The spell was second nature now, requiring nothing more than a single thought. Maintaining the spell required a continued mental exertion, similar to the act of counting in his head.

The problem in this case was that the forest out-side Vanalf was ingrained with traces of magic. Nymphs, dryads, sprites, and other fairies were practically every-where, and their entire beings were mostly magical. Even some of the trees were laced with spells, likely cast by the nymphs and dryads. This was sacred ground for them. He did not sense any trolls, though he did sense a few sprites looking down at them from high among the branches. Using the spell was almost like having a third eye, though he didn't experience things visually. Despite knowing that it would further drain his energy, he cast *detect life* as an extra failsafe.

They kept a steady pace through the forest. The last time he'd been through here, there had been a lot more wildlife and magical entities present, but now it seemed like there was only a fraction of what there'd been before. That had been only three or four years ago. Could things really have changed so quickly? Perhaps the trolls had scared most things away except for the sprites and a few fairies. They were too curious to flee.

They made it a couple miles through the forest without any incident, but the next stretch was steeper downhill as it drew close to Vanalf. It would not accommodate battle formations very easily as the trail was quite narrow and there were mild slopes to either side. If the trolls had a good understanding of the landscape, they'd know this would be a good place to establish an ambush.

Mikel sent a mental message to Serena, and she flew out to the left side.

Trolls were known for masking themselves quite effectively, from both sight and magic, but historically, skilled Watchers had still been able to identify them. Mikel had never sensed a troll before, nor had any of the Watchers in his army. But how hard could it be?

He sensed the whooshing of air as a boulder rocketed toward his head before he ever detected the troll. He dove to the ground and rolled back to his feet as the boulder crashed into the ground directly behind him. "Right! On the ridge!" he bellowed, gesturing frantically at the ridge to their right. "Formations!"

Their presence was evident now. He could sense the trolls as muted blobs of essence, similar to the trees. Even squirrels had more presence to his *detect life* spell than the trolls, but he realized they'd been there for a while now, even before they'd started down this portion of the trail. They'd walked right into a trap.

The boulder behind him launched into the air, reshaping into a jagged pillar as a Vitugr hurled it back at the assailant. It crashed into the troll's shoulder, and the beast fell from its vantage and started rolling down the hill.

There were at least a dozen more up on the right side. They were large, ugly creatures, nearly twice as tall as a human and thrice as thick. Their large, saucer-like eyes glittered as a hail of hurled stones showered down toward the Grimnir Guard.

Mikel jumped ahead to avoid another boulder.

Other Grimnirs were not as fortunate. There were at least three screams behind him as some of his troops were struck.

The army burst into action. A volley of stones erupted back toward the trolls, and several Valtyras sprang up, the launched stones flying right beneath their feet.

The stones from the Vitugrs pounded into the trolls just before the Valtyras drew near enough to stab down with their spears and tridents. Several of the trolls were impaled immediately as the Valtyras crashed down into them.

When he tapped deeper into his *detect life* spell, he sensed several more trolls on the ridge, hiding behind the initial line. Before he could shout a warning, a line of trolls stepped out of their cover, jabbing massive spears up at the Valtyras. Many of them were stabbed.

By the depths. He'd never expected such coordination from the trolls, and the consequences were already stagger-ing. This was no simple clan. These were trained warriors.

Several Watchers scrambled into a broken line as they ran up the incline to assist the Valtyras. Mikel was about to join them when he sensed something else.

More trolls, but coming from the left ridge.

"Shield!" he yelled.

Their many drills had prepared the army for this command. Watchers raised their shields and Vitugrs cast a sealing spell that would form a massive barricade over their heads. It was just in time to prevent another volley of devastating boulders from pulverizing them from the other side.

The trolls chose this time to shout a battle cry that vibrated the very ground. With Mikel's enhanced senses, their thunderous roar felt like a horn blaring directly in his ears.

But the Vitugrs got to work. Large tangles of vines erupted over the trolls on the left while a combined formation of Valtyras and Watchers rushed up the hill.

Mikel needed to fight. He was already closer to the right side of the ridge, so he ran to catch up with the line of Watchers that would engage the trolls in moments. The Valtyras on this side had all moved back, several of them clutching new wounds. Three had fallen dead, and one was being strangled by a troll while using an axe to chop into its side. He'd help her if he could get there in time. He hurried to a sprint, rushing up the hill.

The Valtyra's eyes bulged as the troll lifted her off the ground. It tried to shake the weapon from her grasp, but she hacked at its shoulder one more time before it slammed her into the ground and lifted a foot to stomp on her.

With a double-handed swing, Mikel jumped forward and hacked at the troll's arm right at the elbow. Warm blood spurted up his arms, but he swung again, this time chopping into the troll's head, cracking the bone beneath. It started to slump forward, but he placed his foot against the troll's shoulder and kicked it back so that it didn't fall on the Valtyra.

The warrior gasped for air and clasped Mikel's hand as he pulled her up. Her wings flicked, eyes still wide. He sensed an attack from the side, and the Valtyra barely had time to scream before one of the massive spears took her straight through the gut.

He'd saved her for nothing, and it wrenched his heart, burning him with rage. Mikel roared and spun on the assailant, a hunched troll with grayed skin. Its mouth gaped open and sharp, yellowed teeth jutted irregularly. It tried withdrawing its spear to stab at Mikel, but the Valtyra held onto the shaft, keeping the weapon impaled in her stomach. Mikel rushed the troll. With one slash, he cut across the troll's arm. It released its weapon, and instead of pulling back, it swung its other arm at him with a massive fist. Mikel ducked and spun forward, dodging the punch and slicing across the belly of the troll.

It kicked him, its bare foot smashing into his chest, big toe knocking into his chin, toenail cutting the skin. The downside to his enhanced senses was that he could sometimes detect an attack coming but was often too slow to actually avoid it. This was such a scenario. His sword had been halfway through its arc across the troll's stomach when the kick started coming.

In anticipation, he'd had enough time to start moving back. He stumbled a couple steps backwards but didn't fall. The troll held its injured hand to its stomach, probably holding its guts in as it charged forward, oblivious to its pain. One hand formed a large fist as it prepared to smash down at him. A spear stabbed it in the armpit, stopping it short. The Valtyra had removed the spear from herself, turned it around, and stabbed back. She'd probably die at any second. Blood poured from her gaping wound. This was her final act, face twisted in pain, drained of all color.

Desperation clawed at Mikel's insides. He wanted to save her, but knew he would have no such luck. They were warriors. This was what they'd signed up for.

The troll bellowed as Mikel lunged forward, stabbing it in the knee. It dropped low enough for Mikel to stab again, this time puncturing it right through one of its plate-sized eyes.

Both the troll and the Valtyra fell to the ground.

He'd earned a second to breathe and regain his bearings. The sounds of war echoed around him as people and trolls yelled and died. The smell of metal tainted the air.

A fleeting image from Serena caught his attention, and he whirled to face back down the hill. Charging up the path at an alarming speed were five dire wolves with collars on their necks.

Nature's rays, this was no simple invasion. This was a calculated attack.

The Vitugrs were holding their disadvantaged position on the trail while the Watchers and Valtyras had moved to the ridges on either side to attack the trolls. Those dire wolves would tear straight into the Vitugrs.

Mikel yelled warning to them, but his voice disappeared among the din. He jumped down the hill, trying to run carefully enough not to trip and kill himself on his own sword. One of the Vitugrs noticed the approaching wolves, and a series of stone-crafted spears jutted from the ground. The first wolf was instantly impaled, but the next one jumped right over.

Despite Mikel's request to avoid using fire magic, another Vitugr shot a jet of flame at the wolf, but his reaction was too slow. The wolf pounced and gnashed down on another Vitugr's head. The flames scorched across the wolf and left another Vitugr screaming as his body was engulfed in the flames. More rocks showered down from the left side as some of the trolls broke free from the vines. The Vitugrs erupted into chaos, spells blasting everywhere. They were all falling out of formation, fighting man-for-man.

No, no, no. They were out of practice. Drills had only prepared them so much. Only a few of them had kept with the patrol formation he had them set up before marching through the forest, but most of the Vitugrs remained at the center without backing up their smaller units.

The other dire wolves were already over the spikes by the time Mikel arrived. The burned wolf fell to axes, but the other three were tearing through the Vitugrs. Mikel slammed into the side of one, ramming it with his shield and stabbing straight through it with his sword. Its massive body slumped down with a whimper. A Vitugr jammed a spike of ice through its skull to finish it off.

The remaining two wolves went down quickly. Their initial success had been due to their surprise attack, something that would not have happened if a couple Watchers had remained with them.

Five of the Vitugrs had been taken down.

The casualties would have been completely preventable if he'd had the sense to remain with them. Even now, he had to resist the urge to dash off to either side and assist the battle, but the Vitugrs would need him here in case there were more big surprises.

And there was. A very, very big surprise.

A Valtyra fell from the sky, crashing to the ground just in front of Mikel, but he paid the dead man no mind. The trees further down the trail splintered and snapped, a massive head emerging from the branches as the trees were pushed aside like leaves.

No, there were two heads, joined together on the same body.

A giant. It was as ugly as the trolls, but its limbs were longer and thicker, and it stood over twice as tall as the trolls.

This required no warning.

The giant uprooted a tree with either arm. The fact that an entire giant had been able to crawl through Vanalf was sign enough that their magical defenses had completely eroded.

Behind him, he heard Irena's familiar voice as she ordered the Vitugrs to launch a volley at the giant. A variety of spells exploded over Mikel's head, from glowing arrows to spears of ice and stone. The giant swung a tree, skill-fully deflecting most of the projectiles, but a few of them pierced its hand, and one of the stone spears even jabbed it in the face, just below its eye.

"Fire at will," Mikel bellowed in his loudest voice. They needed to take whatever opening they could get rather than launching calculated volleys.

Even if they didn't hear him, the Vitugrs seemed to understand what was necessary. A near-constant barrage of projectiles launched at the giant as it charged up toward them. It continued using one of the trees to bat them away, but then it hurled the other tree at the Vitugrs.

Mikel, despite his better instinct, ran forward to meet the giant, the tree flying over his head. It crashed down to a chorus of screams. Someone launched a full fireball at the giant that pounded into its knee. Its hand was prick-led with wounds, and it seemed fully intent on tearing through all the Vitugrs. Two Valtyras flew at the giant from either side, and it swatted one away like he was a fly. The other one stabbed down with her spear, puncturing the back of the giant's neck, but it continued lurching forward.

One of the heads glanced down at Mikel. He braced himself, stepping from one side of the trail to the other in a sort of zigzag pattern. The giant didn't seem to want to delay reaching the Vitugrs, as they were the greatest nuisance to him, so he suspected it would merely swat or stomp at him as it continued, and he'd need to dodge it.

His suspicion was correct. Its movements, though still quick, were more easily predictable. At least, that's what all the records had said about them. When it held back its arm to swipe at him with the tree, he knew what he'd have to do. From his observations, this was no fumbling oaf. The giant was keen and precise. It would likely calculate Mikel's projection, so he had to throw that off.

As the arm swung, he stopped and jumped back, though one of his feet slipped against the moist soil. He didn't move back as far as he'd hoped. Although he dodged the trunk of the tree, a few of the branches whipped across his body, several pine needles slashing along his face.

He fell flat on his back, the sting shocking him into stark awareness. He rolled to one side to avoid the edge of the giant's foot and sprang back to his feet. As anticipated, it wasn't going to bother finishing him off. It was set on rushing the Vitugrs.

With the mightiest blow he could muster, he swung his sword at the back of the giant's knee, hoping to sever a tendon. His blade slid across the exact place he'd been hoping, but he hadn't anticipated the roughness of the giant's skin. He'd broken through the skin, but the tendon beneath remained intact, though somewhat damaged.

The giant roared and stumbled, falling to a knee. It smashed down with the tree at the same time, crushing a Vitugr into the ground.

Mikel wasted no time and swung down, this time aiming for the back of the giant's foot, cutting down like he was chopping wood. The first hack broke through with a fleshy thunk, and the second hack partially severed the tendon. The giant whipped a hand back and smacked Mikel before he could get a third chop in. Mikel tumbled down the trail, crashing through bushes. Pain lanced through his left shoulder, and his own shield smacked him in the jaw before getting loosed from his grip.

As soon as he stopped rolling, he launched back to his feet, though his left ankle burned terribly. He spat blood and limped his way back toward the battle. The giant had crawled into the Vitugrs, who had spread out to avoid its reach, but not before it claimed several of their lives. Two more Valtyras stabbed into the giant's back as a flurry of spells exploded against its heads.

A few Grimnirs tumbled down the ridge to Mikel's right as a wall of trolls barreled down. There were about twenty trolls in that formation. How many trolls had gotten through? Was this all a setup? It seemed too well planned.

Perhaps they'd let Lind get away. Maybe they'd watched him the entire time, letting him think he was catching them early.

Dead Grimnirs filled the trail by the dozens, their bodies thrown back down the hill as the trolls took the ridges. The Watchers and Valtyras to either side had started to fall back. They should have immediately retreated back up the trail to avoid getting pressed in from either side. He'd underestimated the trolls. He needed to rally his people.

That was when something struck him on the side of the head, causing his vision to explode into stars. He felt the ground beneath him as he stared up at the sky. Serena soared above him, cawing into the wind.

He blinked slowly. One of his legs had lost feeling, and his ears rang as though Serena's caw would never stop. Something had hit him pretty good. He moved his fingers, but he'd lost his sword. With a groan, he lifted his head to look at his right hand. It was covered in blood. His blood? It was all across the front of his clothes.

His left arm hung limply as he tried to sit up. A wet shiver trembled across his neck. When he went to wipe the sweat away from his face, his hand came away with more blood. Nature's rays. Realization settled on him with a flush of horror. He was going to die.

He turned to look back up the hill where the battle still raged. Or so he'd thought. Instead, it was still. The giant was a crumpled heap. There were probably over a hundred dead trolls, and there wasn't a living Grimnir in sight. The only movement was from Serena, flying in circles over Mikel, her incessant cawing the only sound.

But he was wrong. Something else was moving. A troll. It caught sight of him and started crawling over. It appeared severely injured as well. One of its arms was missing just above the elbow, and a long gash across its face left only one eye functional.

Mikel looked around frantically, though his vision spun. His sword was there, embedded in his own leg. He must have fallen on it. He gritted his teeth and wrenched the weapon free.

The troll laughed as it approached, a bubbling, grinding laughter as though it were drowning in a pile of gravel. "Too late, Grimnir," it said, words barely comprehensible. "Avskild will fall." Its feet shuffled across the ground as it struggled to make its way closer to him.

If Mikel had to guess, the creature was also on the verge of death. Its one remaining hand clutched what looked like a butcher's knife.

Mikel placed his sword across his lap and glanced up at Serena. *I'm sorry.* He roared and lifted himself up using just his good leg. Agony tore through his body, from his head to his open wounds.

The troll only laughed more as it prepared to swing at him. Serena dove down, her beak piercing the troll's remaining eye. It screamed in rage and thwacked her away. Mikel thrust his sword, piercing the troll straight through the chest. He fell forward with the movement, his vision going black.

When had it gotten so dark?

There was darkness everywhere, and he was so tired. So very tired.

CHAPTER TWENTY-ONE

ASHiMAL

Hallik

A deep sound rumbled the ground, and Hallik stared wide-eyed at Bjorn and Elowyn in turn. He and Bjorn had just finished their duel, which, to Hallik's great pleasure, he had won. "Was that an earthquake?"

"No, look," Elowyn pointed toward the Tower of Tarn.

Hallik looked over his shoulder at the tower, just visible over the edge of the wall. Black smoke swirled around its surface as though alive. "By the depths. What is that?"

"I don't know," Elowyn said, shaking her head.

That was a response that Hallik might have otherwise reveled to hear Elowyn say, but not this time.

Lind came sprinting down the stairs of the ramparts. The tip of his axe glowed with an amber light, likely imbued with a spell. Some other students and staff ran out to the courtyard to catch a glimpse.

"Was that a fire?" Hallik asked as Lind strode by.

"No," Lind said without even glancing at them. "Stay here. I will need to investigate." He went straight out the gate into the city at a light jog.

Wordlessly, Bjorn followed after, and nobody tried to stop him.

Hallik looked at Elowyn.

"Hal," she said as though reading his mind, "Lind said to stay here."

"Lind was supposed to stay here too," Hallik said. "If there's trouble, he has no backup. Also, we can't let Bjorn go off and get himself killed. We're the ones that brought him to the city."

Elowyn shook her head and strode off toward the gate.

Hallik smiled and bounced after her. "Too stubborn to agree with me, then?"

"Not verbally, anyway," Elowyn said. "I can't have you thinking you have a good idea for once."

Another tremor shook the ground and a jet of smoke erupted from one of the windows at the Tower of Tarn. Curly tendrils of smoke coiled around the tower before being sucked back in through another window. They increased their pace to a jog as the streets filled with curious citizens.

"Why are you smiling?" Elowyn said.

Hallik's smile disappeared. He hadn't realized it was there.

"You do realize that the Grimnir Guard could have been destroyed and that something else is already ravaging the Tower of Tarn. Our civilization could be on the verge of collapse. Bjorn feels that it's already imminent."

"I don't know," Hallik said. "I just... I have hope, I guess. Things will turn out okay as long as we don't give up."

Elowyn didn't answer, but they did catch sight of Bjorn up ahead. They increased their pace to catch up. When they reached the base of the Tower of Tarn, a crowd of people were fleeing the building. Lind stood at the bottom of the steps leading up into the tower, slowly working his way against the current.

Shouts of a demon came from the terrified crowd. Bjorn, Hallik, and Elowyn all caught up with Lind, who was interrogating a militiaman. The man trembled, face pale, clutching a spear with a white-knuckled grip. His voice was frantic. "It-it's a demon! Covered in shadow! It consumes everyone!" He seemed on the verge of tears.

"Where is it?" Lind asked.

"I-I don't know. It's going room-to-room as if looking for something."

Lind noticed the trio's presence and looked back at them with a scowl. "I told you to stay."

"You need the help," Hallik insisted.

Lind stared at each of them in turn while the militiaman ran away. "Bah. Stay behind me. This sounds like something much more dangerous than your average monster, but if I can't stop it, then the whole of Dalstava might be doomed."

"Sounds like my kind of monster," Bjorn said, withdrawing one of his knives from a sheath on his arm, "though I have not been foolish enough to face a demon yet."

"We'll all be fools together," Lind said. He turned and strode toward the open double doors. "Come then."

Hallik let out a long breath and followed right behind Bjorn.

"Is it a shadow demon, then?" Elowyn asked.

"Perhaps," Lind said. "There are several dark creatures that can control mist and shadow. Some people have said that all they've seen is burning eyes and swirling smoke. I suppose anybody who has seen more than that is already dead."

The large entry room to the tower was completely bare. It was the first time Hallik had seen this place empty, and it only added to the eeriness of their situation. The tall ceiling loomed overhead as they strode through the empty space.

"Stay alert," Lind said. "With shadow magic, this beast could potentially attack from any angle and might even move soundlessly. You'll need to rely on sight. Nature's rays!" Lind shouted and tumbled to the ground, barely catching himself after tripping on a long, tipped-over candle holder.

Elowyn rushed to help Lind back up.

"Should I take the lead?" Bjorn said.

Lind didn't respond, but continued leading the way after getting back to his feet. "It's likely still on the upper floors." He steered them toward the stairs leading up to the second floor.

There was no other sound besides their own footfalls as they marched up the stairs. Hallik had to wonder what force it was that could have shaken the very ground earlier. Would a shadow demon have such strength? He wasn't an expert on monster studies like Elowyn, or Lind, or probably even Bjorn, but they didn't seem to question the likelihood of that kind of beast being responsible.

They cleared the whole second floor, then started up to the third. Shortly after they hit the third floor, another vibration shook the building. They could feel it more intensely this time though, as the source of the vibration was clearly coming from above them. They didn't bother clearing the third floor, but Lind led them straight to the stairs to the fourth.

Lind pointed at what looked like steam curling off the top of the stone on the final step. Hallik might not have noticed it otherwise. This was it. Hallik switched the grip on his sword and wiped his sweaty palm on his pants. As they carefully came up the stairs and rounded the corner, Hallik could feel a pressure in the air, as if it were thick with humidity. There was power here.

We're not going to die, he told himself to assuage the dark thoughts that threatened his resolve.

Lind's axe glowed brighter as they entered the main room, a long, blockish space with tall, slightly opaque glass windows stretched from floor to ceiling, glittering with orange white light that filtered through. The stairs to the next floor were on the far side of the room, but they were obstructed by a wall of bubbling black mist. If Elowyn sat on Hallik's shoulders, she'd probably be able to reach the top of it. Tendrils of the mist flowed across the floor. The mist coiled and writhed with life, refusing to dissipate.

Four flickering flames gleamed out from the depths of the mist, and it took Hallik a moment to realize they were eyes. A voice resonated from the mist, deep and masculine. "Vitugr. Mmm. Delectable."

"Not a demon," Elowyn muttered, her voice a terrified whisper.

Well, that wasn't encouraging. "Then what is it?" Hallik hissed.

Lind hushed them. "Stand back."

"You don't have the blade. Pity. But I can still consume," the monster said. Two pillars of smoke whipped toward them like snakes.

Lind grunted and thrust one of his arms forward. An explosion of wind swept through the room, blowing the mist back. For a brief moment, it revealed the creature hidden within. It looked like a gigantic, hairless, humanoid bear with a frighteningly hulking musculature and a four-eyed face with a hanging jaw and massive fangs.

After the blast, the mist returned like coiling hairs across its body.

"Now that was awkward," the monster said, shaking out its arms as the mist rebuilt.

The fact that the monster was speaking was odd to Hallik. It had an animal head, after all. "Why a bear monster?" Hallik muttered. "Couldn't it have been a rabbit?"

Elowyn hushed him this time. "It's an ashimal. A shadow spirit that has taken a body and manifests in physical form."

"Uh huh," Hallik said, bouncing his sword in his hand. "So we can stab it?"

"Yes, we can stab it," Elowyn said as Lind launched an icy spear at the beast. The beast waved an arm to bat at the spear, but Lind splintered it into four separate pieces, each aimed at different parts. It blocked the one aimed at its head, but the other three disappeared into the mist, causing some unknowable damage.

"We can stab it, Bjorn," Hallik said, turning about. "You'd like that."

Bjorn was... gone. Hallik hadn't noticed the man leave or anything. He'd simply vanished. Perhaps he'd bolted, realizing they were in over their heads. He hadn't survived outside of Avskild by being a fool.

"Mmm. Nothing like a good stabbing," the monster said. It flowed toward them across the floor as though he hadn't just seen it with two legs. Its snakelike, misty tentacles whipped at them again.

Lind took a sharp breath before launching another blast of air, forcing the mist away a second time. The spell dissipated once the air hit the far wall, and Lind gasped at the exertion of using his magic. Without losing a stride, he took another step forward and a small beam of purple light launched from Lind's palm, blasting the bear monster right in the chest.

It let out what sounded like a gruff giggle. Instead of using its tendrils of mist to attack, it barreled forward, still on two legs. Its gaping jaws hung open so impossibly wide it could probably swallow one of them in a single gulp.

Hallik and Elowyn spread to either side of Lind, but the beast closed the distance in the span of a couple heartbeats. Lind jumped toward the beast, raising his glowing axe over his head. He brought the axe down just as the beast crashed into him. Without pausing to see what happened to Lind, Hallik lunged in from the side, thrusting his sword into the shadowy mist. His blade grazed across something, so he thrust again, definitely piercing flesh that time. A massive force crashed into Hallik's shoulder, tossing him aside as though he was a small child.

"Mmm," the beast said again, smacking its lips as though it had just eaten something delicious. Hallik was getting rather sick of hearing it make that sound. "I haven't had Vitugr in a long time."

Lind's glowing axe was embedded in the beast's head right between the four eyes. But Lind was... gone. Four misty tendrils had grabbed onto each of Elowyn's limbs. The beast held her in the air as she kicked and struggled.

Her dagger was gripped in one hand, but she couldn't even use it.

The beast turned its burning eyes on Hallik. It smacked its lips again.

Hallik still couldn't process what had happened. "Lind?" he said. There was no sign of him.

"It ate him," Elowyn yelled, voice quivering with rage.

Just like that? An empty void filled Hallik's brain, shutting off as if to protect him from the quick spike of panic that almost immediately vanished as a coil of mist sprang toward him. Hallik spun to the side to avoid it, his blade passing through the mist without doing any visible damage. He stabbed his sword into the body of the beast, wedging deep into flesh. Before he could pull the weapon free, a solid, fleshy hand grabbed Hallik by the torso and lifted him into the air. He clawed at the hand, digging his nails into it, but the beast didn't even flinch.

"Mmm. I'll eat you next," the beast said, drawing Hallik close to its mouth. Warm, fetid breath blew across his face like poisoned steam. By the depths, he was about to die. For all his hoping none of them would die, he had never actually considered the idea that it could happen so easily.

Elowyn screamed, but no sound would stop the beast. Nothing could.

The jaws opened wide, ready to swallow him whole.

The beast roared, head jerking back. Lind's axe, still embedded in its head, flared with blue fire and sank a little deeper. The beast's misty tendrils lost their structure enough for Elowyn to break free. Bjorn was there, running up from behind, a dagger held in either of his hands. Bjorn jumped and landed on the beast's back, daggers tearing into it. Another dagger whipped through the air, stabbing into the back of the hand holding Hallik.

Pulling the dagger free, Hallik stabbed at each of the beast's fingers. It dropped him and spun around, lashing out for Bjorn. A cloud of black mist exploded into the air with a deep rumble. The shaking building threw Hallik to his knees, unable to breathe through the thickness in the air that seeped into his throat, coating it like sludge.

The beast roared. Its head was still visible even through the dark shroud. Lind's axe blazed like the sun for a brief moment before a burst of light flashed, blinding Hallik even more than the darkness had. He blinked rapidly, but the whiteness didn't leave his vision. Waves of energy pulsed through the floor.

The overwhelming light came to an abrupt end with the sound of a hundred sheets of fabric being torn at the same time.

The feeling of sludge in his throat disappeared, and Hallik gasped for air, his vision slowly returning. He climbed back to his feet, prepared to attack the beast again, but he saw its bearlike shape crumpled on the floor, body split in half through the middle.

Lind's body lay in between the halves of the beast's corpse, covered in gore and gasping for breath.

Bjorn picked himself up off the ground, shaking his head.

"Lind!" Elowyn said, running to his side. Hallik rushed to aid her. Lind said nothing as the two of them helped pull him out of the monster's body. He must have been inside its stomach. The stench was horrible, like that of long-dead fish.

Bjorn gawked at the scene, one of his daggers still clutched loosely in his right hand. A mess of the monster's blood soaked the right half of Bjorn's body.

"You survived," Hallik said to Lind, wiping away some of the muck from Lind's face.

Lind caught his breath, still laying in a heap after they'd pulled him out. "Barely," he said.

Hallik wasn't sure if Lind was injured. His body was so covered in the disgusting mess that he couldn't tell if any of the blood was Lind's.

"Are you hurt?" Elowyn asked. She was looking all around Lind's body, inspecting for wounds.

"Yes," Lind said. "My legs. Both of them. It bit me once before swallowing."

"We'll get a healer," Elowyn said. "My mother will have something."

Selke rarely entered Dalstava, but she'd certainly make an exception to visit the head instructor of Castle Vrodr.

"Also, something pierced me near the hip right at the end there," Lind said, touching his side with his fingertips.

"That was... probably me," Bjorn said, looking down at his bloody hand. "My apologies."

"All is forgiven. That sudden pain actually gave me enough lucidity to cast a couple more spells. I activated a retrieval spell on my axe which forced it deeper into the beast's head, then I used the opening from your dagger to push all the surrounding fluids directly out of its body. I think that sudden force split it in half."

"Yes." Bjorn looked down at himself. "I see that."

"By the depths, Bjorn," Hallik said. "I'm detecting a pattern with you. Waiting until the last moment to finally make your move. We could have all died."

"But we didn't," Bjorn said, eyes on Lind. "Surprising-ly."

Hallik got to his feet, suddenly angry. He jabbed a finger at Bjorn. "Look, I get it. You've been a lone wolf for a while, but if you're going to be a part of this team, you need to learn how to work together. Alone we are weak, but together," he paused to gesture at the dead monster, "we can do the impossible."

Bjorn's frown remained etched on his face like a tattoo, but his jaw shifted slowly until he finally spoke. "I'm not part of any team."

Hallik saw it then. There was a glint of something in Bjorn's eyes, sadness or longing. He liked to pose as this heartless, hopeless person, hardened beyond repair, but the truth was that if Bjorn wanted to be somewhere else, he'd be there. Not here. Not with them. With his skills, he could have snuck out of Dalstava easily, and yet here he remained.

"Sure," Hallik said, "keep telling yourself that while you tag along with us, but the next time we come across a battle, just remember that we try to keep each other alive. Got it?"

The muscles in Bjorn's jaw twitched, but nobody else said anything as he stepped over to Hallik. He held out his dagger, but Hallik didn't even flinch. Bjorn wiped the dagger on Hallik's clothes before sheathing it and taking the other dagger from Hallik's hand and doing the same. "I didn't let you or Elowyn get killed, did I?" His voice was little more than a raspy whisper.

"He's just trying to check off other monsters on his list, Hal," Elowyn said, her expression sour as she inspected Lind's wounds. Lind still seemed like he was just barely holding on to consciousness.

"Probably true," Hallik said, walking around Bjorn to retrieve his sword, "but he can still be a cooperative member of the team while doing that."

"Should we carry Lind out of here?" Elowyn asked, changing the subject.

"I might be too big for that," Lind said.

"Fetch your healer," Bjorn directed. "He could bleed out if you carry him. Elevate his legs. I can keep watch here with him if you need."

Hallik regarded Bjorn once again. His stony facade had returned, but as Hallik had guessed, Bjorn *wanted* to be with them. For now at least. And as long as he was sticking with them, he'd need to play by their rules. Things were different here in Avskild than they were outside.

"Is it dead?" a voice asked from the stairway leading up to the fifth floor.

Hallik jumped at the voice, almost drawing his weapon until he saw a familiar face.

Lorelai came down the stairs in small, tentative steps, eyes glancing between the four of them and the dead monster. She clutched a stunningly unique dagger in her hand.

Hallik sighed inwardly. *Everyone really does have a fancy dagger except for me.*

"It's dead," Lind said. "Do you know where it came from?"

Lorelai slowly came closer, and she did not answer immediately. "I... I'm not sure." She didn't meet any of their eyes, but only stared at the monster.

Hallik assumed Lorelai was still shocked by the whole thing, but he'd never seen the woman in such a state. And what had she been doing on the fifth floor? The Tower of Tarn was known for being practically barren on its upper floors, except for where the Valtyras kept a space at the top.

He was about to ask Lorelai what she'd been doing up there, but he didn't feel like it was his place to question a ranking official when he was merely a Grimnir student. Thankfully, Lind seemed to piece together the same thing.

"Are you sure you have no knowledge of the beast?" Lind asked.

Lorelai's response was delayed yet again. She glanced down at the dagger still clutched in her hands. Her skin had paled. She was nervous. Perhaps she'd done something wrong.

"It's alright, Lorelai," Lind said. "We're only here to help."

Lorelai looked at each of them, bit her lower lip, then nodded. "There's something you should know about the king."

DEFEAT

Jaysen Bjorn

Blood tinged the water red as Bjorn dipped his boot in the basin to scrub it clean. His clothes were drying, and he wore a simple tunic. Thankfully, the list of monsters he'd slain had been unspoiled, which was lucky considering Lind had practically exploded the monster across Bjorn's body.

The courtyard of Castle Vrodr was quiet and still. There was a secondary well at the back of the castle grounds which was used for bathing and laundering. He'd always hated bathing, as it left him vulnerable for a moment, though this time, he'd lined up several daggers beside him in case of danger. Admittedly, this was probably the most secure place he'd ever bathed, surrounded by castle walls. A series of curtains and short walls provided some privacy so he wasn't immediately visible to anyone else walking by, though the only other person who'd come to this area was Elowyn as she fetched buckets of water to clean up Lind.

Lind was in the castle, accompanied by Hallik, Lorelai, and Elowyn's mother, Selke.

Lorelai had told them that the king had been killing Voyagers, seduced by the demon into believing it would strengthen the portal shield. Bjorn hadn't been at all surprised by the revelation. Kings and queens were always doing foolish things to endanger the lives of their subjects. He'd heard of a dozen stories back on the mainland. Manipulating rulers was probably a favorite pastime for the vilest of monsters.

The thing that really stuck with Bjorn, though, was what Hallik had said after the fight with the ashimal. Hallik was young, no more than a boy, but it was clear he held strong convictions. Both he and Elowyn were committed individuals, and Bjorn had to admit that he was impressed by them. He wondered what he might have been like if he'd been raised in such a society. Perhaps he would have been cursed with the same hope they carried. Alas, he was a realist. Death was life's only certainty.

But Hallik's words about being a part of the team wouldn't leave his mind. The boy was too discerning for his age. Bjorn could have left at any moment, but he'd willingly followed Hallik back to Selke's home after saving him from the liowolf. He'd felt some semblance of kinship with the boy, even though he was annoying.

It was true, though. Bjorn could have engaged the monster sooner. It was only when Hallik's life was at risk that Bjorn decided to take his chance at sneaking up from behind the ashimal. He could have stood beside Lind and tossed a few knives or even fired a bolt into its gaping mouth. That would have spoiled its appetite.

Both Hallik and Elowyn had stood their ground, not backing down at all as a superior foe charged at them. They were either brave or foolish. Probably both. It would get them killed eventually, but there were worse ways to die.

Bjorn was a hunter, not a fighter. He was accustomed to tracking his prey and killing it in some clever, stealthy way, not facing it in an outright attack, but Hallik was right. There was more than one way to kill a monster, and as part of a team, he'd have to figure out how to stand with them a little better.

Team.

He scoffed to himself and put his boot aside. Kel's abyss, what had he gotten into? The very idea that he'd somehow ended up on Avskild still seemed incomprehensible.

The silence of the courtyard was broken as he heard Elowyn's footsteps approaching again.

"Bjorn," she said from the other side of the short wall. "We've prepared something to eat if you care to join us."

"I will come, thank you," Bjorn said. He took down his breeches and swung them around a couple times before tugging them on. They were still slightly damp, but he had no desire to wait around all day, and he hadn't eaten in several hours. His armor would need a little more time, but he at least strapped on his sword and headed into the castle, bare feet plodding on the stones.

They'd transported Lind to his room on the second floor of the castle, though it had taken all four of them to carry him there, not counting Selke. Lorelai had stuck with them. With the death of King Knos, Avskild was about to undergo a change in leadership, and she seemed like the kind of person who liked to be around power. With the entire Grimnir Guard away, Lind was probably the most powerful person in the city, even with his injuries. His magical display during the battle almost made Bjorn believe that humanity had a chance. To think that they had an entire army of Grimnirs out there was astounding. The kind of impact they could have made if they'd never hidden away had him gritting his teeth.

The scent of food had Bjorn's mouth watering before he reached Lind's extravagant quarters. As the head instructor of Castle Vrodr, he lived much like a lord. The tapestries, the carvings, the beautiful furniture, and the rich sewn rug that covered most of the floor combined to create the most lavish setting Bjorn had ever seen. Granted, he'd never even seen a building that was larger than a couple stories. For all he knew, everyone in Dalstava was equally as wealthy.

A round table sat at the center of the room, covered by a few wooden plates loaded with steaming, freshly cooked fish and pork.

"Kel's abyss," Bjorn muttered again.

Lind lay on a cot near an open door that led out onto a balcony, Selke sitting attentively beside him. His legs had been wrapped, and he wore a fresh set of clothes. Elowyn and Hallik stood on the balcony as they ate. And at the back of the room was Lorelai, seated on a wooden chair as she ate from her own plate. That gorgeous dagger rested on her lap. It had been the first thing to catch his attention when she'd come down the stairs. There was something mysterious about her involvement with the king, but he didn't read people as well as he did monsters. What she needed was to be stuck alone with Hallik for a couple hours, and that would probably drain her of every secret she'd ever had.

"Help yourself, Bjorn," Lind said, looking over his shoulder upon Bjorn's entrance.

Bjorn grabbed a wooden plate without hesitation and immediately dug into the pork. It was salted just right, and his taste buds exploded with pleasure as soon as it touched his tongue. He was tempted to go hide in an unoccupied portion of the room, but Lind waved him over. Bjorn swallowed the bite of meat and stood beside Lind's cot.

"Bjorn," Lind said. "I know you didn't have to come and help, but you saved our lives back there. For that, I am grateful. Though you are not Avskildian, I want you to know that you are more than welcome among us, and I hope that you might consider staying here, at the school. There can be great opportunities for one such as yourself."

Bjorn wasn't sure how to respond to such a comment, but he didn't have time to answer. Hallik and Elowyn shouted from the balcony.

"Someone is returning!" Hallik said. "A Valtyra." The balcony faced out to the east. They couldn't quite see over the edge of the castle walls, but the Valtyra flew high enough that he or she was easily visible.

Beside him, Lind heaved a sigh of relief. "Perhaps the battle is over, then."

"I'm sure they'll be interested to hear what happened here at the tower," Selke said, one of her thin eyebrows raised in a tall arc.

At the comment, Bjorn glanced over his shoulder at Lorelai. She sat stiffly, and one of her hands had settled over the dagger in her lap. He didn't think she would attack them, but her behavior made him uneasy.

Hallik waved his arms around so that the Valtyra would spot him, but whoever it was had already been heading straight toward them. The idea of a person flying still made Bjorn a little uneasy. They looked too big to be in the sky and not at all like their bodies had been built for such activity, but magic was always a mystery.

Lorelai sank further into her seat, and, despite his inclination to stay to himself, he sighed and moved to stand beside her. There was only so much information he could glean by observation.

Lorelai gave Bjorn a quick look-over as he approached. "You're not from Avskild," she stated.

Bjorn hadn't told her that, but perhaps one of the others had while he'd been cleaning up. "I am not." He eyed her dagger. The gemstones almost seemed to writhe inside. "I like your dagger."

She breathed a laugh. "I can see you are a collector. I'm afraid you'll not be adding this one to your inventory."

Bjorn only nodded. The monster, an ashimal, had mentioned something about a blade before they'd killed it. If it had been seeking to escape the building or to simply kill people, it could have done so. But it hadn't. It remained in the building and had only descended a couple floors. Something had motivated it to stay, but he wasn't sure what. Perhaps that dagger had something to do with it.

He didn't get the time to ask more questions, however, as the Valtyra crashed into the balcony instead of on it. Bjorn was so taken aback by the scene that he drew one of his daggers. The Valtyra's legs had cracked into the railing of the balcony before she fell forward and thunked onto the floor, nearly rolling into the room. She looked like she'd been mauled by a flock of birds, every bit of exposed flesh either bruised or bloody, and her clothes were torn in several places. Her brown wings remained sagged at her side as she slowly climbed her way back to one knee.

"Stay put, Arenda," Selke said as she sprang up from Lind's side. Everyone stared at the winged woman with open-mouthed expressions.

Bjorn took it that they hadn't expected to see her in such condition.

"We," Arenda wheezed, then her face contorted with pain. She dropped her head and shook it, pressing a hand to her side as blood seeped from a wound. A feather fell from Arenda's left wing after it twitched. The woman was clearly dying. It seemed a miracle that she'd even been able to fly this far.

"The battle, Arenda," Lind said. "What happened?"

Arenda let out a pained gasp before she was able to speak. "We lost."

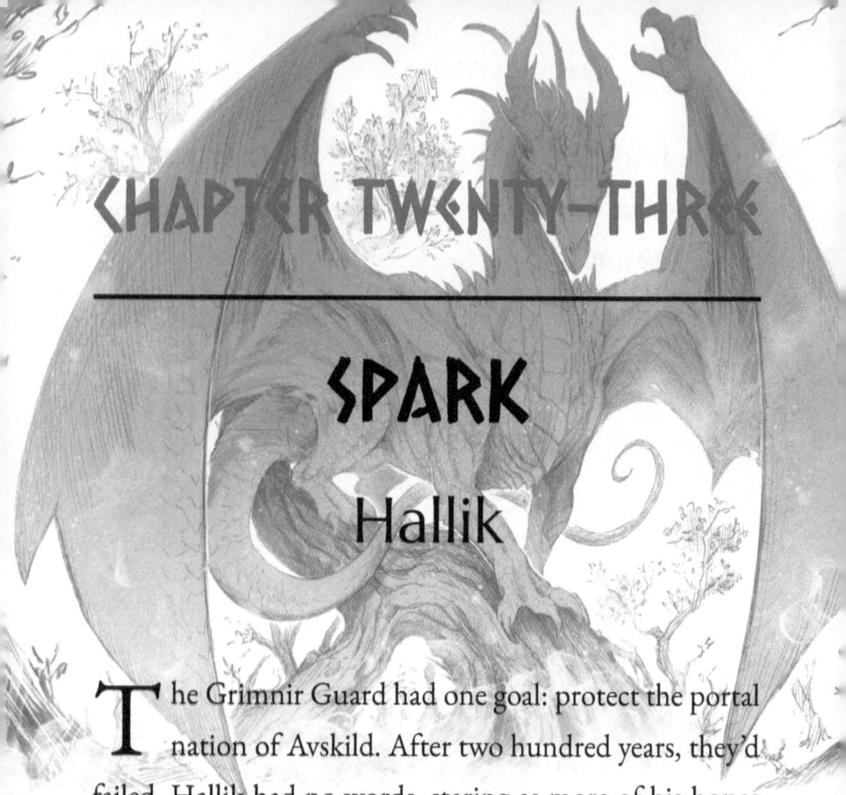

CHAPTER TWENTY-THREE

SPARK

Hallik

The Grimnir Guard had one goal: protect the portal nation of Avskild. After two hundred years, they'd failed. Hallik had no words, staring as more of his hopes started to fall away. His hands went cold. They were freezing.

Beside him, Elowyn's jaw dropped before she clamped her hand over her mouth. Bjorn simply blinked as if he'd expected this all along.

Lind sat up in his cot, brow creasing in a dark frown. "What do you mean we lost? To what extent? When will the Grimnir Guard return?"

Selke was desperately trying to assist Arenda. Rallying Bjorn and Hallik to bring her inside, she directed them to lay her on the plush rug, close to Lind's cot, her life's blood leaving a streak across the whole distance. Selke tore away the side of Arenda's tunic and attempted to stop whatever it was that wouldn't quit bleeding. It didn't stop.

Hallik had no words as Arenda seemed to grow smaller before his very eyes. This was his teacher. She was one of the greatest warriors in Avskildian history, and yet, she was dying. He'd known it as soon as she'd gotten close enough for him to see her wounds.

"We were ambushed," Arenda said. "There were so many trolls. They had dire wolves and a giant. I watched Mikel fall. And Irena. All dead."

Hallik suppressed the panicked, shaky feeling that rolled across his chest and down his back, raising the hair on his neck. He'd processed the words but couldn't fathom the concept of Captain Mikel Vigsen and the whole guard being defeated.

"But what of the trolls? How many remain?" Lind said.

Arenda grunted through clenched teeth. "I think we got them all, though I'm sure some could have snuck away during the battle, and I also lost consciousness for a moment after losing so much blood. I knew I needed to come back and report." She had to pause to gasp, taking a couple sharp breaths. "I'm sorry, Lind." She looked over her shoulder back at Hallik and Elowyn. "I'm sorry."

Hearing the words from his instructor broke Hallik's heart. "Avskild is not lost yet," Hallik said, pushing past the crack in his voice.

Arenda shook her head and squeezed her eyes tight as a fresh seepage of blood escaped her side, staining the rug a violent crimson. "But I did not secure Vanalf. And there could be even more trolls outside its entrance. We never got that far."

"Or maybe you did get them all, and now the path is clear," Hallik said, desperate to find the light as he dropped to his knees beside her.

"Possibly," Arenda said, her wings twitching. Her flat tone suggested that she may have been sarcastic. The lack of faith was unacceptable. They could still save Avskild. They had to.

"Let me just make sure I'm understanding correctly," Lind said. "There were no Grimnir survivors?"

"No," Arenda said, squinting up at the ceiling. "Just me."

"And no troll survivors?"

"None that," Arenda paused again, the pained expression leaving her face. "None that I could see." Her voice had been so quiet that Hallik had to lean in to hear. But from his new position on the floor, he got a clear view of the wound she'd received. It looked like she'd been punctured by an incredibly thick spear. He couldn't even imagine how she'd managed to fly all the way here. "I'm sorry," she said again, her voice weak.

Arenda's eyes glazed over as she looked upward, staring at nothing. Selke looked to Lind and shook her head.

Lind sighed, looking more weary than ever. "Have peace, Arenda," Lind said, his normally gruff tone softened. "You have done your part."

"Peace," Arenda whispered, but the room was still enough that they could have heard a grain of sand falling to the floor. They all repeated the phrase—all but Bjorn who probably didn't understand what the phrase meant.

Selke had stopped trying to patch the wound. She must have accepted that any efforts to fix it would be futile and perhaps only give Arenda a few more seconds. Instead, she grasped Arenda's hand and waited.

They stood vigil until she went still. He wasn't sure what he felt as his instructor died right before his eyes, but all he could do was look at her and struggle to breathe, afraid to speak even though questions swirled through his mind. The others must have felt the same. All but Bjorn, who kept eating from his plate as though this was an everyday occurrence for him.

Perhaps it *was* like that back in Kelig. Maybe this was the way life had been for the rest of the world all this time. Avskild had been at peace for so many years, Grimnir numbers dwindling, not because the world didn't need them, but because they were shielded from all the world's problems. It was no wonder Bjorn was angry at first.

Hallik clenched his fists and shot to his feet as a rising sense of wrath welled up inside him. Defending humanity was the cause that Grimnirs should have been fighting for all along. Perhaps this was why his father had disappeared. He'd known they needed to be out there fighting. "We need to reclaim Vanalf."

Elowyn nodded beside him, her hand slipping into his. He gave it a tight squeeze, her own determination filling him with extra vigor.

"Easier said than done," Lind said. "Though you're right. What we truly need are Voyagers. Without them, we cannot control or repair the portals. This means we need to send the next group of students through Vanalf, but I fear it will be more dangerous than ever before."

"We'll do it," Elowyn said. "I bet every other student would say the same."

"I will go as well," Lorelai blurted from the back of the room. She strode up to join them around Arenda's body.

Lind strained his neck to look back at her. "Lorelai, these students train for years in preparation to enter the cave just for a chance at survival. The dangers are—"

"I said I will go." Lorelai fixed Lind with a stern gaze.

"Hallik," Selke said in a low voice. Her eyes flicked between Hallik and Elowyn. "Now is probably the right time for me to send you to your father."

"Selke," Lind said, but Selke held her hand up in his direction without looking at him. Her eyes remained on Hallik.

Hallik shook his head. "What do you mean?"

"Your father is alive," Selke said. "He is hiding here on Avskild."

"Hiding... why?" Hallik's grip on Elowyn's hand went tight enough that she withdrew her own.

"You will understand when you meet him. It was imperative that he remain there. He said to send you to him *before* you went to Vanalf. That it was critical to your survival, especially if such an event as this should occur."

Hallik only shook his head more. "What, the end of the world?"

"Well, the failing of the integrity of the portals, yes," Selke said. "He was always suspicious about an impending war with the darkness beyond Avskild."

Selke's impassive expression triggered a renewed sense of anger within Hallik. How could she be so nonchalant? His father had been alive all this time, right here on the island, but had hidden from him. How could he do this?

Seeing his expression, Selke sighed and raised both her hands to him. "I understand why you would be angry, but for your father's part, I understand why he felt this was necessary. Please, you must go find him."

"Is that really necessary?" Bjorn said. "I mean, if the end goal is to create some more of these Voyagers, then why not head straight to this cave? With the king out of the way, there should be no more concern for the Voyagers to be abducted or murdered. If we have Voyagers, then we can control the portals."

"Then you can head back to your wildlands," Lorelai said, eyes dark.

Bjorn was not amused. "I want to see all the monsters dead just as much as any of you."

Hallik wasn't sure what he wanted to do, but Bjorn was right. Going through Vanalf should be the priority, but he couldn't deny his eagerness to meet his father. Selke made it sound as if seeing his father was necessary for him to survive Vanalf at all, but why would that be the case? Either way, Selke was at least convinced of the necessity, which was just about all the persuading Hallik needed. Her wisdom far surpassed that of anybody else Hallik had ever met. She had never led him astray.

He let out a long breath. "Where do I find my father?"

"I don't know the exact location," Selke said, "but he gave me something to give to you that is supposed to help you find him." Selke reached into the bag slung around her shoulder and pulled out a wooden box small enough to fit on Hallik's palm.

Hallik took it and stared down at the simple construct. The wood was smooth and polished, with a single hinge connecting it on the back side. There was no latch to keep it closed, but the lid appeared firmly in place. "And you've just... carried this around with you for years?"

Selke placed her hands on her hips. "Your father has a way of being rather convincing at times. But again, believe me when I say it will make more sense when you meet him."

"You're making me worry that he really is some kind of strange creature," Hallik said.

"Nothing like that," Selke said.

"Mother," Elowyn interjected. "What is your relationship with Hallik's father? Why would he entrust all of this to you?" Hallik had been wondering the same thing.

Selke bit her lip and nodded. "He was well acquainted with your father, Elowyn. They were dear friends, if you can even say that your father had friends. I'm quite possibly the only human on Avskild who even knows who

Hallik's father actually is at this point, so it was natural for him to approach me."

Elowyn nodded, but her eyes remained narrowed, as though mistrusting the information Selke relayed.

Hallik would have his answers soon enough. "So do I need to go find my father alone, or can Elowyn come with me?"

"Your father never said anything about you needing to go alone," Selke said.

"Very well, then. Bjorn, will you be coming?" Hallik asked. He knew Bjorn didn't want to sit around in the castle waiting for them, and if they came across more monsters out there while hunting for his father, Bjorn would certainly be useful. As long as he didn't try to sacrifice them in order to kill something on his list.

"Aye," Bjorn said.

Lorelai's mouth opened, then she clamped it shut as if unsure what to say. Finally, she said, "I would like to come with you."

Hallik nodded and looked back down at the box. "Alright, then," he said, wedging a fingernail under the lid. "Let's go see what this is about." He pried the small box open, and a ball of light burst from the box with a scattering of sparks, a couple of them burning Hallik's palm.

The light zipped out toward the balcony in dizzying swirls then stopped just over the ledge, flickering and swaying. Hallik stared, open-mouthed, unsure what he was seeing.

"I think it wants us to follow," Elowyn said.

"Alright, well, glowing light thing," Hallik said. "We can't fly, so you'll need to wait for us to walk down the stairs, understood?"

The sparkling light flickered for a moment, then dashed back inside and hovered just beyond entrance to the room. Perhaps it *did* understand him. Nature's rays. Hallik shook his head in wonder, but that fury that had risen in his chest remained. His father had better have some good answers for all of this.

CHAPTER TWENTY-FOUR

THE FOREST

Elowyn Galdre

Elowyn slung the satchel over her shoulder before joining the others outside the eastern door of Castle Vrodr. A couple of servants had helped them pack some basic provisions. Elowyn saw that the sparkling light, which she suspected was some kind of spirit, was prompting them to head out into the eastern forests beyond her home. Mother had hinted that Hallik's father was hiding out in some secluded place on the island, which might result in them tromping through the forests for a couple days. Hopefully not any longer.

As soon as Elowyn joined the group, Hallik bounded after the sparkling light with a spring in his step. Since Hallik was typically an energetic person, she could only imagine the amount of excitement he was feeling. Elowyn's feelings clashed within her. The idea that Mother had kept this secret for so long felt like betrayal. Mother claimed her intentions were pure, but she still left a lot to mystery. Was she hiding something on purpose? And if the location and identity of Hallik's father were so special, then why were Bjorn and Lorelai tagging along?

She still didn't necessarily like Bjorn. Not only was he an outsider, but he hadn't been trained at all like the Grimnir students. His tactics during a fight did not mesh with theirs, which could easily jeopardize the safety of their whole party. What also upset her was that, despite his combat style misaligning with their trained tactics, he'd still successfully saved Hallik twice now.

And Lorelai? Elowyn grunted just thinking of her. She wasn't even a warrior. No combat experience whatsoever, at least, not as far as Elowyn knew. She held a dagger but probably didn't even know how to use it. If Lorelai truly wanted to venture through Vanalf, then her chances for survival were probably not high.

But Hallik had allowed Lorelai to come, and nobody else had objected. Perhaps there was more to her than met the eye, but she doubted it.

Hallik led the way, following the sparkling light that guided them into the forest. It seemed to have a strange notion of where it was taking them and would sometimes hover straight over obstacles that were difficult for the rest of them to get across. At one point it bounced energetically near the top of a gray rockface that led up a small hill as if impatient with them for not going straight up its surface.

"We can't fly," Hallik said to the blinking light.

Its enthusiastic bouncing ceased, and instead it slunk low to the ground and very slowly went down in front of Hallik, guiding him around the outcropping at a sluggish pace. It was like the spirit was upset they couldn't fly.

Lorelai hung back and spoke to Elowyn over her shoulder. "Is it just me, or does our little guide seem sad we can't fly?"

"I was thinking the same thing," Elowyn said with a smile. Perhaps Lorelai wasn't too bad. And then something finally came to her mind regarding their guide. "Oh, I think I know what it is. This is a valet wisp. They're often excitable spirits, and they'll display highly emotional reactions. In life, they might have been something like a small fairy or a bird."

Hallik glanced back at Elowyn and gave her a short nod. "Alright, well," he said, looking back at the wisp, "thank you, little valet wisp. Sorry we can't fly. You're doing a great job."

The valet wisp gave a swirl before rocking back and forth as it continued to lead the way. Hallik chuckled as he followed.

"You seem a sharp lass," Lorelai said, smiling at Elowyn. She had a clean, toothy smile that Elowyn hadn't seen much of from the older woman. Not *old*. Just older. They'd only crossed paths a few times in the last couple years, but they'd never shared a conversation until this very day. She'd seen her give close-mouthed smiles or smirks before, but never such a genuine grin.

Elowyn smiled back. "Thank you. I have been quite serious about my studies."

"Too serious," Hallik shouted from the front.

"Sufficiently serious," Elowyn said to Lorelai. "I have always thought it necessary to understand all the creatures, good or malicious, that exist in nature. Did you know that some monsters were designed specifically to destroy humans?"

Lorelai frowned and shook her head.

Elowyn couldn't help but continue. "There's supposedly a lost god who was thrown out of Vanheyna for murdering some of his siblings. Not intentionally, mind you, he just liked using his magic to make dangerous creatures, and grew more and more creative with time. One such creature was a basilisk that started devouring his siblings. He ended up getting banished to the Wyrm Tunnels—that's where Vanalf leads if you go too deep—and he emerged into our world through an exit in the ocean somewhere. There are supposedly several islands that were created when he emerged. Anyway, after he came here, he saw all the humans and, out of sheer boredom, decided to start making monsters that would hunt and kill us."

"That... sounds horrible," Lorelai said. "Which god is that?"

"Okan," Elowyn said. "There's a whole series of tales about him recorded in the writings in Castle Vrodr. Some of my mother's songs feature him. There are even tales of him offering aid to people for different quests. His usual motivation is simply curiosity or entertainment."

Elowyn grimaced, realizing suddenly that this information was completely random and unsolicited. "Sorry, I got a little excited there."

"That's alright. I admit I have not invested much time in the tales of old, nor have I had the luxury of hearing songs from your mother. She sounds like an invaluable source of wisdom."

Elowyn nodded fiercely. "She says the chronicles are the most crucial thing she can offer our society, and I agree. I wish she sang to the people more often. Usually she just sings to herself as she goes about her activities at home."

"Do you know the songs as well, then?"

"Yes," Elowyn said with a shrug, "though not all of them. Mother probably sings over a hundred different ones. I might be able to sing twenty or thirty."

"This is a strong legacy you carry, Elowyn," Lorelai said.

Elowyn's eyes narrowed, suspecting some kind of cheap rapport attempt out of the exchange, but Lorelai's expression remained quite serious. "I'm not so sure the songs are my calling," Elowyn said. In truth, she often sang or hummed the songs, but only when she wasn't around Mother. Mother had often practiced with her when she was a lot younger, but she'd stopped after one specific day. It was the only memory Elowyn had of her father. Mother wasn't at home, but Father had just come outside while Elowyn was singing the song of Vanalf.

For all who need a home

The door to their home had slammed open before Elowyn could finish the line. Father ran to her and clamped a hand over her mouth. She could still remember the tightness of his palm as he held her head in his hands, his eyes wide with panicked fury.

"Don't you sing that song," Father had said, his voice a growl. She couldn't remember Father's eye color—couldn't remember his hair or his facial features, or any of his clothes. All she could remember were the whites of his eyes and the feeling of his grip on her face, clamping her mouth shut. She remembered the tears that came and the blurriness of her vision. He'd disappeared only a short time later.

No. The songs were *not* her calling.

Since Father and Hallik's father had known each other before, she had to wonder if Hallik's father would be able to tell her anything about the song and why her father had reacted so vehemently. The idea that this was her only memory of Father struck her with a sudden wave of sadness. Mother didn't speak of him often, and Elowyn rarely felt inclined to ask about him.

Lorelai raised an eyebrow at Elowyn. "Perhaps I struck a chord. That was not my intent."

Elowyn shook her head. "You're fine, but I admit I know very little of you. Were you always interested in politics?"

Lorelai laughed at that, causing Bjorn to cast one of his annoyed glances back at them. "Not necessarily, no. I just find myself drawn to... private information."

"So that's what you're doing here," Elowyn said, knowing there had to be some strange reason that the royal attendant had somehow found herself in their company.

"Not at all, though I do admit that certainly makes this more interesting. After recent events, I find myself more invested in the wellbeing of our people, and I would take any opportunity to secure Vanalf and venture through it myself." Lorelai paused and swallowed as though she might have something more to say.

Elowyn waited to see if she would say more as they ducked beneath some hanging vines to continue following after the wisp. Lorelai slowed her pace, but Elowyn matched strides with her.

"In truth," Lorelai said once they were a little further back from Bjorn, "I didn't like feeling weak. I watched King Knos open the portal. I watched as he conversed with the ashimal. I watched as it attacked him and devoured Daelen. I watched and did nothing, knowing it was wrong the whole time. I hated that sense of powerlessness. I never want to feel that way again. As a Grimnir, I'd be able to fight against monsters like that. I'd be able to stand against a king if needed."

"Ah," Elowyn said. Maybe that was why Lorelai held a dagger now. She still clutched it in her hand rather than tucking it into the satchel around her shoulder, an item she'd "borrowed" from Castle Vrodr so that she could carry some of her own supplies. "That seems perfectly reasonable. When did you get the dagger, then? I've only seen you a few times, but you've never had a weapon until now."

"Oh, yes." Lorelai flashed a nervous smile that never reached her eyes. "The king dropped it. He might have intended to use it to defend himself." She shrugged. "That didn't work of course. I'm still surprised I got out."

Bjorn grunted from ahead of them. "I'm uncertain about something there, Lorelai." He'd apparently been eavesdropping on them the whole time. "How did you get away? I saw how quickly those tendrils of mist moved. It could have easily grabbed you."

Lorelai shrugged, her face becoming a placid mask. "I don't know. It seemed to have some sort of limitation for a while. Its body seemed unable to pass through the portal, and only its arms of mist were able to come out. I'm not sure how it eventually escaped, though maybe that's why it was trying to pull the king through."

"So where was the king when he dropped the dagger? Next to the portal?"

"Yes."

"And then you decided to get that close to it, grab the dagger, then run away?" His eyes were hard, and Elowyn had to admit that she appreciated his no-nonsense approach to conversation. This was certainly an instance where directness was appropriate. "I would have thought you'd just flee. Why bother grabbing the dagger?"

Lorelai's lips twitched before she spoke. "I needed the king's blood to get out. His blood was already on the floor right there, so I figured I'd grab the dagger at the same time."

Bjorn grunted again, but only turned away instead of saying more.

"Are you three talking about daggers again?" Hallik said, stopping to regard them. "I don't see what's so special about daggers anyway. *I* certainly don't need one. Even though the three of you all have one."

Elowyn forced a smile, knowing that Hallik was trying to lighten their spirits. He had a way of sensing hostility. It was painfully annoying knowing that he wouldn't ever let her be upset at him for very long.

"We should find a place to camp soon," Bjorn said, ignoring Hallik's question. "Do you think your moody star will wait for us if we sleep somewhere?"

The wisp zipped back toward them and bounced off Bjorn's head twice, causing a couple orange sparks to pop out. Bjorn flapped his hand at it until it flew back in front of Hallik and settled on a branch.

Elowyn stifled a laugh as Hallik said, "Uh... I think it will wait if we ask it to."

The sun was in fact getting lower and would begin to dip below the edge of the mountains within a few moments.

There would still be about an hour of light after that, but it was good timing to begin setting up camp.

Elowyn hadn't been paying much attention to their surroundings. They'd made good ground as far as she could tell, but the trees were tall, only allowing for brief glimpses of the mountains to their left. Ahead of them and to the right was just more forest. Time had passed so quickly. She could hardly believe that their fight with the ashimal had only been a few hours ago. The memory of her failure and helplessness during the fight had haunted her throughout the walk. Lorelai's commitment to never feeling powerless again was something she could understand.

There were real monsters in the world, and some of them were certainly more complex than others. Magic could make the difference. She only wished she'd known more about ashimals so that she could have handled the fight better, but no matter what knowledge she had, how would she have fought against those arms of mist without magic? Maybe she could have brought a fan.

They came to a flattened part of the ground, and Bjorn had them scope out the area. His grumpy expression seemed darker than usual, and she could have sworn that he was being uncharacteristically anxious as he darted about setting up things that he called "sound traps."

"If we place enough of these around, they should alert us about any approaching beasts," Bjorn explained as he placed a few sticks atop each other in a precarious formation. "Then we just hope that no malicious spirits come after us—since they don't walk, obviously—but in those cases, the spirit is often screaming about nonsense anyway, so we'll still be alerted."

"You've done a lot of camping, then?" Lorelai asked. She did practically nothing to prepare except find a mossy patch to sit on while she picked at a piece of bread and watched them.

"I've slept more on the ground than I have in a bed, if that adds any level of clarity," Bjorn said.

Elowyn shook her head. Sleeping on the ground was only meant to be an occasional discomfort, not a way of life. "No wonder you're always grumpy, then," Elowyn said.

Bjorn's scowl was unchanging as he went to set another trap.

"He's not grumpy, Elowyn," Hallik said. "That's just the way he smiles. I'll be worried about him when those eyebrows of his *aren't* scrunched up."

"Hal," Elowyn warned.

Hallik nodded, smile disappearing as he started addressing them in a *here's the plan* sort of way. "We can have a fire tonight since this wisp shines as bright as one anyway, but we should have somebody staying up to keep watch at all times."

Lorelai opened her mouth to object, but Hallik held a hand toward her and continued speaking. "The lack of sleep is a necessary sacrifice. We don't know what kind of monsters have slipped through the portals, but with the variety we've faced already, having somebody paying attention will help me get any sleep at all."

"Is a fire necessary?" Bjorn asked.

"We could do without," Hallik said, "but since it doesn't make a difference with the wisp here, we may as well sleep warmer tonight."

Bjorn grunted but made no further argument.

"I'll take the first watch," Elowyn offered, though truly, she just didn't want to be woken up in the middle of the night.

"Thanks, Elowyn," Hallik said. "We'll all need to take at least one turn, including you, Lorelai."

Lorelai nodded. "I can't guarantee the best results, but I understand I'll have to do my part."

Elowyn settled down after they got everything ready. Bjorn took his place a little apart from the group, up behind a tree. She still wondered if Bjorn and Lorelai could be fully trusted, but as far as she could tell, they all at least had similar goals. That would have to do for now. Hallik was too kind at times. Hopefully it wouldn't work to his detriment.

CHAPTER TWENTY-FIVE

BORROWED

Lorelai Harkral

Harsh whispers roused Lorelai from her fitful sleep. She wouldn't admit it out loud, but sleeping outside on the moss with only a blanket was not something she cared for. But there was a price to be paid for all things in life, including one's goals.

With bleary eyes, she blinked over at Bjorn and Elowyn who were whispering and gesturing at each other. Their fire had died out, but there was still a wisp of smoke curling away under a calm, early morning breeze. The sky was a dark blue, clear of clouds. The sun would probably pop up at any moment. She sighed and tried to rub the sleep from her eyes.

She was about to ask them what they were going on about, but they shushed her. A shuffling sound came from behind her, and she quickly got to her feet to see Hallik with a finger over his lips.

"Something came through our camp last night," Hallik whispered.

Lorelai pulled her dagger, Dris, out and unsheathed it. She had purposefully avoided telling anybody that the king had been using the weapon to transfer power from the Voyagers over to that ashimal creature in the portal. That didn't stop anybody from asking about it. They could tell it was distinctive, and she'd worried that Lind would just take it from her. As of yet, nobody seemed to have figured out its origins.

If there was power inside of it, perhaps she could figure out how to use it. Maybe she could even use it on monsters. Perhaps the power she was after was already at her fingertips, but she was still committed to entering Vanalf. Maybe the magic she'd obtain there would help her unlock the weapon's use.

"What was it?" Lorelai asked.

Hallik shrugged and shook his head.

They were all still alive, so whatever it was, it hadn't intended to hurt them, though she did notice that her bag looked like it had been ruffled through. The contents were dumped at her feet. Strange.

The wisp that had led them here still hovered over the ground at the edge of the clearing, slowly bobbing up and down as if it were sitting upon ocean waves. Its glowing light was dim, and she worried that perhaps they'd broken it by waiting.

"It didn't hurt us," Elowyn hissed at Bjorn.

Lorelai's senses had returned well enough for her to be at sharp attention now.

"That doesn't mean it has peaceful intentions," Bjorn said. "We should track it down."

"But it didn't do anything to us," Elowyn said. "It could have been a deer or a rabbit. I'm not going to waste our time looking for a deer."

"It wasn't either of those," Bjorn said. "Otherwise, it would have set off one of my traps. All of which are still intact."

"So it was a spirit?" Lorelai asked. She didn't know much about monsters or spirits or anything. She'd never *had* to know much about them.

"Possibly," Bjorn whispered. "There are several monsters that like to toy with their prey, but most of them like to steal something of value, then sneak off to lure people to their lairs. It's a common tactic for those that want to deliver fresh meat to their offspring."

"Did it steal anything?" Lorelai asked.

Bjorn shook his head. "No, unless it stole something from you."

"Then let's be on our way," Hallik said.

"We should try to find it," Bjorn pressed. "It won't leave us alone until we do."

"But you just said it could be a trap," Lorelai said.

Bjorn's jaw hardened. "Yes, but do you want to try going to sleep another night out here knowing that something will be sneaking around our camp?"

Hallik had just finished rolling up his blanket. "I say we continue. We'll get to my father then return to the city. If we're inside Dalstava, it won't bother us."

"That seems rather avoidant," Lorelai said. Whatever was happening, she could at least see Bjorn's logic.

"Look, Bjorn has a point," Hallik said, "but the reality is that it didn't take anything. It was probably just a deer, and it managed to dodge Bjorn's traps. It's not like his traps are infallible, see." Hallik finished putting his bag over his shoulder before trying to sneak out of their camp, stepping on at least three of Bjorn's sound traps in the process.

Elowyn shook her head.

"I'm not as agile as a deer," Hallik said, "but I'm sure it could be done."

As Hallik neared the wisp, its light flared back up, and it started to bounce away with renewed energy.

Lorelai had to remind herself that these were the same people who'd fought and killed that ashimal yesterday. Granted, Lind had done most of the real damage, and none of them had the use of any magical abilities. Hallik and Elowyn had been braver than her despite their youth, though she wanted to think it was because she hadn't been trained to fight like they had. Her training with the militia had been minimal. She could see that it provided them an extra level of confidence that she had yet to acquire. As much as she didn't want to admit it, if the portals remained broken, there'd be a lot of fighting to come.

"Besides, do you think you can even track what came through?" Hallik asked before triggering yet another of Bjorn's noise traps.

Bjorn only grunted. He'd been scouting around the whole area ever since Lorelai woke up. He didn't seem to have any clear direction on where he should be looking. His grunt turned into a growl. "That's another thing that's bothering me," Bjorn said. "The only evidence we have of something being here is that our bags were all rifled through. That leaves me wondering if it was one of you doing it."

"Well, Elowyn does snore on occasion, but I don't think we have anybody digging around in their sleep," Hallik said. "I say we get moving. Who knows how many more days we'll need to be out here. The sooner we meet my father the better. I'm worried the longer we stay away from Vanalf, the greater the risk that more monsters will come through. I have no desire to fight through an army of trolls without even being a Grimnir yet."

Lorelai shook her head. She was decided. She tied her blanket onto her bag and followed after Hallik. "Let's go then. No time to waste." She didn't wait for any more discussion. The wisp was increasingly happy as the group resumed their journey. Its colors undulated between orange and yellow, a red spark sometimes shooting out of the top of it.

Bjorn only grumbled a little before following them.

Lorelai kept her dagger out. She hadn't had the opportunity to use it yet, but she couldn't deny the sense of comfort she felt in holding a weapon. Yesterday's events still had her on high alert. After snatching the dagger and running up the secret stairs, she should have kept fleeing. Instead, she'd crumpled to the floor, hyperventilating, almost crying. She'd sat there for perhaps a whole hour when she noticed steam issuing from the hidden door.

The ashimal had figured out how to get through the doors. She ran down one floor and hid in a room after getting cornered. The ashimal was hunting for her, wanting the magic contained inside of Dris. She could only imagine what the beast would have done had it gotten hold of the dagger.

What worried her more than the ashimal itself was the very plan. Whose idea was it to start killing all the Voyagers? Did that come from King Knos's forefathers? Perhaps the ashimal had come up with the idea and was building up to it for the last hundred years. She didn't know much about ashimals, but how did the creature use Voyagers' magic? It already had some control of shadow or fog magic or whatever that was. Her fear was that there was something else involved in trying to destroy the portals. Something even more sinister than just the ashimal. She knew she should probably ask someone, but Dris was her secret. It was *her* power.

And with the Grimnir Guard apparently destroyed, Avskild was defenseless. The troll invasion would only be the beginning of worse things to come. A tight pain grew in her chest as the thoughts swirled in her brain, and her vision started to fade.

Beside her, a hand gripped her elbow. Elowyn's green eyes glowed with a firm intensity. "We can do this," Elowyn whispered. Her grip tightened as though she were helping Lorelai stand. "Say it. We can do this."

Lorelai swallowed hard and took a sharp, shuddering breath, focusing on Elowyn's eyes. "W-we can do this."

Elowyn nodded.

Lorelai hadn't noticed until now, but she'd been shivering. It wasn't even that cold. The sun was up now, and the air was warming.

"Say it again," Elowyn urged, grip loosening just a bit as Lorelai's steps became steadier.

"We can do this," Lorelai said, though all the odds were stacked against them. She didn't really believe they could do it, but she was determined to fool herself long enough to keep fighting. Perhaps that was the best they could do. If somebody like Bjorn, who had essentially no hope at all, could keep fighting, she could too.

Lorelai patted Elowyn's hand and nodded. This interaction further affirmed her belief that Elowyn and Hallik were both strong individuals. They probably faced the same thoughts she did. After all, many of their teachers and leaders had fought and died yesterday, one in front of their very eyes.

A chittering drew Lorelai's attention. It reverberated down to them as if from several directions at once.

Bjorn had his sword in one hand, crossbow in the other, as if he'd been waiting for this.

"Do you have any animals native to Avskild that make such a sound?" Bjorn asked.

"No," Elowyn said. "Definitely not."

The sound triggered again, the crescendo of a thin piece of metal being bent back and forth. A moment later, a small, furry creature dropped from the trees directly in front of Hallik and right beside the wisp guide. The wisp continued bouncing merrily as if it hadn't a care in the world.

The creature cocked its head up at Hallik. It was no larger than an average dog, but it resembled a squirrel more than anything else, aside from the part where it had three tails, each one equipped with a barb. It opened its mouth and the chittering noise resumed, sounding from every-where all at once. If the sound was meant to disorient or confuse them, it wasn't working, but it was terrifying to see the creature's mouth. Rows of sharp, spine-like teeth completely lined the inside. Its jaw opened significantly wider than it should, and lines of sticky saliva hung and dripped, steaming as though it were some corrosive sub-stance. It probably was.

"Chupara!" Elowyn shouted, whipping her dagger out.

So it was another monster that Lorelai had never heard of. Fantastic.

Hallik drew his sword out then gasped. "What in all the depths?" Instead of a sword, he'd pulled out a stick of equal length. His sword was gone, somehow replaced with a fake.

The monster lunged at Hallik. He thrust the stick forward, straight into the giant monster-squirrel's mouth. It gagged before jabbing its tails at Hallik, who scrambled back as Bjorn fired his crossbow. The monster ducked its head, avoiding the bolt, but it struck the top of the monster's back instead. With a high-pitched whine, it scampered toward Bjorn. He flung one of his knives at it then dove to the side. The beast was agile, however, and pursued him. He tried getting behind a tree for protection, but the chupara jumped onto the tree and stuck its head around, its three tails grasping the trunk for extra support.

Lorelai and Elowyn sprang into action. They both seemed to have the same idea as they swung at the trunk. Lorelai stabbed, holding Dris with an underhand grip. She hit the middle tail just as Elowyn slashed at the bottom one. Dris grazed off the bony spine and stuck into the tree. The injured tails jabbed back at them as the chupara fell. Elowyn slipped away unharmed, but Lorelai was slapped bodily by the chupara's middle tail. A sharp pain pierced her right arm like the sting of alcohol on a wound.

She knew exactly what had caused it, triggering the fear that it was much worse than a simple scratch.

The chupara landed gracefully, but Bjorn hacked across its face with his sword, scoring a gash from its eye to its mouth. It yelped, but despite the distraction, its tails jabbed at Lorelai once more. She stepped back, swinging Dris. They missed each other, but she felt the wind of the chupara's tail as a barb narrowly passed her arm again.

Hallik roared as he appeared beside Lorelai, snatching the base of one of the tails in his hand. The barb twitched as if trying to reach him. The other two tails sprang to jab at him, but Elowyn and Lorelai grabbed those ones respectively. She started hacking down at it with her dagger, but she wasn't sure it was doing much good. What they really needed was for Bjorn to do something at its front.

"Bjorn!" Hallik shouted, yanking back on the tail as the chupara tried turning back to face them.

Bjorn was already on it, hacking down at the chupara with careful swings as though he was trying to avoid its face. The chupara kept biting at his sword, mouth frothing with steaming spit.

Elowyn pushed forward. She slammed down, her dagger ramming into the side of the monster. She stabbed again, avoiding its hind leg as it tried to swipe at her. Lorelai and Hallik pulled back on the tail to prevent the beast from turning around. Elowyn stabbed a third time as Bjorn managed to slice it across the side of its neck.

The chupara yelped one last time before it collapsed.

They released the tails and stepped back, all of them panting.

"What in Kel's abyss is a chupara?" Bjorn asked. "Even its saliva is corrosive. I didn't want it getting on my sword." He tried wiping the gore off on some nearby mosses.

"Yes, sorry," Elowyn said. "It's hard to shout all of its details out to you while it's trying to kill us. They're best killed from a distance."

"Alright, that's great, but where's my sword?" Hallik asked, arms up as he looked around. "And why did I have a stick in my belt? How did none of us notice that?"

Lorelai did think that odd. "I think we know what was taken from us last night, then," she said. "Though I do find it interesting that instead of just taking something, it actually replaced your sword with a stick. I'm not familiar with anything that would do that."

Elowyn shook her head and tried to hide a smile behind her hand. "I think I know exactly what would do something like that."

Hallik was aghast. "And why would that be funny? Please don't tell me you took it. No." He held up a hand toward her. "No, that's not something you would do. So what was it?"

"Well, it probably wasn't done with malicious intent,. In fact—" Elowyn's voice fell short as they heard a crunching pinecone. They all snapped to attention, facing the sound's location.

Lorelai could have sworn that she saw the hand of a toddler waving at them from behind the trunk of a tree.

"Guilty," called a small, gruff voice. A little man emerged from the other side of the tree. He wore a pointed, red cap and had a gray beard that went down to his thighs, but he stood no taller than Lorelai's knees. He had a bag over one shoulder and wore a knit tunic tucked into knit trousers. Most notably, he dragged Hallik's sword behind him.

"A gnome," Bjorn said, slowly lowering his sword.

The little gnome pointed at Bjorn sharply. "It's Nister Gnome to you, slayer," the gnome squeaked, "but the rest of you can call me Nis for short."

"But you're already short," Hallik said.

Nis tugged his beard before bursting into a laughing fit. The sound was such a high-pitched squeak that even Lorelai couldn't resist laughing as well. The response was so unexpected that it only made things that much more hilarious. Only Bjorn remained unfazed, glaring at the little man as though expecting him to attack.

After several moments, Nis wiped tears from his eyes. He pointed at Hallik and said, "I knew you were one of the good ones."

As if suddenly realizing something, Hallik gasped and said, "You took my sword!"

"Bah," Nis said, lips curling in disgust. "If you can call this a sword. It's quite hideous, really. More like a hunk of old metal with a handle." He flung it to the ground in front of him then shivered away from it.

"Excuse me?" Hallik said. He glanced at the others, but Lorelai still had no idea what was happening. She'd heard of gnomes before, but this interaction was… strange.

Nis waved Hallik off. "I was going to try and fix it but decided it wasn't worth my time. Besides, I knew that stick would do you more good against the chupara anyway."

Hallik retrieved his sword, inspecting it before putting it back into the loop at his belt. "How did you know we'd be attacked by a chupara?"

"I saw it," Nis said with a shrug.

"But then when did you take Hallik's sword?" Lorelai asked.

Nis looked her up and down before responding. "When you were all sleeping, of course. Your traps didn't look very good either by the way, so I fixed some of them up."

Bjorn's scowl somehow deepened.

Lorelai had to ask the question. "So you stole Hallik's sword while we were sleeping, knowing that we'd face a chupara later that day?"

"Borrowed!" Elowyn said before Nis could answer. "She meant to say 'borrowed,' not 'stole.'"

Nis's expression had darkened as soon as Lorelai had used that word, but he nodded as Elowyn clarified. "Yes," Nis said. "It noticed you last night, just before it got dark. I couldn't fix the useless chunk of metal though. Not worth my time. Don't dead yourselves. Good day."

Before they could say anything else, the gnome disappeared behind the tree. Lorelai walked over to double-check, but it appeared as though Nis had completely vanished. "He's gone," she announced to the rest of them.

"Wow," Elowyn exclaimed, clapping her hands together. She was absolutely beaming.

"I don't like it," Bjorn said.

Elowyn raised an eyebrow at him. "You're just saying that because it got through your traps."

"By nature's rays," Hallik said. "What just happened?"

"Gnomes are good omens," Elowyn said. "If he liked us enough, he might even help us from time to time."

"I know that much," Hallik said, "but why in the world would he take my sword if he knew we had a fight coming? And if he wanted to help, why wouldn't he just tell us about the chupara?"

Elowyn shrugged. "Gnomes are known as being reclusive. They don't tend to socialize much. Practically nobody has been privy to their society except for when they interact with humans in exchanges similar to this. Most commonly they help around farms and take care of animals as long as you feed them.”

“So who in the world fed the blighting gnome?” Bjorn asked.

Elowyn frowned at him. “That’s enough, Bjorn. Be nice to our new friend. Now that Nis is somewhat attached to us, if we don’t leave him food, he might take some of your knives and keep them unless you make up properly.”

Lorelai shook her head. “So is there some benefit to having Nis follow us around? We don’t have any livestock.”

Elowyn looked around in thought before shrugging. “I guess I don’t know. Nis does seem a little different from what I’ve heard of gnomes. Like I said, they usually help around farms, yet he tried to fix Hallik’s sword while we’re in the middle of the woods. He also said he fixed some of Bjorn’s traps. Maybe it’s just helpful little things like that.”

“Right,” Hallik said, brushing himself off. “Maybe we’ll leave ingredients out for him so he can cook or something. Shall we resume?”

“Yes, please,” Lorelai said, though she was hoping the others would walk ahead of her. There was something she wanted to test. She sidled toward the body of the dead chupara as the rest of them followed after the guide wisp. Dris still glimmered in her hand. She hadn’t sheathed it. If it could contain the magic of Voyagers, could it also capture magic from other Grimnirs? Or, more to her interest, other creatures—especially those of magical origin?

She had no idea if chuparas were considered magical, but she made a quick decision and stabbed into its corpse before withdrawing the blade quickly, trying not to gag from the feeling of stabbing a fleshy corpse. She watched the blade closely. How would she even know if Dris was storing anything?

Her question was answered immediately. The yellow gems had the faintest glow after she withdrew the weapon, a light within the gems winking at her. The handle felt warm to her touch. It worked.

She looked up to see Bjorn staring back at her. His eyes narrowed before he turned away, but in that moment, she realized that Bjorn knew exactly what had just happened.

CHAPTER TWENTY-SIX

NIKAN

Lind Hjordis

Ignoring Selke's protests, Lind gritted his teeth as he steadily rose to his feet. Fire burned in his legs, even with all those healing poultices applied. There were several jagged tooth marks that had pierced his flesh on the lower part of the front and back of both legs, but after Selke cleaned and wrapped them, at least the bleeding had stopped.

"A single day of rest is not enough to heal," Selke snapped. "They will start bleeding again. You need to put your legs back up."

Lind growled a response, not out of anger, but out of pain. "I understand. I just want to know what I'm capable of should the need arise. The city is in great danger, and I may be one of the only people who can help defend it."

He took a few careful steps before sitting. Selke helped him swing his legs back up onto the pillow as he laid down.

"Satisfied?" Selke asked.

"No, but I will exercise patience."

"Wise."

"So," Lind said, shifting the topic, "who is Hallik's father? Part of your husband's entourage?"

"It was the other way around," Selke said. Her green eyes glimmered as she turned her head to look out the opened balcony. Her bright blonde hair hung straight down her back, and her lightly tanned skin was radiant. Her beauty was far beyond that of any other woman Lind had known, and he could almost believe the rumors that she was part elf, or that her father was the fabled Nikan, a demigod of music and running water.

That was the reason people always gave for Selke's unrivaled beauty and enchanting voice. When she sang, the whole world stopped to listen. She'd spent the night in a room two doors down from his own, but he'd heard her singing through the walls. He should have slept, but the song kept him enraptured, heart pumping with the rhythm of her voice. Once she'd finished her song, he'd fallen into the deepest sleep of his life.

He could see where the rumors came from.

Those were *only* rumors, of course. Or so he told himself.

"The story of Hallik's father is not mine to tell," Selke said. She'd told him this years ago, after Hallik and Elowyn joined Castle Vrodr.

Lind nodded, feeling suddenly bold. "What of your story?"

She raised a sharp eyebrow at him. "What of it?"

Lind shrugged. "You've heard the rumors, I'm sure. Do you know much about your own parents?"

Selke laughed, a musical sound that made him smile. "I don't often engage in conversation with the other residents of Dalstava."

"Well, some of them claim that your father was Nikan and your mother was an elf."

Selke's smirk could have disarmed a troll. "They're not completely wrong."

"What?"

"I never met my father, but my mother always claimed he was Nikan. The rumor comes from her directly."

Lind shook his head, flabbergasted by the idea. "How? I always thought Nikan was more likely to lure people to the water just to drown them."

Selke nodded. "I will tell it to you as my mother told me." She cleared her throat, and for a moment, Lind thought she would sing, but instead, she orated a story, not in song, but with a lilting, bouncy voice. "The women of my family have been singers long before the formation of Avskild. The island was once connected to the mainland before the portal shields were established. An elf settlement is now beneath the sea, but one of my ancient foremothers married an elf. They were both ostracized by their respective societies. Each generation has always had a single daughter, and we've always been gifted with musical talent.

"My grandmother had rejoined society to some degree, but my mother was always off in the woods, singing songs or playing instruments. It was on one such occasion that she heard other music carrying through the trees." Selke paused and smirked. "She decided to sing even louder and danced her way toward the sound, but the sound vanished as she reached the edge of a stream. When she finished her song, she heard a fiddle playing the purest note—the same note she'd ended on—but it was so mournful. The song swelled and changed, filling her with the auditory essence of loneliness. She followed the sound upstream to a pond where the water was much deeper.

"As she drew closer and listened, words came to her. She added her voice to the sound as she stepped closer and closer to the edge of the water. When her toes were wet beside the stream, a man appeared from behind a small waterfall on the other side of the pond, strumming away on the fiddle. Half his body remained submerged as he floated toward her. Their song merged into the most terribly beautiful sound. Their eyes locked onto each other as they neared each other, Mother stepping into the water. She had walked until the water was up to her thighs when the song abruptly ended, the man's hand clutching onto her knee. Their eyes remained fixed on each other. His eyes were the deepest, darkest blue. She couldn't look away, but she knew what he'd just done."

Lind was positive this would have been the moment Nikan would pull her mother beneath the surface and drown her, but clearly that hadn't happened.

"She knew he'd lured her there, but she also recognized that he'd enjoyed her voice. If he hadn't, she would have already been dead. Before he could move to drag her under, she said, 'I will return and sing to you tomorrow.' Without saying anything, he released his grip and let her go. That was the first of many visits. After their union, they lived together near the stream."

Lind closed his open mouth. He was actually convinced. "And you… never met him?"

Selke shook her head. "Not to my memory. My mother says that after I was born, they took me to the pool. My father wept and played a song of such jubilation that even the trees danced, but then that was the last time she ever saw him."

"Why? Why would he leave?"

Selke sighed. "The water has eyes and ears. My birth was an abomination. When my mother brought me to the water, it saw. It heard my father's song, and it knew. We don't know who my father had to answer to, but his music has since vanished from Avskild."

"That's... horrible, Selke," Lind said, wishing he could reach out and grab her hand, but he was too far away. "I'm sorry."

"All is well," she said, slapping her knees before she stood. "Such is the curse of my fathers—to love, but not live. We even have a song about it that goes back a hundred years."

"I'm sure you do," Lind said, rubbing his forehead. "Thank you." He dipped his head at her. "For sharing that. I know you didn't have to, but I appreciate it all the same."

Selke smiled. "I figured it would be good to put rumors to rest by affirming them."

Lind chuckled, but his laughing stopped when a familiar raven appeared on the balcony. It landed on Lind's cot and cocked its head at him. There was something metal glistening in its mouth, and he already knew what it was before the bird set it down in Lind's lap.

It was the iron necklace of a Watcher insignia, an encircled eye, though the chain was missing. This was Serena, Mikel Vigsen's companion.

Delivering the token could only mean one thing. It was another confirmation that the army was defeated. Something needed to be done. He'd already wasted enough time. He needed to recover quickly.

Serena bobbed her head at him before flying back out through the balcony door.

A soft knock came at the door.

Selke got up to answer it as Lind picked up Mikel's necklace. There was still blood crusted on the surface of the metal, and he ran his fingers over it.

"I was hoping to have a word with Master Hjordis," a voice told Selke. He recognized it as Skelldwyn, one of the castle servants. It had been a long time since anybody had called Lind by his surname.

"Come in, Skelldwyn," Lind called behind him. Skelldwyn was perhaps just the lad Lind needed right now.

"Master Hjordis," Skelldwyn said, hurrying over to kneel on one knee beside Lind's cot. The lad had always called Lind by his given name, so the change suggested more than Lind wanted to admit. Perhaps it meant that word of the Grimnir Guard had gotten out, and Lind was likely the highest ranking Grimnir in the city. With the royal family dead and the army exterminated, that left very few leaders.

Skelldwyn didn't wait for Lind to respond, but hurried to say more, words spilling out. "I know I have not trained with the students, and I have done little more than carry water and run messages, but I want to pledge myself to the cause. I will do whatever you wish to keep the city safe." He kept his head bowed but looked up at Lind expectantly.

The lad was young, though probably in his early twenties. He had a thin, wispy excuse of a beard and short brown hair, mostly shaved off up the back of his neck to the crown of his head. He was quite lean, but if he'd been running the water, there'd be strength in him. He'd been serving at the castle for the last five or six years, and Lind, regretfully, hadn't really given much thought to the lad before.

"Right now, I need to get word out," Lind said. "We need to round up any remaining Grimnirs in the city. I don't think we can easily notify the villages, but they might be at the greatest risk. We'll need to get word out to all settlements to send delegates and bunker down. Can you get some others to help spread the news for me? We can try to gather people here at Castle Vrodr."

Skelldwyn shot to his feet and nodded. "I can do that. Should I head to the guardhouse at the docks then? We can involve the militia and get word out to the settlements faster by boat."

Lind eyed the lad anew. He was sharp. Perhaps he should have taken note of him sooner. He was often so focused on his lessons with the students that he didn't notice others enough. "Aye. See to it."

Skelldwyn gave another short bow before leaving. "I won't let you down, Master Hjordis."

Selke held the door open for him as Skelldwyn practically sprinted out. "He's... eager," she said.

"We could use a bit of enthusiasm," Lind said. "I need to rally every Grimnir. I'm hoping we still have a decent number left who weren't part of the assault team. Then I'll need to start drilling the militia. If we can't secure Vanalf, then the world itself is lost."

"We still have a chance," Selke said.

"Through Hallik's mysterious father?"

"He is a resourceful man, but I do feel unsure about that woman accompanying them."

"Lorelai?"

"Yes. She was lying to us, if you didn't notice. I'm concerned she has ill intent."

Lind, in fact, *hadn't* noticed. "Erm. What did she lie about?"

"Well, the dagger she held belonged to the king. For some reason, she ran right next to this monster and grabbed it. Of all the things to do before fleeing the room, that was the action she took. She's not a fool. There was a purpose behind it."

Lind scratched at his beard. If the king was truly mad enough to kill all the Voyagers, and Lorelai was his attendant, then perhaps she would try continuing his objectives. They could have very well sent Hallik and Elowyn off with their would-be assassin. Though perhaps they would only be in trouble if one of them became a Voyager after going through Vanalf.

"They'll be fine," Selke said, reading Lind's expression. "I'll send for a meal to be prepared. We can't have you making big decisions on an empty stomach." She departed the room, leaving Lind alone with his thoughts for a moment.

The task that was set out before them was practically impossible. Even if he rallied all the remaining Grimnirs on the island, there may only be twenty of them, and he doubted their ability to regain Vanalf with so few. For all he knew, the troll army would be marching on Dalstava next. They could be here today. How long would they be able to hold the walls against an army of trolls?

Then, even if they were able to get a few students into Vanalf, the cave itself would be far more dangerous than it was when he'd gone through it. Unless Hallik's father knew some way to restore the shield or perhaps make everyone invincible, their fate was likely sealed.

That didn't mean Lind wouldn't keep trying.

He only hoped that Elowyn and Hallik were still alive.

CHAPTER TWENTY-SEVEN

THE WATCHER

Hallik

A light rain sprinkled on their heads as they followed the wisp through rapidly dissipating fog. They reached a clearing on a small rise where Hallik could see all the way out to the ocean. The distant, dark clouds that hung to the horizon of the waves seemed lower than he remembered, perhaps a sign that the portal shield encapsulating Avskild was growing weak. He could only imagine what would happen if that magical shield finally vanished like the morning fog that disappeared under the sunlight. Perhaps there was a host of monsters just waiting to swarm the island once it was defenseless.

At least Bjorn would get to put some new marks on that list of his.

Hallik thumbed the hilt of his sword, partly just to make sure it was still there. He still couldn't believe that blighted gnome had snuck it off of him. Maybe the gnome had its own kind of magic to use.

He looked over his shoulder. Elowyn was close behind him, but Bjorn and Lorelai hung back, bickering about something. He was glad to have them along. Lorelai had proven more useful in their scuffle with the chupara than he would have thought. More useful than Hallik had been without any weapon at all.

"What're they on about?" Hallik asked Elowyn, but she just shrugged and said it was something about Lorelai's dagger.

Hallik paused to scratch at his leg, allowing them to close the distance a little more. He didn't want the group to have any animosity.

"I'll trade you three of my daggers for it," Bjorn said, voice low.

"Sorry," Lorelai said. "I have no interest in trading it."

"Does it hold some sentimental value?" Bjorn pressed.

"No," Lorelai said. "It's just something I don't want to part with. It is mine." She eyed Hallik warily, who still hadn't started moving.

He flashed her a smile and kept walking, though she'd probably realized that he was trying to listen in on their conversation.

"I think she is a spy," Bjorn said suddenly, stopping them all in their tracks.

"What?" Elowyn demanded.

Bjorn nodded toward Lorelai. "She's clearly not a vampire, but she appears to be a thrall of some kind."

"A... thrall?" Hallik asked.

"What could you possibly even mean by that?" Lorelai said, appalled at his accusation.

Bjorn scoffed. "You possess a vampiric weapon. You clearly know what it is, as I saw you demonstrate its use against the chupara earlier, and you've been keeping its true nature a secret. I'm suspecting your mind got infiltrated a long while ago."

Lorelai shook her head. "I have no idea what you're talking about."

"You knew the dagger was magical, didn't you?" Bjorn asked.

Lorelai threw up her hands. "Yes, but I have no idea what you mean by vampiric."

Bjorn scowled. "Those weapons are forged by power-hungry vampires who find that stealing someone's blood isn't enough. The dagger captures the energy of the victim's soul. I doubt there's a long history of vampires in Avskild."

Elowyn shook her head. "There's no history of vampires at all here."

"Alright." Lorelai shrugged. "I don't know anything about the origin of this dagger."

"Then tell us what you do know," Hallik said, stepping closer. She looked like she was on the verge of running away. "It will be alright, Lorelai. If we are to be a team, then it helps not to keep secrets, right Bjorn?"

Bjorn said nothing but stood at the ready, eyes still boring into Lorelai.

Lorelai sighed. "All I know is that King Knos had been using it for some time. Possibly even his father. When Knos would have the Voyagers killed, this dagger was somehow used to capture their power. He would take the dagger to that... portal in the Tower of Tarn and transfer it to the ashimal somehow. Knos was convinced that the ashimal, or something on that side of the portal, could use the power to strengthen the portal shield, though I suspect they were actually using the same power to weaken the shield. I think this is why the portals' power is failing and that monsters are able to get through. The ashimal was trying to get the dagger. That's why I took it before I left. I didn't want that power falling into its hands again."

"We should destroy it," Elowyn said vehemently.

Lorelai clutched it a little closer. "Perhaps we can use it."

"Hand it to me," Bjorn said. It was a demand. He held a palm up toward her.

Lorelai sneered. "You're the last person I would entrust this with. You could very well be the person using it to destroy the portals. How convenient for you to show up in Avskild as our defenses are crumbling. You may have been planning this all along."

"How dare you question my integrity?" Bjorn's face was a mask of barely contained anger. "Destroying evil has been my life's purpose ever since I was a child."

Hallik stepped between them, hands raised. "It's alright for her to be cautious, Bjorn, just as you are right to question her intentions. We are still practically strangers. Perhaps we can come to a compromise." He looked at Bjorn. If he wanted, he didn't doubt that Bjorn would have been able to simply take the dagger from Lorelai, but he'd bothered with asking. That was already a good sign. "Bjorn, what's your intent if you take the dagger?"

Bjorn grunted. "Lorelai is right that the dagger can likely be used in appropriate ways, but Elowyn has a good point about destroying it. That might be our best option. I'm not sure if we can use the dagger, and I'm not sure if we can destroy it. I would like to test both theories."

"Alright, hand me your sword, and hand Elowyn your crossbow, and then you can examine the dagger," Hallik said.

"I didn't agree to that," Lorelai said.

Elowyn raised an eyebrow "I think our trust might be a little more valuable than whatever it is you have to lose. We all have humanity's survival in our best interests, right?"

Lorelai pursed her lips and sighed before giving them a quick nod.

Bjorn growled as he drew his sword and handed it to Hallik. It was certainly a well-crafted blade—much finer than his own. He really needed to see about getting a better-quality weapon. Bjorn then handed his crossbow to Elowyn with even more growling. It was like taking a bone from a dog.

"Lorelai," Hallik said with a nod.

She handed the dagger to Bjorn then folded her arms with a frown.

Bjorn hefted the dagger in both hands. It bore more intricate designs than any of the weapons currently in Bjorn's possession, but he paid little attention to those and focused more on the blue gemstones. Hallik hadn't noticed before, but they did have a sort of peculiar sparkle to them.

Bjorn rubbed his thumbs over both the gemstones, then closed his eyes and muttered, "Kel's abyss." He kept his thumbs moving as his eyes remained closed. "It's... rather remarkable."

"What is it?" Lorelai said. Her hand was half-raised as if to snatch the dagger back. Her near obsession was enough to worry Hallik. For a weapon with seeming malevolence, her interest was unnerving.

Bjorn's eyes snapped open, and he regarded each of them in turn. "This blade is called Dris. Touching the gemstones allows me to access what feels like a sort of... codex. It's like a mental representation of everything this weapon has... killed. Or perhaps just parts of the souls it has damaged, including the chupara and many, many Voyagers." His lip curled in disgust. "Hundreds of them."

Hallik was still horrified by what the king had done. How long had this dagger been under the royal family's possession?

"So is that... useful?" Lorelai ventured to ask.

"I'm not sure," Bjorn said. "Possibly. It would take some rifling through, but there appeared to be a sort of anatomical deconstruction. I could see that being helpful somehow. It's hard to relay the information since it was not conveyed to me in the form of words."

"That sounds equally disgusting and interesting at the same time," Elowyn said.

"Perhaps it requires a magical being to be able to make full use of it," Lorelai said.

Elowyn nodded. "I've read almost everything in Castle Vrodr's library. Enchanted items have two types of magic, referred to as innate or activated. Some have one or the other, some have both. Lind's axe has both. By nature, or innately, it inflicts a dispelling effect on its target. So, if he cuts a monster, the monster's magical abilities can start to fade. He can also activate some of its own magic, which can have a variety of effects depending on the spell Lind uses."

Hallik cleared his throat. "In other words, the innate effect triggers without Lind needing to use magic, but the activated spells require him to use magic?"

"Yes," Elowyn said. "I suspect the dagger has both properties."

Lorelai nodded. "So innately, perhaps it captures the essence and provides this sort of codex access, but we can't use the magic because we don't have a proper spell for it?"

"Precisely," Elowyn said.

Hallik gestured at Bjorn. "What about destroying it?"

Bjorn withdrew one of his knives and tapped the gemstones as well as the rest of the blade. "I suspect it can be destroyed like any other item. I once destroyed a gemstone such as these for a job. Destroying the gemstone in that case ended up killing a blight that was infecting a village's crops. The gemstone was tied to a spell on the blight. Strangely enough, I picked it off the corpse of a deadling I was hired to hunt down."

"A deadling?" Hallik asked, having never heard of such a thing.

Bjorn shrugged it off. "Gross creatures that have an aura about them causing everything nearby to die. The gemstone in this case was tied into its hairs and released into their farmlands."

"Pleasant," Hallik said.

"Not at all."

"It was sarcasm—never mind." Hallik shrugged to Elowyn.

"Could breaking it strengthen the portal shield?" Elowyn asked.

"I'm not sure," Bjorn said. "It could have the opposite effect, especially if some of these Voyagers had been reinforcing the shield during their lives. Breaking the dagger might result in weakening any of their old spells. I don't know much about magic though, honestly. More so about how to kill creatures."

"So can I have it back?" Lorelai asked, holding her hand out.

Bjorn released a long sigh. After a moment, he placed it in her palm. "I will believe your story, but know that I can see great use for such a tool. I'd be willing to trade you for it."

"I'll consider it," Lorelai said, tucking it back away.

Hallik turned back to face the wisp, hiding his smile, knowing that Lorelai's answer was a resounding no. The wisp's hue changed from red to light orange as it hopped into action, eager to lead them back on the trail. It seemed extra bouncy since their encounter with the chupara and the strange conversation with the gnome. Hallik wondered if Nis was out there following them somewhere. He could only imagine how long the gnome had been trailing them, but he had to guess this was a recent development from just yesterday. It would be hard not to notice something like that stalking them, especially with him randomly deciding to "borrow" things.

The group remained quiet as the wisp led them on. They eventually stumbled onto an animal trail. The wisp seemed content to guide them along the trail for quite some time before it finally veered off. As time went on, Hallik found himself naturally walking quicker. Every second counted, and the more time they spent finding his father, the less time they had to get through Vanalf.

At least they didn't get attacked by any other monsters, but the sun passed overhead and started inching down toward the tip of the mountains. Every time they paused for a break, the wisp would turn bright red and start trembling. Hallik couldn't help but feel like it was getting frustrated with them, but their breaks were always short. They maintained a collective drive to keep pressing forward.

For a while, the wisp led them parallel to a stream. At one point, the water pooled into a wide, deep pond with a short waterfall. There appeared to be a small, ancient building off to the side of a tiny clearing there, but it had long since fallen to ruin.

"I like this place," Elowyn said, smiling. She started to hum, and Hallik was, as always, enthralled by the sound of her voice. It was similar to listening to Selke sing, though Elowyn's voice had its own enchanting tone. She claimed that she wasn't as good of a singer as her mother, but these statements frustrated Hallik. She had just as much raw talent, even if their voices sounded a little different. That didn't mean she wasn't remarkable in her own way.

The wisp flew over the stream at a point that it must have considered safe enough for them to cross. There was a questionably stable old tree log that had fallen across the stream, and Hallik risked using it to cross. He wasn't eager to get his boots wet. He was able to cross in three quick steps, with Elowyn and Lorelai right behind and Bjorn at the rear. The log snapped when Bjorn took his second step. He tried jumping but ended up sloshing into the water right at the edge of the stream.

When they all laughed, Bjorn scowled back at them and walked out of the water, but not before Hallik caught a glimpse of what may have been considered a sly smile on Bjorn's face. Perhaps there was hope for the man after all.

The rest of their walk was uneventful, though at one point they did go up quite a bit in elevation, then back down. Part of the trek included a stretch of land that was mostly clear of trees, and Hallik could see all the way to the high peaks on the north of the island. It was wild to think that he'd hardly traveled around Avskild. He'd only visited one other village, and their class had only gone on a couple longer trips through the mountains with Latshal and Lind as part of their nature education courses they took on rare occasions.

Last year, Selke had taken him and Elowyn to one of the lower peaks, a trip that they completed out and back in three days. Those were the only instances of long travel he'd ever done. It still astonished him to think that Avskild was such a small portion of their world and that other realms were even larger.

"We need to set up camp," Bjorn said. The sun was already touching down beneath the western mountains. They were far enough inland that the sea had long since passed from view.

"You may be right," Hallik said. Before he even finished the words, the wisp made an audible ping.

Sparks hissed out of the wisp as it changed to a bright yellow light. It shot up ahead of them to the edge of a short ridge as its colors proceeded to oscillate between red, white, and orange.

Hallik grunted. "I'm not sure Sparky here wants us to stop yet."

"*Sparky* can wait," Bjorn said, adding extra emphasis to the name Hallik had granted it.

Hallik knew they'd already been walking longer than they'd intended, and Lorelai looked like she needed the break.

Sparky was relentless, and Hallik was curious if they were near their destination. "Let's get to the top of that ridge at least, and then we can start looking for a good place to sleep." He just kept walking, not waiting for any kind of objection, but, surprisingly, none came. They quickly climbed the ridge where exposed rocks were a dark gray, almost black hue. The air smelled thickly of pollen and wet wood, a scent Hallik associated with each new year as fresh plants grew from the earth.

A large group of fairies shot overhead, leaving behind a trail of rainbowed light that dissipated slowly. Three deer bounded after them, nearly running into Hallik as they sprinted off. Hallik blinked rapidly as he looked at the trunk of a tree where a dryad's face sank back into the bark.

Something was different about this place.

Sparky grew more and more erratic as they neared the top of the ridge, zipping all around. Hallik felt the weight of a thousand eyes watching him from the trees, and he developed a growing suspicion that if it weren't for Sparky leading them here, their group would *not* be welcome.

As Hallik stepped up to the ridge, Sparky shot down into the bowl-shaped clearing ahead. Hallik's jaw dropped, and he quickly glanced at the others. They were equally awed. Even Bjorn's eyes widened beyond his usual narrowed scowl.

Laid out before them was a glade seemingly frozen in autumn, with trees on the fringes displaying orange, red, and yellow leaves. There were several gigantic flowers, a couple of them almost as tall as the trees. Their petals bulged voluminously in shades of pink, purple, and yellow. A mild glow emanated from them in each of their respective colors, and Hallik could only wonder how such a place had remained hidden. He was sure the creatures—those eyes that still bored down on him—had been keeping this place safe.

"This place," Bjorn said, his hand slowly moving to the hilt of his sword, "is not of our world."

Hallik snatched at Bjorn's hand and motioned to the trees with his eyes. "If you draw that weapon, it may be the last thing you do," he whispered.

Bjorn pulled his arm free but nodded.

Sparky was out of sight now, but it had headed toward the center of the glade. This certainly seemed like a strange place for his father to be staying. He wasn't sure what he'd expected, but perhaps a building at the very least.

"Perhaps your father is a troll after all," Elowyn said. She was the first to step down into the glade.

"Or a dryad," Hallik said, stepping down beside her.

"You mean a drus?" Elowyn said.

"A what?"

"Dryads are all female. A drus is a male."

Hallik shook his head. "Alright, sure." He kept his eyes ahead as the scent of sweet nectar wafted heavily in the air. Their feet trod across bright green grass that swayed lazily in the light wind.

Bjorn and Lorelai padded softly behind them, not saying a word.

Hallik finally spotted Sparky. It was swirling in erratic circles over a space that was densely packed with thigh-high flowers glowing with a soft, yellow light. He proceeded cautiously. He was expecting to find his father there, but he couldn't see anything beyond the blooms. Perhaps the flowers were casting some kind of illusion.

There was a single stretch of short grass that led through the flowers in a subtle swirl toward the center. Hallik resumed the lead as he followed the grassy path. The yellow flowers to either side shivered at his passing. Each breath he took was oddly... filling.

Sparky's circling became smaller as Hallik drew near until it finally stilled, hovering just above the flowers. Hallik made it to a small patch of grass in the middle and stopped in his tracks, eyes going wide. His companions came to his side as well, none of them speaking.

A bare-chested man was lying in the grass, unblinking eyes staring straight up at the sky. Save for a slight sparkle in his eyes, he appeared dead, completely unmoving. Sparky zipped over Hallik's head, rustling his hair with its passing before it curved back around and crashed down into the man's chest, disappearing with a couple sparks.

Stillness.

Until the unblinking eyes shifted to Hallik.

Hallik nearly stepped back, but he stood his ground.

A sharp breath filled the man's lungs, and he rose to his feet, looking Hallik up and down. He didn't even glance at the other three. His eyes were deep, frosty blue, and his bright blonde hair ran down past his shoulders.

Hallik could immediately tell that they bore similarities, but he still hesitated to think of this strange man as his father. What kind of lunatic would abandon his child to lie in a field of grass in the middle of nowhere?

After an awkwardly long moment of them staring at each other, the man was the first to speak. His lips twitched into a smile before he said, "Hallik. My son."

Hallik pursed his lips, still unsure how to address this man. Selke said his father's secrecy would make sense when he met him, but so far, he was only more confused than ever. "Hello. Selke said that I should seek you out before we go to Vanalf, so here I am."

The man's smile widened. "I can't believe it has already been eighteen years. You look strong and you've found good friends. You have done well for yourself."

"Technically, I'm only seventeen, but the need to enter Vanalf has been expedited," Hallik said. "But," Hallik paused to shake his head and find the words, "what are you doing here? Why...?"

The man took a deep breath and dropped his eyes. When he looked back up, he cast his eyes at their surroundings. "The Evergrove is rich with ancient magic, much like the Tower of Tarn, but even older. I have been here," he pointed down, "on this patch of grass ever since I left you with Selke because the magic keeps me alive. As long as I am here, I do not age. My body does not decay, but remains static."

"So, you're... immortal?" Lorelai asked.

"Not entirely," the man said, "but to some degree, yes."

Hallik shook his head as anger slowly boiled in his stomach. A million ways to respond came to his mind, but the anger won out. "You left your own child so that you could remain immortal? You've been so obsessed about living forever that you've lost what it means to live."

The man frowned, but nodded. "I understand your pain, my son."

"No," Hallik said. "I am not your son, and you do not understand what I feel. I knew you'd left me, but I didn't know it was for a reason so petty. Sometimes I wished you'd gone off to do something noble, or that you'd died, as if that might justify you not returning. But here you are. Doing absolutely nothing."

Elowyn placed her hand on Hallik's shoulder as heat rose to his neck. He realized his fists were clenched, but he released them. He reminded himself that Selke was no fool, and he needed to give this stranger an opportunity to explain more. The thing that really hurt and made him angry was that no amount of explaining would give him a father. No words would alleviate the years he'd suffered, feeling unwanted and discarded.

The man nodded more, eyes glistening. Several moments passed until the man spoke. "I am sorry for what you've gone through, Hallik. I realize I should introduce myself." He raised his hands to either side. "I am Tyrus."

Beside him, Elowyn gasped, but Hallik had no recognition of the name. He'd probably heard it before, but he wasn't sure why. "There is a song about you, but then you must be—" Elowyn sputtered as her eyes went wide.

"Yes, Elowyn," Tyrus nodded. "I am the same man from the song. I have been alive since before Avskild was shielded off."

Hallik could only blink. "Wait, so you're like... really old?"

"Yes," Tyrus said, "and I was banished from Dalstava by the king shortly after the shielding, not that it mattered much. I'm a Watcher, you see, but I went through Vanalf a second time in order to aid my first son through. He... did not make it, and I emerged with a curse. If I leave here, I will age rapidly and die."

"Wait, does this mean I have a brother?" Hallik asked, still trying to absorb the waterfall of information.

"He would be 143 years old if he hadn't died in Vanalf, but yes, you had a brother," Tyrus said.

Hallik let out a breath through his teeth and paced the length of the grassy clearing. "And my mother?"

Tyrus' eyes remained on the ground. He rubbed a hand across his surprisingly clean-shaven face. "She was a Voyager from Hemtved, the village northeast of here. Her responsibilities had her keeping watch over portals. She routinely came through the area, though as you've probably noticed, the beings here tend to keep a close eye on any passersby. I found myself among those who would watch as she came near. By this time, Voyagers were being hunted. The people of Avskild still believed that the Voyagers were simply going through the portals and disappearing, but I knew the truth." He tapped his head. "I couldn't resist warning her as she passed. She continued to visit here but eventually went into hiding.

"Eventually, we were wed here in the forest, but when she became pregnant, she had to return to Hemtved. There is no shelter here in the Evergrove, and this is not a safe place to have a child. There are dozens of dryads here, and, despite their good nature, or perhaps because of it, they have a tendency to steal children and try to raise them as their own. Especially baby boys, because they rarely ever have boy children, and your mother was convinced you would be a boy." Tyrus bent down and plucked a single blade of grass, rolling it in his fingers.

"It was only twelve days after your birth that your mother was murdered," Tyrus said. He sat down on the grass and ran a hand across its surface. "I can see many things from here in the Evergrove. Watchers can form powerful bonds with animals, but in my many years here, lying on the grass, I formed a bond with the island itself. I feel much of what goes on but have hardly any power to do anything about it."

"That's awful," Elowyn said.

Hallik still wasn't sure what he felt. Was he sick? Something rang in his ears, like the constant gurgling of a river or the incessant hum of insects. It made his stomach turn. "You couldn't have warned her?"

Tyrus shook his head. "I have no means to communicate across distances like that. It was only once she fell to the forest floor at the edge of the village that I knew what happened. By then it was far too late. She bled out there on the ground, and I felt every last moment. Then her lifeforce was gone. Taken by... something."

Hallik knew exactly what that something was. It was the dagger Lorelai now held. It made him wonder who'd been working as the king's assassin. "We might have the answer to what happened there," Hallik said, gesturing to Lorelai. He'd decided that it wouldn't hurt to share information with Tyrus. His earlier frustration had cooled, though it still simmered deep within.

Of her own volition, Lorelai withdrew the vampiric dagger and held it up to Tyrus. "This is the weapon King Knos was using to execute Voyagers. Bjorn says it captures the energy of the victim's soul."

"Ah," Tyrus said. He touched the weapon lightly, only placing a finger over one of the blue gemstones before withdrawing his hand. "That explains the light spirit left behind over her body then." Tyrus smiled, a toothy grin that reminded Hallik of his own.

"A light spirit?" Elowyn asked.

"Yes, I believe Hallik named it Sparky. I rather like it," Tyrus said. "Some people leave behind a great deal of energy when their souls depart. In some very rare cases, this can form light spirits, though usually they are significantly larger." As if on cue, Sparky erupted from Tyrus's back and swirled about their group. "Your mother was a strong woman, so I was not shocked by the creation of a light spirit from her death, but I was surprised by its size. It makes sense that most of her energy was captured."

"So, the dagger just contains their energy, not their soul?" Lorelai asked.

"Yes," Tyrus said.

Pained stress that Hallik hadn't realized he'd been holding onto released with the statement. Perhaps they'd all been worried about that same thing.

Tyrus continued. "Dris is a very powerful weapon. In the wrong hands, it can be terrible, as you've seen, but hold onto it. Do all of you plan on going through Vanalf?"

They all replied in the affirmative with the exception of Bjorn, who sternly said, "No."

"Its power is likely only accessible to a Vitugr with the right spells, but keep it safe in the meantime," Tyrus said. "We can speak more about Vanalf tomorrow." The sun had since gone down behind the mountain, though the sky was still bright. "We should settle in. You will all be safe here, and I can promise the dryads will not try taking any of you away as you sleep."

Bjorn immediately started scoping out the circular patch of grass as though assessing its defensibility.

Hallik still had a million questions. How long had his father been here? What did he remember of previous ages? What else did he know about his mother? Instead, he asked, "How did I end up with Selke and Elowyn?"

"Well," Tyrus said, lowering his voice. "You see, there's a secret I'll have to share with you. Though it's true I can't leave without withering, every year, I'm able to harvest a bit of the nectar from these flowers." He withdrew a small leather vial from within his trousers. "Consuming it allows me to venture outside of this domain without withering for a time. Usually, when I had collected enough of it, I would go on campaigns with other Grimnirs to fight monsters or secure portals from the other side. Selke's husband was one of my companions the last time I led such a venture, though he was quite young then.

"As soon as your mother died, I grabbed my entire inventory. I burned and buried her body there, then I took you and," Tyrus paused with a catch in his voice before continuing. "You were hungry. You cried and cried, and I couldn't help you. I just held you in my arms and cried with you, but I knew I needed someone who could take care of you." He sniffed and swallowed. "Selke had just given birth to a daughter, so I took you to her. I knew I could trust her and that she would raise you as her own. I stayed there with you for an entire week." He shook his head. "Too short a time, I know, but I was running out of serum. I would hold you all day. Oh, how I regretted letting your mother go back to Hemtved. We could have just always had one of us awake and with you."

Two crystalline tears slid down Tyrus's cheeks. "I would have stayed with you until the moment I died, but Selke reminded me that you would never know me if I died that day. You would never get the chance to remember me. You'd never get to hear your parents' story, so I knew I needed to return here and leave Sparky with Selke to lead you back to me at the right time." His eyes settled on Hallik. "I am so sorry, my boy. I wish with all my heart that things had not happened the way they did, and I have spent so many years in agony because of it, but it restores me in measure to see you here today."

Hallik could only nod. He wasn't sure he'd be able to speak past the lump in his throat. He quickly rubbed at his eyes to prevent his own tears from falling. That simmering frustration in his stomach had been replaced with mourning. Mourning for the mother he'd never known, and the pain that her absence had been to both himself and his father.

Tyrus clasped Hallik's shoulder. "We should rest. I know we are on limited time, but we will speak more in the morning. There is a serious task that remains ahead, but I believe I have a solution."

Hallik cleared his throat. "Of course," he said, fighting off the emotion that gripped at him again. This had not gone as he'd expected, and there was still so much he wanted to say, but Tyrus was right. The sky was darkening, and stars were beginning to appear. "We'll speak more in the morning, then."

CHAPTER TWENTY-EIGHT

A QUEST

Elowyn Galdre

A deep breath filled Elowyn's lungs. She blinked awake, feeling more alive than ever before. Birdsong peeped softly and the sky brightened with morning light. She sat up and saw that the rest of the crew was stirring as well, as if on cue.

Hallik bolted up to his feet. "What in all the depths?" he shouted, looking down at himself. He was completely shirtless, like his father. "Nis! Where'd you take my shirt, you little gnome?"

Elowyn didn't look far. The tunic was folded up and placed right behind Hallik at the edge of the flowers. She pointed it out to Hallik who promptly pulled it on, his shirt now looking crisp and clean.

Tyrus watched the exchange with abject confusion.

"There's a gnome that has taken a liking to Hallik," Elowyn explained. "He keeps trying to be... helpful."

"Helpful?" Hallik said, scoffing.

"Well, your tunic was a little gross," Elowyn said, "but look, it's all clean now. He must have washed it for you." She withheld a smile. She couldn't even begin to comprehend how the little gnome had managed to remove Hallik's shirt while he was sleeping, but she was starting to like Nis's behavior. She wondered if he'd start doing something to Hallik every night.

"Ah," Tyrus said, "don't undervalue such a companion. Gnomes are typically prone to helping on farms. It's very rare for them to follow a person specifically. It would be wise to leave things out for him to do. If not, he will find his own way to try and be helpful. And always, always include good food as thanks."

Hallik didn't respond, but he inspected his tunic after pulling it on. The worn sleeves and a tear in the back had all been mended. He grunted, and Elowyn smiled. She was sure he'd warm up to the extra help eventually.

After getting ready for the day, they gathered around Tyrus again. That curse he'd gotten for going through Vanalf a second time was something she'd never heard of, but it certainly explained why the students always ventured into the cave by themselves.

Tyrus clapped his hands. "There are two things I need to discuss with you, and they are the reasons for your coming here. First, a bit of a history lesson is necessary to understand what is currently at play with the portals. As I've mentioned, I have been alive for a long time. This is part of my responsibility. Much of the truth has been intentionally withheld from passing down. The songs of Elowyn's family and my firsthand experience are the few sources available. Yes, Avskild was sealed off from the rest of the world to save us from impending destruction.

"What happened all those years ago is that the Grimnir forces were spread too thin. We lost a few key battles. Losing all of Groaza to the east was especially devastating when the vampires took over. They'd found a way to turn all the dead into draugrs." Tyrus ran a hand down his face with the memory. "I believe that was the moment that King Bleyda's plan to withdraw completely first took hold. We wiped out the troll stronghold in Kelig, but the losses were so heavy that we couldn't defend Dodlenda. We had to recall Voyagers from all across the world. Many monsters weren't coordinating their efforts, but they were still causing heavy losses. The biggest blow came when a fire demon and a plague lord assaulted a secondary entrance to Vanalf together and killed every person there, including King Bleyda's daughter.

"King Bleyda brought all the Voyagers and Vitugrs to Avskild, and together they cast a spell that created the shield, sealing us off from the rest of the world. At the same time, it also sort of pinched the entire land upward, and everything around us filled in with the sea. Only the portals granted the ability to leave."

"Wait, what?" Elowyn asked, holding a hand up. She felt slightly bad for interrupting Tyrus's explanation, but this was something she'd never heard. "Avskild was lifted up from the rest of the land somehow?"

Tyrus nodded. "Yes. If seen from an outside perspective, the entire island of Avskild would look like an enormous pillar jutting out from the sea. They can't see the island however, since it is covered in a constant, swirling storm."

"This is true," Bjorn confirmed.

"How does Vanalf work then? It descends into the pillar?" Elowyn asked. "I thought it connected to other realms."

"It does," Tyrus said with a grin, "but you must understand that Vanalf functions more as a portal that connects with the Wyrm. It's a realm of itself that cannot be bound to the same physical restrictions we are accustomed to here."

Elowyn nodded, realizing how valuable Tyrus's knowledge was. The songs went into great detail about some of the events Tyrus had just mentioned, especially the battles, but what the songs lacked was the context. He was already filling in a hundred gaps in her understanding that she hadn't known were there.

Tyrus continued. "The important part about sealing off Avskild like that is that there were many of us who disagreed with the idea. I was among them. We had some powerful defenses that we could have used to keep Avskild safe. Some castles were modified to accommodate Grimnir defensive tactics effectively. Using them, we could have maintained a haven while still being able to set out on foot or through the portals if needed, but the king was fully committed to abandoning the entire world. He said it was a lost cause to try and help them. The only reason they kept any Voyagers afterwards was so that they could use the portals to ensure the integrity on both sides, since corruption of a portal from the outside has the ability to weaken the shield. I believe the reason we're in trouble now is that nobody has been able to secure the portals from the other side."

Hallik cleared his throat. "So, in order to save Avskild, we'd have to travel through each portal and make sure it's not corrupted?"

"Yes," Tyrus said. "Though I can already tell you which portal is corrupted. One was already destroyed completely, which we cannot fix, but I can sense the status of all the others from here. You'll need to survive Vanalf first, and, with luck, at least one of you will become a Voyager."

"You're sure you don't want to enter it with us, Bjorn?" Hallik asked.

"Positive," Bjorn said.

"But this was only the first item I had to discuss with you before you go," Tyrus said.

Elowyn leaned back on the grass and crossed her feet at the ankles. She felt as though she could listen to Tyrus for weeks on end. The amount of information he had was endless.

"Hallik," Tyrus said after a heaving sigh. "When I went through Vanalf the second time, I fear that I inadvertently marked our family as targets. Your older brother and I had to fight relentlessly after entering, as if everything knew where we were at all times. I likely took him to his doom. But at one point, we faced a monster that killed your brother and would have killed me if I hadn't trapped it beneath some rubble. It swore to me that it would destroy any of our family who dared enter Vanalf again. I may very well be a little superstitious on the matter, but I want you to be prepared when you enter."

Hallik only bit his lip and nodded.

"If you are adequately prepared, I believe you can make it through Vanalf and emerge quite powerful." Tyrus looked over his shoulder at the distant mountains to the north. "There is a potent weapon here on Avskild. I have felt its presence for several years now as my connection with the island deepened. I have not gone to retrieve it myself for obvious reasons, but I believe the four of you could acquire it." He kept fiddling with his fingers, one of his legs bouncing. Elowyn realized he was nervous.

"What's wrong?" Elowyn asked.

"The weapon is inside the den of a dragon," Tyrus said.

Lorelai started coughing as though she were choking.

"Is this weapon really necessary?" Hallik asked.

Tyrus nodded. "Yes. I'll explain why. The weapon is only perceivable to me while the dragon is absent. When it's in its den and, presumably, laying on the weapon, I am unable to detect either the dragon or the weapon. To me, that indicates that it has the ability to mask its wielder. If there really is some kind of magical beacon marking my family when we enter Vanalf, then the weapon offers a means of cloaking Hallik so he doesn't get assaulted by a horde of monsters as soon as you enter."

Elowyn nodded. That was all she needed to know. "Then we get the weapon. Where do we go?"

Hallik's eyes twinkled as he regarded her.

"Hold on, Elowyn," Bjorn said, though his eyes remained on Tyrus. All of them sat except for Bjorn, who stood with his hand on the hilt of his sword as if he still expected to get attacked at any moment. "There's been a dragon on Avskild all this time?"

Tyrus shrugged. "It stays on the north end of the island. We avoid it on purpose. It doesn't go out of its way to hunt humans since there are a few larger breeds of animals that live in that area, and we specifically have not built any settlements over there."

"Why hasn't it been killed?" Lorelai asked, her expression appalled.

Tyrus blinked at Lorelai as if he didn't understand the question. He opened his mouth as if to say something, but no sound came out.

Elowyn shook her head and said, "Dragons are complex creatures that are immensely powerful. They aren't monsters, so they don't go out of their way to hunt humans, and they are extremely intelligent, but still erratic."

Lorelai raised a hand up. "Which means?"

"It would probably kill everyone," Elowyn said.

"Now, now," Tyrus said. "It might not be that bad. You might even be able to slip inside the cave while it's gone and just grab the weapon and run out. That's the safest route.

It tends to spend a good bit of time out hunting, so as long as you enter soon after it leaves, you should be safe."

"What if it turns around and tries to kill us?" Lorelai asked.

"That likely won't happen," Tyrus said. "Remember, this is my own son I'm sending off to do this. I do not urge him there lightly."

"So the risk is relatively low?" Lorelai said.

Tyrus shrugged. "If you approach it wisely, yes. Just stay clear of the entrance and remain hidden until you see the dragon depart. Its den is a cave carved into the side of a mountain. It's mostly bare rock and some mosses up there, so you won't have any trees to hide behind. Ascend from the southeast side, but be wary in case it flies out that way. I've been monitoring its behavior over the years, and it usually hunts along the northern shore area, so it's not likely to fly out over you in that case."

Bjorn folded his arms. "He keeps using the word 'likely' as if that's supposed to be reassuring."

"It's admittedly dangerous and leaves a lot to chance," Tyrus said, "but again, there's usually a very long span of time where you can easily sneak in. It has a habit of leaving early in the morning, so you might want to hike up while it's still a little dark. If you get there too late, you might miss its exit and then end up waiting all day only to find it coming back."

"Let's make this simple," Hallik said. "I can enter the cave alone so that the rest of you don't have to worry about being eaten. I'll just run in there, grab the weapon, and get out."

"That's very good, Hallik," Tyrus said, "but you might need some help. There are likely a lot of things in that room, and others would be very useful in identifying the right item to take. Otherwise, you might come back here only for me to inform you that you'd grabbed the wrong thing."

"Alright, so how do we know what the right item is?" Elowyn asked.

Tyrus sighed. "It is a sword laying horizontally on the ground of the cave near the center of the dragon's resting spot. I have tried to discern all the details I can from here, but I think there are at least two other swords in the same general vicinity. At least one of those other two swords is magical as well, but it feels cursed, so you don't want to grab that one. As for the sword you want, its grip has worn away. The pommel and guard have some kind of fine carvings on them. That, or it was chewed on extensively by the dragon. The fuller extends about two thirds up the length of the blade. Other than that, it will look rather standard."

"Simple enough," Elowyn said. "Anything else we should know?"

Tyrus shrugged. "Timing is everything. If it sees you, all you can do is run and hope it doesn't care enough to come after you.

Bjorn smirked. "I suppose there are worse ways to die."

Hallik pointed over at a specific mountain. "That one?"

"Yes," Tyrus said. "The cave is about halfway up to the peak. I would send Sparky to help guide you, but I'm afraid her presence would alert the dragon. You'll have to find your own way up there."

"I should be able to handle that," Bjorn said.

"Then I recommend you be on your way. After you acquire the weapon, you'll want to return here so I can confirm you have the right sword. If you have trouble finding your way back here, then—"

"We won't," Bjorn said.

"Very well," Tyrus said as he got to his feet.

Elowyn stood, feeling as though her body were suddenly heavy. She didn't want to leave yet, she realized. Tyrus's use of Watcher magic was so unique and powerful. She could only begin to imagine all the things he'd learned. If she had parchment, she'd give it all to him and make him write everything down. He'd undoubtedly be able to fill out several tomes' worth of knowledge.

Leaving also meant that they were one step closer to Vanalf. That was the heart of it. With every fiber of her being, she wanted to become a Voyager. But if she did become a Voyager, that would mean all the weight of their problems would be on her shoulders, and she wasn't sure she'd be ready.

CHAPTER TWENTY-NINE

THE BEAST

Jaysen Bjorn

Bjorn stood at the edge of the grove, waiting for Hallik to say his goodbyes to his father. Their little meeting this morning had taken only a few moments, leaving them plenty of time to start trekking toward the mountain. The morning sun still filtered through the tall pine trees to the east.

Tyrus's motivations remained unclear to Bjorn. It felt like a strange mission. Steal a magic weapon from a dragon, then bring it back to this mysterious man claiming to be Hallik's father. All while keeping them from getting to Vanalf. He ran his thumb across one of his knives as though shaving the finger.

The density of magic creatures within Bjorn's immediate vicinity was somewhat unnerving. He'd had difficulty sleeping last night, and that little gnome had once again infiltrated their camp. It didn't seem right for the gnome to be so stealthy. At least they were mostly docile creatures. He hadn't seen dryads before, but he'd caught sight of them more than a dozen times since they'd come here. They looked nearly identical to humans, though their skin was tinged with green, gray, and brown in a strange pattern, as though they were covered in strips of bark, and their hair, kept short, was often streaked with strands of blonde, red, and brown.

It wasn't just dryads hiding on the fringes, watching them. There were other faces, less discernible, hiding in the plants themselves. If he observed his periphery, he could swear that some of the bushes were moving, and even some of the smaller flowers. There were many things about Avskild that were different, but the idea of docile or friendly magical creatures was the starkest distinction. Everything in Kelig seemed like it was bent on eradicating humanity. Even with the monsters that were appearing on Avskild, it still felt like a respite to be here.

Finally, Bjorn's three companions joined him at the edge of the grove. "I will lead the way," Bjorn said. He had a lot of experience forging his own path back in Kelig. Many of his hunts had taken him deeper into the wilderness than he would have liked at times. Having this many people with him reminded him of the last time he'd had any semblance of companionship, and that had not ended well.

Despite Elowyn's assertion that Bjorn was more of a lone wolf, he felt drawn to these people. Elowyn and Hallik could be immature and annoying, and Lorelai was slightly suspect, yet the feeling remained. Perhaps it was because of their determination. They actively sought to do what they could to help their island. That same force simmered within Bjorn's own chest. It was why he hadn't given up after his father died. It was why he hadn't given up after watching an entire village burn, or from watching people he cared about die right before his eyes.

No, those things fueled him onward. Every monster responsible for such tragedy would suffer. He would not stop until his list was complete, and then he'd start it all over again.

The going was rough for a while as Bjorn led them through thick undergrowth. It wasn't until the grove was far behind them that they finally reached the tall pines. The undergrowth there was thinner and shorter as the tall trees blocked out much of the light and covered the ground with their fallen needles. They walked in relative silence, slowly gaining altitude as the sun got higher.

Bjorn decided they'd trek through the forest as long as possible until they got up over the next foothill where the trees grew thinner as they gave way to low grasses. It took them more than half of the day to reach that point. Then the route got steeper, and Bjorn had to lead them at a gentler elevation across the foothill instead of straight up. He wanted to hike the next ridge so he could get a clear view of their destination before working on ascending the mountain itself.

They wouldn't have to go to the peak, thankfully, but Bjorn had to wonder how easy it would be to find a dragon's giant cave on the side of a mountain. All he had to work with were Tyrus's vague instructions. The fact that he'd taken directions from a man who'd never actually been there made the task seem that much more elusive. But Bjorn would find a way. Though he'd only had to scale mountains twice before, he was more confident in his own ability than he was in that ancient man's magic.

"Do you think we'll get there by tomorrow?" Elowyn asked Bjorn.

He nodded. "It's possible. We'll need time to locate the actual cave, and then we'll need more time to make sure we approach it early in the morning so we can verify when the dragon actually leaves."

"Agreed," Hallik said. "That way, we can maximize time looking for the sword in case it's hard to find."

"Exactly," Bjorn said.

"I'm good with whatever plan doesn't involve getting eaten by a dragon," Lorelai said.

"Right," Hallik said, "and there's one other detail you missed, Bjorn. My father says that there are several other magical items in the dragon's cave. He advised not grabbing the other objects because he's not certain what they might do, and there's the very real possibility that they could be cursed."

Bjorn grunted. "Don't worry about me. I'm perfectly content with not having any such accouterments."

"Unless there's another good dagger, of course," Hallik said with a smirk, then hurried to add, "but the next dagger we find goes to me. I'm tired of being the only one who doesn't have one."

Elowyn laughed. "Hallik, you're about to get a powerful sword. I'm not sure you'll be needing a dagger after that."

"I'm sure Bjorn has a good argument to counter such a claim. He has a sword and a crossbow, and yet he still finds it necessary to carry a hundred more weapons."

"There's nothing wrong with a spare blade," Bjorn admitted. Lorelai's eyes sparkled at the conversation. She said nothing, but Bjorn suspected if there was anybody they needed to worry about taking a cursed item, it was her.

They'd crested the hill when Bjorn paused to get a good look at the mountain, squinting as he scanned its surface.

The very top of the mountain was still capped in snow, little lines of gray stone peeking out where snow hadn't settled.

A dragon resting in such a cold environment seemed unnatural. Maybe it was lower down than he thought.

"Perhaps over there," Hallik said, pointing to the eastern side of the mountain.

Bjorn couldn't tell where exactly Hallik was indicating, but he simply nodded in acknowledgment. "Let's keep our eyes out to see if we can spot the dragon returning. That will at least give us a better idea of where it goes." He had a good idea of where they should go to reach the mountain. They were already near its base, but they needed to pass over two more foothills before they could start truly ascending.

There were small shrubs that clung to the sides of the hills. Bjorn decided to keep their path going alongside them. In an otherwise open expanse, they would perhaps offer at least a bit of cover should the need arise. They were all gambling. That was the thing that made Bjorn most nervous. Sure, it was unlikely that the dragon would head in this direction, but that was little reassurance. Dragons were not on his list. They were simply beings—primordial beings at that, and practically gods among the natural world—but they weren't monsters.

If it caught sight of them though, he knew there would be no escape. It would be a death sentence.

The sun beat down on them, and Bjorn was soon missing the cover of the trees. A small valley stretched down to their left with a stream running through the middle. From their spot near the ridge of the mountain on the right side, they had a good vantage for a few miles. There was very little activity down in the valley, but he did spot a rabbit at one point and a hawk at another. The day was thankfully uneventful, but that only made Bjorn feel an increasing sense of threat. Perhaps even the monsters knew not to be this close to a dragon's den.

It was early evening by the time they reached the base of the main peak. They'd probably need a whole extra day just to locate the dragon's den. He was hoping they'd be able to spot it today, which would let them know where to hide to ensure the dragon's departure. If they were lucky, they could find the den tomorrow and just run in and grab the sword rather quickly. That would save them a whole day. He could only dream.

There was a stillness on the mountains. No birdsong, no wind, just stillness. The absence of sound made Bjorn uncomfortable.

That was the moment a dark shadow passed overhead. A massive, sun-blotting shadow. Accompanying it was a terrible whooshing sound that made his ears pop. A gust of air batted into him as he glanced up.

It appeared that all of Tyrus's "likelihoods" were wrong.

CHAPTER THIRTY

A KING

Lind Hjordis

Lind hobbled under the castle gate, making his way into the city. Though he used a crutch, both his legs still burned with a dull ache. The pain was manageable. Selke told him that shouldn't walk around too long before putting his legs back up, but there was much business to attend to. They would need to organize a unit to try and get to Vanalf. If possible, they'd want to escort the students so that they could safely enter the cave, then hope for a few Voyagers to emerge.

Skelldwyn walked just behind Lind. He'd been a great help. Word had spread quickly about the need for all the Grimnirs to regroup. Most of the militia had also never returned from the battle, but a handful of them had managed to make it back, which was more than they could say about the entire Grimnir army.

Since swearing himself to Lind, Skelldwyn had been armed with a spear and shield, though he still didn't really know how to use either. Hopefully he'd get a chance to learn before he'd have to use them.

Dalstava felt different since the last time Lind had walked its streets. A lot of the hustle and bustle had simmered down, and people clung together, talking in groups or otherwise standing around outside as if unsure what to do with themselves. Word of the Grimnir Guard's defeat and the death of King Knos had spread quickly. They didn't know what the future held. King Knos had no living relatives. All of the primary leaders had died, and Lind was the highest-ranking person left in the whole city, but few people seemed to know how far down that hierarchy went.

Lind was known, however, as the man in charge of Castle Vrodr, which meant that he'd been bombarded with questions. He could only imagine the rumors that had gotten out regarding his injury. Everyone stared at him as he limped toward the Tower of Tarn.

"Who all did you manage to gather?" Lind asked over his shoulder.

Skelldwyn cleared his throat. "Thirteen Grimnirs, Master Hjordis. There are also some thirty or forty militiamen who have gathered with them, but I think a few other citizens have slipped in among those ranks."

Thirteen. Nature's rays, it was worse than he'd imagined. He knew there were still more than that scattered across the island, but it wouldn't be many. Perhaps three or four in each of the villages.

It made him wonder. If he'd gone with the army, would that have been enough to turn the tide? Could he have saved some of them? But if he'd been with the army, he wouldn't have been here to stop the ashimal.

"Lind," a woman said, approaching him as he proceeded up the street. He recognized her as Huldir, the stern woman who sold her stock of ale, tea, and sometimes clothing to the castle staff. She had two children, but her husband had died a couple years ago after falling off their roof while trying to mend it. She'd been powering on ever since, always the proprietor of some new business venture. "Is it true that an army of trolls is going to attack the city?"

"We still need more details, Huldir," Lind said. "I will see if we can get some eyes out there to get a full report, but I will let everyone know as soon as I find out more."

Huldir reached out and gave Lind's arm a quick squeeze. She glanced down at his legs. "Take care of yourself. We may not all be Grimnirs, but many of us are willing to help where we can."

Lind paused and nodded to her. Just because the ranks of Grimnirs had been dwindling didn't mean that their people weren't strong, or that they wouldn't be willing to lay down their lives if needed. They were still Avskildians after all. "Thank you, Huldir," he said, and continued on.

He'd been hoping the pain in his legs would recede if he just got to using them, but he was wrong. The pain remained consistent with each step. There were many times in his life that he'd been grateful the Tower of Tarn was not immediately beside Castle Vrodr, but now was not one of those times.

More people approached him with questions as he made his way. He was not prepared to answer all the concerns, but it was clear word had gotten out that Lind was sort of in charge. A crowd had gathered outside the tower. If the questions were constant before, now it was a full-on assault.

"Is the king dead?"

"Where is Captain Vigsen?"

"Did we lose Vanalf?"

"Are the portals destroyed?"

"Are we going to die?"

"Are there monsters all over the island?"

Lind wished he could reassure them, but all of the worst possible things were indeed that: possible. Very, very possible. Lind raised his free hand to them and tried shouting over all the questions. "Thank you for your concerns. I need to discuss everything with the others. Once we have a plan, I will let you all know. We may all have a role to play in the next few days, but we will pull through this, as we always have."

He didn't want to say more for now. He didn't dare. If they all knew how bleak their chances were, perhaps more of them would enlist in retaking Vanalf, but he still wasn't sure what they were up against.

They slung questions at him up until the moment the tower doors closed behind him. The pain in his legs continued to burn and he yearned to sit down, but there was another crowd of people gathered just inside, waiting for him. Rest would come later, but now he needed to address them.

This group was a little more patient, and they were mostly armed for battle. It seemed the general public expected an assault on the city at any moment.

Skelldwyn remained at his side as Lind addressed them. "Thank you all for coming. There are many questions that we cannot yet answer. My purpose in gathering us together is so we might assess the situation and plan accordingly.

We will need reconnaissance and proper defense teams. We have two primary objectives." He held up a single finger. "We need to ensure the safety of our citizens, not only those here in Dalstava, but in the four villages as well." He held up another finger. "We need to secure the entrance to Vanalf. We currently have no Voyagers among the ranks of Grimnirs. Something is causing erratic reactions from the portals, which means monsters will continue to appear on Avskild. We cannot regain control of them without Voyagers. I have plans for how we can accomplish these goals and have already set some things in motion to secure victory."

Lind spent the next several moments getting them grouped up. There were three other Vitugrs, six Watchers, and four Valtyras. With such a force, they would even struggle to overthrow another draugr attack like they'd had the other day. With so few Grimnirs, there wouldn't be enough energy for any kind of sustained effort; a Vitugr was exceptionally susceptible to magic fatigue if they had to cast spells continually. Another attack would be devastating, but he supposed if they could keep vigilant watch for danger, they could retreat behind the walls and hold out for a few months from within the city.

But even in such a case, it would only be a temporary delay of their utter destruction. The number of monsters would swell until the island was overtaken. Their only choice was to retake Vanalf or die a slow death.

The Valtyras were broken into two parties. Each group would take a Watcher with them to fly out and scout the area around Vanalf. Lind wished he knew what had allowed the troll army to remain so elusive, but hopefully this method would allow them to learn more. If they were outnumbered, they'd have to play it smart in order to take them out in small numbers or perhaps try to sneak students into Vanalf.

The rest of the troops were split into squadrons to maintain the city defenses. Ideally, they'd round up more people for the militia. From what he could guess, there were several thousand people in Dalstava, and they should be able to get most of the adults to take up arms. There simply wasn't an alternative.

"Where is she?" the voice echoed through the room like the scream of a ghost.

Lind recognized that voice, but it was more haunting than he'd ever heard. His axe glowed as he withdrew it from his belt in one hand, still clutching the crutch in his other.

From the back of the room emerged none other than King Knos. He looked like he'd been dragged across the forest floor for hours. His hair was disheveled. His clothes were torn to the point of rags, and he had several cuts and bruises across his mostly exposed skin. He looked angrier than a mother bear whose cubs had been eaten by a dire wolf.

"Where's that cur, Lorelai?" Knos demanded.

Nobody in the room said a word.

Lind regarded the troops. "Scouting squads, head out immediately. We have no time to waste." They hesitantly moved toward the exit. Then he turned his attention to Knos. "Knos, you have some explaining to do."

CHAPTER THIRTY-ONE

DRAGON'S DEN

Lorelai Harkral

Screaming seemed like a perfectly appropriate thing to do as Lorelai gazed up at the enormous winged lizard that flew overhead. No air escaped her lungs as Bjorn clapped a hand around her mouth and pulled her to the ground.

The dragon was large enough that it held an entire whale in the claws of its hind legs as it flew. It didn't even seem to notice them as it passed over. If Bjorn hadn't pulled her down, she assumed that the powerful gust of wind created by its beating wings would have been enough to put her on her back.

It went over them in a flash, its scales shimmering in shades of blue, gray, and white as if to camouflage it with the sky. The beast must have been moving faster than anything she'd ever seen.

Bjorn released her from his grip as they all whipped their heads around to see where it was going. The dragon tipped its wings and pumped them a few more times as it rounded the mountain's side and disappeared from sight.

They all remained in their places, silent as night.

"Well..." Hallik said, straightening up. "We're not dead, and we at least know we're in the right place. I say we find somewhere to bunk down and hopefully hide."

Bjorn exhaled. "We definitely don't want it to see us in the morning. Seeing us at the end of the day after it had such a massive catch is one thing, but if it sees us in the morning before it has had an opportunity to hunt, we might not be so lucky."

Lorelai still couldn't comprehend that something so large was able to fly. It didn't seem possible. But then again, that wingspan was absolutely enormous while its body was long and thin.

"Was it holding a whale?" Elowyn asked, face twisted in confusion.

Lorelai released a nervous laugh. "Yes, that's what it seemed like."

"Nature's rays," Elowyn muttered.

"I suggest we keep moving," Bjorn said, following the dragon's path.

Lorelai went after him, still in a daze but conscious enough that she knew they needed to find their hiding place before it got dark. Soon enough, they'd be on the east side of the mountain where the sun was already casting a deep, long shadow. They hadn't seen exactly where the dragon had gone, but they at least knew it was around this way.

Bjorn was leading them quicker than before, but Lorelai was all for it. A new surge of energy blazed through her. She tried not to show it, but her excitement was growing. She fantasized about the contents of the dragon's cave. Tyrus had left such a mystery around the various magical items inside, and she could only wonder what kind of powerful things the dragon had hoarded over the years. He'd warned against taking anything besides the sword, but she had to admit, the very idea of the magical objects had her chest thumping.

They walked on as the light in the sky continued to dwindle. The path Bjorn led them on was increasingly difficult, with more rocks and boulders to climb over. A small swarm of insects zipped by in a writhing mass, but that was the only other life they saw.

Bjorn stopped suddenly, holding his hand out behind him. He pointed further up the edge of the mountain. A spout of steam issued from the mountainside then slowly cleared, revealing a massive opening in the side of the rock-face.

They'd found it.

Wordlessly, they all started looking for a good place to bunk down. Hallik found a spot where he could hide under a leaning boulder, and Elowyn said she could squish next to him.

Bjorn found another nook within a fissure in the mountain. "You take this spot," Bjorn said to Lorelai. He handed her a small bush with little leaves that he'd plucked up. "Put this down over the top of you after you settle in."

And that was it. They'd hunker down and try to get some sleep before waiting for the dragon to leave its cave in the morning.

As Lorelai nestled into her crevice, shoulders pressed uncomfortably against the stone, she knew she wouldn't get much sleep. Even with her blanket wrapped around her, the night air was frigid. She shivered, whether with nervous energy or the cold, she couldn't tell.

Tomorrow, they would raid a dragon's den.

***

Lorelai stirred awake even before Bjorn patted her foot. Her sleep had been so restless that she wasn't sure it had helped at all. The sky was a dark shade of blackish purple as the first signs of sunrise filtered through the shield's misty shroud on the horizon. The bush he'd given her was wedged over her in the crevice, providing a bit of cover should the dragon fly by and look down. At the speed that creature flew, she'd be surprised if it could spot her at all, but she certainly didn't mind the extra security.

"Just wanted to make sure you're ready to go," Bjorn said in a growly whisper. "We're not sure when the dragon will leave, but we're keeping an eye on the cave. We'll want to run in as soon as it's out, but it looks like a bit of a climb to get inside, which will take a fair amount of time. If it returns as late today as it did yesterday, then we'd have several hours to scour the cave, but I'm hoping we can get in and out as quickly as possible. I don't want to linger here any longer than necessary."

That was quite the long explanation coming from Bjorn. Perhaps the stiff man was opening up.

"Alright, thank you," Lorelai said, sitting up and stretching her aching muscles. She hadn't done this much hiking since, well, ever, and her hips were not accustomed to the exertion. After crawling out, she got ready before joining the others. Bjorn had since disappeared somewhere, but Elowyn and Hallik were crouched under their boulder.

"Did you sleep much?" Lorelai asked them.

"Hallik sure did," Elowyn whispered. "He passed out as soon as we laid down."

"It was a long day," Hallik said with his classic smirk.

A rumble in the ground made Hallik's smirk vanish. They all braced themselves, but the rumble was gone as soon as it happened.

"I think our friend is awake," Elowyn said, slinging her bag over her shoulder.

Lorelai did the same, and they all waited. Several more moments passed, but they felt no other sign of the dragon's movement. The sky was getting brighter by the second, and Bjorn still hadn't returned. Right when she started wondering if he'd gone by himself, his footsteps betrayed his approach as he slid down beside them.

"Be ready," Bjorn said. "I think it's about to go." Before he finished the last word, another rumble shook the ground and the unsettling sound of massive, batting wings vibrated the air.

Bjorn scrambled away, climbing back up to wherever he'd been hiding earlier.

Lorelai leaned toward Hallik and Elowyn, but the noise of the wings diminished. The only sound was their breathing as they glanced around at each other.

A whistle came from around the other side of the boulder followed by Bjorn's voice. "Go time."

The three of them hurried out from behind their cover.

Bjorn waited to see they were following before he dashed across the side of the mountain.

Lorelai was positive she already had a blister on her left foot, but she ignored it and moved to keep pace with the others. Elowyn and Hallik seemed completely unaffected by all their hiking. She had to remind herself that Grimnir students underwent daily rigorous training that kept them in peak physical condition. And from what she'd gathered, Bjorn must have spent much of his life traveling on his hunts.

Lorelai didn't like to be the weak link. She wasn't unhealthy or unfit by any means, but the comparison with the others was evident. The lack of sleep hadn't helped much either, but the brisk morning air brought her right to her senses.

They kept a steady pace as Bjorn hurried ahead. Oftentimes, they had to climb up the rockface, but there were thankfully plenty of handholds that Bjorn was able to locate as they navigated up. She was grateful she didn't have to find the path herself.

As they grew closer, she realized the entrance to the cave was even more enormous than she'd thought. It looked as though it had been carved by the dragon's own claws, as there were several deep gouges in the surrounding stone. Whether those came before or after the dragon had claimed this as its lair remained a mystery.

It was one of these gouges in the stone that ended up being part of their final ascent to the cave. Their bodies fit inside the groove, Hallik's head nearly touching the top as they stood sideways to work their way up. It continued all the way up to the lip of the cave.

Hallik heaved a sigh of relief, but Elowyn shushed him.

Lorelai looked back out over the land below. At the bottom of the mountain was an immense collection of bones. The stretch directly beneath them was practically a cliff, but a thin forest arced out to either side, forming around a crescent shaped fjord that led out to the sea beyond. A fall from here would be certain death. She gulped and stepped back into the cave.

"It's... warm," Elowyn said, holding her arms out as they all moved deeper.

Lorelai felt it as well. It was like somebody's muggy breath washing over her entire body. A trickle of fear rippled down her back. "Are we sure the dragon left?" Lorelai whispered.

"Yes," Bjorn said, "I saw it with my own eyes." He didn't hesitate to stride directly into the cave.

Lorelai allowed herself to observe the cave in greater detail. She'd expected it to be shallow with a rounded back wall, but it extended further than she thought, and there was an initial upward incline that prevented her from seeing all the way to the rear. She had to follow Bjorn further up in order to see better inside.

Hallik practically ran.

As Lorelai rounded the incline, her eyes widened. Something toward the back of the cave glowed orange-red, dark and deep like simmering embers. She prayed in her heart to any gods that might listen that there wasn't some other dragon curled up back there, but certainly Tyrus would have known about something like that.

More bones littered the cave, some of them still fresh with strands of flesh. An eagle darted away from them at their passing, and even some kind of lynx hurried out of the cave. Perhaps they ran in here after the dragon left to eat the scraps. She could imagine a whole ecosystem centered around the life of this one creature.

They passed the half-crushed remains of a giant crab, one that could have snipped Lorelai in half with one of its claws. The northern shores of Avskild were said to be riddled with the animals.

Besides rocks and bones, the floor of the cave also glittered with several trinkets. Perhaps the dragon had a penchant for collecting metal objects. All of Lorelai's trepidation vanished in an instant. She held her bag against her body to keep it from bouncing and ran in behind Hallik.

"Hurry," Hallik said. "Let's find that sword and get out of here."

There was a bowl-shaped recession in the floor at the back of the cave. Within that bowl and around the edges, metal items were strewn about—nails, joists, helmets, shields, pins, cutlery, and even coins, which seemed like the most prevalent item of all. There were other objects as well, like bits of amber and several, oval-shaped objects that glistened like silver-blue glass.

She remembered Tyrus's warning about the potential curses, but she bent down to look at some of the objects, realizing that they were actually scales from the dragon's own body.

"Tyrus said it would be near the middle," Elowyn reminded them all.

Lorelai slowly progressed forward, but her eyes darted across the floor of the cave, hoping to alight across another magical artifact. She recognized her own dangerous inclination, but the idea of finding something else powerful itched at her mind. Besides, the dragon had no use for such things. It would be a waste to let them rot in here for eternity when she could use them herself. Now, of all times, was the perfect opportunity to take such risks, for the sake of Avskild.

A growing sense of urgency gnawed at her stomach, and her search became more frantic. How would she know if an object was magical or not? Would it glow? Would it speak to her? She went so far as to bend down and touch a few things of interest, particularly weapons she saw, but none of them stood out to her.

"I found a bunch of swords," Bjorn said, voice echoing through the large, open cave.

Lorelai ignored him and kept searching, panic rising, but then she saw it. It was a simple ornament attached to a thin, silver chain. It looked so delicate, but despite probably being trampled endless times by a dragon, it was remarkably undamaged. The symbol was that of a serpent, woven and knotted all around itself, with two eyes made of tiny amber stones. Without hesitation, she pulled it over her head and tucked the necklace into her shirt, the silver chain hidden behind her hair.

The swelling panic in her chest and stomach subsided. She had no idea if the item was magic, but her instinct told her it was why she was here to begin with. When it settled over her skin, the metal was not cool as she'd expected, but warm.

"Lorelai." Bjorn's voice was gruff as it echoed toward her.

His voice startled her. He gestured with his head for her to join them.

Lorelai smoothed her tunic reflexively. She was accustomed to wearing dresses, but when she'd joined up with their venture, they'd given her the standard outfit of a Grimnir student with pants and a tunic. It was a much better fit for their type of activity, but she missed that extra layer with the pinned apron. She liked to keep a second belt underneath where she could conceal her possessions a little better. She cleared her throat and walked over to join them.

Hallik was rifling through a few weapons that were lined up.

"Careful," Elowyn chided as Hallik touched each one. "Tyrus said one of them seemed cursed."

Hallik only grunted. "I think I have it down to these two," he said, pointing two of them out. Both were missing the grips for the handles.

"That one," Elowyn said, pointing at one with an elaborately carved pommel and guard. "The other sword is worn away along the blade more and the fuller extends too high."

"I think she's right," Bjorn said.

"That's my inclination as well," Hallik said, placing his hand over the hilt. "Please don't be cursed." He picked it up, using his other hand to hold the blade. He tried holding it aloft to see it better in the light coming through the cave entrance, but at that moment, something flicked across the opening. A familiar, deep thrum reverberated from outside.

Lorelai shared a horrified expression with the rest of them. She looked around frantically, wondering if there was anywhere they could go. Was it possible to hide in here?

Bjorn moved first, patting Hallik's shoulder before he ran toward the back of the cave where water ran down the stone wall. Lorelai hadn't noticed the water before, but it probably streamed down deep into the mountain.

A sound like thunder vibrated through her entire body as she stumbled after them. Perhaps Hallik had picked up the cursed sword instead of the right one, but one glance back told her that wasn't what had gone wrong.

The ground rumbled beneath her as she beheld the massive head of the dragon snake into the cave. Its mouth opened in a roar that made thunder seem like a water drop. The very sight of the beast's head, with rows of teeth longer than she was tall, nearly paralyzed her, but Elowyn grabbed Lorelai's hand, pulling her onward.

The dragon continued clawing its way into the cave, and when its eyes settled on them, a sound issued from its mouth like that of water splashing against a hot pan.

They were dead. By the depths, they were so dead.

"It's our only chance," she heard Bjorn say, but her heart pounded so hard in her chest that she could hardly breathe.

"Maybe it's a nice dragon," Hallik said.

The dragon's teeth were fully bared as it flashed a dangerous sneer. In two more steps, the dragon would probably gnash at them. Its tongue flicked out as if to taste them, and she felt her head start to get lighter.

"We have to jump," Bjorn said.

Jump? What were they talking about?

"I guess drowning can't be much worse than getting eaten," Elowyn said. She slapped Hallik's shoulder and jumped down into the stream of water that ran down the side of the cave. She disappeared into the hole, wherever the water led.

Lorelai's eyes widened with even more horror. That stream would lead through the heart of the mountain. There was no way they'd survive that.

"Elowyn!" Hallik shouted just before jumping in after her.

Bjorn turned to Lorelai. "Big breath," he said.

Lorelai couldn't believe what she was doing. She could hardly breathe as it was. The air behind her grew insanely hot, but she didn't dare look back. She sucked in a sharp breath and fell in after Hallik.

CHAPTER THIRTY-TWO

DROWNING

Hallik

Blackness surrounded Hallik as he continued to fall, water all around him. At the back of his mind, he was afraid he was about to die. More than that however, he was angry. Angry that Elowyn had jumped down without much consideration. Perhaps the dragon wouldn't have killed them. But this? This was certain death.

He clutched the sword in his hand, holding it close to his body, worried that all his bouncing around off the stones would result in stabbing himself. He wasn't sure how much longer he'd be able to hold his breath, but if it came down to drowning or getting stabbed and bruised, he'd take drowning.

His descent curved out sharply, and one of his heels caught hard against something which tugged his leg back with a crisp pain. A second later he fell to a sheer drop-off with nothing around him but water. He splashed down, hanging suspended beneath the surface for a while. Everything was still black. He stroked, trying to find some kind of surface, though he felt he was getting dragged to the side at the same time. Just as his lungs felt like they would burst and he'd be forced to try and breathe the water, his head broke the surface. He took a gasping breath.

"Elowyn!" he shouted immediately, but there was no answer. The water kept pulling him. He flailed around him in the darkness but felt no surface. Perhaps this was some kind of lake deep inside the mountain. The air was stale and left him gasping as though it did little to help.

The current picked up speed. His head thunked across something, and he took another deep breath, bracing himself for yet another drop-off. Sure enough, the rushing water pushed him through another narrow tunnel, too steep for him to try and swim. He had to let the water carry him. He braced the sword against his body and held his other arm up around his face, hoping it would prevent him from getting bashed too hard. The last thing he needed was to go unconscious, but that seemed inevitable. His eyes, ears, mouth, throat—everything burned with a tight pressure.

He came to yet another lull where his head was able to surface. He gasped more, breathing the insufficient air before plunging for a third time. Or was it the fourth? It could have been hours. For all he knew, he was already dead, and this was merely part of the abyss he would suffer unless his body was recovered. He had no idea how long the process repeated itself, but a fire in his heart urged him to open his eyes.

Despite being beneath the surface of the water, he thought he saw a glimmer of light. He swam toward it with whatever remaining strength he had. *Elowyn.* Reaching her was all his mind would cling to. If he managed to get to her, he'd give her the sternest talking-to of her life.

The light ahead grew larger as the tightness in his chest continued to increase. Bubbles rippled out in front of him, distorting the light, refracting it into fragments, each one as unreachable as his destination. He realized too late that those bubbles were the air leaving his own lungs.

The light ahead vanished.

***

Water ejected from Hallik's throat with such violence that it burned his throat. He spewed again and gulped air in great, heaving gasps. He rolled over to hands and knees, trying to gather his strength. His bare fingers curled into dark, thick mud. A light breeze felt cold against his soaked body, but most importantly, there was light. He was outside on the bank of a pond that gurgled with water.

He was outside.

The sun glared down from directly overhead. How long had he been falling through the streams?

Miraculously, the sword was still clutched in his hand. He loosened his grip and shook out his fingers.

"Elowyn," Hallik said, voice hoarse. He struggled up to his feet. His lungs still burned. He had no idea how he'd survived or where he was, and the feeling that he needed to vomit didn't subside. "Elowyn!" He coughed more, chest tightening with every heartbeat.

Elowyn was not dead. She couldn't be.

He climbed the bank of the river and mounted a large rock beside the grasses growing near the top. Despair clawed at him, but he fought it back and kept shouting for her. "Elowyn!"

"Hallik!" The voice that called for him was distant, but he recognized it instantly. He jumped down from the rock and ran along the side of the river, following the sound of the voice as he kept calling her name.

The voice repeated, shouting for Hallik. It got closer and closer. A smile split his face and he ran harder, wet boots sloshing on the sandy shore. She would be just around the next bend. "Elowyn!" he said as soon as he came around, his smile as big as it had ever been.

His smile disappeared immediately, elation replaced by rage.

He whipped the sword out in front of him and ground his teeth at the new sight. Before him was a monster, not unlike a spider, with six legs protruding from its elongated body that ended in a massive, round abdomen the size of a canoe. The entire body was black and poxed with brown, but its face was like a featherless bird's, dark pink skin shining atop a bald head. Its beak opened and a perfect mimicry of Elowyn's voice emitted from its throat. "Hallik!"

Elowyn lay upon the creature's back, parts of her wrapped in silky threads as if the beast had been in the middle of putting her in a cocoon.

An extra set of mandibles descended from the beast's beak, and it rose up to its full height, standing on four of its legs while the front two were held high, prepared to strike.

Hallik didn't hesitate as he roared and stepped toward it. The legs jabbed at him, twitching as fast as a striking snake. He ducked to one side, sword flashing. Managing to dodge one leg, he completely severed the other. The disgusting, hairy limb fell in a spew of green and orange goop. He swung again, aiming for one of the legs it was standing on. This leg too fell away in a slimy mess. The monster hissed and snapped at his neck, but he whipped the sword up, blade arcing across its bald-skinned face. It reared back, jabbing at Hallik as it did so. He moved quickly, hacking off the very tip of that leg before lunging forward and thrusting the tip of the sword through what might have been considered the monster's chest.

It tried to limp away from him, hissing all the while. Elowyn bounced on its back, her eyes closed, her skin pale. She could already be dead for all he knew.

Hallik did not relent. He pursued, hacking again, severing the final leg on the same side. The beast tried crawling with its broken appendages, their severed ends still leaking foul smelling ichor as it hissed. It tried using Elowyn's voice again, telling him to stop. That alone wrenched his heart, but her body was still clearly laid across its back. When it snapped at him again, it jarred him back to his senses. There was only one way forward. He chopped across its middle. In two swings, he severed the thorax in two.

The beast stopped hissing, but its legs still twitched. He ignored that and went straight for Elowyn's body. "Don't you dare be dead!" he said to her as he scooped her off the monster's shuddering corpse. The skin of her neck felt cold, but that did not deter him. He carried her back a bit to where the sand was flat and laid her down. He tore the strands of web from her body and ran a hand down her face, brushing the hair aside.

Her mouth hung open.

Further up the bank, Bjorn came sputtering onto the beach, followed almost immediately by Lorelai.

Lorelai gasped upon seeing Hallik, but he shook his head at her, still unsure if Elowyn was alive.

"Come on, Elowyn," Hallik pleaded.

Lorelai ran over and dropped beside Hallik. She said nothing, but held her hand over Elowyn's open mouth and left it there for a moment. "She's breathing," Lorelai said.

Hallik released a long sigh of relief. "There was some monster that had her," he said, gesturing behind himself. "I killed it, but I don't know if it did something to her."

Bjorn growled at that and tramped behind Hallik.

"Does she have any wounds?" Lorelai asked as she started looking around Elowyn's body.

Hallik found a couple scrapes and cuts along her arm and one on her ankle, but nothing seemed too amiss. It was then that he realized he was shaking. His hands trembled and his chest quivered. How could Elowyn be so careless as to jump into the water? Didn't she know how important she was? She couldn't do things like this that would threaten her life.

But they were all alive, and the dragon might have very well just eaten them.

Elowyn's eyes fluttered open, and she took a sharp breath. As her green eyes settled on Hallik, all his anger, fear, and frustration melted away.

"Elowyn." Hallik bent over her and gave her the tightest hug.

"We made it," Elowyn said, weakly patting Hallik's back. "Wait." She pushed Hallik off her and sat up. "There was a monster!"

"I got it," Hallik said. "I came looking for you as soon as I surfaced. That monster had you on its back. What happened?"

"It's over here," Bjorn said, interrupting the conversation.

Elowyn not-so-steadily got to her feet.

"Are you alright?" Hallik asked.

"No," Elowyn said. "I feel as though I got chewed on and spit out by a toothless whale. As soon as I came out, that creature was already here, staring down at me from the bank. I turned to run away, but I think I must have blacked out. My vision was already spinning when I first stood up. That's all I remember before waking up just now." She gripped Hallik's arm as the two of them walked back over to look at the monster Hallik had killed. He'd definitely never heard of something like this before.

Bjorn growled. "Lorelai, do you want to use Dris on it? I've never seen one of these before. Perhaps we can learn something about it."

Lorelai covered her mouth and nose with a hand, but she nodded and drew out the dagger.

"It seems like some kind of arapede," Elowyn said, her nose crinkling in disgust.

"That sounds familiar," Hallik said, vaguely recalling a reference to them from a class sometime last year.

"Lind shared a story that mentioned one a couple times," Elowyn said, "though the one in the story was quite large. It had run its webs across the treetops of half a forest."

"Oh yeah," Hallik said, remembering in gruesome detail how the story mentioned several dangling corpses that had been sucked dry and left as hollowed husks. The arapede was supposedly half as tall as the trees. "But this thing doesn't seem that big, and honestly," he paused to heft the new sword, "it was relatively easy to kill. It was even on the verge of running away after I chopped off some of its legs."

"Perhaps this was a young one," Elowyn mused.

"Let's not linger to meet its parents, then," Bjorn said, dumping the water from one of his black boots.

"Agreed," Lorelai said, looking to the sky. "Any idea how we get back?"

Bjorn regarded the mountain behind them. "Yes. We've actually emerged on the southwest side of the mountain, so we're already on the right side. We just need to head further south, though we should probably follow this stream for a while."

"Let's get to it, then," Lorelai said. She clutched a hand to the base of her neck. The motion disturbed the neck of her tunic just enough to reveal a thin silver chain that he hadn't noticed before.

Hallik pulled the old sword that still hung from his belt. It had smacked across his leg more than a few times while going through the underground stream, and his skin felt raw. He placed the new sword in its place and sighed. "Lorelai, Elowyn, do either of you want this sword?" He held the draugr's weapon before him.

Lorelai politely declined, and Elowyn shook her head.

Was it really that bad? He gave it one last look-over. It had several chips he hadn't been able to fix, and some of the rust had been impossible to remove from some grooves in the metal. There was also a decent-sized dent on the back, and he wouldn't be surprised if it snapped in two after its next use. He sighed again and stabbed the sword into the sandy beach. "Alright, well... it was good while it lasted."

The others were already on the move, heading parallel to the stream.

He left his first sword behind but was already feeling excited about the new weapon. He still hadn't seen any indication that the weapon was magical, so perhaps it only had the innate effect that prevented Hallik from being detected by magical means. Or perhaps he'd grabbed the wrong sword altogether. Would he have to go back to the dragon's den? He wasn't sure he'd survive another dive down that terrible path.

The weapon itself was rather sleek. Other than the missing grip and the handle being a bit worn, the sword was in excellent condition. He imagined it had to be quite old for the dragon to be holding onto it. As far as their history went, that dragon had lived in the mountain forever. This sword could have been hiding in there for hundreds of years.

He inhaled deeply and returned his attention to following after his friends. He was confident he had the right sword. This put them one step closer to Vanalf, and even though getting this far had already been a struggle, he knew the worst parts were still ahead of them.

CHAPTER THIRTY-THREE

IMARÚN

Elowyn Galdre

They were only a couple hours into their trek down the mountain before Elowyn started recognizing some familiar terrain. Bjorn had spoken true about knowing where they were, and it seemed they'd actually be able to find their way back to the Evergrove. It took all her willpower not to run down the mountain. An urgency tugged at her with such force that it made her stomach ache. Or maybe she was hungry. Probably both. All her food had been ruined by going through the water, and everyone else's supplies were the same.

But hunger wasn't what drove her.

She felt as though time were running out. Every second they wasted was another monster finding its way onto Avskild. They needed to get to Vanalf as soon as possible. She'd been willing to take a detour if it meant Hallik would survive when they got there, but now finally going to Vanalf was at the forefront of her mind.

If only she knew how to ensure that she'd become a Voyager. A heavy weight rested on her shoulders. She knew she wasn't their only chance. There were several other students who would try getting through Vanalf along with them, and there would undoubtedly be some Voyagers among them, but she couldn't help feeling that she needed to be the one who'd fix the portals.

A familiar light sparkled up ahead, zipping toward them in an energetic flare of yellow.

"Sparky!" Hallik practically squealed.

Elowyn smiled at Hallik's enthusiasm. She still found Sparky's existence to be peculiar. To think that the wisp was formed from the spirit of Hallik's mother was... strange. At the same time, it was almost like a piece of Hallik's mother was here with them.

Sparky swirled around Hallik's head as the young man chuckled. It shot down to Hallik's new sword and traced across its surface, its color changing to a dark red as it did so. After sliding down the entire length, Sparky's color simmered back to an almost white glow, then it bounced on Hallik's shoulder and hovered in front of the group as it had before.

"I think Sparky approves," Hallik said, patting the sword.

"So we didn't nearly die for nothing. How satisfying," Bjorn said, his voice flat.

Lorelai laughed. "I have to admit, surviving a run-in with the dragon was quite something."

"Yes," Hallik said. "We'll have to try it again sometime and maybe grab a few coins and a dragon scale for proof."

Elowyn smirked and reached into her bag. "You mean one of these?" she asked, pulling a dragon scale from inside.

"Brilliant," Bjorn said with a raised eyebrow. If she didn't know any better, she'd say he actually seemed impressed. She could imagine that if the man had room, instead of checking off items on that list of his, he'd probably collect trophies from the monsters he killed.

The urgency Elowyn felt hadn't diminished. She returned the scale to her bag and went to follow Sparky. The wisp led them through the forest with even more gusto than before as a trail of slowly falling yellow lights streamed behind it. The lights rested on the ground as shimmering sparks until Elowyn walked over them, making them wink out.

At the front, Elowyn was able to set the pace, which helped ease a bit of the tension in her stomach. She practically jogged down the mountainside, and thankfully none of the others complained. They were making much better time going down than they had going up. If she had to guess, they'd reach the Evergrove soon.

After another hour of nearly running, Sparky's undulating colors indicated that they were already near. She guessed they still had over an hour left in the day by the time Elowyn started noticing the dryads peeking at them from on, behind, or sometimes *within* the trees, as some of the faces were quite literally protruding from the wood. She didn't fully understand how that worked, but it was like the dryads' bodies could become one with the trees and separate at will.

As soon as the Evergrove came into sight with its colorful trees and flowers, Sparky zipped back toward the ring of flowers where Tyrus resided. Hallik ran after Sparky, but Bjorn tapped Elowyn's shoulder.

"Be wary," Bjorn warned. "I'm not sure if he can be fully trusted."

Elowyn nodded, but she was also aware enough of Tyrus's power to realize that the man had probably overheard. If he could detect a sword all the way up in a mountain, he could probably hear anything within his sight range.

Bjorn was always a bit cautious, and Elowyn would be genuinely surprised if Hallik's own father were to somehow betray them.

Hallik and Tyrus were already in the midst of a conversation by the time the rest of them got there. Tyrus held the sword in his hands, eyes glowing with new light. They walked to join them, winding through the grass path that led to the center of the flowers.

"So, I got the right one?" Hallik asked.

"Oh, indeed," Tyrus said, eyes still sliding up and down the length of the blade. "I knew you had the right one as soon as you touched it. I couldn't detect you at all." A smile lifted the edges of his mouth. "It works exactly as I'd hoped." He blinked down at Elowyn as she stopped beside Hallik.

They nodded their greetings, then Tyrus's smile faded. "We haven't much time," he said, lowering the sword from his inspection. "There are many threats that stand before Vanalf, but the cave itself will still be the main trial." He handed the sword back to Hallik. "At least I can feel better about your chances now that you have the sword."

"You realize the dragon almost killed us, right?" Bjorn stated. "Getting that sword nearly cost us our lives."

Tyrus frowned. "I did not anticipate such a thing. I sensed when the dragon returned, and I wondered if the reason I could no longer sense Hallik was because he'd been slain." He clenched and unclenched one of his fists. "There must be some kind of spell in place that warns the dragon if people trespass. I've never had the luxury of testing the theory."

"Well, we are alive," Hallik said.

Tyrus nodded. "Yes, and I am grateful for that. Now, about the sword. Its name is Imarún."

"It has a name?" Elowyn interrupted.

"Yes," Tyrus said. "Many unique objects have names or meanings ascribed to them over time, which become imbedded into the essence of the object. When touching such an object, I'm able to cast a spell unique to Watchers that allows us to identify its true nature. In this case, the sword's name means something to the effect of concealed embers. Innately, it conceals the wielder from magical detection, which we already knew. Additionally, it has an activation enchantment that can deal damage to an entity's essence or soul in the same way that fire does. As such, it would be quite effective against an undead opponent, like a draugr or harmful spirit."

"Well that certainly would have been useful," Elowyn commented.

Hallik's jaw hung open, eyes sparkling with excitement as he regarded the sword in his hands. "How is it activated?"

"That's the interesting part," Tyrus said. He folded his hands in front of it. "It has a rare binding that can be established with its owner. Once the owner completes the binding, the activation is in effect for as long as the owner is alive. I recommend we do the binding now, then send you straightway to Vanalf."

"We must get to Dalstava first," Elowyn said. "Lind plans to send an entire class of Grimnir students down with us."

Tyrus frowned but said nothing.

"How is the binding done?" Hallik asked.

"It is quite simple," Tyrus said, but he bit his lip before continuing. "It will likely be a bit painful, and the weapon will consume a sliver of your soul's energy as part of the binding."

"I'll do it," Hallik said without hesitation.

Tyrus smiled at his son. "Just be aware that the sliver of your soul it consumes will restore with time, but souls heal differently than bodies."

Hallik nodded. "Understood. Let's do it."

"Very well. Grip the handle with both hands." Hallik did so, holding the weapon before him as he stood at a right angle beside his father. "Now just say the name of the sword."

"Imarún," Hallik said, Tyrus saying the name at the same time. Immediately his arms seized, muscles flexing as though the sword was trying to rip from his grip. He groaned through his teeth before his body writhed with a massive shudder. He gasped as the shuddering ended and looked around at them as he panted.

The sword took on a glow of pale blue for just a moment before the light faded back into the blade.

Tyrus patted Hallik's shoulder with one hand while pinching the blade of the weapon with his other. He nodded. "It is done. You are not a Grimnir yet, so I had to speak Imarún's name with you for the spell to work. It will be a potent weapon."

Something about the weapon made Elowyn nervous. She'd heard of such things before. "Is it possible for him to destroy something's soul without also destroying the body?"

Tyrus gave her a serious look. "Indeed. In fact, I assume the weapon is likely to deal more damage to a soul than it does to a body. If a body is left soulless, then it remains a husk. I doubt this is something that will happen often, if at all, because souls tend to be significantly more powerful than bodies. If a husk is created however, there is the possibility that other souls or energies can possess the body. It does help to be aware."

"I'm sure that won't be a problem, Elowyn," Hallik said, admiring his sword anew.

Elowyn merely shook her head.

"Alright, well," Tyrus said, looking at each of them in turn, though his eyes lingered on Hallik. "I've taken enough of your time to get the sword. You must be off to Dalstava and then Vanalf. Regardless of the kind of Grimnir you become, your powers will be necessary and quite potent. I can sense it in each of you already. It is no small matter that the four of you have come together." He pointed at Bjorn. "Bjorn, I want you to consider entering alongside them."

Bjorn opened his mouth to respond, but Tyrus raised his hands and spoke first. "Don't dismiss the idea yet. Just consider it. I understand your animosity toward Grimnirs, but becoming one would help to accomplish what you're truly after."

Bjorn grunted. Elowyn certainly wouldn't mind having Bjorn along. His experience with monsters was much more practical than the rest of theirs.

"Now off with you," Tyrus waved a hand dismissively. "I will keep watch from here, though my vision is often blurry inside of Vanalf. For that, well, pray that Kel is not after your souls quite yet."

Vanalf.

Elowyn let out a long breath.

It was time. She was coming.

CHAPTER THIRTY-FOUR

DEMONS

Lind Hjordis

Lind stood across from King Knos. The sky outside the Tower of Tarn grew darker. The people hadn't listened to Knos's request to stay. Though many had hesitated, they'd already gone out to fulfill Lind's orders, knowing full well what was necessary to keep Avskild safe.

Lind's legs ached with a dull burn. He hadn't been planning on standing this long, but the king's appearance was completely unexpected. As King Knos kept insisting that it was not necessary to send reconnaissance troops to the portals, it became very clear that he was bordering on insanity. Their defenses were so clearly degrading that it was impossible to deny the need to maintain security.

Knos claimed that Lorelai and Daelen had forced him into some hidden floor and were trying to compel him into a sacrifice with the ashimal. This was far too different from Lorelai's story, so Lind had to trust his instinct.

"Knos," Lind said, "we know the truth by now." Everyone else had already left the room, leaving Lind, Skelldwyn, and the other Vitugrs. "Lorelai told us everything."

Knos shook his head. "And yet you trust her over your own king."

"Her story makes sense," Lind said. "Yours does not. Finally we understand why the Voyagers' numbers have been dwindling for the last fifty years. How did the ashimal deceive you? Where did the idea of murdering Voyagers even come from?" His voice was filled with more anger than he'd realized. His stomach turned at the very idea of how many of his fellow Grimnirs this man had killed. *Despicable.*

The venom in Knos's words dwindled to the point that he looked like he was on the verge of tears. Something was not right with him. He kept flashing between pure rage and deep sorrow. He'd broken. "It was my father. He told me to keep killing them. Promised it would secure the safety of Avskild. I did only what I thought was best."

This was Knos's first admission. Lind looked over at the other Vitugrs, their expressions varying from rage to disgust.

"You must understand," Knos said, eyes pleading. "My father had been doing this for years. I was told about it as the time got closer to pass the crown. He explained that it was necessary for the safety of our people. I knew it was wrong, at first, I truly did, but I didn't want to believe that my father was doing something so terrible without purpose. I... deceived myself into believing that it was alright, that this was the way it had to be done. It wasn't a day after my father died before I started hearing the voice."

Lind narrowed his eyes. "What voice?"

The sadness in Knos's eyes was gone, replaced only by a grim darkness. "Here. In the tower. I could hear whispers. They weren't words that I could understand, but I tried to find them. I spent many hours searching the rooms on each floor until I found the portal at the bottom of the tower. That's where I met Skuga, the ashimal. It said it had been helping my father."

"But your father never mentioned this creature?" Lind asked. The story felt stranger the more Knos explained.

"Not once. For all I knew before that moment, the idea of killing Voyagers had been his plan. Skuga said that it had given the dagger to my father. The fact that it could at least pass the weapon through was evidence enough that the portals were weaker than he'd thought."

Lind nodded with some semblance of understanding. So there had already been some hint of a flaw in the portal defenses, perhaps causing terrible anxiety in the late king. An obsession with keeping the portal shield defenses strong probably drove him to do these things, and he'd even convinced his son to continue it.

Knos shook his head, new tears forming. "When monsters started coming through, I didn't want to admit it was because of the failed defenses."

"And yet," said one of the other Vitugrs, "you killing the Voyagers is what caused the portal shield to fail. All of the worst instances started occurring once the last Voyager disappeared."

Lind nodded. None of the others had said anything until now, but he could tell they were livid. It was all Lind could do not to simply throw the king into a cell, but he had too many questions.

"Well, I killed the ashimal," Lind said. "It didn't seem like the kind of monster to be trusted."

Knos blinked at Lind with a confused frown. "Skuga is dead?"

Lind grunted. "Yes. It ate me, and I ripped it in half from the inside."

Knos covered his mouth and mumbled something to himself.

"What is that?" Lind said, leaning forward.

Knos frowned and hesitated before responding. "I... I still hear the whispers."

"We should kill him and be done with this!" shouted the same Vitugr, a woman with amber brown hair and a gnarly scar across her forehead. Lind knew her by the name of Rav. "It would be a mercy. You can see how mad he is."

Rav was probably right, but there were still things that Lind didn't understand. "Where have you been for the last couple days? Lorelai said you got pulled into the portal. How did you get back?"

Knos's eyes slowly shifted to Lind. The expression was blank, but something about the way Knos's mouth moved as he spoke just seemed off, like he wasn't sure how to use his lips. "All I remember is blackness. Thick blackness that pressed against me like warm water. The next thing I remember was standing on the sixth floor of the tower. I came down to see you all here. Has it really been two days?"

Lind searched his memory, trying to think if there was any reference to something similar, but he could recall nothing where somebody went into nonexistence for days. The bit about hearing voices was too familiar, though. There were several monsters or even different sapient beings that could communicate psionically. Ashimals were not known to have such an ability, which meant that something else had been pulling King Knos down to that portal. Was there some other infiltrator already here among them? Could a voice really travel through the portal to assault Knos directly, or was the king himself possessed by a sinister spirit?

There were too many possibilities.

He wished he hadn't let Lorelai go with that dagger. He'd recognized that it had some magical quality to it, but he hadn't realized how powerful it truly was.

The others were right, though. Knos's actions were well worthy of execution. Nobody would question such an action on moral or legal grounds, but something about killing Knos worried Lind.

"You say you started hearing strange whispers in your mind the day after your father died?" Lind asked for clarification.

Knos tugged his beard and nodded. "As soon as I awoke that morning."

Lind turned to the other Vitugrs. "We need to lock the king up. He cannot be trusted, but I worry about what might happen if we kill him."

"What could you possibly mean by that?" Rav asked, the muscles of her arm twitched. She had a shortsword sheathed at her belt, and the knuckles of her hand were white as they clenched the handle.

"I believe we need to cast a dispel on him first," Lind said, glancing at the others in hopes that they would understand his meaning.

"We should trust Lind on this, Rav," said another Vitugr. "He's been teaching lore at Castle Vrodr for years. Things like this are his expertise."

Rav pursed her lips. "Alright, why don't we dispel him now and then take him outside for the execution."

There was a subtle shift in Knos's demeanor. He stood at a wide stance, arms hanging casually at his side, shoulders rolled back. The sorrow and fear were gone from his eyes. An execution was what he wanted. They had to be careful with what they did here.

"Not tonight," Lind said. "At least not the execution, but we can try dispelling whatever it is that haunts him. I need to consult with the singer. The voice Knos is hearing concerns me."

"If it's possession you fear, then just burn me with magical fire," Knos said nonchalantly, as if he weren't offering a suggestion for them to take his life. "That's certainly at your disposal." His eyes lingered on Rav.

"True, that can work in most cases," Lind said, "but I need more certainty about what we're dealing with." He was now fully convinced that Knos knew exactly what his malady was and that fire would absolutely *not* be sufficient to destroy whatever had taken hold in him.

Whatever this was, it needed to be resolved immediately. "Skelldwyn, find Selke. I will meet her in the library at Castle Vrodr as soon as possible."

Skelldwyn bowed his head before dashing out of the building.

"The rest of you keep Knos in the cell until I return," Lind said. The cell was really just a single room in a small building next to the tower that could only be unlocked from the outside. It was something that Lind had only heard of being used maybe four or five times in his entire life. Locking somebody up was readily acknowledged as the least effective way to help someone correct their behavior. If somebody got locked in the cell, it was really just a delay of their execution.

"The dispel," Rav reminded Lind as he took a painful step toward the exit.

"Ah, yes." Lind still wasn't sure if a simple dispel would be the right thing to cast, but all four of them faced Knos together. They held out their hands, and Lind took a sharp breath. Many people misunderstood the magic of a Vitugr. Casting a spell was not a simple task. At least, not at first. Repeating a spell certainly made it easier with time, but learning it was difficult. It required knowledge of true names, utterance or mental dictation, and an opening of magical channels to direct the will—which Lind often described as a third lung, or a muscle that could be flexed and strengthened. Spells could even be tied to muscle memory, where all three components could be harnessed into a gesture.

The *dispel magic* spell had been taught in the same way for generations, tied to a single gesture. To make the gesture, they would cross two fingers and quickly pull them apart. Lind no longer needed to actively think the words—it was second nature. Once their group had all crossed their fingers, their other hand was lifted toward Knos, open palm facing him. This would help direct the spell. When they cast the spell together, it would magnify the potency. To help with synchronization, Lind said the name of the spell, "*Ekk galdr.*" They released their crossed fingers. The only signs that the spell had been cast were a mild pressurization in the air that made Lind feel the urge to pop his ears and the very distant, muted sound of glass breaking, but the sensation and sound lasted less than a single heartbeat.

Lind felt the telltale sign that their spell had worked. It was almost like he'd sprinted across the room. The others would have felt it too. Something had been unbound from Knos, but he just didn't know what.

Knos remained standing exactly as he had been before, only now there was the most subtle hint of a smirk on his lips. Or was it a sparkle in his eye? Perhaps Lind imagined it. By the depths. He just wanted to kill the king and be done with it, but he didn't want to act hastily. "Take him to the cell," Lind said.

Not even Rav questioned him this time.

Whatever was happening, King Knos was not alone inside that body of his, and no simple casting of *dispel magic* would expel another entity.

Selke would know what this was. She had to. Lind ignored all the pain in his legs and ran as hard as he could. She was going to be furious when she realized he'd been standing all this time, but that issue paled in comparison with whatever they were still facing.

Forces were at work. Grimnirs had made many enemies over the years. There were some entities that lived thousands of years, and they had memories that went through the ages. Most of them were sworn enemies to humanity. It was only humanity's affinity for magic and their resilience that had saved them.

Lind did not have enough information to know what kind of forces would be at work out there, trying to break through the shield and assault Avskild. Regrettably, he was one of the most educated people regarding their history. Between him and Selke, they probably knew more than the rest of the island combined. He felt that weight now more than ever. Voyagers were absolutely necessary, but enough forces had already leaked into Avskild that simply strengthening the shield wouldn't be enough.

It was practically night by the time Lind reached Castle Vrodr. Selke stood outside the gate, arms folded. Skelldwyn fidgeted beside her.

Selke shook her head at him. She left her disappointment unspoken, choosing instead to inquire about Knos.

Lind heaved a deep breath and continued toward the library, Selke and Skelldwyn following behind. "I was hoping his condition might sound familiar to you. He says he hears a voice muttering another language, and that the words only became discernible when he was near the portal in the tower. He started hearing it the morning after his father died."

"You're saying Knos is being haunted?" Selke asked.

"Possibly," Lind said. "We also cast *dispel* on him, and that turned off something, but we don't know what."

"Wouldn't he have had some spells on his body anyway?" Selke asked.

Lind blinked. "It's possible." It was not uncommon for King Knos to have spells of protection cast on him that would last a day or two. "He'd been missing for a couple days though. You heard Lorelai. He got pulled into the portal. In speaking with him, he never denied that happening, but he said he doesn't remember being inside the portal and for him, it was only a moment before he was suddenly at the top of the staircase that led beneath the tower."

Selke tapped her chin in thought. "There are a few songs that mention people going mad or hearing voices. One was even the sister of a late king. There is mention of a man who was possessed and burned with fire, which destroyed both the body and the evil spirit possessing him. I don't know as much about the monsters though, unfortunately. That is your expertise."

"That is an interesting detail though, because Knos suggested we burn him with fire."

"He suggested it?" Selke grabbed Lind's arm.

Lind nodded.

"Are there any monsters that would not die if you burned them with magical fire?"

"Not many," Lind said with a shrug. "Though practically any demon could potentially be resistant. We are instructed just to use ethereal or ice spells against them."

They'd reached the library, and Lind found an entire page of various demons listed out on a leather parchment.

A demon. His pulse quickened at the thought. They were among the most powerful opponents to crawl through the other realms.

"Any demons that could possess a body?"

Lind rolled his finger down the list. "That's a difficult question. Demons are complex, and their abilities vary. Many subtypes of them are fairly standard with similar characteristics, but there are also some unique demons that could have any number of spells or abilities at their command, except there is one that..." he trailed off, finger hovering over a specific demon. It was unique enough that it was simply the demon's name.

A chill ran across his skin as he uttered the demon's name, "Ontr-anda."

Under the firelight in the library, Lind could see the bumps rise across Selke's skin.

"What's Ontr-anda?" Skelldwyn asked.

"It's the name of a demon. The name is mentioned in the original song as one who first sought the destruction of humanity about a thousand years ago," Selke said.

"He started his obsession by possessing the body of a dead woman, who he used to assassinate other members of their community," Lind explained further. "That caused so much distrust that they warred with each other. After their numbers were decimated and many people fled, he tore free and started eating them."

"He's mentioned a few other times," Selke said. "Every instance is equally unpleasant."

"Do you think it's really him?" Skelldwyn said, grip on his spear growing visibly tighter.

Lind ground his teeth. Battling a demon that had been tormenting humanity for a thousand years was the last thing they needed right now. "Yes," Lind said gravely. "He's quite a powerful entity. It would have been hard for him to get through the portal physically, but he could have been haunting the king with his psionic abilities with ease. He's certainly capable of that. The whole plan for destroying the portals and convincing somebody to secretly eliminate the Voyagers sounds perfectly aligned with his usual tactics. I suspect King Knos's soul is split. Ontr-anda could have left just enough of it inside the body for him to assume control and send the king back through the portal almost as a husk. He wanted us to dispel the body to remove the other protections. He also wants us to burn the body because it would allow him to absorb the fire energy. Possibly enough for him to manifest here fully."

Lind slapped the parchment back down and hurried toward the door, now limping worse than ever before. "I must get back to the others." Selke and Skelldwyn hurried with him. There was a reason Ontr-anda was still alive after all these years. He was resilient and clever. "Perhaps now is the only time that he will be vulnerable. We have to make sure he doesn't break free from Knos's body."

He'd made it halfway down the hallway before the world spun and he collapsed to the floor. The pain in his legs burst with an extreme flare. Was he bleeding? His vision faded to black.

CHAPTER THIRTY-FIVE

A GNOME'S GIFT

Hallik

The sky was a dark shade of purple when they awoke. The first thing Hallik noticed was that all the blueberries he'd set out last night were gone. They'd found a few bushes just before stopping to set up camp, and, at Elowyn's urging, Hallik had *not* eaten all of his, but had left some out specifically for Nis. It seemed the little man had actually taken them.

"That wasn't you who took my blueberries, was it?" Hallik asked Elowyn as they all quickly got ready.

Elowyn grinned. "I would never."

"That seems exactly like the kind of thing you would do, actually."

She just shrugged at that. Hallik shook his head at her, chuckling.

They didn't waste any time. Bjorn said he knew how to get them back to Dalstava. They would regroup with Lind and any other students who were willing to enter Vanalf, then head straight to the cave. Since they were fairly light on supplies and the trail was most often downhill, they jogged at times. Lorelai was the only one who seemed to struggle with this, but she made no complaint. She had a strong character. In time, her body would grow stronger as well. She'd made the right choice in joining them, and Hallik felt eager to see what kind of Grimnir she would become. Possibly a Vitugr. Hopefully a Voyager.

Hallik still wasn't sure what to expect for himself.

They always placed bets before each group went to trial in the depths, guessing which class each student would have, and more grimly, who would probably die. There were always *some* deaths. It was never a perfect run.

But it had always been Hallik's goal, probably foolishly, to get his entire age group through without any deaths. Not likely of course, but weren't goals meant to open up possibilities? They'd never get a perfect run if they didn't at least try.

They descended into a thick part of the forest. Bjorn had been trying to keep them above the tree line for a while, probably to keep their trajectory more accurate, but now it was impossible to avoid being swallowed up by the trees. The woody, piney smell of the forest was always such a soothing scent. Though things were bleak, he couldn't help but smile.

"What are you so happy about?" Elowyn asked.

Hallik grunted a laugh. "I've just spent so much of my life wondering why my father left me behind, hoping that it was for some noble cause or that he'd died just so I didn't have to feel abandoned for nothing. Do you know how relieving it is to be justified?"

"I can imagine that it must offer you some peace," Elowyn said. Then she placed a hand on Hallik's arm and smiled back at him. "But no matter what, Hallik, you are always valuable, always needed, and always worthy of love, regardless of who is or is not showing it."

Hallik nodded, ignoring the lump that caught in his throat. He squeezed her hand. Did she have any idea how much strength she gave him?

Ahead of them, Bjorn held a hand out behind him as he slowed down. With his other hand, he slowly slid his sword from its sheath.

Elowyn and Hallik didn't question Bjorn's instinct, so they scanned their surroundings. A chill passed through Hallik's entire body, as if something cold and wet had just brushed across him. He suppressed a yelp and drew his sword to face off whatever had touched him. In his hand, he held a wooden stick in the general shape of a sword. "Nis!" he bellowed. He'd hoped that they'd somehow managed to lose the little gnome after the escape from the dragon's den, but apparently to no avail. Now Nis had taken his most valuable possession.

Hallik resisted the urge to hurl the stick into the forest and tried instead to assess the situation. *Something* had touched him. The only sign he could detect was some shimmering blue light that wavered across his vision.

"He took your sword again?" Elowyn asked, sounding genuinely surprised this time.

"Yes, and it could certainly come in handy if we are about to be attacked by some malevolent spirit right now," Hallik said. "Nis! If you can hear me, bring back that sword."

The shimmering blue light grew sharper, and a chilling touch grazed across the back of Hallik's hand. This time, it inflicted a sharp pain as though he'd been pierced by a shard of ice. He shouted and stumbled back, whipping the stick through the light, scattering the glowing particles. A high-pitched scream tore at his ears, that of a woman being murdered.

For a split second, the shimmering light became the clear image of a tall woman. All her features were blue, and it looked as though she were underwater, her ethereal hair and clothes floating with small ripples.

"Ghost!" Elowyn shouted.

Hallik swung the stick at it again with similar results, though it didn't seem like he'd be able to destroy it this way. Its strange matter always reassembled. The ghost screamed and reached out to Hallik, long nails jabbing toward him like the legs of a spider.

Bjorn's water skein passed through the shape of the ghost, water arcing across the ghost in a line. Before Bjorn could do anything else, Lorelai stepped up beside Hallik and slashed her dagger across its intangible body.

Just like that, the ghost disappeared. The gemstones on Dris flared briefly before the light went out. The whole interaction had taken mere seconds, but it left Hallik panting for breath. He looked back at his hand. The skin was slightly reddened, but it otherwise looked undamaged.

Hallik pointed at Lorelai's dagger. "Sorry, ghost, but that is not the proper way to get a man's attention."

"Oh, Hal," Elowyn said, slapping his shoulder with the back of her hand. "Good thinking, Lorelai. I hadn't considered the idea that Dris could damage a spirit like that."

"Me neither," Lorelai said. "Until just now, anyway. Tyrus's description about souls made me consider that if Dris captures soul energy, then it should be effective against non-corporeal opponents."

"Nis!" Hallik shouted again, disengaging from the conversation. He waved the wooden stick over his head. "We talked about this."

Not a second later, Imarún flipped down in front of Hallik, blade piercing into the softened ground. Hallik had no idea where it came from. It was followed by a leather sheath. A second later, Nis appeared from behind a tree, as usual.

Nis released a squeaky growl. "That sword looked like it was a thousand years old—older than me! Besides, using Dris was the best option for that ghost anyway."

Hallik scowled back at the tiny man.

"Oh, Nis, we're so glad you found us," Elowyn said, nudging Hallik.

"Easy to find," Nis said. "Hallik smells like a troll. Hard to lose."

"Aha," Elowyn said. "Nis agrees on your stench."

Hallik ignored them and went to retrieve Imarún. To his surprise, a new leather grip was in place. The metal was polished, and the blade was glistening and sharp. "Nature's rays," he said, picking up the sword and holding it in both hands.

Nis looked up at him expectantly, hands on hips. "That sword is much better than that rusty bar you had before. Good metal. Magic."

"Thank you, Nis," Hallik said after a momentary delay. "Perhaps next time, you can leave the items beside me when I wake up so that I'm not weaponless for another fight."

Nis gave one quick wave to Hallik then disappeared behind the tree again.

"Alright, goodbye, then," Hallik said. He picked up the sheath. It was a simple item, but the leather looked well-treated and was secured with careful stitching. A metal ring capped the entrance to prevent cutting. Overall, it was one of the finest sheathes he'd ever seen. It looped easily onto his belt. The sword fit perfectly.

"Where does he keep all his supplies?" Lorelai asked.

"Gnomes are a mystery," Elowyn said with a shrug. "Nis is more interactive than gnomes usually are, but he also doesn't seem like your typical gnome."

"So I gather," Lorelai said.

"Check your inventory more closely each morning, Hallik," Bjorn said, turning to resume their trek.

Hallik held back his response and instead said, "Should we jog to make up time?"

"Gladly," Elowyn said.

Lorelai groaned but made no objection.

They were still perhaps three days away from entering Vanalf, but would the portal shield last that long? Then the cave itself would take an entire day as well.

The shield had to stay strong. All of this couldn't be for nothing. That is what he told himself, but there were still doubts that churned at the back of his mind like a waterfall. He ran harder.

CHAPTER THIRTY-SIX

BURN

Rav

At the age of ten, Rav and her twin sister Rethr had joined the students at Castle Vrodr. Though they were twins, Rav always considered Rethr to be the beautiful one, with her thick hair and straight teeth. Rav had the brains, but Rethr was more sociable, easily making friends. They made a good duo, though, and they always had each other's backs.

At the age of eighteen, they entered Vanalf together, and they emerged together. The details of their experience remained fuzzy to Rav, which was apparently not an uncommon experience, but she knew they'd stuck with each other through the whole venture. In the end, Rav had become a Vitugr, and Rethr had become a Voyager.

They'd both been so excited for Rethr's class. Voyagers were already nearly gone back then. Little did they know that it would turn out to be a curse. It was a few months later when Rethr disappeared. Her body had never been found. She was just... gone. It left an emptiness inside Rav, a pain in her chest that never went away. All because of some murderer.

It was only just barely that she'd learned it was because of the king. The man whose cell she now guarded. It was taking all of her willpower not to simply turn around and torch the entire little building with flames. Fire magic was a specialty of hers. She knew a dozen ways to summon it depending on what she wanted. It would be so easy.

"Lind is taking too long," Rav said. She and the two other Vitugrs had been left to guard the king, though one had just left to relieve himself.

"Well, he did get eaten by a monster," Benson said, one of the other Vitugrs who stood guard with her. Four Vitugrs were all that remained in the world. There was possibly another Vitugr on the west end of the island. But that was it. This was what they'd been reduced to. All because of this *king*.

"He won't let you kill me," Knos said from inside.

"You will not speak!" Rav shouted at him, her voice carrying over the still night air.

"Rav," Benson warned with his eyebrows raised, voice low so that Knos wouldn't hear them from inside the cell, but she glared back at Benson.

"Lind is trying to decide if I am still your king or if I'm a monster," Knos said. "I wouldn't say I'm a monster. I just did what I thought was best. Like when I killed your sister, Rethr."

Swirling traces of fire were already snaking across Rav's palms before she even realized it. "You will not speak my sister's name!" She kicked at the wooden door to the small building.

Benson's eyes widened at Rav's outburst.

"I remember her," Knos said. "Whenever I see you, I'm reminded of her. She was one of the first Voyagers I killed personally."

Rav banged the door with the side of her clenched fist. She'd balled her hands to extinguish the flames that threatened to burst out. She'd never felt such rage against someone in all her life. Knos was a monster—like any other beast that sought to exterminate humanity. He was no better than them.

"Don't let him get to you, Rav," Benson said. "Perhaps you should go for a walk. Let me watch him for a moment."

Rav forced herself to step back from the door, releasing a seething breath between her teeth. She wasn't sure what Knos was after, but if he was trying to make her upset, it was working. All she wanted was to see his eyes as she set him on fire. This was her sister's murderer. The man who'd taken her only family away from her. The man who'd taken her dearest friend. The pain that had been festering in her chest ever since her sister died was growing with every second.

"She was watching the sunrise on a rock overlooking the sea," Knos said. "I stabbed her from behind, right in the back, just below the ribcage."

Rav's arms trembled. She wanted to take another step away, but her feet remained planted.

"When she looked back at me, she was so surprised," Knos continued. "I stabbed her again, this time in the neck. Her soul's energy sucked into the blade as she bled out. I dumped her body in the sea. She was probably one of the draugrs that attacked. I guess you could say I made *her* a monster. Then you were likely the one who burned her cursed body."

"That's enough!" Benson shouted at Knos.

But the damage was done. Rav set her jaw and pivoted. Knos had no other information to offer them. Lind would not get his interrogation. The only beneficial thing Knos had left to give was the closure she would take from seeing him die, burned alive by her magic.

"Rav," Benson said, holding a hand up to her.

She ignored him. The pain in her chest would never subside until Knos was nothing but ash. She threw open the door to the cell. Knos was leaning against the wall, arms folded, a blighting smirk on his face. Fire coursed through Rav's very being as she pointed a hand at Knos. Flames erupted from her arm, singeing the sleeve of her dress. She'd never summoned so much all at once before. Knos didn't even flinch, maintaining eye contact with her. A jet of flame crashed into him with the sound of a dozen roaring bears, continually pouring from her arm. She didn't care how much energy she used. All that mattered was watching him burn.

Benson shouted at her, but she couldn't hear him. She couldn't avert her gaze. Knos stared straight back at her as the fire burned at him, his entire body going black within seconds. He started dissipating into ash, but not before his crusty lips curled into a full smile. It was sick, and it twisted her insides almost as sharply as the pain that was now stabbing through her chest. Perhaps killing him wouldn't alleviate the suffering she'd endured since losing her sister. Perhaps this was in vain.

Knos's body was completely unrecognizable by the time it erupted into black ash. The building imploded and the flames extinguished all at the same time. An explosion of soot burst around her. She shielded her eyes against the blast, and when she peeked back out, she saw a jet of smoke trailing into the sky as if something had launched out of the building.

Benson grabbed Rav and dragged her away from the building, coughing as he did so. Only then did she realize how extremely exhausted she was. She'd expended everything she had into that fire, as though she couldn't let go until she'd given her all. A few people had already begun gathering around, many of them pointing to the sky.

"No!" Lind said as he stumbled onto the scene, supported by Skelldwyn, Selke at his back. Lind shook his head at Rav. "You've just released a demon," Lind said, though his tone was not angry, it was... sad.

Rav looked back at the jet of smoke that was now slowly drifting away. She realized now what it meant. The demon had taken flight. What had she done?

"Where did it go?" Benson asked, blinking up. His face and clothes were covered in black soot.

"He will hide and then do what he does best," Lind said. "That was none other than Ontr-anda. He will try to drive us against each other or kill us slowly. With his presence here, he may even be able to draw more monsters through the portals."

"Then we need to get those students to Vanalf," Benson said.

"My thoughts exactly," Lind muttered.

Rav was too stunned to say anything. She'd let Knos—no, Ontr-anda—get to her, playing right into his plans. Her breath came in rapid gasps as the realization settled in.

"Are you alright, Rav?" Lind asked, looking down to where she still knelt on the ground after Benson had pulled her back.

She shook her head. "I'm so sorry, Lind. I should have listened. I don't know what overcame me."

Lind was silent for a moment before he responded. "I understand. I suspected it could be a demon, but I didn't realize how effective he'd be at manipulating emotions. Records suggest that's how he's ruined us in the past. He played on the king's fears, just as he took advantage of you."

"Ah." Rav dropped her head. "For me, it was grief for my sister. He turned it into rage."

"Well, at least now we know what we're up against," Lind said. "That is half the battle." He reached down a hand to help her up.

"Are you sure you should be doing that?" Rav asked.

Lind looked down at his hand, then dropped it back to his side. "Probably not."

Rav stood on her own.

Then Lind spoke to no one in particular. "We'll ensure the students are ready to leave at a moment's notice. The Watchers and Valtyras we sent out should be back with their reports at any time now."

As if on cue, a pair of Valtyras drifted down toward the tower, a Watcher held between them. Rav was surprised they'd flown back despite the late hour. The squad of three landed beside them, regarding the smoldering building.

"What happened here?" asked one of the Valtyras, a woman named Zaakira, as she stretched one of her arms across her chest.

"There was a demon hiding inside the husk of Knos's body," Lind explained. "He got away, but we can address that later. How is the path to Vanalf looking? Where's the other squad?"

"We noted several monsters in the valley," said the Watcher, also stretching his shoulders after having been carried. His name was Anders, and he was perhaps in his fifties, but his Watcher senses were as sharp as ever. "There were actually eight militiamen hiding out at the old outpost, but they were all injured, and a couple were on the brink of death. They'd survived an ambush from the trolls on the day of the battle. There was also an injured Valtyra with them, but one of her wings had been severed. She's not doing well. The other squad remained with them. They're going to try and get them back to Dalstava."

"Survivors nonetheless," Lind said. "That is good news."

"I got all their names," Zaakira said. "I'll get word to their families."

Rav straightened her posture. Even this fragment of good news was so welcome. It reminded her that they needed more than just vengeance for the dead, but courage to defend and protect the living.

"Did you detect any trolls?" Lind asked.

"Not sure," Anders said. "They are tricky to identify, but there were three questionable lifeforms that remained grouped together. They were up near the northern end of the valley, so if they were trolls, they've pulled back from the battleground. I'd guess that both our army and the troll army were equally devastated."

"If I may pose a recommendation, Lind," Zaakira said, "it may be wisest for us to get the next students through Vanalf with a more covert approach. We can focus on clearing out the monsters once the shield is restored."

"Agreed," Lind said, eyes scanning the darkened sky, "though being discreet just got a lot more difficult. Ontr-anda will likely try coordinating the efforts of the monsters that have already gotten through. The monsters he can manipulate, anyway."

Rav subconsciously cast a spell over their group. If Ontr-anda were still within the vicinity, he could already be listening in, but the spell would help keep their conversation muted from outside its area of effect. "Is the demon near?" Rav asked Anders.

"Ah," Anders said, "no. I sensed him earlier, but I was unable to track his energy after he disappeared somewhere on the west end of the city. He got out of my reach, though his elevation did not descend for as long as I could sense him."

"Hopefully he left the city," Lind said. "We should try to get some rest, and then you and Zaakira should look for it tomorrow. I need to put my legs up before I get any worse." Lind gestured at the other Valtyra, Bryn. "Let's get a carrier to that outpost. Perhaps we could transport the wounded back to the city. Rav, we'll have you lead the escort tomorrow to Vanalf."

Rav sputtered for a moment. "Me?" She'd just made one of the greatest mistakes in her career, and he was about to trust her to take the students to Vanalf? "What about you?"

Lind gestured to his legs. "I'm not traveling anywhere in my condition."

"What of Elowyn and Hallik?" Selke asked.

Lind sighed. "I'm not sure we should delay on their behalf. I also wouldn't be surprised if their group would be able to reach Vanalf without an escort. They may even have better luck getting to the cave more discreetly than a larger group of thirty."

Selke frowned but still nodded.

"Rav," Lind said. "Stay with us at Castle Vrodr tonight. Tomorrow, we'll get you sent out with the expedition to Vanalf."

Rav could only nod, ignoring the heaviness that weighed on her heart. She'd failed, and yet he'd still rely on her. This is what it had come to. There simply were no other options, except for Benson, but maybe Lind felt more comfortable having a Vitugr here who wouldn't so easily jeopardize things.

She clenched her fist and followed the small group that walked back toward Castle Vrodr. More than anything, she wanted to kill Ontr-anda, the demon who'd instigated all their troubles. But first, they needed to secure the portals and cut off the demon's support before he'd be able to enlist other monsters. *Then* she could kill him.

CHAPTER THIRTY-SEVEN

TO RISE, ONE MUST FIRST HIT THE BOTTOM

Jaysen Bjorn

Bjorn huffed and slowed to a walk. Lorelai heaved a sigh of relief, but Elowyn and Hallik weren't even panting. He could only imagine how much more formidable he would be if he'd experienced some of their training while he was younger. Sure, he'd started hunting monsters at a younger age, but the evidence of their training left him feeling like he could have done more. Either way, he'd still be killing monsters, the one remaining thing that brought him satisfaction.

"We should be near Dalstava," Elowyn said.

They were deep in the forest, but Bjorn could catch glimpses of the mountains through the trees. It didn't take long before Elowyn said that she recognized their surroundings. He could tell that she'd been holding back an urge to sprint ahead, even across the uneven ground of the forest floor.

"How can you tell?" Lorelai asked.

Elowyn pointed to her right at a gap in the trees. "Over there, where the mountain dips down. That's where a trail leads down into the Valley of Vanalf. My mother and I would come out here a lot, especially to gather berries. We should be intersecting the main trail at any moment."

This part of the forest seemed peculiar to Bjorn. There were several creatures he'd never seen before, like a squirrel with an owl head and a deer that he could have sworn had fangs. The rest of them didn't seem bothered by these animals when he'd pointed them out, so he had to assume they were normal creatures and not monsters of some kind. It could never hurt to be too cautious though, so he still watched each animal carefully.

Before long, Elowyn's words rang true as a path became clear in the forest ahead, wide enough to fit a wheeled cart.

"We can follow this straight back to Dalstava," Elowyn said, but then she stopped short as soon as they all entered the trail. Voices carried over to them through the forest.

Wordlessly, they all drew their weapons and hurried off to the side of the trail, hiding among the foliage as the voices got closer. The voices were distinguishably human, and some of them even seemed young, like they were little more than children.

From his position low to the ground, squatting back against a tree, Bjorn looked over at Hallik questioningly.

Hallik shrugged and shook his head.

Bjorn peeked around the tree and between the leaves of a small bush. The voices became clear just as he saw the first person. It was a woman with amber-red hair, pulled back and braided. She wore padded armor, a sheathed sword at her waist, and a pack over one shoulder.

"Get all your talking done now," the woman said. "I don't want to hear a peep once we reach the pass."

Elowyn, Hallik, and Lorelai all put their weapons away and emerged from hiding. Bjorn joined them slowly, weapon still in hand. Now that he could get a better look, it seemed like a sort of procession. Most of the people trailing out behind the woman at the front were young. In fact, they were all young, like Hallik and Elowyn. They were dressed up in armor as if prepared to go to war.

Kel's abyss, is that what they were doing? Sending these children off to finish what the army could not?

Several of the youth called out to Hallik and Elowyn.

The woman at the front paused so that they could all mingle.

"I was informed that you had been sent on some necessary mission," the woman said, but her eyes drifted to Bjorn. "I take it you've completed it, then?"

"We have," Lorelai answered, then gestured at Bjorn and introduced him as the man who'd come through the portal. "And this is Rav," Lorelai told Bjorn. "She's a Vitugr."

Bjorn said nothing, unsure how the woman would take the news that he was not Avskildian. She didn't seem to care at all, but continued her conversation with Lorelai. "I have been instructed to lead the students to Vanalf. We'll meet up with some other Grimnirs at the outpost who will guide us through the valley. Will Hallik and Elowyn be joining?"

"That's the intent," Lorelai said. "I... will also be entering with them."

Rav blinked at Lorelai. "You did not train with the students."

"We need more Grimnirs, do we not?" Lorelai said.

"Lorelai, the cave is dangerous."

"I am aware, Rav. Our group of four has successfully fought and killed several monsters already. I am fully confident in my ability to survive the depths of Vanalf."

Lorelai's expression was hardened, lips tight with determination.

Rav nodded back to her. "Very well, let's be on our way. We plan to camp at the outpost, then be down to Vanalf in the morning." She resumed the march at a steady pace. The students hurried on as Elowyn and Hallik continued to mingle with them, Hallik showing off his sword. If there were truly many dangers inside of Vanalf, then Elowyn and Lorelai both seemed equally ill-equipped to enter. Each of the other students had been more properly armed with axes or swords, though no spears. He imagined spears would not be ideal if the cave ever had tight spaces to maneuver.

Bjorn walked at Lorelai's side, just behind Rav. To his relief, the students behind seemed content not to talk to them.

"Should we not report back to Lind?" Bjorn asked Lorelai.

She shook her head. "No. We were probably gone longer than he was thinking we'd be, so they would have completed all the reconnaissance around Vanalf already and concluded that sending the students was the next best thing to do. We'd be wasting time if we went all the way back to Dalstava now."

All the better. This saved them some time. They'd collectively been worried that the valley would be filling up with more monsters every day, so the sooner they got to Vanalf, the better. If these other students were as skilled as Hallik and Elowyn, then he imagined they'd do alright for the most part. "This trial in Vanalf, how long does it take?"

"About a full day," Lorelai said. "We have to travel all the way to the bottom of the cave before we come back, otherwise it doesn't work. The bottom of the cave functions like a portal that connects the realms. There's a sort of network down there between them that we call the Wyrm. You've heard of the other realms, right?"

Bjorn grunted. "I know of Kel's abyss."

Lorelai smiled. "That's one. Can you imagine—an entire world inhabited by the dead and damned? The old name we have for it is Dothvarld, but there are many others, perhaps some we do not even know about. There's the Jotvarld. That's where the trolls come from. There's also the Essvarld, realm of magic, inhabited by the primordials, and the Alfvarld, realm of elves."

"Are there not elemental ones as well?" Bjorn asked. He'd heard of the elf and troll realms, but there were also supposedly some related to ice, fire, and shadow.

"I've heard of other realms, but Elowyn is probably the one to ask if you want all the details there. I think there's another realm called Myrkvarld, the realm of darkness, but it's possibly connected to Dothvarld. It's hard to truly know about places we've never been."

Bjorn wasn't sure what to think of all this. It only further solidified his idea that killing monsters could only delay the inevitable. If there were entire worlds populated with monsters, then all his killing barely made a difference. "Can the caves be traveled in order to reach the other realms?"

Lorelai smiled. "That troll army got here somehow, didn't it?"

"Yes, but what of people going to other realms?"

"We don't try it. You saw Tyrus. Nobody wants to get cursed by entering the cave a second time."

Bjorn grunted. "Does that happen to everyone?"

"I don't know. Another question for Elowyn or Lind. All I really know is that if I go through it, I come out with magic. That's what matters."

Bjorn was learning more every day. He'd always wondered how monsters from other realms ended up here in theirs. This concept of access to the different realms was interesting, but if these monsters were simply encroaching on their world for the sake of expanding their territory or hunting grounds, then it gave him all the more reason to exterminate them. Why not stay in their own realms rather than come here and hunt people? Maybe people were easy prey, and thus giving them powers through their journey in Vanalf was even more necessary. It was a stretch, but perhaps killing enough monsters might send the message that Mennesvarld was not a safe place for them to hunt.

But these were concepts well above his ability to understand. There was much more to this that he did not know. He hadn't thought it possible, but he actually found himself wishing he could go back and speak with Tyrus more.

The trail got steeper as the group ascended the mountainside. The anticipation filling the air from all the students was so charged that even Bjorn felt like storming ahead. This was a moment they'd been training their whole lives for. To think that an army of people like this had just been destroyed felt heavier on his heart than he cared to admit. If the Grimnir army could be destroyed, then what hope did they really have?

The answer was the same as it had always been.

None.

Despite that, the students were still eager to obtain magic and fight to maintain their freedoms as long as possible. That was a sentiment Bjorn could share with them.

They continued hiking for another couple hours before they reached the pass where two pillars stood to either side of the trail, one of stone, one of wood. The carvings on them were ancient, which somehow gave Bjorn a sense of primal connection. This place was not only significant to Avskildians, but to all of humanity. Whether Grimnir or not, they all struggled against the encroaching darkness.

He looked back at the students, who had all gone silent. A sense of reverence muted their excitement. Many of them reached out their hands to touch either pillar in passing. This was going to be a significant moment for them. After tomorrow, they would no longer be the same.

As they went through to the valley on the other side of the pass, the trail bent to one side. The valley was small, nothing like the ones back on the mainland, but there was still another forest stretched out across the bottom of it.

Ahead of him, Rav gasped and drew a short sword. "They're under attack," she said, hurrying to a jog.

Bjorn finally noticed what she was talking about. Off to the side just a little way down was a stone tower. A large beast that looked like a bald, gray-skinned ape with hulking musculature swung a club around as though fighting off insects. Bjorn hurried after Rav, Lorelai at his side as the students behind them roared for battle.

Elowyn was beside Bjorn in a flash. "It's an ogre," she said easily, as though they weren't jogging.

They weren't even halfway toward the engagement by the time a Valtyra flitted across the front of the ogre, a metal flash glinting in the light. The Valtyra hooked a blade into the creature's skull, jerking its head back as he flew over. The ogre fell backwards, a long point bursting out of its stomach as the Valtyra stabbed it from behind. It collapsed with a rumble.

The Valtyra withdrew his spear from the ogre's gut and stood watching the students approach. It was the first time Bjorn had seen one of them in action, and he had to admit that he was impressed. He'd made that battle look like child's play. There'd been over a hundred Valtyra in that battle with the trolls, and they'd somehow been defeated? A chill went up his spine.

"Bryn brought us word earlier that you'd be arriving," the Valtyra said as they came to a stop before him.

Smoke rose to the sky from a nearby fire where several bodies burned, but most of them appeared to be some kind of monster.

"You've been busy, Kaldir," Rav said, gesturing at the fire.

The Valtyra shook his head. "It's like our arrival has been drawing them out. This ogre was the most intelligent of the species that have attacked, but at least it's not a coordinated effort. The injured taking refuge in the tower only had to fight off a single monster before we arrived, but since we got here, we've killed seven."

One other soldier stood near the door to the tower, though he didn't have wings and looked like he hadn't slept for a couple days. The necklace he wore bore the symbol of an eye, which Bjorn had learned was the symbol of Watchers.

"Where is Bryn now?" Rav asked.

"She and Halva flew one of the injured back to Dalstava," Kaldir said. "They are supposed to be back any moment now to get another. Hopefully we can get the worst ones out today, and then the others will go off tomorrow, but a couple of the militiamen are still offering to hold posts here until the students get back from Vanalf. Their wounds are much more manageable than the rest of them, so it might not be a bad idea. I'm not too keen on holding this position by myself, even if I can fly. I think I saw a couple dark fairies when we did our fly-over across the valley."

Dark fairies. Deceptive little blights. Bjorn clenched a fist. Those were certainly on his list.

Lorelai drew her dagger and went over to stab the ogre with a brief explanation to the Valtyra.

Rav told the other two Grimnirs to rest while they could, and they hesitantly obliged, though the Valtyra flew to the top of the tower. "We'll set up camp here," Rav said to everyone else.

The plan was to camp at the outpost, then head straight to Vanalf first thing in the morning with all thirty-three students. He wondered how many of them would survive.

Bjorn surveyed the outpost, questioning its defensibility. The only real structure was the tower itself, a tall, rounded, brick building dotted with arrow slits and crowned with crenulations at the top, suggesting there was an inner staircase. That, or it was designed specifically for Valtyras.

None of them were armed with bows except for the Watcher. Not even the students were armed with any ranged equipment, which meant their defense simply wasn't reliable. A pile of bricks suggested that another building had once stood here but had since collapsed many years ago. There was also the remnant of a wall, though not a single portion of it reached higher than Bjorn's knee, rendering it useless. Staying here would scarcely be better than anywhere else, with the exception of the wide visibility down the hill.

It would have to do.

The voices of Hallik and Elowyn carried to Bjorn as he stood near the pitiful remains of the wall.

"I still don't understand why we have to wait until tomorrow," Hallik said. "Can't we just go straight there?"

"They don't want to traverse the forest at night," Elowyn said.

"But you and I could reach Vanalf before nightfall, couldn't we?"

"Probably, but they are supposed to keep somebody on watch outside the cave for when we emerge."

Hallik grunted. "Still feels like a protocol that's only preventing us from fixing things sooner."

"What do you think, Bjorn?" Elowyn asked, folding her arms as she stared down at the valley.

Bjorn sighed, but before he could respond, a sound like ice cracking over a frozen lake rippled across them. The ground trembled. Bjorn could have sworn he saw two large fractures in the sky as though it were made of glass.

"By the depths," Hallik muttered, his eyes also on the sky. "Did they destroy another portal?"

"Gather close, everyone!" Rav shouted from the tower.

The earth groaned again as though something were on the verge of snapping.

Avskild was falling apart. There was no denying it now. Perhaps they were too late.

"You want to know what I think," Bjorn said, eyes on Elowyn. "I think Hallik's blighting right. There's no time to waste. We can hide here at the tower for a day, or we can get to Vanalf now. If we skim a few hours, we might still have a chance to save Avskild."

"Elowyn, Hallik, gather round," Rav hollered over to them.

Lorelai stood near the edge of the group, staring over at them as well.

Elowyn bit her lip, looking back and forth between the outpost and the forest below.

"You feel it too, don't you, El?" Hallik asked. "It's that pressure on your shoulders. We can't wait."

"Oh, nature's rays," Elowyn said, bending down to tighten her boots.

Bjorn actually smirked. This would be fun. The odds were not in their favor, but at least it would be an adventure. Lorelai was walking toward them as the earth continued to rumble. By unspoken word, she seemed to understand what was coming. All four of them did.

They would travel to Vanalf together.

Ignoring Rav's shouting, they took off down the slope as the ground shook around them. It didn't take long before they reached the forest. Though he hadn't been to Vanalf before, a clear trail led the way ahead. Their pace only slowed slightly as the ground leveled out. Lorelai caught up to them, and they all jogged together.

"We're really doing this, eh?" Lorelai asked in a huff.

"Somebody has to," Elowyn said. "May as well be us."

They proceeded in silence for a while until Hallik let out a low whistle and pointed to something on the side of the trail. It was a dead man, completely missing a leg. He looked like he'd been there for a few days.

It meant they were getting closer to the battleground where the army had been defeated. They slowed to a brisk walk and pulled weapons out.

"Lorelai, Elowyn," Bjorn said in a gruff whisper, "if you see some other weapons or gear, it may be beneficial to arm up more appropriately. I'm not sure daggers will be sufficient for Vanalf."

They nodded but said nothing. The trembling in the ground had stopped, and the air was humid, buzzing with insects. The stench of death wafted at them in a light breeze, though they didn't see any other signs of battle for several moments. Further ahead, the trail was covered in lumpy masses. It took Bjorn a moment to realize they were the corpses of trolls.

There were more flies about than he'd ever seen in his life. He covered his nose in the crook of his elbow and proceeded around the dead bodies. There was occasionally a fallen Grimnir among them, with the humans seeming to attract more insects than the trolls, and the smell was absolutely horrendous.

The trail ahead descended between two ridges, and the scene that stretched out could have been pulled straight from a nightmare. Bjorn had seen massacres before, but never of such magnitude. None of them spoke. Bjorn didn't even dare open his mouth. A few scavenging animals darted away at their passing.

Bjorn saw a relatively clean axe on the ground and nudged it with his foot. Lorelai nodded and picked it up, and then put on an unsullied helmet at Bjorn's urging. To their collective surprise, a whole giant lay face down on the ground, covering the trail. They had to go around it to proceed. How in the world had a giant gotten here? He was sure they all had the same question.

Hallik paused at a body near the edge of the scene. He bent down and looked up at Elowyn, tears glistening in his eyes. The man was on his side, lying next to the corpse of a troll. A sword was still clutched in his hand. A raven perched upon the dead man's foot, unperturbed by their arrival.

Elowyn bit her lower lip, but that didn't prevent it from trembling.

Bjorn recognized the body as that of Captain Mikel Vigsen. This had been their leader.

Elowyn bent down and retrieved Mikel's sword, prying it away from his rigid fingers. It was still strange, seeing a dead man like this, still and lifeless, when only a few days ago he had been well. Bjorn wasn't sure he'd ever get accustomed to it.

He stepped down ahead of Elowyn and Hallik, unsure of how long he could stand to watch them. This scene made everything too real. This wasn't just any army that had fallen, it was *the* army. The last human army that remained. He didn't want to admit that coming here and seeing the city had given him some trickle of hope, but that trickle was taken away so immediately and violently that he couldn't help but feel stricken.

"Let's get on with it," Elowyn said, passing Bjorn to take the lead. Mikel's sword, still marred by dried troll blood, was clutched in her hand.

"Are we close?" Bjorn asked, all too eager to leave that nightmare behind.

"Yes," Hallik said. "We came to wait outside when last year's initiates went through. It's just around here."

Bjorn glanced up at the sun. It was evening, but they probably had nearly two more hours before sunset. "And you're certain it's fine to go through Vanalf at night?"

"Not certain at all," Hallik said.

"How did I rope myself into this?" Lorelai asked.

"Probably by getting too interested in finding out who my father is," Hallik said. He smiled at her. "You're stuck with us now."

The edge of a rocky outcropping came into view. The formation itself was like nothing Bjorn had seen before, like an impossibly large skull with a crown. This hardly seemed like a natural cave.

"Whose idea was it to go inside there?" Bjorn asked.

Elowyn laughed. "The people who first entered were trying to hide from monsters."

"By entering a cave that connects to the homes of those monsters?" Bjorn's steps became more tentative as he followed them down the slope to the front of the massive stone structure.

"Something tells me they didn't know that back then," Lorelai said.

They were nearly to the bottom of the hill when Bjorn thought he saw something atop the rocks. He paused, staring hard, sparing only quick glances elsewhere.

Hallik reached the bottom first, and he too paused, pulling his sword from its sheath.

Bjorn readied his crossbow, winding back the string as he kept his eyes up. A deep, throaty laugh echoed up at them from inside the cave as a dark shadow grew closer.

Bjorn fitted the bolt and held the crossbow out to his side, slipping a throwing knife into his other hand.

"We was told ye might be coming," a voice croaked from the cave. A creature emerged. It was humanoid in shape, but it had reddish gray skin with long black hair and sharp, pointed ears as long as Bjorn's forearm. Its face was circular, and even its nose was more of a rounded stub, but it had two fangs jutting up from its lower jaw. It wore a patchwork of metal plating and wielded a long, slightly curved blade in one hand.

It was a hobgoblin.

Bjorn had killed them before, so it wouldn't be new for his list unfortunately, but he'd gladly remove any more of them from the face of the planet. They were malicious, usually doing whatever the nearest dominant, evil being told them to do. However, they usually worked in groups, so he kept his eyes up. The hobgoblin speaking to them was possibly doing so as a distraction.

"That's strange," Hallik said, taking a step closer. He held his sword over one of his shoulders casually. "I don't remember telling you we'd be here."

"What?" the hobgoblin said, confused. "No, I don't mean you told us." It took on a wicked grin. "I mean we have informants."

"So it was meant as a surprise, then?" Hallik said. "Lovely."

Another hobgoblin peered out from behind the largest of the stone spires, a shortbow in hand. It started nocking an arrow, but Bjorn pointed his crossbow and released, piercing the hobgoblin straight in the neck. It slumped, falling from its post to the ground below.

"No!" the hobgoblin from the cave said. "I mean—" The dead hobgoblin from above smacked down directly in front of the one talking with a dying squeal. The live one's eyes widened, and Hallik sprang forward, slashing his sword down.

The hobgoblin barely reacted in time, raising its sword to deflect the blow, but it was too slow. Hallik's sword slid across the metal plate on its shoulder and pushed its sword down. He moved in with another quick strike and his sword ripped across the hobgoblin's neck.

Three more hobgoblins shrieked and jumped out from around the cave. One was only a few steps away from Bjorn. His hand flicked, throwing knife embedding into the hobgoblin's clavicle, though he'd been aiming for its neck. The creature hissed at him and charged. It too was armed with a long, curved sword, which it swung wildly at him.

Bjorn stepped back and drew his own sword, still holding the crossbow in his other hand, as he hadn't had time to tuck it back away. Their blades met twice, the hobgoblin's sword nearly cutting Bjorn's leg if not for a dagger blade strapped to his thigh that blocked the blow. That was too close. He parried another swing then jabbed, stabbing through the hobgoblin's gut, but the creature still swung at him. He spun away, blade arcing around him, blocking the attack.

The hobgoblin stomped at him, but Bjorn kicked the leg away, throwing it off balance. One more swing of his sword across the back of its legs and the beast was down, finished with a final jab.

Hallik had fared better than Bjorn. The boy was more skilled at swordsmanship, and only one hobgoblin remained, though it appeared Elowyn had stabbed it in the eye. He looked up just in time to see Lorelai hack it across the back with her axe. It fell on its face with a final, guttural scream.

"Will it be like that through the entire cave?" Bjorn asked.

"Possibly," Hallik said, turning to face Vanalf. Elowyn and Lorelai went to stand beside him, but Bjorn held back.

"You're sure you aren't coming?" Elowyn asked Bjorn.

Bjorn was still unsure. All his life he'd struggled against these monsters, knowing that the Grimnirs had abandoned them. And yet, now he had the chance to become one.

Hallik turned back to face him. "It's like my father said. You'll still be your same stoic self that likes to kill monsters, and becoming a Grimnir will just make you better at it."

"That's not how Tyrus said it," Elowyn said.

Still, Bjorn certainly hadn't forgotten the insight. He recalled the Valtyra from earlier, killing that ogre with a few complex strokes that he'd never be able to do in his present state. It was true. Grimnir powers would aid him, but he didn't know if there was any other kind of corruption involved.

He didn't *need* the power. He'd survived this long at least. Didn't normal humans need to have some reassurance that they could still fight back? He clenched his fist and shook his head at Hallik.

"We've wasted enough time," Lorelai snapped, flexing her fingers as she stepped toward the cave.

Elowyn gave Bjorn a sad look but followed Lorelai.

Hallik sighed. "We could use your help, Bjorn." He remained for just a moment, but Lorelai had already stepped into the entrance to the cave, so he turned to follow.

Bjorn ground his teeth and hooked his crossbow back in place. The cave was no doubt filled with more monsters. He'd hate to have gotten this far only to see the kids die inside the cave. Humanity's last hope was going in there without him.

Could they really rely on him? Bjorn had tried to save countless others only to watch them get destroyed, but in reality, their odds wouldn't be much better or worse with him there. He might as well see it to the end. He growled and said, "Wait." He quickly retrieved his throwing knife and jumped down.

Hallik stopped right at the edge of the cave, a smile splitting his face.

Bjorn next got his bolt from the hobgoblin's neck and entered the cave. Hallik went to give him a hug, but Bjorn stiff-armed him. "We're a team, but don't think that means you can get all sappy with me."

Hallik laughed, but the four of them stood still, staring down into the darkness beyond.

A weight settled on Bjorn's shoulders.

"Won't we need light?" Bjorn asked.

"No," Elowyn said. "Vanalf provides what we need." She went and gave Hallik's hand a squeeze.

"Odds are that one of us will die, aren't they?" Lorelai said, only one step further than them.

"We'll all make it out," Hallik said.

Despite his assurance, Bjorn couldn't help but think they were looking down into their own graves.

"Remember the saying," Elowyn said, looking at each of them. "We can't go up if we're already on top. To rise, one must first hit the bottom."

Hallik spoke the last sentence with her, but then added, "From the bottom, there's only one way left to go. Up."

They seemed to be quoting something. Likely some indoctrination to convince Avskildians to send people through Vanalf. But there was wisdom in the words.

Bjorn repeated the phrase in his mind. *To rise, one must first hit the bottom.*

Kel's abyss, was he ready to hit the bottom? He thought he'd hit the bottom once before, but this gave the metaphor a whole different meaning. He clenched his fist around his sword. "No use pondering about it," he growled. "Let's see what magic awaits us." He led the way into the depths of Vanalf.

Chapter Thirty-Eight

INTO THE DEPTHS

Lorelai Harkral

Footsteps reverberated hollowly through the darkened passageway. It wasn't long before the light from the entrance faded behind them, leaving them enveloped in complete and utter blackness, the likes of which she'd never experienced before.

Lorelai's heart thundered in her chest. At first, she considered the possibility that everything was wrong. Perhaps they'd entered at the wrong time and things wouldn't work. There'd be no light to get them through. Maybe the damage to the portals had rendered Vanalf dysfunctional. Again, the thought of retreating came to mind, but it was like Hallik had said. There was no turning back now.

She held her hand out, running it along the side of the wall.

Bjorn grunted ahead of her, then said, "Watch your heads."

Lorelai lowered her head, but it still thunked into a low-hanging stone, and she was instantly grateful for the helmet Bjorn had convinced her to wear. They continued this way, walking deeper into the darkness, the only sounds coming from them. At least nothing would be able to sneak up on them. Hopefully.

As if summoned by her thoughts, a chittering sounded in the distance. They all halted, but the sound did not repeat. They'd only been going for a few moments, but this whole journey was supposed to take most of a day.

Not bringing any light seemed like a ridiculous notion, but Hallik and Elowyn seemed so confident about their approach that she hadn't thought enough to question them. Lorelai had brought both flint and kindling in her bag, but neither would be any good if there wasn't anything to light.

After a bit of silence, Bjorn simply resumed. They'd only gone a few more steps when the sound came again, though this time it was behind them.

"We are *not* going to die when we've barely gotten through the entrance of the cave," Lorelai whispered. "Can you imagine how embarrassing that would be?"

This time, they didn't stop. Bjorn kept them moving.

"Are you certain we weren't supposed to bring any light?" Bjorn asked.

"Yes," Hallik said. "Well, I don't know. Maybe daylight matters, but they don't really give us any specifics."

"What?" Lorelai hissed.

"The students always go in without any torches," Elowyn said.

The chittering sound was even closer this time, like it was somewhere just over Lorelai's shoulder. She resisted the urge to swing her axe around her back. Elowyn was behind her, and she'd be more likely to hit her than whatever thing was making that sound.

"Ouch," Hallik muttered from the rear of the group. "It feels like something just pinched the back of my leg."

A second later, there was something that sounded like crunching on a pile of leaves atop a hunk of pork. Hallik gasped. "I stepped on that."

More chittering sparked from all around the cave.

"Faster!" Elowyn urged. She pressed a hand against Lorelai's back.

Bjorn growled and trudged ahead, stumbling through the darkness. Lorelai tripped and crawled back up, but not before her hand slapped down against a hardened carapace of possibly some kind of insect. She scrambled to her feet, boot crunching on whatever it was. The chittering intensified.

They were going to die, and not even from regular monsters, but from some giant bug. They kept moving through the darkness, but to Lorelai's great astonishment, light glowed ahead of them.

"There's light!" she said a little too loudly, though she wasn't sure her volume would matter with all the creatures around them. They all saw it, and their pace increased as they stumbled over rocks. Something pinched Lorelai's arm, then something else seemed to scrape down the front of her leg. Whether it was a rock or one of the mystery creatures, she didn't know, but she kept running forward regardless.

She slipped Dris out, prepared to cut through anything that touched her. As soon as they reached that light, she'd turn around and get hacking.

The light ahead looked strange, like a bulb of white dangling from the roof of the cave. Jagged stalagmites and stalactites shimmered around it, glistening with moisture. Something scratched at her leg again, and she kicked it away, scrambling after Bjorn.

Both Hallik and Elowyn cried out from behind her, but they kept coming as well.

Lorelai worried there'd be too many of these things and they'd get overwhelmed.

As they reached the light, Bjorn muttered a curse and staggered back.

The light bobbed up, and the nearby stalagmites and stalactites widened further than Lorelai's eyes. Those were not stone at all, but the teeth of some large, fish-headed monster. It gnashed at Bjorn, but he'd apparently recognized it early enough to stay clear of its reach. The monster hissed and flopped toward them, but it was slow and clearly depended on the lure to actually catch any prey.

"What do we do?" Lorelai said. She was close enough to the light to see around her, though far enough away to be safe from the monster's slow, lumbering attempts to reach them. A single glance back into the darkness revealed small creatures skittering across the floor with many-legged bodies, like centipedes the size of her forearm.

Elowyn and Hallik had stopped behind her and were sweeping their weapons across the giant bugs, holding them at bay.

"Kill the monster. Take its light," Elowyn said as she hacked through another disgusting insect.

Lorelai didn't want to go anywhere close to that flopping mass of teeth. That was still the only part of it she

could really see other than its massive, black eyes that glint-
ed dully under its own glow.

"On it," Bjorn growled. "Lorelai. We need to get to
either side of it. Maybe target those eyes." He hopped back
again as the monster lurched toward him with a heaving
flop and a gnash of its enormous teeth.

Lorelai bent down to stab one of the creepy bugs in the
head before facing off against the large monster. "Keep
watching our backs," she said to Hallik and Elowyn.

"Likewise," Elowyn said.

Hallik was a flurry of swipes as his magical sword cut
through the bugs like they were nothing but water, the
sound of their crunching bodies echoing off the cave walls.

Bjorn shimmied to the right while Lorelai angled left.
The creature's bobbing light dangled from side to side as
its head swiveled to either of them in turn. She considered
the possibility that the monster was much more agile than
it let on, and that stepping closer would put them within
easy reach of a single, fatal snap.

It was a risk they'd have to take. They needed light if they
were going to survive Vanalf, and this monster's dangling
lure was the only source of light they'd seen so far.

Bjorn flicked his wrist, and the monster grunted, snapping at him in rage. He'd probably just thrown a knife into
its face. He stabbed his sword high as the monster flopped

at him, and Lorelai realized this was her opportunity to attack. Abandoning all the anxiety that told her not to, she sprang forward, hacking with the axe as she did so, aiming right for the giant disc of the monster's eye. The axe met with surprising resistance, like the eye was made of thick, bouncy glass.

She sucked in a sharp breath as the fish monster turned to bite at her. Jumping back, she tripped over the uneven ground and landed on her back. The bottom of its mouth grazed the heel of her boot, but she was too low for it to snap at her. She rolled away and got back to her feet as it snapped again, but Bjorn stabbed it from the other side.

Clearly frustrated, the monster wobbled back and forth, and she realized it had some kind of flipper leg on either side. When the monster tried snapping at Bjorn again, she jumped to its side with more confidence this time, using Dris to try and pierce the beast instead. This time, her dagger went through its flesh, but she missed the eye and instead stabbed right below it. She withdrew before the monster could react, but she could almost *feel* the dagger's warmth as it absorbed something from the monster.

Something snapped onto Lorelai's back, and she released an involuntary scream. It felt like whatever it was, it was trying to tear through the back of her shirt. As quickly as it was there, it was gone again as Elowyn swept by and tore the insect from Lorelai's back.

"Sorry," Elowyn said, "though you might want to hurry it up."

Lorelai dared to look back only to see that the number of centipede monsters had increased considerably. Hallik and Elowyn wouldn't be able to stop them all.

Bjorn's grunting drew her back to the task at hand. The light had shifted away as the monster went after Bjorn, leaving its side completely exposed. Now that she had a better look at its whole body, she realized that practically half of the monster's mass was devoted to its head, making it seem much larger than it actually was. The other half of its body was no longer than Lorelai was tall. It did in fact have large flippers, but it also had hind legs that looked like they belonged to an incredibly chubby frog.

She tried the axe again and hacked at the monster's frog leg with all her might. It cut through the flesh much easier than she'd expected, nearly severing the limb completely before catching on bone. She swung again, this time aiming for its back. This swing was also successful, and the monster shuddered and croaked.

The monster tried turning to face her, but it could no longer maneuver very well, and she easily stayed behind it, hacking away. She gasped as Bjorn was suddenly there, running up the monster's back. He jumped over the top of its head, blade flashing as he severed the dangling limb that hung over its head. The light dropped to the ground.

Several of the bugs scrambled past Lorelai, diving greedily at the wounds she'd punctured into the monster's body. The monster wriggled in place but no longer seemed able to defend itself.

Lorelai hurried back over to Bjorn. He'd picked the glowing limb up, but the insects were no longer trying to attack them. A large pile of bug corpses littered the cave floor, and they seemed to get thrown into some kind of frenzy, either eating their fellow bugs or the monster.

The four of them backed away, deeper into the cave.

"This is definitely as exciting as I expected," Elowyn said, wiping bug gore from her forehead, lips curled in disgust.

"We've only just begun, Elowyn," Hallik said with a smirk, flicking a bit of bug chitin off Elowyn's arm. "Now let's hurry off while those things are distracted."

Bjorn was quick to oblige, and together, the four of them trod even deeper into the depths of Vanalf.

CHAPTER THIRTY-NINE

GETGALK

Elowyn Galdre

The air inside Vanalf was sometimes warm, sometimes cool. Certainly not something Elowyn had expected. She'd been in a different cave before, and it had been pretty cool inside, but this was only more evidence that Vanalf was not like other caves. It would undoubtedly have strange ways of sustaining life with its magical environment. How much of Vanalf was part of their realm, and how much of it was actually a hybrid of all the realms? Was there a point at which it was more of one place and not another?

There was not enough information about Vanalf to really know. Many Grimnirs emerged from Vanalf with foggy memories, thus perpetuating the mystery of what happened inside. Tyrus seemed to remember his venture better than others did, particularly when he shared details of entering that second time. Perhaps it was the transformation itself that did something to them.

"So what was that thing?" Bjorn asked.

"A krokrfisk," Elowyn said. "They have frequently been remembered by other Grimnirs. And the bugs were giant centipedes. They've been seen outside the cave sometimes as well."

"I killed one that was probably as big as me," Hallik said with a shake of his head.

"They're supposedly more venomous the larger they are," Elowyn said. "If you got bitten, just be mindful of how you're feeling. I don't think anybody has died from their venom, but it can make you woozy."

"Lovely," Lorelai said sarcastically. "I think I got bitten three different times."

"Can I see?" Elowyn asked. "I haven't seen one of their bites before, but it's supposedly a little difficult for them to actually bite humans, and they usually just scratch."

Lorelai held her arm up under the light. Her skin was red and slightly swollen with two distinct punctures.

Elowyn gave Lorelai a frown. "Looks like a bite to me. Be mindful of your steadiness."

"Did that dagger give you any information on those monsters?" Bjorn asked.

"I think Dris collected something from both of them," Lorelai said, "though more so from the krokrfisk. I actually felt it take something away from the monster after I stabbed it the first time, while it was still alive."

Elowyn shivered, still unsure how she felt about the weapon. Once they were Grimnirs, she'd be more interested in seeing what kind of power it could unlock. The trail ahead narrowed until she could easily reach out to either side and touch the walls. As it started getting even closer, her discomfort only grew. They wouldn't be able to pass each other, and if something attacked, only one person would be able to fight it.

Bjorn stopped from up ahead and lifted the glowing appendage higher. He glanced back at them, eyes narrowed, and pointed to his ear. Elowyn heard it as well. Something was coming toward them, shuffling up the cave ahead, occasionally grunting. Bjorn slid his weapon free until, further down the path, something came into sight.

It had the head of a ram, with curled horns on either side of its horse-like face, though its four eyes glowed with crimson embers that reminded her of the ashimal. Its body was blackish-blue, and for some reason, it shimmered as though it were wet. She instantly recognized it as a getgalk. "Climb!" she yelled to them, bracing either side of the cave wall.

The getgalk let out a steaming huff of air and lowered its head.

Ahead of her, Bjorn tucked the glowing appendage in his tunic and crawled up the wall. Elowyn came right behind. The stone was slick with moisture, but she was still able to grip it well enough to start clambering upward.

Lorelai tried to climb up after them as the getgalk kicked its feet and started charging forward, but she slipped down the surface, unable to gain any altitude. "I can't get up!" she shrieked.

Hallik growled from behind her and crawled under her legs. He stood, sword braced in both hands as he faced the charging beast, his cheeks puffing out as he released a breath.

Lorelai dropped back behind Hallik and bent down, grabbing something from the cave floor. All Elowyn could do was watch.

"I don't want to die, Hal," Lorelai said.

"We're not going to die. Back up and brace yourself," Hallik said.

The getgalk brayed just before it would crash into Hallik. A scream caught in Elowyn's throat as the beast passed beneath her.

Hallik dropped to one knee and ducked, thrusting his blade forward and up. His body was beneath the getgalk now, but its momentum had halted. Lorelai threw gravel into the getgalk's face. It shook its head and bellowed.

Bjorn dropped down the cavern, one of his knives flashing out as he cut down the rear of the getgalk. Not a bad idea. She was almost directly over the getgalk herself. She shimmied back a bit, the getgalk stamping below her. For all she knew, it was trying to trample Hallik. She loosened her grip on the walls and pulled out her sword as she slid down. With one full thrust, she slammed her sword between the getgalk's shoulders.

The getgalk shuddered and slunk down, but not before Hallik rolled out from beneath it, blood covering half his face. He coughed and stayed sprawled on the ground, but Lorelai stepped over him and rammed Dris into the creature's head.

Elowyn, practically seated on the getgalk's furry back, gripped the sides of the walls again as the monster fell with a groan.

"Hallik, you're a fool," Elowyn said, going down once she concluded the beast was truly dead. She had to crawl over its body to get to Hallik, though he seemed more concerned with his left leg than anything.

"I wasn't about to let Lorelai get trampled," Hallik said.

"But you could have died," Elowyn said. She didn't want to say it out loud, but she certainly valued Hallik's life more than Lorelai's. "Where did it hurt you?" She kept looking around his body, especially his head, to see where the blood was coming from, but quickly decided it probably belonged to the getgalk.

"It stomped my leg," he said, tapping his left thigh. Bjorn held the light high so they could see better. Hallik's trousers bore the slightest tear, but she couldn't see the skin beneath, nor was any blood soaking through. "I stabbed it right through the chest though. It didn't lower its head enough. Its horn actually caught on the wall a bit so I don't think it was able to reach me."

"Can you walk?" Bjorn asked, looking back at the direction they still needed to go.

Hallik shrugged and tried to get his feet under him, bracing either side of the wall. He grunted, baring his teeth, but he managed to stand. He nodded to Bjorn and shrugged to Elowyn. "Onward," he said before stooping to pick his sword back up. Elowyn still needed to wrench hers out of the getgalk's back.

"Thank you," Lorelai said to Hallik.

"We're a team," Hallik said, stepping forward with a slight limp.

Elowyn retrieved her own sword, but she was still worried about Hallik. He'd play it off like his injury was nothing, but she'd need to keep an eye on him.

"Alright," Bjorn said, turning back around. "Deeper we go."

RAGE

Jaysen Bjorn

Bjorn tried to ignore the bit of gore that had trickled down his chest from the krokrfisk's appendage he'd stuffed in his tunic so he could climb. After they got out of here, he'd need to bathe for half a day.

They continued down the narrow tunnel for a while longer before it opened up into a larger cavern. If Hallik's injury was serious, he was doing a good job of hiding it. He made no complaint whatsoever, though through brief observation, he could tell the young man was hurting. The fact that he was walking at all meant that nothing was broken, so it was more likely just some bruising.

The cavern ahead of them was not quite what Bjorn would have expected. There was almost a mild glow to the place, making the walls more easily visible. As they got deeper, the effect intensified until it was apparent that some sort of ambient light existed in the air as if the dust itself glowed.

He stopped short, noticing reflections in the floor. There was water interspersed across the floor of the cave. "Watch your step," he said, his voice projecting much louder than he'd intended. Something was off about this room.

Lorelai had bent down beside the nearest puddle, brows furrowed in a frown. "It's strange," Lorelai said, her hand slowly moving toward the water, triggering a primal fear in the depths of Bjorn's gut.

"Don't touch it," Bjorn said.

But Lorelai ignored him and dabbed the surface of the water with her finger. There was no ripple. "I can see a perfect reflection of myself." A split second later, a hand emerged from the water, grabbed Lorelai's wrist, and pulled her in. Before Bjorn could even blink, Lorelai was gone, leaving no trace but her axe that clattered to the floor.

Hallik dropped to his knees beside the pool and splashed his hands across the surface. "Lorelai!"

But there was nothing. The cave was silent.

They looked at each other, stunned.

A moment later, there was another splash. Further down the cavern, Lorelai was rolling across the floor with something assaulting her.

Bjorn dashed over to help, but as he neared, he realized he was looking at two exact duplicates of Lorelai, both of them drenched in water, both holding copies of Dris as they tried to stab each other. "What the blight?" he muttered, unsure of what to do.

The two Lorelais continued to struggle with each other. "Gah, help me!" one of them cried. Hallik and Elowyn also stood beside Bjorn, having no clue which one was real. They shoved and tried to stab at each other, yelling for help.

"We have to do something quickly!" Hallik said.

If they didn't act soon, the real one could get killed. Bjorn could only think of one possible solution. "Hand me Dris," he said, kneeling down beside them. One of the Lorelai's was currently on the bottom, a dagger getting dangerously close to her shoulder. "Hand Dris to me, and I'll kill the mimic," he said, "but if I save you, I get to keep the blade."

"What?" said the one on the bottom. "That's ridiculous!"

Bjorn put his own knife to the neck of the Lorelai on top. "Get up. Stand apart from each other." He was mostly certain which one it would be, but he needed to be positive. He couldn't just stab one if it meant accidentally killing Lorelai.

They continued struggling with each other, despite the fact that Bjorn accidentally nicked the skin of the one he suspected to be false.

She gasped. "Bjorn, just let me finish this imposter!"

"Take their daggers," Bjorn said, putting his knife away. Elowyn and Hallik hurried over. They were able to wrest the knives away from both Lorelais. Once disarmed, they still struggled against each other. "Calm yourselves. The only way out from here is for us to decide which of you is real."

"But what if you choose incorrectly?" one of them screamed, eyes watery. They both got to their feet.

"I'm not sure you know me well enough to guess correctly," the other said.

"Don't you even speak, you deceiver!"

"Silence," Bjorn said. "Let me just discard these first." He held both the daggers over the edge of the water.

"No!" said the one to the right, diving for Bjorn. Bjorn immediately swung around her lunge and stabbed both daggers into the other Lorelai.

The stabbed Lorelai dropped to her knees, lips trembling, eyes filled with tears. "Why?" she asked. He withdrew the daggers and she fell to her back. One of the daggers felt warm in his hand. That would be the real Dris, drawing on the soul's energy. The other was a fake.

"How... how did you know?" asked the uninjured Lorelai.

Bjorn shrugged. "Mostly a hunch, but I just assumed the real you would die before she let Dris get lost in this cave."

The dead woman's body started to change, color shifting to that of the cold, dark stone around them. Her body was formed of corded sinews all wrapped together, like exposed muscle with a thin, nearly transparent layer of skin over the top. He'd never seen such a being before. When the body finally stopped changing, it looked like a squat humanoid, its purplish blood flooding onto the moistened stone around it.

He kicked it into the water. One of the daggers in his hand disappeared, and he handed the other to Lorelai. "I said not to touch the water."

Lorelai brushed her soggy hair back and didn't respond.

"Brilliant," Elowyn said with a smile.

"Let's keep moving. I don't like this section," Bjorn said, taking the lead once again. This place still made him uneasy, and after kicking the body into the water, a mild steam started fogging up over the surface of the water.

As they went further, he realized there were several more puddles.

"It'll be alright," Hallik whispered to Lorelai. She was still dripping wet, and her boots squished as she walked.

"That was... scary," Lorelai said.

"I can only imagine," Elowyn said.

Good. They'd help her through it. Bjorn didn't have much to offer when it came to helping people recover. The world was filled with terror, and it wouldn't be the last time something horrific might happen before they got out of this cave.

Bjorn chose his steps carefully. Much of the cave floor was smooth in this part, as if it were trying to make itself indistinguishable from the puddles. There could be more of those doppelganger creatures, and he wasn't eager to have any more of them get duplicated. When they got to the far end of the expanse, there were no more puddles, and the path further down led around several stalagmites. The same, strange dusting of light lingered in the air.

The ground was uneven, with a layer of loose rocks covering the surface. He thought it was peculiar, but the reason for the gravel only became clear after they took a few more steps and noticed the ceiling was shaking. At first he thought they were some kind of monster hanging down, but on closer inspection, it appeared that the entire ceiling was covered in stalactites. They shook slightly as if on the cusp of falling.

"Blight," Hallik said, and a stalactite fell straight down toward him. He jumped aside and the stone spear shattered onto the ground.

They all held still, eyes on the ceiling. Oddly, a new stalactite slid into view, replacing the one that had just fallen. They shared a look as they recognized the same thing. Things did not function here as they should. Bjorn had to remind himself that this was no normal cave.

He held a finger to his lips then motioned for them to proceed slowly. If his suspicion was correct, making a distinct sound would cause a stalactite to fall on them, which was hard not to do when the ground was covered in gravel. Their boots grinding on the stone was louder than his teeth grinding in his mouth. They'd only made it a few steps before another stalactite plummeted, this time aiming for Lorelai with her squishy boots. She dodged, but the shattering of stone caused another stalactite to drop, then another, though these weren't directly over them. Others continued to fall. The haphazardness of it all would make this place unpassable.

Elowyn groaned. "Run," she hissed at them.

Bjorn did not hesitate. The four of them started sprinting down the slope, dodging around the stalagmites. Stalactites started falling in a constant barrage behind them. If they slowed down at all, they'd get skewered. They also needed to keep pace with each other. If one of them ran too far ahead, they'd cause those behind to get hit as well.

Maintaining their footing became difficult as gravel slipped beneath each of their steps. When the slope became steeper, Elowyn said, "Slide."

He wasn't sure what she meant until she jumped ahead and started sliding down the gravel with both of her feet planted. He tried as well without looking behind. The gravel slipped beneath him as gravity propelled him down. Eventually, the slope began to taper off, but much of the gravel was pouring over the edge of a drop off.

"Cliff," Bjorn warned.

Elowyn dropped to her back and started rolling to the left. He mimicked her maneuver and was able to catch a glimpse of Lorelai and Hallik at the back. They were already further to the side where a lip of stone would prevent them from falling at the drop off. That meant Bjorn was the closest to danger.

He rolled, surprised at how well it worked. Elowyn hit the lip and crawled away to leave room for Bjorn. He caught the ledge with his hands and worked on pulling himself up while gravel continued to pummel and tug at him.

Hallik and Lorelai landed well in the safe zone, and the three of them rushed over to pull Bjorn up. With the rest of the team's help, Bjorn heaved his legs up, clearing the landslide. It stopped not long after.

They all sat for a brief moment. Bjorn didn't even want to think about trying to go back that way, but perhaps the route up would be different. He cringed at his own thoughts. Hallik's optimism was rubbing off on him too much. It was better to plan for the worst outcomes.

After drinking the last of their water, they agreed to continue on. He realized he had no sense of time, and it felt like they'd been in Vanalf for several hours. He'd almost expected there to be more monsters, and it was hard to understand how an entire army of trolls had made their way out through this cave. It only supplemented his idea that perhaps the cave continually changed or evolved.

They left the gravel slope behind, rounding a large stone pillar. A new light burned ahead. Orange veins in the cave walls glowed as though roiling fire lived beneath the stone, casting an amber hue across the whole space.

The glowing appendage in Bjorn's hand added little light, but it didn't take long for him to realize that they weren't alone. Several monsters looked up at them. There'd be no sneaking about in here. It was like they'd been waiting for them, though that came as no surprise.

The sound of all that gravel crashing through the cave would have drawn the attention of every living thing nearby.

"By the depths," Lorelai said.

The cave was easily wide enough for them to stand side-by-side, and they did so now, looking down at the monsters that all started creeping their way toward them. This was more in line with what Bjorn had expected of Vanalf. Despite the host of monsters that stretched out below them and the lack of food he'd had in the last few hours, Bjorn had a peculiar energy tingling through him, tantalizing him, pulling him.

"Do you feel that?" Hallik asked, rolling his shoulders.

"It's like a song in my heart," Elowyn said, placing a finger to her chest. "It's the depths. Calling to us. We must be close."

Some of the monsters started to growl at them as they drew nearer. Bjorn prepared himself, holding his sword out before him.

"Then let us go to it," Lorelai said, hefting her axe in one hand, Dris in the other.

"Stand together," Hallik said. "These monsters don't seem coordinated."

They weren't all the same kind of monster. Two of them looked like rabid dogs with frog-shaped faces, one was a roiling mass of legs, and another—with a small body, bulbous head, and long limbs ending in claws—was flying at them. There were three other monsters coming toward them as well, if not more.

"At least this will be good for your list, Bjorn," Hallik said.

Bjorn grunted. If they survived.

The first to reach them were the frog-headed dogs. A tongue shot from one's mouth, and Elowyn deftly stopped it from slamming into her face by blocking it with her sword. Instead of cutting, the tongue grabbed her sword around the blade and pulled. Elowyn gasped, but Lorelai hacked the tongue clean off with her axe.

Another tongue launched at Hallik, which he also deflected with his sword, but the tongue sizzled on contact with Imarún. Both the frog-dog monsters whimpered. They were only a few steps away when this happened, but Bjorn didn't want to break position to finish them off. The flying monster was nearly upon them. He took one more step to the right as the rest of his team stood to his left. The flying monster swooped, its long, spiked appendages aimed at them.

Bjorn ducked and swung a horizontal swipe, cutting off the tip of one of its barbed ends. He spun back, hoping to get in another attack, when something slammed into his side before falling away. It was the stump of a chopped tongue, the frog-dog monster still trying to use it. Instead, it croaked a whimper at the pain. Blood flicked from the end as it whipped the tongue around.

A ball of fur launched across the cavern and latched directly onto Hallik's arm. He screamed and spun, slashing his magical sword across one of the frog-headed monsters. "Gah! What is this thing?" He flicked his arm, trying to dislodge the furry creature, but to no avail.

"Lorelai," Elowyn said, "use Dris to help Hallik. I'm not sure that will come off otherwise."

"It bit me!" Hallik called, his voice a high-pitched shriek.

Bjorn could not discern what the creature was before Lorelai hurried over and jabbed Dris into it. The creature yelped and disappeared in a flurry of ash.

Hallik began to yell in rage and charged forward with frightening zeal. His blade was a blur as he took out two other monsters before they even had a chance to react. He was clearly not acting normal.

"What was that thing?" Bjorn asked, hurrying to back up Hallik.

Elowyn gave an exasperated sigh. "They're called rage lemmings."

Bjorn dodged under the flying monster's slicing limbs as it took another pass over them, then cast Elowyn a bewildered look. "What? A monster lemming?"

"Yes," Elowyn said. "They aren't actual lemmings. They have fangs. When they bite somebody, their venom inflicts people with some kind of delirium that often results in something like... well, that." She gestured to Hallik, who was still yelling and swinging madly.

Bjorn wasn't sure he minded, so long as it was only temporary. Hallik was tearing through the monsters. Practically the only creature left was the one that kept flying over them, trying to jab them with its hooked claws. "Does it wear off?"

"It does, but we may need to keep some distance from him for a moment." Elowyn hacked at the flying monster's jabbing limbs but missed.

Bjorn threw one of his knives at the monster. The knife tore through the side of one of its wings and embedded in the body. It lost its ability to fly and plummeted, crashing headfirst into the ground. It groaned and looked up at Bjorn, a gash on its bulbous head. Lorelai dashed over to it and smacked one of its jabbing limbs away with her axe before stabbing it with Dris. The monster's groan cut short, and it collapsed to the cave floor.

Hallik was almost all the way on the other side of the cavern.

"Oh, blight." Elowyn hurried through the cavern after Hallik. "We might not want him to get too far away. He could easily get into danger."

Bjorn groaned and followed, trying to take note of the various monsters that had been slain. He counted over a dozen in total, at least nine of them killed by Hallik in his enraged state.

"By the depths," Lorelai exclaimed as they rushed by the carnage.

When they reached the bottom, Hallik was sitting back against a severed stalagmite. His tunic was pulled loose and his body was covered in sweat as he panted. He brushed his hair back and wiped the sweat from his forehead. "Wh-what happened?" he said between breaths.

"It was a rage lemming," Elowyn said, checking the bite on Hallik's arm. "Fortunately, you never turned to attack us, but simply charged down the cave."

Bjorn hated to think what would have happened if Hallik had turned on them.

"Oh, yes," Hallik said, holding a palm against his head. "I honestly didn't think those were real."

"Are you well?" Lorelai asked.

"I think so," Hallik said. "I could use a drink."

"We're all out," Bjorn said. The only thing they had left to do was to finish this and climb back out.

Hallik grunted and got back to his feet, breathing finally slowing. "By the depths, it's hot." He wiped his sweaty face against his shirt sleeve. "Let us proceed."

Bjorn gave Elowyn a questioning look, but she only shrugged.

"We need to finish this," she said to him in a low voice.

Bjorn nodded and followed Hallik. They ducked through a crack in the wall. It got particularly narrow, which made Bjorn question if they were going the right way. In all likelihood, there were probably a dozen paths they'd missed. He had no idea how they were supposed to know which way to go.

All doubt vanished as soon as they emerged on the other side. He went to stand beside Hallik on a ledge, breath catching in his throat. Before them stretched an entire universe, a massive tunnel that went on forever. It seemed impossible, but above, it went as high as the sky, the surface of the cave clearly visible, but at the same time appearing vastly far away. Everything glittered as though emblazoned with distant stars, and clouds of amorphous material that looked like sand billowed across the expanse in myriad colors.

"We made it?" Lorelai asked, mouth open as she gazed out at the scene, her eyes sparkling.

"Not yet," Elowyn said, pointing down to their side. A gradual slope led to the bottom of the cavern that lay before the expanse. "We must first hit the bottom."

This was it. Bjorn was about to become a Grimnir. He glanced the way they'd come, concerned about their path back, but the crack through which they'd crawled was gone. He shook his head, realizing he'd have to trust whatever crazy process this was.

To the bottom they'd go.

CHAPTER FORTY-ONE

THE BOTTOM

Hallik

Fire coursed through Hallik's veins as his heart hammered within. He didn't want to share with the others that he was still suffering some side effects of the small monster's bite, so he continued on. Time was too valuable to wait for this sensation to calm down, and he'd at least regained his senses.

The whole fit had been quite the experience. His vision had been acutely focused on each enemy, and he'd moved faster than ever. He wondered if there were any spells a Grimnir could cast that might have similar effects with fewer downsides.

But they needed to get this over with. And quickly.

Reaching this deep into Vanalf was unlike anything he'd expected. Other Grimnirs had described the depths as beautiful, but their words could never do it justice. Through that vast expanse that stretched beyond, all the realms were tied together.

Ancient lore referred to the expanse as the Wyrm, like it was some living being that somehow pulled all of existence into a single connection. He could see now why such a word had been used. Vanalf seemed very much alive, and the stretch of the Wyrm did have the vague appearance of a long, rounded body. He shivered at the notion. Perhaps he was finally cooling down.

They descended as a group, Hallik at the lead. The instructors always said that they'd know when they hit the bottom. It was such a distinctive experience that there'd be no denying it. Once they had confirmation, the path back out would be clear before them. A lot of this rode on faith, which was no problem for Hallik. He'd been riding faith for years.

A whooshing sound filled the chamber then ceased, and he couldn't help but think that it was like the sound of giant lungs filling and exhaling.

"I could spend a lifetime here," Elowyn said. She pressed a hand to her chest, barely able to watch her steps as she walked beside Hallik.

Hallik only nodded. He couldn't agree more. He could only imagine all the things they could learn down here.

Elowyn, destined to be a singer, was probably the only one of her kind to ever descend here. The songs she'd sing one day would rock the foundations of the world.

If he had to guess, portals were a very natural part of how things operated down here. There didn't seem to be any other way to explain how the realms connected. It couldn't be so natural as a physical connection through this Wyrm. Or perhaps he was wrong, and they really were all connected in such a way. There truly was so much left to learn.

His remaining symptoms continued to recede as they went down the incline, which was shaped like a natural, uneven staircase with interspersed rock formations. The very bottom was the darkest place in sight, shrouded as though the light could not reach it.

Their view of the Wyrm's expanse started to diminish the lower they got, impeded by the uneven floor of the vast network, many parts rising quite high. He'd expected more resistance to this point, but he knew it wasn't over yet. That feeling in his chest that urged him onward continued to expand. He had to actively resist the impulse to start running down the slope. The feeling only crescendoed as they neared the bottom. He couldn't help but smile as he looked at Elowyn.

Hallik was only a couple steps from the bottom when the ground trembled like the passing of a dozen galloping horses. "I'm sure that's normal and not at all indicative of something terrible coming," he whispered to the team, but Elowyn gripped his arm to try and silence him.

The sound persisted, and Elowyn did not release Hallik's arm as they stepped down. Hallik could have sworn the sound was oddly rhythmic, as if intentional. That feeling that drew him onwards seemed to be coming from the source of the sound. Ahead, the area was covered in darkness. A low mountain stood between them and the rest of the Wyrm, blocking the colorful light beyond.

"Wait," Bjorn said as they continued to walk. Even he didn't stop at his own word. "I think we might have been tranced."

Hallik knew what Bjorn meant, but this seemed like it was part of the process. The feeling and the sound were drawing them to the bottom of Vanalf. Once they reached that point, they would turn around and climb back out. This was how to become a Grimnir.

As they drew nearer to the deepest point, however, the dim light still held in Bjorn's hand brought something else into view ahead. The first things Hallik noticed were the twinkling green eyes of an animal watching them approach. Then he noticed its teeth, revealed under the snarling snout of a wolf. The beast was so tall that its head was eye-level with him. Unconsciously, he withdrew his sword, the surface glowing with the slightest hue of orange.

A battle was before them.

The others spread out to either side of him. The giant wolf did not attack. It was held in check by a chain wrapped around its neck. Another figure stepped into view, holding the chain. It looked like a long-limbed man with a thick, wiry beard. Deer horns protruded from the man's head, and his skin was dark gray, not dissimilar to that of the trolls. In his other hand, he held a staff made of iron.

Hallik couldn't tell if the man was some kind of troll or a twisted elf of some kind.

The man smirked at them. "I thought some of you might try coming down here. I knew it was too much to hope that the trolls would finish you all off."

"And you are?" Hallik said, leveling his sword.

"You don't recognize me?" He lifted his staff and shrugged. "I thought your songs kept record of Dvelden."

Elowyn hissed the words out as she whispered, "An evil dark elf." That was Hallik's only warning before chaos erupted. Elowyn, not waiting for any signal, rushed forward. Hallik certainly didn't recognize the name, but apparently Elowyn had, and she'd instantly deemed him worthy of death. This was no friend.

Hallik ran beside her as Dvelden released his grip on the chain that restrained his wolf. The creature snapped forward. Elowyn skipped to the side, but the beast wisely held its ground and snapped again. She could not advance.

Dvelden lifted his staff, its entire length thrumming with deep energy. A bolt from Bjorn's crossbow pinged harmlessly off its surface. The singsong sound that had rumbled through the ground earlier trembled once again at Dvelden's utterance. The cave floor cracked, and Hallik had to dive forward to avoid being crushed by stones that ripped up and smashed together from either side of him.

A throwing knife lodged into the giant wolf's shoulder, but it gave no sign of being injured.

Hallik got back to his feet and thrust his sword straight at Dvelden's gut. The dark elf did not block, but instead became blurry. Half a heartbeat later, Dvelden was no longer where Hallik's sword was but was just to Hallik's right, his glowing staff smashing into Hallik's shoulder. The blow sent him rolling toward the wolf, which eagerly bit at him.

But Lorelai was on the other side of the wolf already, both her axe and Dris piercing the wolf's side. It nipped at her, tearing her sleeve and clipping the side of her arm with its teeth, but she stabbed again, grazing the wolf's face with Dris's tip.

Hallik rolled in time to avoid a couple more blows from Dvelden's staff. He tried cutting at the wolf's legs with Imarún, but it stepped over the attack easily. Ignoring the miss, he swung for Dvelden as he got back to his feet. Dvelden knocked Hallik's sword away, then jabbed Hallik's gut with the butt of the staff.

It felt like he'd just been punched, but it ignited a fury within him. He did not come this far just to have his chances at becoming a Grimnir get snatched away by some angry, twisted elf. He sprang forward, striking with rage over and over again, trusting that his friends were taking care of the wolf that was now behind him.

Each time he swung, his blade either passed through nothing or it was deflected by that metal staff. It was almost like the dark elf was incorporeal while still wielding the weapon. The fifth time his sword passed through nothing, he realized he was being duped. This was somehow only a projection. The elf had cast multiple spells, not just the one where he'd tried crushing him with the stones.

The real enemy was probably hiding in the dark somewhere, his staff being controlled by some sort of manipulation. But where was the actual enemy?

It was Bjorn who spotted him a few paces away and charged, fighting the true Dvelden while Hallik kept defending himself against the staff, which was somehow fighting him even without the dark elf's aid. He grunted and parried it then grabbed the staff with one hand, but it merely jerked him around. Instead, he tried something else, letting go and sprinting after the real Dvelden, hoping to aid Bjorn.

At a gesture from the elf, a burst of black energy swarmed over Bjorn, and Hallik showed up just in time to leap forward and hack at Dvelden. His blade cut across Dvelden's ribs, and the elf looked back at him with wide eyes.

"Imarún," Dvelden said, muttering the sword's name as though it were a curse. How he'd learned the sword's name was beyond Hallik, but he didn't need to understand something in order to kill it. He swung again, this time severing a couple of Dvelden's fingers.

The elf yelled, ground shaking. The staff appeared in Dvelden's good hand just in time for him to deflect another blow from Hallik, but then a dagger slammed into Dvelden's eye, hurled by Bjorn who'd emerged from the dissipating darkness.

Hallik acted quickly, feinting a swing before stabbing Dvelden straight through the chest. He could feel the magic of Imarún warming his hands as the magic sapped Dvelden's very soul.

With an earth-shattering pop, the ground shook even more than before as Dvelden disappeared in a cloud of black ash. The ash burst away, blown toward the low mountain as though carried by a powerful wind. The wolf howled and retreated, also disappearing into the darkness.

"Did you kill him?" Bjorn asked. He looked haggard, his face spotted with blood.

"I'm not sure," Hallik said, wishing he could see where the ash cloud had gone. That didn't seem like the way a monster died. He'd heard of eruptions before, but nothing like black ash getting sucked away.

"That seemed like a manipulation spell if I had to guess," Elowyn said. "But the wolf was pretty severely injured as well. I wouldn't be surprised if they die."

"Let's hurry in case they decide to come back with more help," Lorelai said, rushing off to follow that tug they all felt in their chests.

None of them argued. They ran now. This was the moment they'd all been working for. The ground was still shaking as they approached a large stone. When they finally got to it, Hallik could barely make out the runes on a flattened surface. It reminded him of the runic stone he'd seen outside that portal he'd found when he first met Bjorn.

"It says 'the bottom,'" Elowyn said, pointing to the large runes at the very top. Below that were thousands more runes which Hallik recognized as names.

A tingling sensation caused his body to shake, and he placed a hand on the stone. All of them did. But the rumbling suddenly intensified, and he worried it was not part of the typical routine.

"We made it," Hallik said, experiencing a sensation like something shifting beneath his skin. He wasn't sure what it was that happened inside of him, but he'd changed somehow. All that was left was to get out alive. "We should run back."

Elowyn nodded, but Hallik became flushed with a strange drowsiness, and an image crossed his vision, that of a pair of eyes peering at him. The runic stone became a vibrating blur. A voice was calling him in a language that he did not understand.

The ground erupted into darkness and Hallik was only vaguely aware that his body was falling. Deeper. Deeper into the depths of Vanalf.

CHAPTER FORTY-TWO

GRIMNIR

Lorelai Harkral

Lorelai coughed, attempting to clear her lungs. All around her was blackness. She felt around, crawling slowly. "Elowyn," she called. No answer came. "Bjorn? Hallik?" Nothing. She crept on hands and knees, continuing to feel around in the darkness until her hand finally connected with the wall. When she looked up, there was still no light at all, though she could have sworn that she'd just fallen straight down. Perhaps Vanalf had deemed her unworthy to become a Grimnir and had swallowed her up in its rejection.

No. She set her jaw and stepped more firmly. No, that was not what happened. She'd made it to the bottom. That was the only requirement. Now she just needed to escape. She pressed forward, climbing over rubble. She called for the others a few more times, but there was still no response. Wherever she'd fallen, it was vast, and there was nothing else to do but keep moving.

She had no idea how much time passed as she walked, often stumbling over the uneven ground. At least there were no more monsters. With her hand on the wall, she walked and walked, realizing it was quite possible that she was only going in circles around the same, empty chamber. Had something broken? Perhaps the portals no longer protected anything at all. Maybe the source of Grimnir power had just been destroyed by that angry dark elf.

Regardless of how futile it seemed, she would not stop walking. This was her power. She'd gotten to the bottom. She'd earned it. Reining in her frustration took just as much effort as each step forward. She was nearing the end of her wits and wanted to let go of the wall and head to the other side. Maybe she really was walking in circles.

When she was just about to give in, she saw a light. It could have been her eyes playing tricks on her again, but she took heart and pressed on. Her ankles were bruised and aching from blindly kicking stones, but nothing would stop her now.

"Bjorn," she called to the light, hoping beyond reason that it was somehow him up ahead, holding his light out to guide her back to them. She still didn't want to admit it, but they must have all died when the floor caved in on them, swallowing them beneath the runic stone. Why else would they not answer?

There was, of course, no response. She tried to swallow the lump in her throat as she got closer to the faint light. It was small, reflecting only off the surface of the stone, hiding its true source around a bend up a tunnel. She took longer to reach the opening of the tunnel than she might have thought, having to climb up a crumbling wall of stones to reach it. When she got there, she had to get down on hands and knees to crawl through the hole. She continued in such a manner for some time, knees and elbows getting sore as they grated against the hard surface, but she would not give up.

The light only increased in intensity ever-so-slightly with each passing moment. At times, she wondered if it was growing darker. Eventually, a new scent, like that of rain, urged her on even more.

Before she knew it, the light was so intense that she had to squint her eyes as she crawled out, her hands grazing against soft vegetation. It took her a moment to realize she could stand, and as she rose to her feet, her jaw dropped, her eyes slowly taking in the vision that lay before her.

"Lorelai!" Elowyn cried, dashing over and embracing her.

Bjorn also stood there, arms folded as he leaned back against a sharp stone spire that rose behind him. They were outside, and the sun was setting to the west, though the late evening rays still shone directly on them. They stood atop a stone surface which she vaguely recognized as the top of the rocky structure that formed the entrance to Vanalf. When she looked back, the hole through which she'd crawled was nowhere to be seen.

Her lips moved with unspoken questions, still unsure what to even ask.

"We don't understand it," Bjorn said, noting Lorelai's disorientation. "Even with you, I couldn't see you until you were standing up. I don't know where you came from otherwise. The holes we crawled through appeared to us individually, as if Vanalf wanted us to take different paths to get here. Strange."

Elowyn shook her head, pulling back from her hug with Lorelai. "That's even more than I remember. I just remember touching the stone, and then we fell. After that, I was simply crawling until I was here with Bjorn."

Lorelai nodded. How had she gotten here? What stone was Elowyn even talking about? She looked down at herself, her filthy hands, her tattered clothes. Hadn't she been wearing a helmet at some point? "Is it done, then? Are we... are we Grimnirs?"

"Oh, yes," Bjorn said. "I certainly am. At least, I believe so. I'm experiencing things... differently. I can see and hear sharper than ever before." He shook his head.

Elowyn smiled. "He's a Watcher."

"And what about you?" Lorelai asked, expecting Elowyn to say she was a Vitugr.

Elowyn shook her head. "I'm not sure. I can't tell if I'm a Vitugr or a Voyager. Hopefully the latter, of course. We may need to get back to the outpost to find out."

Bjorn grunted. "No Hallik."

"How long did it take for us to emerge behind you?" Lorelai asked.

"Seconds," Bjorn said, folding his arms.

"Then we will wait," Elowyn said with a nod, but moments passed. The sun started dipping down behind the nearby mountain. Both she and Lorelai tried experimenting to see what kind of Grimnir they were. Indeed, Lorelai felt something different. Her mind felt as though there were some distant memory that she couldn't exactly recall, but it was there, and it was vivid.

There was a dark feeling, though, when she considered Hallik. She didn't want to voice it, but she was quite certain Hallik would not be joining them, but she admittedly did not know the mysteries of Vanalf.

The sun was completely behind the mountain by the time Bjorn shushed them, and they all ducked behind the stones. Something was coming. He pointed to the sky before pulling out his crossbow and winding it up.

It took Lorelai a moment to see, but she finally identified a shape flying in their direction. She peeked out from behind her rock to look as it drew closer, but she recognized what it was rather quickly.

"It's a Valtyra," Bjorn said after a quick glance. "He's got somebody with him."

The three of them stood together as the Valtyra approached. The Valtyra, who Lorelai vaguely remembered as Kaldir, carried Rav in his arms and silently landed on a stone nearby them. He placed Rav on the ground before their group.

"Nature's rays, you did it," Rav said, smiling only with her lips as she regarded them, but there was a downcast look to her demeanor as she noticed one vital detail. "Where is Hallik?"

Elowyn shook her head, but Bjorn answered. "He has not returned."

Rav shook her head, eyes wider. "Peace," she said, her voice little more than a whisper.

Elowyn shook her head again. "He is not gone."

"It is far past time," Rav said. "He would have come out with you already. He is one of the lost."

Elowyn looked at all of them, fierceness in her eyes. "No."

Rav shook her head. "I'm afraid it's the same every time, Elowyn. The survivors always emerge almost simultaneously. Are you sure he reached the bottom?"

"Yes," Lorelai said, remembering the blurred image of Hallik there beside her, touching the strange stone. "He got there with us, all at the same time."

Rav frowned and ran the fingernail of her thumb across her lips. "That does seem peculiar." Kaldir nodded in agreement. "But we must plan for the worst. There's the chance that one of you is a Voyager, and as you can see," she paused to look up where the strange crack in the sky remained, "we have no time to waste." Rav waved a hand in front of each of them in turn, her eyes flashing with a yellow light each time.

Lorelai looked down at her hands, wishing she understood what power she had and how to use it.

When Rav waved a hand in front of Bjorn, she muttered, "Watcher." She got to Lorelai and waved a hand. Something warm rolled beneath her skin. Rav then said, "Vitugr."

Lorelai lost her breath at the utterance. She was a Vitugr. It was not the kind of Grimnir they needed, but even Lorelai knew that Vitugrs were often considered the most powerful. She looked down at her hands, letting the idea of being a Vitugr sink in. Great power was now at her fingertips, but she had no idea how to access it yet. That alone sparked a flame of frustration.

Rav waved a hand in front of Elowyn, everyone tense as they waited to hear what she was. Rav let out a breath and nodded to them. "Voyager."

Elowyn didn't even react. Her face was still twisted in a frown as she glanced back at the seemingly invisible hole from which she crawled.

"This is what we've needed," Rav said, placing a hand on Elowyn's shoulder. "You understood the risks long before now. Hallik did too. The two of you knew the price it might take to save our people. Now let us get on so that the sacrifices we've all made can hopefully save the rest of us."

Rav had a point, but that didn't make Lorelai feel any better. She really hadn't expected that Hallik, of the four of them, would be the one who wouldn't emerge. In truth, *she* had been the most likely one to die inside. But Hallik? It was not fair.

Elowyn clenched her fists. "Very well." She regarded Bjorn and Lorelai. "We must go to Tyrus."

Lorelai nodded. She understood what had to be done. They needed to find the portal that was on the verge of destruction, and Elowyn's Voyager magic would somehow be able to restore it. Then they'd have to check the other portals and see if they could cleanse those as well to reinforce the shield.

Elowyn was strong. Even losing Hallik would not set her back from their goal. They could push through this. They could survive.

A thrum resounded beneath them, and the crack in the sky spread even farther.

She could've used one of Hallik's stupidly optimistic phrases right then.

From the corner of her eye, she thought she saw something move down below. She hurried over but saw nothing. "What was that?" she asked.

Rav peered over the edge with a frown and said, "Something just entered Vanalf."

CHAPTER FORTY-THREE

DRAKKED

Hallik

Sweat dripped from the top of Hallik's head. Or was it blood? He was so hot. A fire burned nearby as he swayed back and forth. He was dangling from his legs. It smelled of smoke and seared flesh. Part of him suspected it was his own flesh that burned, but his senses were so muddled that it took him ages to even realize he was upside down. His sides ached abominably, and his arms hung limply at either side of his head.

As he swayed, something creaked, and he heard the occasional tap of wood on metal and crackling embers. His vision was blurry and his head felt like it was stuffed full of wool. He was certain he'd lost consciousness or something, but he was still struggling to put his thoughts together.

At one point, something pricked him, and a low, satisfied growl vibrated the air.

His mouth tasted of vomit, and he had no recollection of how he'd gotten into this predicament. He could have sworn he'd been in the depths of Vanalf, fighting to become a Grimnir. Not... here. Where was here?

His vision slowly started to clear, the light of the fire becoming more distinct. Shadows danced on a cave wall nearby as something hunched over the fire, stirring a metal pot that hung over the flames. Hallik blinked his eyes rapidly, hoping to clear his vision more, but his body swayed away. When he finally swung back around, a creature was staring at him, clutching a wooden spatula in its hand.

It spoke to him then with a voice somewhere between a growl and a rasp. "I was certain I'd get another chance at the blood of a Tyrusson." A tongue flicked from the figure's mouth. It was harder to gauge while upside down, but Hallik guessed the monster was as tall as a troll. Its body was covered in scales, and several horns crowned its head and ran down its neck. Its face was fairly round, save for three more spikes that jutted from its chin, and it stood on two legs that weren't completely visible in the shadows. A plain linen robe hung from one of its shoulders, held in place by a spike that jutted from its bone.

A lizard creature, fairly humanoid in structure. Had he heard of monsters like this? He could have sworn its classification was on the tip of his tongue. For whatever reason, it had chosen not to kill him. Not yet. Worst of all, he feared it was the same monster that had killed his brother and nearly killed his father.

"Quite deceitful of you," the creature said, returning to stirring the pot. "I should have been able to detect you after you entered. All of us should have." Its voice was intelligible despite its growly tone. "I caught only a whiff of you at some point. Must have been a moment where the blade wasn't in your hands. All I had to do then was track your companions."

It looked up from its stirring to regard Hallik, its dark eyes glinting from the light of the fire. After retrieving something from the floor, it stepped toward him. Imarún shimmered in the creature's grip. "To think this might have saved you." A gravelly sound issued from its throat, which he eventually realized was laughter.

"What do you want?" Hallik asked, unsure why the creature was bothering to talk to him. He knew there were some monsters that liked to torture their victims. Perhaps this was the case. He swallowed, recognizing that he'd actually failed his mission. His heart pounded, probably from hanging upside down, but also with the devastating realization. The pace of his breathing increased rapidly. He'd always known there was a chance that he wouldn't survive Vanalf. It was pounded into them from the very beginning. Casualties happened. That was part of the job. Even still, he'd never imagined that he'd be one of the students who never made it through.

The creature grunted. "I fought your father before when he came through the first time. And the second. He wasn't supposed to do that, you know. The magic of a Grimnir is something unique. Not to be disrespected. Gifted by the Wyrm itself. It's not like most of the other races' innate magic. And a Grimnir human can be used to make some of the most potent spells, potions, and enchantments. A delicacy, if you will." It flashed a wicked grin that revealed a row of jagged teeth. "A Grimnir's magic is easily detectable here in the Wyrm since they are one and the same. Their very blood acts as a beacon."

It crouched down so that its warm, rotten breath blew across Hallik's face, ruffling his hair. "And your blood has a long line of Grimnir magic flowing in it. That makes it more potent. You may not be a full Grimnir yet, but the seed of the Wyrm's energy is planted within. That is all I need."

Hallik didn't understand the relevance of what the monster was saying. Perhaps he should have paid closer attention in some of Lind's classes. He just hoped the other three had gotten out safely, though he wasn't sure that was possible. The ground had seemingly swallowed them all whole. "Need for what?"

The creature ran Imarún across Hallik's arm, drawing blood. Hallik gasped at the pain, but the creature simply held its hand to Hallik, catching some of the blood in its scaly palm. "I can take your power for myself," it said. "Your kind still have no idea what power you wield. It belongs to those of us born of the magical races."

"Who are you to decide the will of the Wyrm?"

It dropped the sword to clamp a hand over Hallik's mouth, fully enveloping his face, its sharp claws pricking the back of his head. "Your people will know soon enough who I am." It released him with a shove, and he started to sway back and forth. The creature tipped its hand over the pot, Hallik's blood dripping in. "In your tongue I would be called Kottatare, a drakked."

Kottatare. Hallik knew enough of the old language to recognize that it meant "flesh-eater." He shivered at the insinuation. The monster was going to eat him. "I taste disgusting," Hallik said.

Kottatare only chuckled.

"I'm serious. The last thing that tried to eat me quite literally got torn apart from the inside." He didn't share the part where it was Lind that had actually been swallowed, ripping his way out.

"Worry not," Kottatare said. "There are only select parts of you that I will need to consume." It pricked its own arm, letting the blood drip into the pot.

"You say you'll get my power somehow, but I'm not even a Grimnir yet. Maybe once you drink that, you'll just start growing hair."

Kottatare chuckled again. "Your blood will allow me to enter your realm, Mennesvarld. Once there, I can eat all the Grimnirs I please."

That did not sound good. Hallik started struggling against whatever bound his ankles. It stretched his body, making his joints sore. There had to be a way out of this. Dying was one thing, but being the final piece that allowed another monster to get into Avskild was another. He was not about to become such a key.

His struggles were fruitless. Whatever it was that bound his legs, it held firm. He coughed a couple times, lungs heaving to expel some of the dust that must have filled his lungs after the fall. He needed to inspect the binding more closely, but he doubted the drakked would be very accommodating.

Kottatare took a deep breath through its nostrils as it sniffed the curling, steamy tendrils of whatever it was brewing. It shivered visibly, its eyes closed in delight. "It's finished." Its tongue darted out, licking at the steam.

A rumbling trembled through the stone, and dust trickled from above.

Next came a bellowing voice that sounded like it belonged to a giant talking cow. "Drakked. We know you have the Grimnir. We come for its flesh."

Kottatare hissed. "They will regret this trespass." A fiery axe appeared in Kottatare's outstretched hand before it turned and roared, charging up a dark path.

Hallik didn't hesitate to pop up, bending at the waist to examine his feet. His lips curled back as he realized that whatever held him there was some kind of dark goo. His boots were held fast, but he could very possibly just pull his feet free from the boots. After some serious wiggling, he got one foot out.

Sounds of a horrible battle raged nearby, like the monsters were tearing each other apart. He had no idea that monsters were *this* intentional about hunting people. It was almost like he was a trophy.

His stomach and arm muscles burned as he tried to get his last foot free, but the toe of his boot was clamped down tightly by the black material. A flash of red light burst behind him. He didn't even bother looking. None of it would matter if he couldn't get free. He decided to just try dropping his weight after lifting up again, which got his heel to move at least a fraction. That was it. Maybe one more. He dropped his weight again, jerking his leg as he did so. His leg tore out from the boot, and he fell to the stone floor of the cave, barely getting his hands in place before crashing down on his head. He rolled but still smacked his left elbow hard.

Nature's rays, he'd gotten down. Now how in the depths was he going to get back out of Vanalf? Imarún lay right where the drakked had thrown it. He knew that once he touched it, he'd be undetectable by their magical senses, but he needed all the monsters out there to believe that he was still bound.

First, he needed to destroy that concoction. Then he could spare Avskild from facing at least one more monster. He went to knock it over, and was surprised by its scent, like that of spices and fresh-cut wood.

An idea came to him.

"Oh, Elowyn would call me mad," he whispered to himself. Maybe he was mad. He wasn't particularly known for having safe ideas. He grabbed the wooden spoon that Kottatare had discarded. After two quick breaths to pump himself up, he scooped the liquid, blew on its contents, and slurped it up. The taste was not too surprising, not dissimilar from the smell, but a little coppery. He gulped it down. If there was something magical about this, then he would be the recipient instead of the drakked. Unsure of how much he would need, he scooped up more and more, burning his tongue a couple times, but the sounds of battle slowed, reducing to a couple voices shouting at each other in their rumbling tones. He could not understand any of the words, but he figured a change in pace out there meant he needed to find a way out.

He tipped the pot over, pouring its contents into the fire, then glanced around quickly, his stomach roiling as it reacted to whatever he'd just drunk.

There was only one way out.

He growled to himself, bracing for what lay ahead before snatching Imarún from the ground.

"Tyrusson," The voice of Kottatare snaked down the tunnel, reverberating off the walls, shaking his frame. The other monsters had paused their fighting. They all knew that he was coming.

Hallik took a deep breath and plodded up the tunnel, woolen socks padding on the cold stone beneath him. He rolled his neck and shoulders. Orange light shimmered ahead. The tunnel wasn't long, and when he emerged, he saw four monsters there waiting for him, Kottatare among them. The mangled bodies of at least a dozen other monsters littered the ground. It seemed Kottatare had worked through them with cruel efficiency.

The drakked had a single gash along its arm but was otherwise unharmed. It had been too much for him to hope that they'd all be severely injured or that they would've been too distracted by their fighting to notice him.

Of course things wouldn't be that easy.

"It's mine," squealed one of the other monsters, its face like that of a giant boar, long spines covering its entire back. It was missing an eye, and one of its own tusks had been broken off and stabbed into its shoulder.

"You are not worthy of the blessing," Kottatare said, raising its axe to the boar monster.

Blessing? Hallik would have to think more on the implications of that word. A different monster attempted stabbing Kottatare in the back, but the drakked twisted and yanked the blade from it, severing the arm of the monster who'd attempted the jab. They all roared at each other and resumed their fight, though the boar monster charged straight at Hallik.

Hallik skipped to the side, narrowly dodging the boar's massive fist as it crashed into the stone where he'd been standing. Rocks shattered behind him, showering against his back. One of the monster's quills nearly jabbed into him, but he barely slashed it away with his sword. A flash of fire scorched across the boar as Kottatare's axe exploded into its body.

Hallik ducked under the liquid flame that scorched by him. A different monster was there, gnashing at him with its long jaw and rows of teeth. With a quick swing of Imarún, the lower jaw of the monster tore away, and Hallik continued running up the cavern. He had no idea where he was going, but up seemed the right direction.

Where was the Wyrm? This seemed more like he was somewhere inside the caves of Vanalf.

"He's trying to get away," roared another monster.

A different monster with four sharp horns atop its head charged at Hallik on all fours. There was no way he'd be able to outrun any of these things. They were all easily twice his size. In fact, they generally seemed larger than anything they'd come across on the way down. He wondered if perhaps there were different monsters that had become aware of him when he was not connected to Imarún. Likely. He could only imagine what his father and brother had faced when they'd tried coming down.

He'd never be able to fight all the monsters. He had to get out somehow. And meanwhile, the charging monster was almost to him. There was no time left to think and no room for error. It lowered its head to ram him, but Hallik sprang toward it with a high jump. He completely dodged the horns and placed one foot on top of the monster's shoulders, stepping up and over its body. He slashed his sword down at the same time, drawing a long gash across its body.

Hallik fell awkwardly, just behind the monster. He rolled into the landing and sprang back to his feet, pivoting to sprint up the incline. A ball of something dark green flew past his left shoulder, some of it touching his shirt, burning at his skin beneath. He gasped at the shock of hot pain as the ball exploded in a goopy mess on the cave wall, steam rising from the spot.

He charged on, ignoring the pain as he stomped on a small rock with the ball of his foot, his wool sock doing little to cushion it. Farther up the slope, he could see a dull light, his one beacon of hope. His lungs screamed at him as he sprinted onward, but a roar came from just behind him. Going purely on instinct, he dove down and turned, holding his sword up like a spear.

The monster bearing down on him was a three-headed troll, but it stopped short before stomping on Hallik as a flaming axe tore through its middle head from behind. Hallik crawled back. He hadn't realized how powerful Kottatare was, and he suspected the other monsters didn't truly know what they were up against either. What surprised him the most was that they were all fighting to get their hands on *him*. It was like Hallik was the prized hog at a market fair. They were risking their lives just for a chance to eat him.

Perhaps his father was right. There was a curse in their blood that drove monsters wild for them. But at least he had Imarún, and as long as he held onto it, he'd be able to avoid these hunters.

The two unscathed troll heads looked toward each other, the third no longer anything more than a simmering stump. Both heads roared and the troll spun around, swinging a massive root that had been stabbed through with swords and daggers, the metal protruding to form a spiked club.

Kottatare caught the weapon with his hand, seemingly oblivious to the jagged sword end that jabbed into the side of its arm. It kicked the troll's leg from the other side before hacking into its torso with the flaming axe. Then Kottatare bit down on one of the other heads, tearing it away.

Something must have hit Kottatare from the back because it reared its head and threw the nearly dead troll to the side.

Hallik didn't bother watching the rest. He turned, climbing back up toward the distant light. As he got closer, he could barely make out the sparkling twinkle of lights that he recognized as the immeasurable top of the Wyrm.

Hope endured. He could still emerge as a Grimnir. From behind him, there was a shriek and then silence. He was so close to the exit that the myriad colors cast a glittering light on the floor of the cave he ran on. One massive hand grabbed him around the waist, squeezing tight enough to empty his lungs. He was lifted off the ground as Kottatare turned him.

"You're not—" Kottatare started to say, but Hallik didn't wait for it to finish before slashing across its wrist once, and then again across Kottatare's mouth, causing one of the monster's teeth to go flying out. He stabbed into Kottatare's arm, hoping to loose himself. Kottatare screamed in pain, a hissing sound that made Hallik's insides squirm. Its grip loosened, and Hallik slashed one more time across Kottatare's hand. He dropped.

Kottatare seemed to lose interest in communicating and instead slammed its axe at Hallik. Hallik ducked, feeling the heat of the axe as it passed right over his head. He swung up, gouging a finger on the hand that held the axe. The drakked roared, and fire licked out from its mouth in little embers, causing a wave of heat to blow across Hallik's skin. Even parts of his clothes got singed from the heat.

Hallik knew he wouldn't be able to run. The other monsters were dead. Kottatare had killed all of them. There was no remaining distraction. It took a limping step toward him, hinting that the other monsters had not left it unscathed, and brought its axe down again. Hallik threw up his sword with the most minute parry and sidestepped the attack. The axe hit the cave floor in a shower of sparks.

Seeing no other option, Hallik took a strong step forward, swinging Imarún with all his might. The sword sliced across Kottatare's knee. Kottatare leaned to its other side and elbowed Hallik, who grabbed the arm with his free hand, latching on. It was the same arm that held the axe, and the other hand was injured already. The wind fled Hallik's lungs again, but he stabbed the underside of its shoulder before letting go. He dropped hard to the ground and rolled, a rock jabbing into his back. He sprang back up with a groan as Kottatare swiveled.

Hallik stepped close once again, this time stabbing the back of the same leg he'd cut earlier, aiming for the tendons he assumed would be around its ankle. Or... whatever that section was. Regardless, something snapped in there, and Kottatare fell, unable to turn around as it had intended.

Instead, Kottatare swiveled off its injured leg and used one of its arms to turn then snap at Hallik with its jaws. He took Imarún in both hands and jabbed the weapon straight through Kottatare's nose and into its mouth, but the drakked's forward thrust still shoved Hallik back. Hallik's grip on Imarún was the only thing that prevented him from going straight into the monster's mouth.

When the momentum ended, Hallik yanked the sword out and cut a glancing blow across Kottatare's neck. It was nothing that would stop such a monster, but he at least knew that every cut Imarún made across Kottatare's body meant that he was draining some of its soul.

"That weapon," Kottatare growled as it possibly recognized what was happening. Perhaps it hadn't expected Imarún to be so powerful, or that Hallik could be bound to it already, even without being a Grimnir yet.

Hallik swung again, going around Kottatare so that he could try and make a break for it again if he successfully maimed the beast. Its jaw hung open as scarlet blood leaked from its mouth. He'd stabbed all the way through the back of its head, piercing its tongue.

It slapped at him with its other bloody, clawed hand, but Hallik stabbed the palm as it came at him. The force of the slap jolted him back, but it was manageable. He had the upper hand.

He withdrew his sword and stepped around the monster, slashing once at its remaining good leg just in case it tried to get up. Kottatare's panted as it glared at Hallik, but he slowly backed away.

"I drank that concoction of yours," Hallik said, still feeling the roiling pain in his stomach. It must have been some prideful side of him that wanted to shove it in Kottatare's face that not only was it dying, but it had failed, and Hallik had taken its potion.

Dark, rumbling coughs came from Kottatare's throat. A laugh. It didn't even say anything. The laugh made Hallik's mind twist. Perhaps this was what Kottatare had intended all along—but there was no way it could have known that Hallik would risk drinking it, right?

Hallik backed away. He was wasting time. Kottatare would not be able to pursue in its condition. He needed to run. Keeping Imarún gripped in his right hand, he turned and dashed toward the only visible exit, Kottatare's laughter echoing behind him.

Sure enough, after emerging from the large cavern, he found himself at the base of the mountainous structure that stood between the entrance of Vanalf and the rest of the Wyrm. At least, he hoped the rocky surface that stood before him like a massive, cracked wall was Vanalf. How strange it would be to crawl up through a cave that led to somewhere completely different. And there was still the very real possibility that his entire team had died.

Worry clawed at him as he ran with all his might, ignoring the growing pain in his side. The pain of all his bumps and bruises faded as he focused on his objective. He would not be defeated.

But then he noticed he was not alone in the darkness around him. Snarling faces and glowing eyes peered up at him as growling filled the air. He skidded to a stop. There were hundreds of them, creatures like wolves with jagged spines down their backs and teeth large enough to be knives.

"By all the blighting depths," he said, suspecting the words might be his last. Now would be a much more appropriate time for a rage lemming to leap out and bite him.

CHAPTER FORTY-FOUR

BLIGHTING DEMONS

Lind Hjordis

Lind's grip tightened over his axe as he strode through the streets to the western wall. Three militiamen marched with him, as well as Zaakira. She and Anders had spent much of the day scouring the eastern end of the city in pursuit of Ontr-anda. If they could discover what the demon was after, perhaps they'd be able to thwart it.

This was vital because, if Lind was correct, the demon would try to deceive them into working toward its desires. Ontr-anda was renowned for his manipulation. Lind would have to figure out a way to get a step ahead of the monster.

Blighting demons.

At least they'd had some good news recently. The students were going to enter Vanalf first thing in the morning, and some of the survivors from the battle had already been shuttled back to Avskild, though one concerning detail was that apparently Elowyn and Hallik had run ahead to enter the cave early. It was always ill-advised to enter Vanalf when their journey might stretch into the night. How would they find the light to emerge?

There was nothing he could do about that at present. He needed to address the issue with Ontr-anda to ensure the city did not destroy itself from within.

They reached the site of a disturbance that had been reported at the base of the western wall near the gatehouse. A few militiamen surrounded another fellow who'd huddled up against the base of the wall, arms wrapped around his head as he sobbed. Blood spatters covered his body.

Anders was there too, though the Watcher's eyes scanned the rooftops and battlements. He was not concerned with the sobbing warrior.

Lind didn't even bother approaching the group of militiamen. He went straight to Anders. "What's your take?" he asked the sturdy, older soldier.

Anders grunted and shared a look with Zaakira. "That militiaman there, Kalle, killed his longtime friend while they were up on the battlements. Hacked him to death with his axe before throwing him off the wall. Then he cut the ropes for the portcullis and jammed the rig. He supposedly snapped out of it and started crying like that. Doesn't even deny what happened. Tells everyone."

"Wait," Lind said, lifting a hand as he sorted through the implications. "Do you mean to say that the portcullis is stuck closed?"

"Yes," Anders said. "And it's jammed, so we can't even try to open it manually. It's like there are piles of rocks stuck throughout the whole thing."

Lind nodded. It was clear what had happened. Ontr-anda had influenced the man to perform these actions. A quick assessment told Lind that this situation was far too extreme to have been anything as simple as whispered influence. It was a direct possession.

That meant one obvious thing. "The demon wants us stuck inside the city, and he wants us to know we're stuck."

Anders nodded. "That would appear to be the case."

"I will check the other gates. Warn the guards," Zaakira said.

"Wait," Lind said, placing a hand on Zaakira's shoulder. Her muscles were tense. "This was too obvious. Perhaps that's what Ontr-anda wants us to do."

Zaakira grunted. "You did say he was a master manipulator, but what does he gain by having us secure the city gates?"

"He could be playing with us," Lind said. He toyed with a single, simple iron ring on his left small finger. "He used one of our own guards for this. Perhaps he's trying to say that our threat isn't from outside the city, but within."

"He wants us to fight each other," Anders said. "Sow suspicion."

Lind rubbed his chin. It was probably more complex than that. Certainly that may have been a part of what Ontr-anda wanted to convey, but this was all a game to him. Lind had to remain focused on the end result. What did Ontr-anda want? The downfall of Avskild, of course, but on a deeper level, he wanted them to suffer. Perhaps he wanted to enslave them and make their destruction last for years to come.

But what did he need in order to make that happen?

Lind grunted. "Maybe this really is just a distraction. If he was the mastermind behind getting all the Voyagers killed using that dagger, then he wanted the portals destroyed. He didn't simply want to sow chaos. He wanted this place ravaged by monsters, and there's still only one way for him to make that happen. The walls aren't the concern. I think we need to remain focused on securing the Tower of Tarn. That's where the portal was erected. That's where we must maintain our defenses."

Zaakira folded her arms. "So we just let him ruin the city gates?"

"No," Lind said. "We'll play his game. That's what he wants, but we need to make sure we keep our Vitugrs at the Tower of Tarn and leave this preventative work to you two. I think he'll use the distraction as a means of finding a way back to that portal in Tower of Tarn. The best way for him to overcome the city is to get more monsters through there."

"What's to stop him from using a different portal completely?" Anders asked.

Lind felt a weight slowly settle over his shoulders. None of the portals were secure. "I suppose... nothing is, really."

Anders raised his eyebrows at Lind. "There aren't enough of us. We need to hunt him down. Playing defensive will probably ruin us."

Lind sighed and clapped Anders on the shoulder. "You are right." He nodded to Zaakira. "Let's keep pursuing him with all our efforts. If we can stop him outright and get some new Voyagers, then we'll have saved Avskild."

"All your talk of Ontr-anda trying to complicate things is really just him getting into your head," Zaakira said. "Let's keep it simple. We'll follow the traces."

Lind nodded. They were right. By the depths. Without them, he may have played straight into the demon's plans.

Zaakira smiled at Lind. "Don't worry so much. You're not alone in this, Lind," she said. "We've still got a city full of Avskildians who will not back down without a fight."

"Thank you, Zaakira," Lind said, that pressure on his back lifting ever-so-slightly. "So where do we find Ontr-anda?"

Anders grunted. "I think that part may be easier than you think," he said, pointing his chin down the street.

Lind squinted, but his eyes were nowhere near as sharp as the Watcher's, nor was his hearing as keen.

Without waiting, Anders started up the street, Zaakira right behind him.

"What is it?" Lind said, hurrying to keep up. The ache in his legs was not nearly as bad as the day before, but his shins still hurt when he pushed too hard. The three militiamen followed behind. They'd learned to stay close until receiving orders.

Not a moment later, an elderly man came staggering out from a side street, hand clutched to his bleeding shoulder. He screeched in desperation when he saw the three of them coming closer. "You must help!" he said. "She's going mad."

The six of them quickened their pace to reach the side street. The injured man continued to tremble, eyes wide with fear. They paused beside him so that they could assess the situation before proceeding. Lind could hear some kind of commotion up the street.

"Are you well?" asked Anders.

The man nodded, then shook his head and said, "N-no. She stabbed me! Something dark passed through our home and entered her mouth. She didn't seem to recognize me anymore." He burst into tears. "My wife—it must be the demon. It did something to her. I already lost my son, and now her." A fit of sobs overtook the man.

Lind averted his eyes and pointed at two of the militiamen. "Remain with him." He jerked his head at the third soldier, and the four of them continued up the street.

A woman's screaming voice erupted from a home. The building was constructed of large stones and a wood-and-thatch roof. She stood in the doorway, a knife clutched in her hand as she screamed at a younger woman trying to prevent her from leaving.

"That's not your Hanfar," the aged woman screamed at the younger woman. Her hair was a stark white, but she looked strong for her age, her muscles still well-defined. Her clothes hung oddly on her body, and one of her eyes had a milky appearance to it, suggesting she was at least partially blind.

Zaakira gasped, her wings twitching tight against her back. "That's Grende's mother. He was one of the Valtyras who fell at the battle outside Vanalf."

"Aye," Anders said, "and she was a Valtyra as well."

"Was?" Lind said, eyebrows furrowing.

"Let's speak with her," Anders said.

Lind stretched his fingers in anticipation of signing for spell activation. If Ontr-anda had taken possession of a Valtyra, even an older one at that, then she could quite possibly be rather strong. He realized that the reason her clothes hung strangely was that there were two bumps on her back, over which her dress was draped. The younger woman, perhaps a granddaughter, was trying to calm her down.

"All Valtyras are taught about her," Zaakira whispered to Lind. "They call her Mother Afmor. She was struck by lightning while flying. She fell to the trees below and broke both of her wings. They would not heal and had to be amputated."

Lind nodded. He'd heard of her as well, though he'd never met her before. Her family had generations of Grimnirs. They were a sorry target for Ontr-anda's games.

"Grandmother, please don't fight!" the young woman pleaded.

Afmor's one good eye blinked across them as they hovered outside the door.

"Ah," she said, voice much louder than necessary. "Did you stop him? You better not have let him get away! He's possessed by that demon." She brandished the knife and pushed past her granddaughter.

"We have him detained," Lind said, realizing how complicated this was getting. Was it possible for Ontr-anda to possess two people at once and turn them against each other? He wouldn't doubt it, but these conditions seemed too peculiar.

"Then come, let us finish him!" Afmor hurried out, surprisingly spry for her age. "Free the city!"

Zaakira had to physically stop Afmor from charging off. "Hold on! How do you know he is possessed?"

Afmor screamed, trying to free herself from Zaakira's grasp. "I know my husband. He does not speak like my husband. My husband is too much of a coward! Not some warrior!"

Lind looked to the granddaughter while Zaakira kept hold of Afmor. "Were you there? Do you know what happened?"

The young woman shook her head. Her arms were folded across her chest and her expression was that of exasperation. "I'd just informed them about the attack at the wall earlier. A while later, Grandfather demanded to know where Grandmother's dagger was." She shook her head. "They started fighting. I don't understand."

Anders did not look pleased with her explanation, and he shared a worried frown with Lind.

"How long ago did this start happening?" Lind asked.

"Just barely," the girl said.

Lind leaned in to whisper to Anders, though with the Watcher's enhanced senses, he would hear better than anybody. "The demon is nearby."

Anders nodded.

Zaakira's muscles strained as she held Afmor back. The old woman was flailing, that dagger of hers getting dangerously close to Zaakira at times.

"Afmor, we want to help you," Lind said. "Why did Hanfar want your dagger?"

Her eyes were wide, her skin red as she struggled against Zaakira. "The demon wants to kill us. Please, let us finish him. Don't let him defile my husband any longer." She managed to jerk free of Zaakira's grip, a swing of her dagger running a small cut across Zaakira's arm.

Afmor sprinted down the street.

Lind made a quick gesture with his left hand and shifted his left foot ever-so-slightly, just enough to trigger the spell as he thought the command. The cobbled street erupted into a pillar directly in front of the old woman. She ran straight into it and bounced back. He'd forgotten she was practically blind.

Zaakira and Anders caught up with her quickly as she turned to face them. The wingless nubs on her back twitched beneath her dress as she looked across them, eyes squinting. She was bleeding on her right cheek. She must have cut herself when crashing into the wall Lind had summoned. A scream tore from her throat, so wretched it made his ears ring with pain. There was much more happening inside of her than physical anguish.

She was a distraction. She had to be. The real enemy was here somewhere, perhaps hiding in a house or on a rooftop, watching them. Laughing. This was all mere amusement to him.

"Where is he, Anders?" Lind growled at him. It was rare that Lind regretted his limitations as a Vitugr, but not having a spell for detecting other lifeforms was undeniably frustrating.

Anders shook his head, face squinted in focus. "Hiding, though I detect traces of him in the air. It's like a stench with no distinct location—he's been everywhere. There's a darkness upon her as well." His eyes were saddened.

Lind's grip tightened. He'd been wrong earlier. Ontr-anda wasn't fully here physically. It was some fractured part of his soul that was roaming about the city. The extent of the ancient demon's power was still beyond Lind's comprehension, but Ontr-anda would be detectable once he wasn't hiding in a vessel. That only left one option.

Lind cast *dispel* over Afmor. She gasped and fell to her knees, though he knew that spell wouldn't be enough. There was only one way out.

He put his hands together then jerked one away in Afmor's direction as he muttered the word, "*Liosgeir.*" A spear of yellow light lanced forward and pierced Afmor straight through the chest, impaling her against the stone wall that still lingered behind her. The old woman's face twisted in pain, and her granddaughter ran over to her with a scream.

"Oh, Grandmother," the young woman said, kneeling in front of her dying matriarch.

The pain in Afmor's expression vanished as she slumped back. The magical spear disappeared, and she fell to her knees in front of her granddaughter.

Anders nodded to Lind and said, "It is cleared from her."

"Sonda," Afmor said, raising a hand to touch the young woman's face. "I am free. Keep this safe." She held the dagger up to her granddaughter, but she fell back, hand dropping before Sonda could take it.

Zaakira walked over and placed a hand on Sonda's shoulder. Tears welled in her eyes but never fell, and her lip curled in contempt.

Lind knew she was teetering on the edge of outrage. They would need to leave her to her grief, but he needed that dagger. Ontr-anda was after it for some reason. He stepped over and extracted the dagger from Afmor's limp grip, then he cast a spell that flattened the pillar of earth back into the street.

"Stop," Sonda said, rising to her feet. "That dagger belongs to me. She asked *me* to keep it safe. You must honor her."

Lind set his jaw and regarded the weapon in his hands. It was seemingly plain. The metal was worn in a few places, but it looked like it had been recently polished. There were some small prongs on one side, though the gem it once held was now gone. "Of course," he said to Sonda. She was right. It would be an affront to claim the weapon. "I must ask Anders to look it over before we do that. We all have the same goal." Anders came over, and Lind handed him the dagger. "If the demon was after this weapon, then it would be wise to consider what he wanted from it."

Sonda simmered, but she said nothing as Anders looked over the dagger.

"It's magical," Anders said. "Minor quality. It has a true-strike enchantment, nothing else, though the missing gemstone may have previously given it some other attribute."

Lind nodded. Nothing about it was particularly unique. That only left him with more questions.

"Missing gemstone?" Sonda asked.

Anders handed the weapon over to her. "Yes." He tapped the small empty prongs on the side. "Used to go here. Was it always missing?"

Sonda shook her head. "I don't remember."

Lind bit his tongue as he and Anders shared a look.

"Sorry for your loss," Lind said, giving Sonda a somber frown, but they still had her grandfather to address. "Za-akira, stay with her for a moment, if you will."

Zaakira gave him a curt nod and remained put as Lind went back toward the head of the street. Hanfar stood with his arms wrapped about himself, shivering, although it wasn't chilly at all.

Anders knew the drill. "It's on him as well," he said to Lind in a low voice.

Lind ground his teeth. Even if they stopped Ontr-anda today, the damage he'd done was far too much. There were so many innocent lives brutalized. Lind's heart still ached with the pain of killing Afmor. He was no stranger to death, but more people had died in the last few days than he'd seen in his entire life.

"She is free, then?" Hanfar said.

"Why did you need the dagger?" Lind asked, ignoring his question.

Hanfar frowned in confusion. "For... the demon. It's magical. It could hurt it." His eyes narrowed at Lind. "I will go see my wife now." He took one step forward before pulling a knife from the belt of the nearest militiaman. Before Lind could do anything, he'd stabbed the knife into the militiaman's neck.

Though he was a few steps away, Lind threw a fist. The *force* spell connected with Hanfar's throat, and he stumbled back with a choked cry. The other militiaman, who was standing just behind him, recovered from his shock and jabbed Hanfar in the back with the point of his spear.

Lind stepped up, activating the radiant magic of his axe before slamming it into Hanfar's torso. Hanfar's chest sizzled as the dark soul was slowly purged. Ontr-anda's possession was like a plague that infected every fiber of its host.

Hanfar fell in a heap, body withering, but his face broke into a dark smile. "It's too late," he said, cackling.

"Too late for what?" Lind said, leaning over the body. He wasn't sure if he was speaking with Hanfar's afflicted mind or if he was speaking with Ontr-anda indirectly.

Hanfar only cackled more, hands clenched over the seeping wound in his chest. His eyes shifted, looking in the direction of the Tower of Tarn. His smile grew wider. "You failed, Lind."

Something deep within the earth trembled, and the distant Tower of Tarn resonated with the sound of a mountain collapsing. Lind's eyes widened. "What have you done?" he demanded of the dying man, shaking him, but Hanfar was already still, final words poisoning the air.

Lind shot to his feet. They had to get to the tower before everything was lost.

CHAPTER FORTY-FIVE

SACRIFICE

Hallik Tyrusson

Before Hallik could even make his first attack, he witnessed a body of one of the dark, shadowy wolves go flying toward the front of the pack, skimming the others' backs, flung by something coming through the rear. It was another monster coming to claim Hallik for itself, no doubt.

Hallik stepped back. If they surrounded him, there'd be nothing he could do. His demise was inevitable. Short of a Vitugr or Valtyra, he doubted anybody could get out of such a predicament.

Sensing the tension, the creatures moved as though triggered by the same impulse. They charged for him, casting all caution aside, coming in straight for the bite with no regard for his flashing sword.

Hallik's fatigue vanished as his body pumped with invigorated blood. He would hold off death as long as possible. Imarún parted flesh and soul as Hallik whipped it through each opponent, skillfully maintaining a constant arc and avoiding jabs at all costs. If his sword got caught in their flesh, he'd have no defense against the gnashing teeth.

These monsters were skilled hunters. Several started slipping around behind him—they were too fast for him to outmaneuver. Even as he spun from side to side, slashing each snarling snout that nipped at him, he couldn't avoid them all. One managed to bite onto his foot from behind before he was able to cut along the back of the wolf's neck. Some of its teeth had pierced the leather, but he barely noticed the pain in the heat of the moment.

Something was still barreling through the mass of monsters packed around him, and much of the attention of the large pack was drawn away by the new arrival. The distraction was still not enough. One more bite caught Hallik on the hip. Though only a nip, this bite stung more than the one on his foot. He wouldn't survive long enough to see what other monster was coming to finish him off.

To Hallik's utter surprise, an armored body flipped through the air, crystalline blade slashing across the back of a wolf. The person landed and bashed another beast away with a rounded shield, throwing it through the air as though it had been nothing more than a small rabbit. Whoever the person was, they were covered head-to-foot in plated armor that the monsters could not seem to penetrate with their teeth. One of them attempted to bite Hallik's would-be savior, but it yelped as its teeth crashed against the hardened metal.

Hallik and the mysterious warrior fought back-to-back, both swords wreaking havoc against the unarmored, non-magical monsters. Before he knew it, there was only a handful of the wolves left, but they held their distance, growling.

Instead of waiting for the monsters to act first, the warrior sprang forward, spinning around a high bite aimed at his throat before slicing across two of the monsters. One monster turned to run away, but the warrior stepped up on a corpse, using its body as a springing board to jump toward the retreating beast, stabbing it through the back.

The battle shifted as the monsters seemed to realize they were defeated. With only five of them left, they slunk back into the shadows.

Hallik regarded his savior, the eyes of whom looked vaguely familiar.

The soldier pulled off his helmet to reveal that he was none other than Tyrus, Hallik's father. "No time for conversation, my son," he said. "We must hurry." His eyes strayed to the wound on Hallik's hip.

When Hallik followed his father's gaze, he found his side drenched with blood. It must have been more than a nip after all. He took one step toward his father as his vision started turning black.

CHAPTER FORTY-SIX

TRAVELER

Elowyn Galdre

Elowyn's feet couldn't move. To leave now meant accepting that Hallik would never emerge from Vanalf, and she wasn't sure she could do it.

"Elowyn, you must hurry to find this Tyrus before all is lost," Rav urged.

Bjorn and Lorelai already stood at the edge of the stony slope that would take them down from the rocky outcropping over the entrance to Vanalf. The sun was down, and the sky was just taking on the first tinge of dark purple. Stars would begin to appear at any moment and night would reign. Despite the darkness, that strange crack in the sky remained distinct.

Elowyn glanced at the invisible exits one last time. Lorelai nodded to her and a shuddering breath leaked from

Elowyn's lips. She took one step toward them before she noticed a tiny light shooting toward them through the darkening undergrowth of the forest below.

Rav grimaced and cast some kind of spell, and a faint, mystical light surrounded them.

Elowyn braced herself for an attack, but as the light grew closer, it shot up at them from the ground and flashed with colors red and yellow. "Sparky!" she said with a gasp.

"Perhaps Tyrus sent it to guide us," Lorelai said.

But instead of dashing off to lead them away, Sparky lowered itself to the ground, swirling around the bottom of the rock wall from which they'd all emerged.

"A wisp? What is it doing?" Rav asked with abject confusion.

"It wants us to stay," Elowyn said, lowering to her knees.

"Elowyn," Bjorn said in his growly voice. She expected him to tell her she was crazy, but instead, he came to stand beside her. He placed a hand on her shoulder and said nothing else.

Even Lorelai joined her on the other side while Elowyn explained to Rav. "The wisp is bonded with Tyrus somehow. It has guided us where to go before, and now it's telling us to stay."

Kaldir, the Valtyra, shook his head. "Perhaps we should concern ourselves over the other students, Rav."

"Of course, but these still lack training," Rav said. "Especially for a Voyager—she needs to know how to purify the portals, and a Vitugr—she could kill them all if she attempts too much."

"Then teach us something while we wait," Lorelai said, her voice a little too snappy for Elowyn's liking.

Elowyn could practically feel Rav's glare on their backs at the tone of her voice. "It's dangerous out here. Let's head back to the outpost before it gets any darker. I can teach you more there."

"No, we wait," Elowyn said. "If Hallik does not emerge by sunrise, then we will go." Sparky had come here for a reason. She had to believe that Tyrus had sent it here so that they would know not to go to the Evergrove.

Kaldir grunted. "We may as well teach them what we can. The others should be able to hold out at the outpost in our absence."

Rav clicked her tongue. "Very well. For all three of you, I will teach you the method for casting spells. Please avoid doing so at all costs unless you have training in specific spells, but this is the starting point for making use of your magic."

Elowyn knew all this, but Lorelai and Bjorn were unfamiliar with Grimnir practices. It would be difficult for them to start from scratch, whereas she had already gone through many such routines, only she hadn't possessed any magic at the time. Now? She flexed her muscles, feeling through her whole body. Something was different about her, like her very anatomy had changed, but it was hard to pinpoint what exactly had been impacted.

"Magic is controlled by language," Rav explained, her voice taking on a bored tone, "though this may be confusing if you don't understand the depth of language. This could be obvious in singing, runes, or utterance, but action and thought are also language, which is why you see many Grimnirs or even creatures activate magic without vocalizing. Please don't try and complicate this. For now, just know there are two parts to casting a spell: the word, and the will. Both need to be present at the same time for a spell to work, because that way people aren't accidentally summoning fire when they're just talking about it. That being said, activating a spell is actually rather easy, but controlling it is difficult."

To make a point, Rav held out her hand and said, "*Brun*," summoning a ball of flame that lit up just above her palm. "How is the fire just in my palm? Why is it not over my head? Why is it not streaking out in a jet of flame? These things can be further controlled by the will. Additional words can be used to help clarify the action or position of a spell, but that's more complex."

These were all things that Elowyn knew, but she hadn't been able to utilize them yet. She resisted the urge to interrupt Rav, but Lorelai and Bjorn were both intent on listening. Inside, she kept oscillating between excitement for her magic and anxiety for Hallik.

"Lorelai," Rav said, her eyes settling on the fresh Vitugr. "I recommend keeping things simple. If you plan to practice with fire or any other dangerous spell, do so on a beach and clear from others who do not also have Vitugr abilities, or you risk harming them."

Lorelai only nodded in response.

"Elowyn." Rav sighed before continuing. "I admit I do not know much of the Voyager spells. Perhaps Tyrus knows a few of the words, but from what I know, there are manipulations of the words *utrym*, *tme*, and I used to hear a Voyager say *snabfot* rather frequently. From what I understand, Voyager spells are significantly less dangerous though, so you should have more liberty to experiment as long as you're in a relatively..." she paused to look at their surroundings before finishing, "flat area."

Elowyn nodded. "I know many words." In truth, she and her mother probably knew more Voyager spell commands than anybody else, especially since a lot of the songs were in the true language. There were doubtless many other spells that could have been lost or forgotten, but she would have time to figure that out. "The command for the shield is in one of the songs, though I'm not sure about the purification."

"Perhaps they are one and the same," Rav said, though Elowyn wasn't so sure.

"What about spells relevant to me?" Bjorn asked.

Elowyn smirked and couldn't help but jump in to explain. "Simple. Watchers have two primary spells, *synliva* for detecting life, and *synseith* for detecting magic. You are welcome to practice, though it can become quite disorienting. As Rav said, you will need to focus your will on the objective."

Bjorn grunted before muttering, "*Synliva*," and immediately gasped and stumbled back a couple steps. Kaldir moved to prevent Bjorn from falling off the outcropping, but Bjorn flopped to his back. "How do I turn it off?" His eyes were clenched tight as he placed both hands to his head.

"Focus on something else!" Elowyn said. "Open your eyes!"

Bjorn did so with another gasp, his breath labored. He scowled at nobody in particular. "Well, at least I know it works."

"It will take getting used to," Rav said. "You should all practice something. A battle is no place to try a spell for the first time."

Elowyn resisted rolling her eyes. They probably wouldn't get the luxury of much practice before being thrown into the fire, but she tested a spell anyway, whispering the word, "*Tme*," to herself, though she didn't know exactly how to direct her will into it. She wasn't sure what happened, but she felt something, like a muscle twitching. What it had done, she couldn't tell.

"Do you have something I can actually practice with if I'm not supposed to be using fire?" Lorelai asked.

"*Vindr* is probably safe," Rav said. "I haven't used wind related spells much myself because I tend to lean toward inflicting more... damage, but I think it can be helpful to use for training."

The three of them practiced into the night without any monsters coming to disturb them, but as the stars passed by overhead, Elowyn's anxiety grew and grew, gnawing at her stomach. When the sun came up, Elowyn would be faced with keeping her word and leaving, with or without Hallik.

Elowyn started awake. She must have dozed. In fact, everyone seemed to be asleep with the exception of Kaldir, who stood with his arms folded, looking away from the group. She'd almost forgotten that Valtyras benefitted from needing less sleep. Nearby was a bowl-shaped piece of wood on the ground filled with water. Perhaps Nis had paid them a visit to provide much needed water.

To her horror, the first light of dawn was barely visible through the murky horizon. *No. Not yet! It can't be time already.* There was still no Hallik, but Sparky was a dark red, yellow sparks shooting down from it in rhythmic pulses. Then Sparky flashed to a white-yellow light and swirled upward.

Not a second after Sparky blasted up, two figures shot out from a hole she hadn't seen before. They landed on the stone floor in a grunting heap before she realized Tyrus was looking up at her, a semi-conscious Hallik beneath him.

At the sound, everyone launched to attention.

Elowyn gasped, eyes unavoidably straying to the wings that spread out behind Hallik's back. Valtyra. He would be beside himself when he noticed, but something was wrong with him. There were several knicks and cuts across his body, but Tyrus was already pulling back Hallik's clothes to reveal his hip.

In the darkness, Elowyn couldn't make out the details, but Rav summoned a flame overhead that removed any of Elowyn's doubts.

Hallik was mortally wounded.

"They made it," Kaldir said, voice struck with wonder.

Lorelai remained where she stood, hand over her mouth, but Elowyn fell to her knees at Hallik's side, careful not to land on his wings. His eyes fluttered.

"Tyrus, where did you come from?" Elowyn asked. "What happened?" She didn't fail to notice that Tyrus was covered in gleaming plate armor padded with fur.

Tyrus dropped a helmet to the ground and patted Hallik on the cheek. "Wake, boy, or you will die," he said without answering Elowyn's question. "He's a Valtyra, this is good. They are the most resilient of Grimnirs."

Hallik looked up, eyes flicking between Elowyn and Tyrus. "I made it," he sputtered.

Tyrus shushed him and withdrew a vial. Elowyn recognized it. Tyrus had said that he created an elixir from the flowers of the Evergrove allowing him to leave its borders and remain alive. "Indeed. You did well, my son, but I need you to drink this."

Hallik sat up and looked down at his hip. "By the depths," he grunted. "That's a lot of blood."

"Exactly," Tyrus said, holding the vial up to Hallik. "Now drink this."

Hallik took the vial but then narrowed his eyes at his father. "Wait, isn't this what you use so you don't die when you leave the Evergrove?"

"Yes, it's quite powerful. Now please, drink."

Hallik nodded slowly before throwing back his head and downing the contents. "Ah, it tastes like honey." He dropped to his back again and looked over at Elowyn. "We made it, El." He reached a hand to her, and she clasped it in her own.

"I'm a Voyager, Hallik," she said carefully, trying not to reveal that she'd been on the verge of tears. He would still make it. The tonic would restore him.

He squeezed her hand tighter. "I knew it. And it seems I'm the one stuck with wings." One of his new, splayed appendages lifted up so he could look at it better.

"What's wrong with wings?" Kaldir asked.

Hallik looked around to see the whole crowd and smiled at them all. "We all made it out."

"Barely," Tyrus said, inspecting Hallik's wound. There was quite literally a piece of Hallik's flesh dangling off the side, and Elowyn averted her gaze as Tyrus started fiddling with it.

"Who are you, exactly?" Rav asked, voice stern.

Tyrus regarded Rav silently after a moment of finishing up whatever he was doing to Hallik. "I'm a Watcher. A very old one." As if to make a point, he seemed to start aging right in front of her eyes, his hair tingeing from light brown to gray.

"He's my father," Hallik said, gingerly poking at his hip. Elowyn dared to look again, and to her astonishment, his skin already looked like it had knitted together.

"And... you went into Vanalf... again?" Rav asked.

"Yes," Tyrus said, "though this was my third venture."

Rav and Kaldir looked at each other with the same dazed expression.

Hallik struggled back to his feet. Elowyn didn't even bother telling him to take it easy. The words caught in her throat as she watched him stand. He flexed his wings and brought them up before him, touching the feathers that matched the same blonde color as his hair, though they were a bit darker on the underside. The wings had torn through his tunic, and he'd need to get the custom clothing worn by other Valtyras. That was one other reason Elowyn had been afraid to emerge as a Valtyra. She knew how difficult those clothes were to don.

Elowyn retrieved the water and took a quick sip before handing it to Hallik.

Hallik took a long swig. "What of the rest of you?" He looked at Bjorn and Lorelai.

"I'm a Vitugr," Lorelai said. "Bjorn is a Watcher."

"One of each," Elowyn said with a shrug.

Hallik nodded with a smile. His wounds looked even better, and he started fixing up his trousers. Imarún still hung from his belt, and his body was spattered with blood, most of which, she assumed, *wasn't* his. Some of it was even a different, darker color.

"Thanks for saving me, Father," Hallik said with a smirk. "I didn't know you were such a capable warrior."

"I have done a lot of fighting in my years," Tyrus said. There were noticeable wrinkles around his eyes, mouth, and forehead. "I kept an eye on the group the entire time and noticed when you separated from Imarún. I knew I wouldn't be able to come to you as you made your way through the depths, but I tried to be ready in case something else happened when you reached the bottom. That was where I lost your brother."

"I killed the monster that came after us, by the way. The drakked," Hallik said. "The one that killed my brother."

Tyrus shook his head, and his eyebrows, which were now thick and wiry, furrowed deeply. "I sensed it when I came for you. It was dying, yes, but you should have severed its head. I worry only the soul was mortally wounded and not the body."

Hallik nodded slowly and said, "I see."

"Tyrus, you're... aging," Elowyn said, unsure of how to word it as Tyrus's body started to stoop.

"Ah, yes," Tyrus said. "The effects are wearing off. Not to worry." He loosened a strap and reached within, pulling out another vial.

Elowyn's heart dropped. There was no air in her lungs. Hallik's mouth hung open as he too realized what they were looking at.

The vial Tyrus held was dented on the side, its lid gone, its contents long gone.

"Father," Hallik said, his voice but a breath. "You have another, don't you?"

Tyrus frowned at Hallik, his skin starting to sag along his cheeks and neck. "I'm afraid I do not, my son."

Tears welled in Hallik's eyes. "No. You must. You can't have given me your last."

"It's alright," Tyrus said, reaching out a hand to cup Hallik's cheek. "I've lived a long life already. I just wish I'd had the courage to spend more of it with you. At least I die somewhere that matters with someone I love."

"Can we fly him back?" Hallik asked Kaldir, then he swiveled back to his father. "How long do you have?"

"A couple moments is all, I'm afraid. It progresses quickly. Flight cannot save me," Tyrus said.

Elowyn's eyes flooded with tears. This was not fair. Hallik had only reunited with his father days earlier. To lose him again so soon was unthinkable. Even Elowyn had grown fond of him in these brief moments. Tyrus was a treasure that could never be replaced.

"Father, I'm so sorry," Hallik said, tears sliding unabashedly down both of his cheeks. "I should have at least saved half the drink for you."

"You needed it all," Tyrus said. "Even had I known that my other vial was broken, I wouldn't have it any other way. This will be an honorable death. Perhaps then you will forgive me for all those years of absence."

"You are already forgiven, Father," Hallik said. "Now please, help me find a way to spend even more years here with me now that we are reunited. Please." Hallik's voice choked off, and Elowyn could barely watch for the deep sorrow that flooded her chest.

How she wished with all her heart that she could comfort Hallik. That she could extend their time just a little bit. That they'd had so little time together only to have it taken away so quickly was cruel.

But then again, Elowyn was a Voyager. Didn't she have power over time and space? Wasn't she the very possible solution? Wasn't there anything she could do? She scoured her mind, heart pounding as she watched Tyrus wither before her, his skin getting more shriveled with each passing second.

"Remove his armor!" she shouted at them. Her hands shook as she hurried over to help Tyrus from his armor. For her plan to work, she'd need to be able to hold him and at least take a few steps.

A few steps.

Blight, she was so far from reality.

But if there was a chance, she had to try.

The others stared at her dumbly until she repeated herself. "I can try something. Hallik, come on." Elowyn was strong, but not strong enough to carry a man in full armor.

Hallik did not question her, but helped to remove Tyrus's shoulder and chest armor. He wore only a simple tunic beneath. They got him down to smallclothes in a matter of seconds, and Tyrus's body shivered as he looked up at her.

"It is too late, my dear," Tyrus said, piercing blue eyes sharper than ever before.

She ignored him and took him into her arms. Without explaining herself, she envisioned the Evergrove in her mind. She pictured the flowers and the soft grass. She remembered one flower in particular, one that she'd cupped in the palm of her hand, smelling its sweet aroma. Once the vision was captured in her mind, she muttered, "*Ferth*," and stepped forward at the same time.

Her eyes remained closed, and her muscles strained to keep Tyrus in her arms. "*Ferth*," she said again, taking another step. Wind blew around her in a torrent. The scent of those flowers, the touch of the soft grass, the deep blue sky stretching overhead—it was more than a memory—it was truth.

All her energy flashed from her body as though she'd been sucked dry. She fell to her knees, Tyrus dropping from her arms, a weight she could no longer bear. She collapsed as darkness filled her vision.

Soft grass cushioned her fall.

CHAPTER FORTY-SEVEN

KEL'S ABYSS

Jaysen Bjorn

Bjorn blinked at the afterimage of Elowyn's and Tyrus's bodies. The lingering effect of his *detect magic* spell was still causing him some disorientation, but he could see an ephemeral, wispy tendril of light green smoke in the air that he realized was a visual result of magic itself.

Everyone stared blankly at the place where Elowyn had stood. When she had taken that step after muttering her spell, it was like watching her whole being stretch before vanishing in a small stream of smoke.

"What do Voyagers do again?" Bjorn asked.

"They can open portals and move quickly," Rav said, "but I am not at all sure what Elowyn just did."

Hallik shook his head, his hands upturned as he tried to grasp what had just happened.

"Where could they have gone?" Lorelai asked.

Bjorn had only one suspicion for what Elowyn had tried to do. "Perhaps she tried getting him back to the Evergrove somehow."

"How did she do that?" Lorelai said.

"Elowyn knows more language than anyone I know except her mother," Hallik said. "That, and she studied everything she could. I wouldn't be surprised if she knew every spell possible."

The wisp spiraled around the group before bouncing off Hallik's head and swooping over to the slope that led off the outcropping. It remained there, bouncing and sparkling as if expecting them to follow.

Hallik moved to oblige.

"Hold on, what happens now?" Rav asked.

"We follow Sparky," Hallik said. "And those other students need to get through Vanalf."

"But what about the Voyager?" Kaldir said.

"Elowyn knows what she's doing," Hallik called back. He wasn't waiting around for anybody. His confidence was reassuring.

Bjorn shrugged and followed after him. They'd trusted this glowing, far-too-enthusiastic ball of light before, and he supposed it would be fine if they did so again. Lorelai hurried after them.

Rav seemed without words. Elowyn disappearing was not part of the plan. They were supposed to find the corrupted portal and use her magic to strengthen the shield. Perhaps she'd gone there already and the wisp would lead them to her. Or she could very well have used her power incorrectly and torn herself apart.

Bjorn shrugged. Nothing he could do about that either way. Might as well trudge on and kill more monsters. He hoped he would acclimate to his changed senses quickly. It was already apparent to him how useful it would be to have keener sight, smell, and hearing. And if he could find a way to temper his senses with *detect life* and *detect magic* spells, nothing could hide from him. Though truthfully, he had been hoping to perhaps gain the abilities of the Valtyra. Their enhancements made them quite formidable in combat.

Rav and Kaldir said nothing more, but they remained behind as Bjorn, Lorelai, and Hallik followed the wisp down into the still-dark forest, the soft morning sun too weak to filter through the thick branches. They'd only made a few paces into the forest when Bjorn felt something strange in the air. A second later, Bjorn's ears popped, and it felt like a splash of water whipped across his forehead.

Before he could react, Elowyn was back, crashing headfirst into Hallik as though she'd somehow appeared directly in front of him, diving into his body.

They fell to the ground together, laughing or crying—he wasn't sure. He could never guess if they seemed more like siblings or longtime lovers.

"Elowyn," Hallik said, squeezing her before they both got to their feet. "What happened?"

Elowyn shook her head, wearing a confused smile. "I'm not sure exactly. There's a spell meant for fast-travel. I didn't expect it to be quite so effective. There are a couple songs about Voyagers where they picture a place vividly in their mind, somewhere so familiar that it can feel like they're there. When they use the spell, it can carry them there."

"And my father?" Hallik's face was torn.

"Oh, yes," Elowyn said. "I'm sorry, I should have led with that, but we went straight to the Evergrove. Tyrus said he will survive, though it will take quite some time for him to recover. He said he'll try to get the dryads to help return his armor. He's familiar with the spell I used, and he said I likely would have died if we'd gone anywhere besides the Evergrove."

"Nature's rays," Hallik said, his wings flicking upward in apparent jubilation. "I can barely believe it."

"Why would using that spell kill you?" Lorelai asked.

Elowyn shrugged. "It's an extremely powerful spell. In fact, I blacked out as soon as the spell ended. My body was not ready for such exertion. Tyrus said my very soul would have shriveled, but the Evergrove helps restore souls. That's why I had to wait to come back."

"And how did you make it back?" Hallik asked.

"That part was interesting," Elowyn said. "He taught me a safer spell that is very similar, though I haven't heard it in any of the songs. Then he used his magic to share a vision of you." She pointed her eyes at Hallik. "It was the most vivid thing I've ever seen in my mind before. I was able to use that as a sort of beacon that let me return here. He said traces of my magic would make it easier to return along the same path. It's not quite like a portal that has innate energy connecting two places, because it dissipates over time."

Hallik raised his hands. "Alright, best not get too deep on the specifics there or you might lose Bjorn."

Bjorn stared flatly at Hallik. He'd been following the logic quite well.

"He also said that Sparky would lead us to the portal, but we should be careful," Elowyn said. "There is something there... or a collection of entities of some kind. He couldn't quite discern them, or it, or whatever, which is already concerning given how powerful Tyrus is."

Bjorn fiddled with one of his daggers. He too felt uncertain about such a prospect.

The ground shook and a nearby tree fell, stopping halfway down its descent by crashing into the branches of another tree. They were running out of time.

"Can you get us there faster?" Lorelai asked.

"Not the best idea," Elowyn said. "I've already drained much of my energy getting back here. We weren't able to talk about it earlier, but using too much of our magic can cause our souls to burn out, though I haven't heard of this happening with Valtyras. It's most common with Vitugrs, and several Voyagers outright died when the original portal around Avskild was created."

"Then let's go," Bjorn said, going straight to a jog as he followed the little wisp. He still didn't like the idea of giving the strange being a name, so calling it Sparky was out of the question. "We've wasted enough time talking."

The others joined him.

Despite having gone through the depths of Vanalf and getting far too little sleep, he was oddly enlivened. It was like their time in Vanalf had been little more than a quick stroll. He wondered if that came with being a Grimnir or if Vanalf itself had merely been a dream. Its magic was inexplicable.

"You never told us what in all the blighting depths happened to you," Elowyn said as though they weren't jogging.

Hallik grunted. "I'm still not sure." Bjorn still couldn't fathom what kind of conditioning the two of them had been through for them to be able to have an effortless conversation as they kept such a pace. "After touching the stone, I think I just blacked out and woke up with some lizard demon wanting to eat me and drink my blood so that it could come here to Mennesvarld. It must have tracked me when I let go of Imarún for a moment. I'm guessing it, as well as some other monsters that came for me, has a similar *detect life* spell, like a Watcher, that alerted it to me."

Monsters with the same abilities? Bjorn noted that detail for later. He was also increasingly curious about Lorelai's dagger. Would they be able to see more information from it now that they had magic of their own to command?

"So, anyway, I basically just killed everything and got back out," Hallik said. "Father came in to help of course, or I may have been eaten by a pack of shadow wolf monsters."

"How strange for it to appear when it did," Elowyn said.

"Yes, I think it had something to do with the monster wanting me to reach the bottom before it took me, like that condition somehow impacted my blood. He said I was already a Grimnir, even though I hadn't emerged from Vanalf with my wings yet."

"More mysteries," Elowyn said.

For all their years of entering Vanalf, Bjorn was still surprised by the lack of information they had about it. Elowyn's ignorance was especially telling, given that she, even at her young age, was supposedly one of Avskild's most educated individuals.

They kept a hard pace, and the wisp led them to the base of the mountains southeast of Vanalf. It was trying to find an easy path for them to scale the steep incline, often dotted with rocky edges. Bjorn took the incline in stride, leaning forward and keeping his legs pumping. Even Hallik started panting to keep up, but Elowyn's inhuman endurance made him wonder how much elf blood she truly had. Perhaps she was right, and the blood of a primordial was mingled in there as well. That, apparently, had not restricted her from becoming a Grimnir, something that he'd thought exclusive to humans.

More mysteries. Just as Elowyn had said.

The sun was up by the time they climbed well above the tree line, though they were still behind the shadow of the mountain. Their trek so far was eerily calm. The monsters they'd been anticipating were nowhere to be seen. After having to fight their way everywhere they'd been so far, and with some nefarious force out there trying to take down all of Avskild, shouldn't there be something trying to prevent them from reaching the portal?

He kept his thoughts to himself as they continued to climb. The tremors in the ground came at sporadic intervals, and at one point they had to dodge a few rocks that came tumbling down the mountain. It made him wonder what would happen if the shield was completely broken. Perhaps the whole floating island of Avskild would crash back down to the rest of Mennesvarld. Probably most everyone would die.

They were about three hours into their brisk pace when Lorelai groaned from behind and demanded a break. The wisp continued swirling around, trying to convince them to keep going, but even Bjorn was feeling exhausted. "We should take it easy from here," Bjorn suggested. "We don't want to collapse from exhaustion if something decides to attack us."

He stretched his muscles but remained on his feet. The mountain here was bare, save for rocks coated in low grasses and bushes, some of them speckled with tiny pink flowers. Insects buzzed around, and with his enhanced senses, he could even spot a bear farther across the way, digging through some rocks.

"I wish I knew how close we were," Elowyn said.

"It must be here on the mountain," Bjorn said. "Otherwise the wisp would have led us around rather than up."

"Whoever placed the portal on top of a mountain should be ashamed of themselves," Hallik said.

Elowyn smiled at him and rolled her eyes.

"Let's keep going," Lorelai said, looking up at the crack in the sky.

Bjorn resumed the lead, hoping they'd cross a stream at some point to refill their water. They hadn't eaten anything since finishing the last of their food while inside Vanalf. It wasn't uncommon enough for him to go without food for a couple days at a time on occasion, but he doubted the rest of them were accustomed to such conditions while living in a city. He could probably hunt something for them to eat, but that would take what little precious time they had to save Avskild.

The wisp seemed aggravated by their lumbering pace, but its frantic movements eventually shifted to a gradual swaying back and forth as it led them onward. They reached a ridge and crossed down to the other side. The edge of the mountains to either side gradually narrowed up to a point, the top of which was hidden from view by several trees.

"If I had to guess, that is where the portal will be," Bjorn said. He squinted ahead, though with his vision so sharp already, it did nothing to aid him. He didn't quite trust his ability with the spells enough, but he muttered, "*Synseith*," anyway to see if it would reveal any magic. He skipped a step forward and stumbled as his vision became awash with colorful images that appeared to him in a wave. He rubbed his eyes, but even with them closed, he could still see all the strange colors. The spell had no dependence on eyesight to function.

He waded forward, trying not to get lost in the new sensation while taking careful steps. Behind him, the others were talking, but he couldn't focus on their words as he tried to discern what he was seeing. Shapeless colors wafted through the air like tiny, stretched clouds. Threads of shimmering light were laced across the ground in uneven, random patterns. Some of the trees ahead seemed pockmarked by dark, viscous spots along their trunks. All the other plants had some kind of similar marking on them as well, even down to the grasses.

Bjorn shook his head as the vision went away within a blink of his eyes. There was even more magic lingering around here than what he'd seen around Vanalf. He looked back at the team, their weapons drawn.

"What did you see?" Hallik asked knowingly.

"Be on guard," Bjorn said, unsure how to explain the traces of magic he'd seen. From what he could gather, with a significant amount of experience a Watcher would potentially be able to identify what kind of spells had been used, but he had no idea what he'd been looking at. He clearly had a long way to go.

As they drew closer, Bjorn realized something was off about the place. Many of the plants were brown and shriveled. Some of the trees were rotted with disease, most of their needles having fallen to the earth. He drew his sword, feeling suddenly envious of both Hallik and Lorelai for possessing magical weapons. He only hoped he'd still be able to have their backs. They were capable warriors, and now that Lorelai was armed with Vitugr spells, she had the potential to be the most powerful one among them all.

The wisp led them to the edge of the trees and paused, its light fading to a dim, dark red. It jerked forward then returned to its previous position as if waving Bjorn on.

Bjorn looked back at the others, who nodded to him. He shrugged and moved forward, Hallik marching up to be at his side. Once they entered the shade of the blackened trees, the wisp zipped away, vanishing from sight.

It seemed that where they were heading, even the wisp did not want to go.

So be it.

To Kel's abyss.

Bjorn strode forward, already anticipating all the new things he'd be putting on that list of his.

CHAPTER FORTY-EIGHT

PLAGUE AND PESTILENCE

Lorelai Harkral

Having been through several battles now, Lorelai thought that she might not get so nervous each time, but that cold sensation of subtle fear clung to her spine like an insect, crawling up and down her skin. Every word of every spell she'd heard kept running through her mind as she prepared herself to use them. What she really needed was a few months of practice. She had little understanding of magic and had never anticipated becoming a Grimnir. She was no Elowyn.

Her brief moments of practice over the night would not be sufficient, but at least she had Dris. Stabbing was something she understood. Blowing air at an opponent did not seem like the greatest tactic if they got into a fight.

They slunk together through the deadened trees. Whatever had happened here, it was like poison. There were even blackened vines that stretched across the ground, all of them seemingly coming from the very back of the pointed mountain formation.

Hallik glanced over his shoulder at her and whispered, "We'll be alright, Lorelai." He had a strange way of sensing the anxiety others experienced.

"I am not a warrior," Lorelai said. Though she'd worked with the militia, they'd never fought anybody during her time there. She'd merely caught robbers. This was different. Talking helped release some of the tension in her back.

"What is a warrior, anyway?" Hallik said. "It's more than training to fight. It's the spirit of a person that makes them a warrior. It's having something to fight for, even if the odds are not in our favor. It's being brave even when we are afraid."

Lorelai didn't often care for the young man's speeches, but this was one such occasion where she appreciated it. She nodded back to him with the smallest of smiles.

Even Bjorn grunted at Hallik's monologue.

Ahead of them, the trees cleared, and the portal was plainly visible as a large arch, completely covered in thick vines. The vines undulated like squirming veins, giving the impression that the structure was alive. Perhaps it was. This was much different than the portal she'd seen in the Tower of Tarn. It was also twice as tall, which possibly allowed even bigger beasts than the ashimal to get through. That idea alone frightened her, but their quarry was already there, waiting for them.

On the top of the portal was the figure of a woman, body laced with the same vines that wove around the structure. At first Lorelai thought that she was a statue, but the eyes blinked, a dull blue light glowing from within. Her skin was pale and decayed, much of the skin around her mouth completely missing, leaving the muscle and crooked jaw exposed.

"Pesta," Elowyn hissed the word, her upper lip curling and nose crinkling as though there was a foul stench.

In fact, there was. It hit Lorelai in a nauseating wave. She could only imagine what Bjorn was experiencing with his enhanced senses, but his face was as grim and grumpy as usual.

"She is the pestilence," Elowyn said.

"Whoa," a new figure said as it emerged from the side.

Lorelai's eyes had been so drawn to the portal that she hadn't noticed the small, ruined temple off to the side. The building was so dilapidated and concealed in vines that she wasn't surprised she hadn't noticed it before, but a man approached them from inside, his hands outstretched. He had white hair slicked down the back of his head. His skin was almost equally pale, and he wore fine black clothes that looked like they hadn't been cleaned in years. Pointed ears suggested that this was no mere human.

"Surely you weren't just calling my dear love a pestilence," the man said.

"That thing?" Hallik said, pointing up at Pesta.

The man smiled at Pesta and placed a hand over his chest. "Yes. Isn't she remarkable? Her beauty surpasses all. Indeed, I count myself lucky to be in the presence of her radiance. What great fortune you have to behold her before she consumes you."

"You are talking about that disease-ridden woman thing on top of the portal, right?" Hallik said. "Are you well?"

The man snarled in rage. "How dare you! Your eyes have been graced long enough!"

Slithering vines crawled closer to them.

"I love her. I will burn this whole island in fire for her!"

"There will be no burning anything today," Hallik said.

A vine touched Lorelai's ankle, and she shrieked the word, "*Brun*," as she jumped back, swinging Dris at the vine. An explosion of fire burst from her arm, scorching the vine and lighting a nearby tree on fire.

"Blight, Lorelai, now I'm a liar," Hallik said.

"Blight, indeed," the man said, raising his arms.

Bubbling green ooze issued from his fingertips, spewing toward them. It splattered out in an unavoidable spray, which Lorelai dodged only to be tripped by one of the blackened vines. Some of the ooze flicked across her skin, instantly searing at her flesh, but Hallik had blocked the brunt of it, stepping forward and extending his wings. He was a madman.

From her place on the ground, Lorelai dug Dris across the vine, and it slithered a retreat. She wiped the ooze off onto her clothes, but her skin continued to sting and blister. When she looked back up, Bjorn launched a bolt that struck the man in the shoulder. Unperturbed by the damage, he raised his upturned hands and several blobby masses rose from the ground, like zombies made from blight itself.

"A blightmancer and a pestilence. How quaint," Elowyn said, while she too was trying to wipe the blight from her skin.

Hallik just roared, probably from the pain, and stepped forward, slicing one of the blight zombies with his sword clean in half before it could fully form. How he wasn't rolling on the ground in pain was beyond her.

Elowyn stepped to Lorelai's side and cut down another vine that reached for her. Lorelai thanked her and hopped back to her feet. Seven blobby figures had formed and were moving to attack them. It was only then that Lorelai realized they possessed real body parts, though they were basically bones encased in the gelatinous green substance, some of which seemed human, while most belonged to animals like deer, bears, or rabbits.

The rotted tree beside Lorelai started to writhe, and a branch swiped at her. She ducked beneath it and realized that the blotted marks along its trunk were not simply killing the tree but possessing it.

Most of the tree's limbs were ablaze, its dried surface kindled to flame. It swayed, another branch swinging for her as the top of the tree fell off completely, crashing down beside another tree, causing the flames to spread.

Lorelai ducked again and felt needles from the branch whip across the back of her head. That had been too close. Another branch swung, and she used her axe to try and block it, but that only ended up jarring the weapon from her grasp. Brute force would not be sufficient.

The burning tree succumbed to the flames and split in half as the fire spread. More vines whipped toward Lorelai. She used Dris to cut across one of them, but another tendril slammed into her like a punch to the ribs. Meanwhile,

Hallik and Bjorn battled against the grossly animated bodies.

"We need to get to her," Elowyn said, referencing the decaying woman.

"Aren't you the Voyager?" Lorelai said.

Another spray of burning ooze sprinkled across them, but it wasn't as bad as the first since it seemed to be aimed at Hallik. She wasn't sure how much more of that the young man could take. They needed to remain focused on the objective.

The earth shook with another tremor, and the portal itself shimmered with blue-green light like ripples across water. She could have sworn she saw something else through the hazy surface of the portal.

"This has to end," Lorelai said. She switched Dris to an underhanded grip and took off at a sprint, jumping over a vine and ducking beneath another. Elowyn kept pace beside her until a couple of the vines slapped her down. Lorelai paused just long enough to stab one of the vines that grappled at Elowyn's leg, but then another wrapped around Elowyn's arm.

"Go!" Elowyn cried. "Attacking the vines does nothing. You need to get her."

Lorelai grit her teeth and spun just in time for a vine to whip across her face. She gasped at the blow and yelled the word, "*Brun*," as if it were a curse. Fire fanned out around her in a smokey blaze, burning the nearest vines. She spun forward, Dris slicing across another vine. She could feel the small blade lapping up tiny portions of soul energy.

Somewhere behind her, Hallik screamed. All she could do was pray that he hadn't been killed, but if she didn't take out Pesta, they'd all be dead in moments.

A vine latched around Lorelai's arm then coiled around her fingers, squeezing the hand that held Dris. She tried yanking her arm free when more vines slammed into her, knocking her off her feet. The touch of the vines was strikingly cold, and it felt like they were sucking the moisture from her skin.

She spared a glance at the rest of the team, hoping for aid, but they were no better off. Bjorn was pinned down by a tree, Elowyn was almost completely wrapped in vines, and Hallik was down on one knee, one of his wings pressed to the ground by a vine. An ooze creature beat him with what appeared to be a rib bone while the strange man strode toward him.

This would be the end of them.

Lorelai tried to pull her arm free, but the vine gripped her even tighter, the pestilence draining her energy with each passing moment. She hadn't seen pestilence in action before, but from what she knew, it would probably leave her as little more than a withered husk as the poison choked her out.

Hallik wasn't giving up, and she wouldn't either. These were not just her allies, not just her team. They were her friends. Even Bjorn with all his doom and gloom. He'd known exactly how to tell the difference between her and the doppelganger. Friends had been foreign to her before, but they'd each reached out to her with care and compassion. They'd fought and bled for one another, even when she'd been the weakest among them.

But she was not weak now. She was a Grimnir—a Vitugr at that. She'd earned her magic by her own strength and the strength of their team. These monsters would learn what they were up against.

Another vine wrapped itself around her leg, forcing her to kneel. As if sensing the danger she presented, a vine tried to get around her mouth, but she jerked her head away and yelled, "*Brun*," calling forth all the will in her body. Fire licked all around her, the heat of it even causing some of her hairs to singe as she leapt to her feet. The vines around her withered as flames scorched them to blackness.

All the vines came for her then, but with the distraction, Hallik too was able to break free, though the strange man blocked Hallik's path to Pesta. It was up to Lorelai.

She roared as she spun forward, Dris slashing across a vine. She willed the fire all around her. Her spell was erratic, but she didn't care much as the distance from her friends grew. She found that if she swung Dris with the spell, it helped her body more naturally direct the flames. Fire licked out with each slash, slicing through the vines with the force of a great axe.

Instead of waiting for Lorelai to arrive, Pesta screeched and rose from the top of the portal, decaying body supported by the throbbing tendrils of vines that spread out where her legs would otherwise be. A dark cloud of mist sprayed out of Pesta's mouth at Lorelai, but she shouted the word, "*Vindr*," by instinct, and a force of wind blew into the mist, dissipating in Lorelai's wake as she ran toward the monster.

With a hiss from Pesta, several vines came slamming down at Lorelai.

Lorelai called on the fire again, another burst of flames holding the vines at bay, but her body fatigued. It was cold. Each time she summoned fire, it grew even colder. *It's draining me*, she realized.

She needed to end this quickly.

Pesta was coming in fast. The number of vines she summoned never seemed to diminish. Destroying them only delayed the assault.

Instead of focusing as much on deflecting the vines, Lorelai swung Dris directly toward Pesta, casting the fire spell at the same time, willing the burning energy toward the monster. An arc of fire burst from the fist that clenched the dagger. It sailed straight toward the monster and burned right across her chest.

Pesta screamed, cringing away from the flames, but in the attack, Lorelai had let down her guard, and a vine slapped into her back, sending her tumbling forward. She rolled and popped back up to her feet, hurtling yet another sweep of flames at the monster. This one streaked across the vines that spread from the woman's lower body. She sent another, getting ever closer.

Pesta used some vines to block the attack, now redirecting her own efforts to defense, but she could not defend well against Lorelai's fire.

The blightmancer yelled in outrage from behind her. She needed to finish this. Several coils of vines came once again, but Lorelai used another hectic burst of flame to keep them at bay before pouncing forward. With one more step, she stood directly before Pesta, though the vines held the woman up head and shoulders taller than Lorelai.

Lorelai panted from the exertion, feeling like she'd been sprinting to get here. She swung Dris once again, sending another flaming arc as the weapon itself bit across Pesta's lower body. Pesta recoiled, vines whipping everywhere like writhing tentacles. Lorelai jabbed this time, jumping higher to drive the dagger into Pesta's chest. The monster blocked the stab with her arm, but Dris pierced her flesh all the same.

Dris drank deeply from the monster's soul, and Lorelai stabbed again, this time striking Pesta on the lower torso. Dark ichor splattered across Lorelai's arm, licking away her skin. She screamed and staggered back, calling upon her fire magic instead, and aimed for Pesta's head. The flames burst from her arm, scorching across Pesta's decaying face. Pesta fell back, her uninjured arm clutched over the wound in her stomach.

"No!" the blightmancer screamed. "Her face—her beautiful face!"

Lorelai looked around at him just in time to see Hallik's sword tear across the man's stomach. He screamed but ignored the pain and dashed to Pesta's side. Elowyn and Bjorn had both been released, and they hurried over to Lorelai, who didn't know what to do now. The vines had all stopped writhing and pulsing, and instead they'd deflated like crushed worms. She took a step back as the blightmancer dropped to his knees, his blood a strange iridescence of red and green as it spilled, but he scooped Pesta into his arms with tears streaming down his face.

"My dear, Pesta," he sobbed, shoulders bouncing as he held her disease-ridden body against his own.

Lorelai looked back at her friends, but they too seemed unsure of what to do. Hallik limped over, his body covered in burn marks. Several of his feathers were completely missing. It looked like he'd been getting plucked like a chicken, and his face held a slight grimace.

Bjorn took one look at Hallik, then set his jaw and strode up to the blightmancer's back. With one swing of his sword, he lopped the man's head straight off. "Weep together in the abyss," he said.

When the others stared at him, he shrugged. "Somebody had to do it. Now, Elowyn, go do your thing."

He was right, of course. It was a mercy, perhaps. One the strange man did not even deserve. He'd come to ruin Avskild, and for what purpose? They'd never truly know, but from what Lorelai knew of pestilences, they had no true goal. Destruction was merely their nature.

Elowyn nodded and strode toward the portal. Most of the pulsing vines had receded, revealing a surprisingly sleek, black surface beneath, not dissimilar from the structure of the Tower of Tarn. This was what their entire last few days had led them to. Restoring the portals would restore the shield around Avskild. It would prevent more monsters from leaking through. It would restore peace to their people after so much destruction.

Lorelai smiled at Elowyn as the young woman raised her hand.

And then the sky shattered.

The earth shook as the mountain trembled.

They'd been too late.

CHAPTER FORTY-NINE

NOT DEAD YET

Lind Hjordis

Lind, Anders, Zaakira, and their handful of militia-men reached the compound of the Tower of Tarn just as the earth shook and the sky shattered. The sound reverberated from everywhere and everything, like all of Avskild was exploding.

Lind tumbled, summoning a shield as though that would somehow protect them. Several buildings collapsed, but the Tower of Tarn was as steady as a compass. The sky, instead of falling in on them after shattering, simply became clear and bright as though a film had been removed. The other sensation was that he was falling slowly, like he was sinking in water. He clutched the ground as though his life depended on it, and everyone else either did the same thing or fell over.

Anders was on his back, staring up at the sky with widened eyes. Lind couldn't even imagine what the Watcher was experiencing. Zaakira wisely shot to the sky, her wings pumping as she stayed aloft.

This could only mean one thing. It was the end of the world. The shield had broken. Hallik, Elowyn, Bjorn, and Lorelai had either died or they'd been too late. The island of Avskild was rejoining the rest of Mennesvarld. The pillar upon which it stood was tumbling back to the sea. The other students were probably working their way through Vanalf even now. They would emerge to find the entire island in ruins.

No. I'm not dead yet. Lind cast a spell, binding the earth around him and his little group. They'd survive the fall.

A moment later, the rumbling intensified, and Lind's hold on the earth around him started to waver. His body trembled with fatigue as the spell was ripped from his grasp. He gasped, closing his eyes as dust billowed up around them.

And then it was over.

He coughed, hearing others around him doing the same.

So they'd at least survived the fall. "Anders," he grunted before casting a light wind spell to disperse the dusty cloud. Anders remained in the same position, though he withdrew an arm from covering his face after Lind cleared the view.

Zaakira dropped down beside them a second later with a deep frown. "Avskild has fallen," she said. "Almost the whole rock formation is below surface. The waters have joined. I must warn the people at the docks to seek higher ground."

"Go," Lind said.

Zaakira nodded acknowledgement before launching back into the air.

"Anders," Lind repeated.

The older Grimnir's expression was dark with concern. "We are not alone here in Dalstava," he said grimly before sitting up with a groan.

"What do you mean?" Lind said, looking around.

Anders drew his weapon. "On your feet!" he shouted. The dust settled, and there were many survivors who started to rise—thankfully more than Lind had thought there would be. "Every living citizen must be armed for battle."

Lind brought out his axe. "Elaborate, Anders."

Anders nodded toward the Tower of Tarn. "The portal is open."

A few people came sprinting out of the tower, running toward Lind and Anders. Behind them, clawing its way out the of entrance, came a monster shaped like a squid with twelve tentacled legs, each hooked at the end. It had a single eye and a mouth lined with jagged teeth that could devour an entire horse.

"An amgrunda," Lind said, recognizing the creature immediately. They were notorious for subjugating humans as slaves. Without a second thought, he hurled a spear of light toward the monster, piercing it through the eye before it had a chance to reach the fleeing people. It screeched and fell, tentacles flailing.

Three more came behind it.

"By the depths," Lind muttered. Some of the people who'd fled ran behind him.

"Grab your weapons," Anders shouted to everyone who passed.

"How many are there, Anders?" Lind asked, hurling another spear of light. This one missed the eye but still lodged into an amgrunda's face.

"Enough to ravage the entire island," Anders said.

"Lind!" came a huffed voice.

Lind barely spared a glance to see Skelldwyn running to join him. He released a tense breath at the sight of the lad.

"What can I do to help?" Skelldwyn asked.

"Rally the whole city," Lind said. "Everyone needs to be armed. Our only hope for survival is to retake the tower and eliminate whatever has activated the portal."

"Aye, sir," Skelldwyn said, running off and shouting at the top of his lungs for everyone to arm up and head to the tower.

Lind's place was here. He knew exactly who was responsible. It was no doubt Ontr-anda. Whatever energy had been inside that gem must have been enough for him to unlock the portal completely.

Even if they secured the portal, they'd have to seal it off physically. It made him wonder what horrible place that portal connected with. Did it go straight to Kel's abyss? Why would the Tower of Tarn be built with such a thing inside of it? Perhaps the mysteries of this place were darker than he'd ever thought.

Benson appeared, coming up the street to take position beside Lind. They nodded to each other and started flinging spells at the outpouring of monsters.

More militia members had arrived as well as several citizens armed with their spears and shields. They'd run drills at least once a year, and they were about to learn just how effective that single practice had been. Anders was rallying the people into formation just before the first couple monsters reached the line. Lind and Benson wouldn't be able to hold them all. They'd need to push forward and regain the tower.

Two other monsters broke into the sky, flapping scaly wings. Small flickers of fire left embers behind them every time they flapped. Lind launched a spear at one, piercing it through the leg. It dropped, but the other monster veered away, flying out over the homes. It would burn down the city if nobody could stop it.

The citizens fought back bravely, realizing that they must win or be wiped off the planet, enslaved, or kept as livestock.

Lind would die before he let that happen. His axe burned in his hand as he activated it and swung, severing the grasping tentacle of an amgrunda before running it through with a magical spear.

The monster dropped, but several more were break-ing through. A new figure emerged from the tower, great wings spreading out from it on either side, though it did not require flapping them in order to fly. It merely gained altitude, grinning out at the terrible display of carnage as the monsters tore into the defensive ranks. A smirk settled on the demon's face.

Ontr-anda watched as his plot unfolded.

Other people were running to help, but it would not be enough. Mere humans were not strong enough to fight against such a horde. There were too few Grimnirs to defend against the onslaught, all thanks to the troll army that had ravaged them.

Lind was witnessing not just the end of an era, but the end of humanity.

He growled, filled with fury.

If they were to die, then Ontr-anda would go down with them. This would not be a day of victory for the demon.

Lind raised his axe and charged.

CHAPTER FIFTY

FIRES

Hallik Tyrusson

A groan issued from deep inside Hallik's chest as he cautiously rose back to his feet. Other than a new crack in the mountain beside them, the world seemed unharmed. Even the sky was more blue and clearer than ever before. They weren't dead. Not yet.

Without any prompting, Elowyn started casting her spell, words spilling out in a frantic voice.

"We're already too late, Elowyn," Bjorn said. He looked as battered as the rest of them, some of his leather armor had torn on the shoulder, and his dark hair was completely wild. The man hadn't shaved in days.

"That won't stop us from trying," Hallik said, making his way over to Elowyn's side. She was still muttering the spell, her hands touching the base of the portal. Green and blue light pulsed within the dark structure, a positive sign that her efforts were having some effect.

Elowyn dropped her hands and looked back at them all. Her face was smudged, and her skin was speckled with little sores where the blight had gotten her. "Well, it's sealed," she said simply. "I did everything I can think of, but we should probably go find out how everyone else is doing." She eyed Hallik carefully, her eyebrows knitting with concern. "Are you well?"

Hallik scanned himself over. He looked terrible. Many of his feathers had been burned away completely, giving his wings an almost skeletal appearance. If Valtyras were meant to fly, then he wouldn't be taking to the air for a long, long time. The blight had burned him in so many places that he thought he'd die, but something about being a Valtyra had made him considerably resilient. More resilient than he should have been. Other Valtyras had died to blight before, so why hadn't he? There was one possibility that he suspected, though he felt like it would be something to address with Tyrus or Lind.

"We should get back to Dalstava," Lorelai said, already looking away.

"I want to check in on my father," Hallik said.

"Which we can do after," Lorelai asserted. "We should be wise and coordinate our efforts in securing the other portals. Then we can go back to Tyrus. There may very well be more Voyagers later today. Getting everyone together would be in our best interest."

"She's right, Hallik," Elowyn said.

"Yes, of course," Hallik said, trying not to limp as he walked. Pain lanced up through his left thigh. Not only had he been cut, but the grasping tendril of vine had squeezed his leg with such a crushing force that it left his entire leg tender. The pain in his wings was an entirely new sensation, one that he was positive he'd get accustomed to eventually, but for now it was a strange agony. He did what he could to avoid moving them at all, keeping them splayed out to some degree. A thorough sea-bath would do him some good.

"You did well, Lorelai," Hallik said to her as he passed. He pointed at his wing where a couple feathers were terribly singed. "You got me a little though. I guess what Rav said about control is very real, but for not having any formal Grimnir training, your directional control of that fire was impressive."

"Agreed," Elowyn said.

Lorelai smiled, despite their grim circumstances. "Sorry for burning you."

"It was worth it, given the circumstances." In truth, he'd suffered so much pain that the burn hardly seemed to make things worse.

It was very possible that they'd walk to the edge of this mountain and see Dalstava was nothing but rubble.

They reached the edge of the mountain's slope, and indeed, Dalstava was visible in the distance. The black spire of the Tower of Tarn stuck out like a dark sentinel.

And it was wreathed in fire.

The city of Dalstava was burning.

"We are too late," Lorelai said, her mouth agape.

Dalstava was lost, and with it, all of Avskild would follow.

ONTR-ANDA

Elowyn Galdre

Hallik led the charge down the mountain, Elowyn right beside him. Nobody questioned what they were about to do. There had to be *some* survivors inside the city. He had a clear limp, but Elowyn was surprised he wasn't worse. His clothes were in tatters and his skin was dotted with little burns, but there was little time to address this.

She too was in pain, but all four of them were still able. None of them bore wounds that would not heal. At least, so long as Hallik's wings would mend. She wasn't sure how that worked.

Branches whipped past as they ran. They weren't fast enough. From their vantage atop the mountain, she wagered that despite their quick descent, they were at least two hours away from the city. As Grimnirs, they all seemed more physically fit than before. Even Lorelai was keeping pace. Perhaps they were all spurred on by that same great weight of responsibility. They were some of the last few Grimnirs. The defense of Avskild rested on their shoulders.

To see the shield break and to witness Dalstava burning—it was the most poignant form of failure Elowyn had ever experienced. *She* was the Voyager. This was what she'd been training for her entire life, and she'd been so close to success. The sickness that roiled within her was almost unbearable. Only a sliver of hope kept her pushing on. The sweat that beaded on her forehead as she ran was not because of the physical exertion.

They ran and ran, and as they got closer, the flames within the city seemed that much larger. Fear pounded against Elowyn's chest as she worried what they might see when they actually arrived at the gates. Had everyone died? Where was Lind? Where was her mother? She wanted to let the rage overtake her and scream, but she couldn't. She had to cling to hope.

Their pace did not slow as they approached the walls.

Castle Vrodr stood undisturbed, and the walls were high enough that most of the flames within the city were not visible. The gates were open, unmanned.

When they ran through the entrance to Castle Vrodr, a few people were huddled just on the inside of the wall. It was most of the servants, students, and many other children that Elowyn didn't recognize, preparing to run into the forest if whatever was ravaging the city came nearer.

"Where's Lind?" Hallik asked, their team pausing just long enough to ask a couple questions of the students.

They regarded Hallik's wings with widened eyes.

"The tower!" said one of the servants, arm trembling as she gripped a spear. "Monsters started spilling out."

Elowyn clenched her jaw. They must have entered through that portal. She needed to reach it. "Stay with the children," Elowyn said. Each student was armed with some kind of weapon, even down to the twelve-year-olds. Hopefully they wouldn't have to use them.

They went to the far side of the castle grounds to the gate that led into the rest of the city. The portcullis was half raised, just enough for them to crouch under. Two older students and a servant stood guard beside it, and they said nothing as Elowyn and her friends crawled under, finding themselves in a nightmare.

Many of the buildings were ruined, only a few standing unharmed. The fire centered around the Tower of Tarn. Their footfalls sounded hollowly in the deserted streets. The lower portion of the city was currently draining of water from the waves that must have crashed in after Avskild's fall. They proceeded cautiously at a jog, wary that a monster might jump out at them at any moment.

Elowyn kept her dagger in one hand and sword in the other. There were no signs of battle until they neared the first burned building. Half the home had collapsed, but a tentacled monster and two fallen people lay dead just outside of it. "Amgrundas," Elowyn said. "How fitting."

Bjorn growled with more anger than usual.

"What are those?" Lorelai asked.

"They are known for enslaving humans," Elowyn said. "I'm not surprised to see them here. They were probably hoping to take Avskild for themselves."

There were more bodies as they got closer to the tower. It was an absolute massacre. They started moving faster, as if all of them were subconsciously spurred to find survivors. Elowyn was actually relieved when she heard shouting. That meant that somebody was alive.

Bjorn grunted. "Beings near the tower," he said, shielding his eyes with a hand as though it was causing him pain to use his abilities.

Elowyn sprinted ahead. She hadn't eaten for over a full day now, and she'd been burning every ounce of energy up to this point, but all that fatigue and weariness was pushed aside as she clung to the hope that she might save somebody. She cleared the short wall that ringed Tower of Tarn and skidded to a stop to assess the scene. People and monsters were dead all over the place, including the burned husk of Benson, one of the last Vitugrs. His body was shriveled and dusty, a clear sign of somebody who had expended more magical energy than their body could sustain. He'd given his all.

But there was still some activity.

Lind had one of his arms impaled by a spear into the wooden siding of a ruined building, pinning him there. A demon stood in front of Lind, its feet hovering over the ground, wings outstretched but not beating. The demon was relatively human in size and general form, but his skin was red, two small horns arched back from its scalp, and his lower half was hairy enough that it could almost be described as fur.

Lind's body sagged, and he was barely on his feet. His face was cut and battered, and his axe lay just behind the demon.

When he caught sight of Elowyn, Lind roared and lifted his free hand, light sparkling in his palm, but the demon kicked his hand away. A spear came hurtling from a crumbled roof, straight toward the demon's head, but he caught the spear and hurled it back at the assailant. The scream that came after was an indication of the demon's perfect aim.

Elowyn charged. She didn't know what use she would be against something that even Lind couldn't defeat, but if she could at least draw its attention away, that would be enough.

Hallik's shout echoed behind her as he joined in the charge. She knew Lorelai and Bjorn would be right behind her as well.

The demon turned to look at them as a smile disappeared from his face.

Lind took the moment to remove the spear pinning him to the wall. He thrust it into the demon's side before falling to his knees. The demon roared, but Elowyn arrived just in time to hack at the monster. Her sword met the demon's elbow, barely piercing flesh as the blade slid across a sharp, horned protrusion that stuck out from the demon's arm.

The demon made as if to slap Elowyn with a clawed hand, but she ducked beneath the attack and slashed her dagger across the demon's shin. She rolled away to get out of its reach as Hallik arrived, his sword swinging in several quick strokes. The demon, clearly surprised by the magical weapon's capability, found his arm severed in one blow before Hallik stabbed it in the shoulder.

The demon shrieked and dove at Hallik, clawed hands outstretched, when a spear of light struck it through the midsection. The demon tumbled, still clawing for Hallik, but he stepped aside, slicing his sword across the demon's wing. Slamming his sword into the other wing, Bjorn pinned the demon down on that side as Lorelai jammed Dris into the demon's ribs. It swiped at Lorelai, sharp claws tearing across her arm, forcing her to scramble away.

An amgrunda smashed into Bjorn, entangling him with its tentacles, teeth gnashing. The Watcher warred with the beast, stabbing it with daggers this way and that.

Hallik hacked the demon's foot off at the ankle. Whatever they'd done so far, the demon had lost its ability to float, and instead was kneeling in the ashy dirt. The demon regarded the dagger protruding from its chest with widened eyes. Despite the damage it had received, it smirked.

"No!" Lind shouted, stumbling over with his axe dragging on the ground. He was too far.

Elowyn realized it then. This was Ontr-anda. This was the very creature that was plotting Avskild's downfall. He had been using the power of murdered Voyagers to wear down the portal shields, power that had been drained using the same dagger now settled in its own body.

Ontr-anda reached with its remaining hand to grasp Dris in its bloodied claws, smile changing to a broad grin. "Oh, what fun we will have," he said.

Ontr-anda could *not* take the power within Dris for himself.

This would not be their end.

Elowyn jumped onto the demon's back, sword plunging through its back, dagger tearing into its neck. Ontr-anda's body glowed with a purplish-red hue. He ignored Elowyn's stabbing weapons, a laugh escaping the demon's throat.

What would it do with such power? Avskild was already ravaged. They would all become slaves. Whatever hope remained for people outside of this island would be gone as well. The blood of so many Voyagers rested within that one, simple item.

With Bjorn distracted, Hallik stabbed Ontr-anda again, thrusting his blade into the demon's chest. He kicked Hallik in the chest with a sickening crunch. Elowyn gasped as Hallik fell, his eyes wide with shock. The demon shot into the air with a burst, throwing Elowyn from his back. He hovered a few spans off the ground, his body knitting back together.

No.

Hallik was sputtering on the ground, Bjorn was entangled with the amgrunda, Lorelai stood dumbfounded knowing her two spells would do nothing, and Lind was struggling to stay upright.

It was up to her. Elowyn was their chance.

Her eyes focused in on Dris. She knew the spell she needed to use. "*Dimhastig*," she hissed, then jumped, eyes honed in on the dagger. She'd barely moved and she was already there, crashing into Ontr-anda's arm. Without a second thought, she hacked with both her weapons, cutting into the demon's wrist, then let go of her own dagger so she could reach for Dris.

Dris was in her grip as she fell to the ground.

Ontr-anda regarded her with sheer fury, but Lind had just hurled his glowing axe at the demon. It rammed into the demon's hip with a burning light. He roared and dropped back to the ground. Lind fell back, his flesh looking slightly shriveled as the demon continued to yell, its body trembling.

Lind was channeling all his energy into the axe, still embedded in Ontr-anda's body.

He's going to burn himself out, she realized with horror.

Hallik stepped up with a wheeze and hacked directly into the demon's head, Imarún flaring with a bright orange glow.

Despite the wound, Ontr-anda glared up at Hallik with a snarl. "This is just the beginning." The demon's body froze, turning to gray stone. A second later, he began to crumble, collapsing into a heap of dark sand.

Dead.

They'd defeated the demon.

"Bah," Bjorn growled, stepping away from the corpse of the amgrunda.

Hallik clutched his chest and smirked at Bjorn. "Don't worry, you can mark them both off your list."

Lind's eyes were half-lidded as he stared up at the sky.

Elowyn hurried to Lind's side. A few other people emerged from the nearby buildings. Not everyone had died.

Lind heaved for breath. Another man came limping to Lind's side, an older man with a Watcher medallion hanging from his neck. "He almost withered," the man said.

"I'll find him some food," Elowyn sputtered, knowing that nourishment and rest would be the best remedy for Lind's soul.

"No," the man said. "You're a Voyager. Send another. You must ensure the portal inside the tower is secure."

"Are there no other monsters?" Bjorn inquired of the man. He held a hand to his forehead as though shielding his eyes from the sun, despite several clouds rolling in. He'd taken to doing that whenever he was trying to use his new Watcher abilities.

"This was the last one within my view," the old Watcher replied.

Hallik and Elowyn looked to Lind.

"Go," the Watcher said. "We will take care of him. Securing that portal is vital." A few people were running off, and somebody came dashing toward Lind with a horn mug of water. It was a young man whom Elowyn vaguely recognized as one of the servants at Castle Vrodr.

Elowyn nodded.

"I will take you to the portal," Lorelai said, holding her hand out to Elowyn.

Realizing what Lorelai was after, Elowyn handed Dris back. Lorelai nodded and led the way into the Tower of Tarn.

Hallik held a hand to his chest and leaned against the wall of the tower.

"Hallik should wait here," Bjorn said. "He may have broken ribs."

Hallik looked as though he might object, but instead he nodded and rested his head back with a grunt.

Bjorn continued on with them as they strode in silence through the skeleton of a building. So much death. So much carnage. Elowyn could scarcely believe it had come to this. No matter how well they recovered, the destruction of this day would remain a scar that would never go away.

Words of a new song already formed in the back of her mind, but she was not a framer of words and music. At least, she hadn't ever borne the full mantle of such a task. That duty still rested on the shoulders of her mother, wherever she was. Thinking of her mother brought tears to her eyes as she worried that perhaps she hadn't survived this assault.

Rebuilding Dalstava would take ages, but this war was not over. Avskild was no longer shielded from the rest of the world. Monsters would be able to reach the island physically, if not through the portals themselves. The peace they had known for so long was gone forever. It seemed her concerns regarding the disappearance of Voyagers and the potential threat to their island had been real all along.

They climbed up the tower, then all the way back down through a secret passage, Lorelai leading them deep beneath the tower. Instead of being transparent like the other portals Elowyn had seen, this portal maintained a dark, shrouded fog within, as though something was hidden behind it. A quick glance around the strange room filled Elowyn with more questions. The Tower of Tarn was older than all the songs. What purpose could such a room hold?

"I do not like this place," Bjorn said.

Elowyn felt the same, though she placed her hands against the portal's arch. She cast the sealing spell, energy slipping from her body like she'd just been drained of blood. She sagged against the portal as magical tendrils squirmed beneath the structure's smooth surface. Then it stopped. The sealing was done.

She stepped away. Her body was weary. Weary from Vanalf, from battles, from worry and fear. She needed rest.

But she knew her exhaustion would find little relief. This was only the beginning.

CHAPTER FIFTY-TWO

A TEAM

Jaysen Bjorn

A light rain pattered down on the flower petals as Bjorn stood at the edge of the Evergrove. Hallik and Elowyn sat inside the circle with Tyrus, who had assumed his normal position, lying on the grass, staring up at the sky. He looked ancient. Bjorn could still barely believe the man was alive. He would supposedly be restored to his normal condition, but the process would take upwards of an entire year.

Lind had also been allowed access to the Evergrove, and he too was beside the ancient man. Lind's wounds had been severe, and they'd had to carry him all the way here in a wagon pulled by horses, Hallik sitting beside him for much of the ride.

Everyone cried. The devastation was too much. The tears hadn't stopped falling.

Everyone but Bjorn. He had seen this kind of devastation before. Too many times. He'd lost every tear in his body by the time he was twenty.

Of the twenty-eight thousand residents of Dalstava, there were probably only ten thousand who remained. Entire generations had died, fighting back the monsters that had poured through the portal. Still, Avskildians were hardier than Bjorn had initially thought. The peace had softened them of course, but at a moment's notice, they'd all rallied to defend their people. He had not seen such bravery among any of the other people he'd fought beside.

Lorelai stood next to Bjorn, silent. Dris was still looped in her belt. Her clothes were as tattered as the rest of theirs. Hallik was practically in rags. Bjorn gave Lorelai a sideways glance. Her eyes were puffy and red, matching the color of her disheveled hair. He wasn't sure how to react to their sadness. There was no reassurance he could offer. The world was a bleak and terrible place. He at least was pleased that they had put up a good fight. Many monsters had died. They would not underestimate the readiness of Avskildians again.

And from what he understood, defeating Ontr-anda was a great victory. He'd been a foe to humanity ever since the first monsters found their way to Mennesvarld.

Hallik looked over to Bjorn and Lorelai before beckoning them over with a jerk of his head.

Bjorn stepped forward, pausing as Lorelai grabbed his wrist and squeezed. He looked at her, expressionless. If she took comfort in his presence, he could not understand why, but he merely nodded to her and moved to join the others. She released him and came as well.

When they reached the inner circle, Tyrus looked up, straight into Bjorn's soul. There was a connection between them. Bjorn could feel it, like an invisible thread that bound them together. They were fellow Grimnirs, and more than that, they were both Watchers. Bjorn had felt the same thing when he'd caught the eyes of the old Watcher at the Tower of Tarn.

"There is much to be done," Tyrus said, his voice hoarse. Rain pattered against Tyrus's eyes, but he did not even blink. "The four of you were meant to come here. Bjorn, I believe you stepping through the portal was no accident. You needed to be here with Hallik, Lorelai, and Elowyn. And to see the four of you representing each Grimnir class is no coincidence. Vanalf called to you."

Bjorn tried not to scoff at the notion. Destiny was not something that happened, it was something one carved out for oneself. Avskild had not been destined to be decimated, their kings had merely been fools. He listened anyway. Now was not the time for such a debate.

"Hallik is not only a Valtyra, but he has partaken of a blood-binding potion belonging to the drakked," Tyrus continued. "I would never have advised such a risky action, but in so doing, I can detect that he has developed a unique resilience to magical elements. This will make him a strong protector. Lorelai has been given the gift of much power. Paired with her unconquerable spirit, she will become a Vitugr to rival those of legend. Bjorn, you were already keen before, but a true mastery of your senses will make you formidable indeed. And Elowyn, as a Voyager, you provide all Grimnirs with the hope to fulfill what we failed to do so many years before."

"But we killed the demon, and the king is gone," Elowyn said.

Bjorn narrowed his eyes, waiting for the old man to explain what he meant about Elowyn.

"Ontr-anda was not alone in his efforts." Tyrus cleared his throat. "Work remains. The portals throughout Avskild connect to many places. Places that have needed our protection, but we abandoned them." Tyrus blinked for the first time, gaze shifting back to the sky. "You must travel the portals. Cleanse the lands."

Bjorn couldn't hold back his scoff this time. "That would be impossible. Even with an army of Grimnirs, it could not be done."

"And still, you will do it," Tyrus said. "One by one, you will save the nations of Mennesvarld. Some will be more corrupted than others."

"But we must also rebuild Avskild and keep the lands safe," Lorelai said.

"As you say, but others will do that. Somebody must bear the mantle of protecting all people. This is where we failed. This is why the Grimnirs have fallen. The shield should have never been raised, but the spear."

Tyrus closed his eyes. He was clearly weary. Whatever healing process he had to undergo was a mystery to Bjorn. The magic of these flowers was well beyond anything he'd seen before.

A few dryads were suddenly there, heads rising from around the flowers. He got the distinct impression that they wanted them to leave.

"Rest for a few days," Tyrus said, eyes still shut. "Encourage the people. Ensure the other villages of Avskild are safe. There are some new Grimnirs who will be returning to Dalstava within a few moments, having succeeded at their journey through Vanalf. They will need to see what you have done. Train. Then return to me, and I can share what I know of the portals."

No other words escaped Tyrus's lips. His chest rose and fell in great breaths, and the dryads rose ever taller as though they were spawning up from the ground itself.

"We must go," Bjorn said, eyeing the dryads. He did not think they wished them ill, but he did not want to test the theory.

Lind hadn't moved, still in the same spot where they'd laid him down. He'd fallen asleep as they entered the Evergrove, and remained that way even as they set him on the ground. Tyrus had told them that Lind would remain for a full day, then the dryads would carry him out of the grove where he would awake and return to Dalstava.

Some spell lingered on Lind's body, keeping him asleep. If he'd been better at using his *detect magic* spell, Bjorn would have noticed the dryads cast Lind into his slumber, but the skill of detecting magic was a difficult one to grasp.

Bjorn took a deep breath, the scent of the pollen filling his lungs. Hallik was the last one to leave the flowery circle as they departed. His wings were noticeably improved, and the fact that he was now walking upright without too much grunting was remarkable. The Evergrove was a powerful place. Bjorn had only stood within the circle for a few heartbeats, but the aches and pains of battle had diminished, though a weariness weighed upon his eyelids. Perhaps the sleeping spell the dryads cast on Lind had some lingering effect on those around him. That, or the healing of the flowers caused fatigue.

As soon as they were out of the grove, the rain ceased. It was as good an opportunity as any other. Bjorn withdrew the sheet of parchment from within his tunic. His armor was damaged and in need of repair. He would be sure to mend it all. It sounded like he would need it again soon. The piece of charcoal he used to write on the parchment had seen better days, but he was still able to scribble in a few monsters.

"Ontr-anda?" Hallik said, peering over Bjorn's shoulder.

Bjorn clucked his tongue and tucked the parchment away.

"I seem to remember that I landed the killing blow," Hallik said.

"It was a team effort," Bjorn said.

Hallik smirked. "That's fair. It's a shame I didn't get to help with that amgrunda though."

"My thoughts exactly," Bjorn said, but when he saw the smile on Hallik's face, he knew the younger man was simply teasing him. And... Bjorn didn't mind. At least, not today.

"I'll be curious to see what Dris discovered about that demon," Elowyn said.

"Indeed," Lorelai said. She held Dris in her hands, rotating it in her fingers, thumbs occasionally passing over the gems.

It was a dangerous weapon. The demon had used it to restore himself. There was much about it that they still didn't understand. They would need to discuss this with Tyrus when he awoke.

The group was somber as they walked in silence, a momentary reprieve.

Hallik broke the quiet. "There is a lot we have to sorrow for, but at least today we have won. Today we have proven that Avskildians are a force to be reckoned with. My father is right. If there are more people out there, then it is my responsibility to help them."

"I'm with you, Hal," Elowyn said, looping her hand around his arm.

"Me too," Lorelai said.

They looked to Bjorn, expecting a response from him. He grunted. He realized he'd have a choice here. If he were to ask Elowyn to help him get back to his own land, she would likely oblige. He could resume his own path of taking jobs to kill monsters, and with his new abilities as a Watcher, he would certainly be better at it. Though he didn't believe in what Tyrus had said about coming here for a purpose, he couldn't deny that he felt something when he was with Hallik, Lorelai, and Elowyn. Whether he fought beside them or not, they were still going to risk their lives trying to save this doomed world. Didn't they stand a better chance with him by their sides? "We're a team, aren't we?"

Hallik patted Bjorn on the shoulder, his face beaming with a smile.

Bjorn almost let a smile creep onto his own face. Almost.

The others still had no idea what kind of horrors truly lay outside of Avskild, but he knew they'd be in for a rude awakening.

ACKNOWLEDGEMENTS

A lot of work went into this book's production. I'd especially like to thank Alexandra Leonhardt for her editing work on this piece. She added the extra level of professionalism the manuscript deserved. I'd also like to thank my wife, Julia, for letting me bounce ideas off of her and for sharing in my excitement and enthusiasm. It is from her that I learned how much love can strengthen me. I understand the sacrifice this labor is for her, and she has been so extremely accommodating, for which I am endlessly grateful. She enables my dreams.

I also had some wonderful friends helping with artistic ideas—the whole Ringdweller Facebook group was great—and especially Tori, Audrey, Rachel, Alyssa, and Samantha for keeping my hyped up even though I sent them ALL of the spoilers.

Zac Hall, Andrea Wilson and Tori Grounds (again) also provided some excellent feedback that directly resulted in some adjustments from the original draft, and I appreciate their help.

ALSO BY

Brady Hunsaker is also the author of the Ringdweller Series, featuring a tidally locked planet.

1. Scorned Prince

2. Cursed King

3. Broken Empire

The Impervious Series features a world where the blood of dragons is used to fuel technology

1. Dragonsbane

2. Dragonsworn

GLOSSARY

Realms

Dothvarld, or Kel's Abyss: Realm of the dead.

Jotvarld: Realm of trolls

Vanheyna: Realm of gods

Essvarld: Primordial realm

Alfvarld: Realm of elves

Myrkvarld: Realm of shadow

Mennesvarld: Realm of men

Grimnir Classes

Voyager: Spellcasting role specializing in time and space manipulation

Vitugr: Primary spellcasting role with a large arsenal of spells they can learn

Watcher: Enhanced senses and few spells

Valtyra: Easily identified by their feathered wings, they have enhanced strength and stamina. Their spells are not often learned

ABOUT THE AUTHOR

Brady was born in a stronghold at the base of the Rocky Mountains. He currently resides there with his wife, their three daughters, and a few domesticated house lions of a rare breed. He set out with the goal to write fantasy that anybody could read, with characters who face real life struggles. Everyone deserves to feel like there is hope.